PRAISE FO

"Karla Sorensen's books are pure magic!"

—Penny Reid, *New York Times* bestselling author

"An expert at her craft, no one writes heartwarming characters with emotional depth like Karla Sorensen. She's a perfect fit for readers who love to laugh, build a found family, and fall in love."

—Kandi Steiner, #1 Amazon bestselling author

"If Karla writes it . . . I'm reading it."

—Devney Perry, *Wall Street Journal* bestselling author

"It was beautiful, heartbreaking (yet it put me back together, too), and the perfect mixture of spicy and sweet."

—Megan Reads Romance on *The Best Laid Plans*

"Sparkling tension between our main characters, a slow burn that doesn't leave you unsatisfied for too long, witty and smart banter, all blended together with romance that feels right and natural."

—Helpless Reads on *The Best Laid Plans*

"A perfect blend of raw emotion, tension, and humor, it was everything I didn't know I needed."

—All in with A on *The Best of All*

"With a torturous slow burn that finally snaps with the most electric kind of tension, a seriously swoony tortured hero, and a storyline that made my chest ache, this was even better than I expected."

—Jeeves Reads Romance on *The Best of All*

Lessons in
HEART
BREAK

DISCOVER OTHER TITLES BY
KARLA SORENSEN

The Wilder Family

One and Only

Head over Heels

Promise Me This

Forever Starts Tonight

The Wolves: A Football Dynasty
(The Second Generation)

The Lie

The Plan

The Crush

The Ward Sisters

Focused

Faked

Floored

Forbidden

The Washington Wolves

The Bombshell Effect

The Ex Effect

The Marriage Effect

The Bachelors of the Ridge

Dylan

Garrett

Cole

Michael

Tristan

Three Little Words

By Your Side

Light Me Up

Tell Them Lies

Love at First Sight

Baking Me Crazy

Batter of Wits

Steal My Magnolia

Worth the Wait

The Best Men

The Best Laid Plans

The Best of All

Lessons in HEARTBREAK

The Kings, Book 1

KARLA SORENSEN

 Montlake

Text copyright © 2025 by Karla Sorensen
All rights reserved.

Published by Montlake, Seattle

www.apub.com

Amazon, the Amazon logo, and Montlake are trademarks of Amazon.com, Inc., or its affiliates.

ISBN-13: 9781662526626 (paperback)
ISBN-10: 9781662526619 (digital)

Cover design by Letitia Hasser
Cover images: © Michelle Lancaster PTY LTD; © Pasta La Vista / Shutterstock

Printed in the United States of America

To the friends in our life who know exactly when to push us past our fears

Chapter One

RUBY

Despite the fact that worst-case-scenario thinking was my default state of mind, I never could have guessed that my friend's gift of a monster sex toy would kick off the most dramatic series of relationship events I'd ever experienced.

It wasn't the sex toy, per se. How could it be? Not that it wasn't dramatic, of course. That thing had more bells and whistles than most of the electronics in my possession.

It was more what it represented.

Because the first thing I felt when I laid eyes on it—buried underneath tasteful wrapping paper and a beautiful shiny bow—was pure, unadulterated terror.

How was anyone supposed to slip under their sheets—mine, in this instance, were high thread count, with a cute little-blue-flower print—spread their legs for a giant rotating, vibrating thing with appendages, and feel even the slightest bit relaxed?

In truth, this was a me problem. Lauren was great, as was her gift-giving ability. There was an element of thoughtfulness to this terrifying gift that I wasn't quite ready to see. It stemmed, of course, from our repeated conversations about my lone sexual experience and how I was seemingly incapable of creating more experiences—*better* experiences—to wipe that one out.

The longer I went without those more frequent and better experiences, the harder it became to put forth the slightest effort. Now I had the strongest notion that when my gynecologist asked me to spread my legs for my next exam, a stray moth might fly out.

It wasn't that I didn't want to try. Not really. But letting someone in—to me—was as scary as jumping out of a plane with no parachute.

I know, I know . . . *control freak* was right above *worst-case-scenario thinking* on my list of personality traits.

The hardest part about being a control freak was admitting it, and it took me until my thirtieth year to be able to do so. And here's what makes it so hard to admit—when you struggle with control issues, especially as a younger person, most people look at you in such a positive light.

My parents were constantly told things like, *Oh, she's such an old soul.*

Ruby never causes any trouble, does she?

You're so lucky. She's such a serious little thing. You must never have to worry about her.

But you know what that really meant? It meant I took on about a hundred times more responsibility than I should have at a young age. It meant that I was juggling mental weight that was far too heavy for someone in my age bracket.

Old soul was just another way of saying *can't relax enough to express their emotions.*

And as I got older, that positive reinforcement just kept on coming in.

I was responsible. Organized. Motivated. High-achieving.

That list showed up in so many places in my life: In my grades. My extracurricular activities. The complete and utter lack of a social life. While most kids in high school were going to football games and getting asked on dates, experimenting with their sexuality and hooking up with harmlessly inappropriate peers, I was locked away in my room, doing homework and reading and making sure that every single domino was lined up to get all the things I wanted out of life.

Valedictorian? Check.

Student body president? Check.

Debate team, yearbook staff, event planning–committee chair—the list went on and on.

To no one's surprise, my parents ate all this up. It was the clear benefit of being the only child of two high-achieving people. They were the ones who wanted to keep every test marked with an A, the ones who loved hearing about any project I was working on; who happily encouraged me to take on more responsibility, to volunteer for more committees because it would look great on a college application. Achievements were the way we related most.

Was I doing all the right things at the right time? Check, check, check.

Ours wasn't a relationship based on deep, emotional talks, but more of a "Look at this bright, shiny thing I'm bringing home!" declaration. They loved those little trophies, real and unseen. And oh, it was how I'd always felt the most loved. The discussions about books and the deeper themes found in the text; the pulling apart of the things we all read, the things they taught in their respective college courses—my mom was a statistics professor, my dad a lit professor, both tenured at Colorado State University in Fort Collins.

Because of that, college wasn't as heavy on the extracurricular, and instead of living in the dorms to get the messy experience there—I could do without the great social experiment, thank you very much—I chose the safer, much more practical option of commuting. They supported the choice because it was responsible. It was financially smart. It was prudent.

Just what every twenty-year-old girl likes to be called. *Prudent.*

Believe me, I still got the college experience. The number of hungover frat boys who tried to cheat off my papers in class was truly staggering.

But I was consistent. I always got good grades. There was no stumbling in late at night or tripping into class with bleary eyes and two-day-old mascara. It never bothered me back then because I was admired by my peers, my professors, and my parents.

It wasn't until later that there was a creeping sense that maybe something wasn't quite right.

There were always reasons, of course. Valid, believable, sympathetic reasons why I held the reins of my life with an iron grip, keeping every day scheduled and structured in a way that eased my mind. Because it was safe, and I could predict each outcome with surgical precision.

And it was on my thirtieth birthday, when my coworker Lauren surprised me with a present, that I knew I couldn't avoid the truth any longer. We'd gone out to dinner at her insistence, and after a shared bottle of wine at my house (I never drank in public, because, honestly, someone could spike your drink when you least expected it), she said, "Ruby, I got you the most perfect gift in the world. Something you need desperately."

"A new planner?" I asked, perking up instantly.

She rolled her eyes. "Thank you for proving my point."

The box was immaculately wrapped—tiny pink and white flowers on a silver background, tied up with a rose-gold bow—but when I opened it, the thing staring back up at me had my jaw falling open, heat crawling up my neck at an unstoppable rate.

"What is *that*?" I gasped.

She laughed, reaching forward to pull it from the box, where it was nestled in brightly colored shreds of paper. It was big. Light blue, with a small arm that hooked out of the front and buttons along the bottom.

"You know what this is," she said slyly. Then she hit one of those buttons, and it started vibrating. A lot. And the little arm on the front moved.

"That's supposed to go inside?"

She patted my arm. "Trust me. It'll do you a world of good, honey."

My eyes widened, and I snatched it from her grip, dropping it immediately when the feel of it had heat billowing from the surface of my skin. "I am not using that, Lo," I hissed. "It's obscene."

She merely smiled. "It sure is."

I slammed the top back on the box and shoved it away from me, watching while it slid across the wood floor.

Bzzzzzzz. Bzzzzzzz. Bzzzzzzz.

Now the box was vibrating, and it was moving from the force of those vibrations, the sound echoing through my living room like it was plugged into a massive speaker. I pinched my eyes shut while she laughed.

"Ruby," she said gently. "Look at me."

"No." I buried my face in my hands. Something about the gift made me want to burst into tears. I knew why she was doing it. I knew why she was trying, even if I was not the right audience for that sort of . . . apparatus.

Gently, she wrapped a hand around my wrist and pulled. "Take a deep breath, all right? I'll take it home with me so you never have to see it again." She sighed. "Probably should've started smaller. Maybe a nice little vibrator instead."

I gave her a look. "You think?"

Her eyebrows shot up. "Would you have used that?"

"No." My hand fluttered to my chest, my heartbeat hammering away. My eyes slammed shut as I counted the beats to center myself. "I don't think so."

Lauren was one of my only friends. Don't get me wrong, I was friendly with everyone in town. There wasn't much of a choice with how small our town was, but when I moved to Welling Springs as the new head librarian, she'd basically forced me into being friends with her.

She was funny and irreverent, with a loud laugh and the kind of irrepressible warmth that seeped into every corner of the room when she was around.

And if there was anyone who knew the corners well, it was me. In a group of people, that was often where I found myself—out of sight, where no one would notice me and I could observe from a place of relative safety.

People like Lauren, the ones who did so well as the centerpiece of whatever conversation they were in, fascinated me. A puzzle I didn't quite understand and could never really figure out. But as a friend, I was grateful for her.

Usually.

Except when she gave me a monster-size penis replica and expected me to be excited about it. If I tried introducing that to my poor lady parts—which had only ever been viewed in detail by my doctor—I was quite sure I'd hear panicked screams coming from the general vicinity of my vagina.

"I'm sorry," she said quietly. She never did anything quietly, so I peeled my eyelids open to study her. "I just know you've been"—with a tilt of her head, she searched for the right words—"struggling to let people in."

I'd spent my whole life in white-knuckled control of the things within my power, so it was terrifying to have someone challenge one of the things that wasn't. It felt like a rush of icy frost racing up the surface of my skin, eclipsing all the heat her gift had generated.

"That's a very kind way of saying it, Lauren."

The facial expression she made was half smile, half grimace, because she knew it was true. I didn't just have walls up—I was wrapped in barbed wire, encased in a ten-foot block of concrete, surrounded by a deep moat teeming with rabid sharks.

And it was lonely.

I didn't want to be there anymore, but the longer I sat, the scarier all those barriers got. Bigger and bigger in my mind.

Lauren started cautiously. "Sometimes we need to be alone in order to loosen up a little. Maybe that would help you, even if you don't use that."

That being the box, still doing pulsing vibrations on my living room floor.

"I don't know," I said skeptically. "I don't even know what I'd be able to think about to distract me from all the . . . moving parts."

God, I sounded pathetic, didn't I?

What thirty-year-old woman was afraid of a sex toy?

Lauren's eyes sparkled as she laughed. "What about when you were younger?" she asked. "Did you ever have any harmless crushes or teenage sweethearts?"

My answering laugh was wry, and I rubbed at my forehead. Two faces instantly popped into my head. Two versions of the same face, really.

"There was this family who lived behind us for years." I twisted my fingers into the fringe of the throw pillow resting against my thigh. "They had twin boys. We didn't go to the same school, and they were a couple years older than me, but I always climbed this big tree in our backyard and watched them. They were constantly practicing football or soccer or baseball. They were good at *everything*."

She smiled. "Did they know you were there?"

"Oh yeah. The younger one, Griffin—or younger by a couple minutes, I guess—he was always teasing me. He'd climb up into the tree and snatch my book away, trying to coax me down. He was such a pest." I shook my head. "The other one—he was more serious. Never teased me the way his brother did. But when he smiled . . ." I laid a hand on my stomach. "I felt it right here."

"You didn't feel it when the younger brother smiled?"

"I was too busy being annoyed," I answered dryly. "But yeah, I felt it watching him too. They were just . . . everything I wasn't. Strong and fast and outgoing, and everyone loved them. We moved away when I was fifteen, so it's not like anything happened, but sometimes I think about how I felt sitting in that tree, and I get sad that I didn't just do something about it."

"You can do something about it now."

"Can I? I just want . . ." My eyes burned, and ruthlessly, I willed the buildup of tears away. That was within my power, within my control. "I'm sick of not knowing what any of it feels like, Lauren. When I've tried . . ." The way my voice trailed off really pissed me off.

Wary and unsure. Quiet.

It was timid.

Ugh. Screw that. I was so sick of feeling that way.

And yet, despite the tumultuous reaction, I couldn't stop it, no matter how badly I wanted to.

But her face was soft with sympathy, as was her voice when she spoke. "I know, sweetie."

The difference in our ages was just shy of a decade, but that nickname, only brought out when she was feeling particularly motherly, tested my ability to hold back those tears.

My dog, Bruiser, wandered down the hallway—after he'd likely slept sprawled on top of my bed—drawn by the noise from the box.

Bzzz. Bzzzzzzz.

His head tilted as he approached, his butt sticking up in the air as he crouched down in a playful pose to inspect the package.

"I swear, if he pulls that out and asks me to play fetch with it . . . ," I said in a warning tone.

Lauren reached over to grab the box, deftly pressing a button to stop the vibrating, and I exhaled a short laugh. "Thank you."

Determination blazed in her eyes. "You need a professional. You need someone who can help you build your confidence and show you that you have the ability to let someone in again." This time, she was the one who tapped a hand to my chest, but she did it gently. "You have it all right here."

Maybe it was because I'd been an avid reader my entire life, but trying to get a mental picture of what a word meant helped conceptualize the way it was affecting me—for good or for bad.

What did desire look like?

Was it the flexing muscles of a tanned, strong boy with a big smile and knife-sharp jaw? Was it dancing in a dark corner and not worrying that anyone was watching? Was it kisses that stole your breath and greedy hands tearing at clothes?

And love. What did that look like?

Parents hanging your test on the fridge or hugging you when you got the acceptance letter for your master's program. Friends giving gifts to help you push past your self-inflicted boundaries. A neighbor bringing soup because she knew you were sick.

I couldn't picture love in other forms. Not in my own day-to-day.

Control, though . . . I could picture that so very clearly as I sat cross-legged on the floor.

A miniature version of myself, held in a tight, giant fist of my own making. No matter how I squirmed or fought to get free, every movement was futile. Like King Kong about to ascend a giant spire with the screaming maiden in his hand.

Except I was the maiden *and* I was King Kong. Wasn't that a head trip?

For years and years, I'd slowly increased the strength of the grip on my own life until there was no breathing around it. No ignoring its presence. It was a stifling jail of my own making, and I sat in the cell, key in hand.

I was entering my thirtieth year, and I'd never really let myself live. There were no crazy stories, no good memories that I wanted to play in my mind over and over. And I wanted them. Just a few.

"What do you mean, *a professional?*" I asked warily. Bruiser flopped his big body onto the floor next to me, and I smoothed my hand over the sleek muscles on his side, smiling faintly as he turned onto his back and exposed his belly for scratches.

"Think of it like any problem that needs solving," Lauren said carefully. "When there's something wrong in our house, we call an expert to fix it, right? I wouldn't try to update the wiring or put in new plumbing by myself. I'd need someone who knows what they're doing."

I sighed, rubbing a hand over my forehead. "I should know better than to drink around you. I feel like I'm going to regret this entire conversation."

Lauren smacked my thigh with a laugh. "You had one drink, calm down. Plus, you know I'm right."

I cut her a look, pairing it with a haughty sniff. "I know no such thing. You've yet to arrive to your point for me to make that kind of judgment."

She inched closer, angling her legs toward me. "Everyone who knows you knows that you are funny and smart and beautiful." When I rolled my eyes, she merely raised an eyebrow like I'd proven something. "But you need help believing those things. You hide, Ruby, and I don't want to hear a single argument, because you know it's true. Your confidence took a hit, and I understand why—that guy was a giant fucking douchebag. He was the absolute worst choice for your first, and I hate that for you."

I kept my eyes down. "He seemed nice enough at first."

"They always do." Lauren covered my hand with hers. "But you were never comfortable around him, were you?"

I bit down on my bottom lip and eventually managed a quick shake of my head.

"You need someone who knows how to make you comfortable and understands how to build your confidence."

"And where, pray tell, will you find such a man among our nonexistent dating pool in town?" The glint in her eye made me nervous. Then again, every idea Lauren had made me a little nervous. "Oh gosh, what?"

She pulled out my laptop and opened a private browser. "I have an idea that you will probably hate at first, but if you fire up that gorgeous logical brain of yours, you'll see it's the very best possible solution."

Her serious tone had me sitting up straighter, eyeing her doubtfully. "Okay."

Before Lauren started typing, she gave me a quick, searching look. "How badly do you want to do something about this? Because if you're genuinely content right now, I'll back off."

I laughed quietly. "It's not that easy, Lauren."

"It *is* that easy." Something in her gaze made it impossible for me to look away. "It is, Ruby."

"How?" I heard myself whisper.

Then her smile spread, something so devious that I probably should've ran scared right then just to avoid the knowledge of whatever her brain was plotting. "I need you to trust me."

"I really, really don't."

Lauren grinned, then turned the laptop screen around. Leaning in, I had to squint to read the print. When I did, I looked back at her with wide, horrified eyes.

"You cannot be serious."

"It's either this, or I leave you alone with the giant dildo, Ruby. Which is it gonna be?"

For a moment, I actually considered both options, envisioning that giant fist around my own life, squeezing to the point of danger.

Wasn't I already in danger, though? I'd lived thirty years, sure. But what had I really experienced?

I'd lost the ability to allow myself anything spontaneous in life, because I was afraid of what might happen. It was so easy to imagine standing up in front of a group of people and making my own small admission: *Hi, my name is Ruby Tate, and I'm a control freak.*

Blowing out a slow breath, I looked at the pink-and-white-wrapped box, then back at Lauren's face.

"Fine. Tell me what to do next."

Chapter Two

GRIFFIN

How many almost-thirty-three-year-old professional athletes got their asses grounded by their agents?

Not many, I'll tell you that.

Oh sure, he told me over and over that I wasn't grounded when he sent me away for three weeks to his big fucking house in some tiny town outside Fort Collins, Colorado. He told me over and over that it was for my own good, that I should go somewhere quieter, get some rest, stay out of the public eye. He told me over and over that I'd end up appreciating the peace and quiet.

I didn't believe him the first time he said it. Didn't believe him the third or fourth time he said it.

And it took me exactly thirty-six hours before I was bored out of my skull.

Obviously, there were people in the world who would love this shit. A big-ass house to themselves, sprawling land all around, mountains in the distance, green fields, unobstructed views of the sunsets. I'm sure those people would do things like read books and nap and cook meals. They'd probably meditate and become one with nature, deep-breathing while they cleared their minds of everything that was troubling them.

My first attempt at meditation lasted less than a minute. There was no slowing my thoughts. No centering of anything.

In fact, the attempt just made me feel like I was crawling out of my skin, immediately sending me downstairs, in the direction of his home gym, where I worked out until my muscles shook. Then I searched all the cupboards, wandered through the bedrooms, lay on the big couch and tried flipping through one of the many books lining the shelves of the two-story family room with the gorgeous mountain views, and generally wondered exactly how much money my agent made.

After tossing the book onto the floor, I pulled out my phone and brought up his contact information.

Me: Your house is nicer than mine.

Steven: That's because my wife has excellent taste and no problem spending the money I make.

Me: That sounds like something you should bring up with a marriage counselor.

Steven: Oh, I'm not complaining. She spent a fortune on lingerie last week after I finalized your new deal with Nike. She loves you just as much as she loves me right now.

Me: It's my deal, but you're the one getting laid and buying the giant house. Why do I feel like something's wrong here?

Steven: You're also the one who ran his mouth to the press about his brother now coaching in the division in which you played. Maybe if you'd refrained from doing that, you wouldn't have to disappear for a few weeks to let it die down. Or change teams, for that matter.

The scowl appeared on my face before I could stop it.

The truth of both things sat like a rock in my gut. Changing teams wasn't ideal, but I'd been unhappy in New York for years—friction with a new coach, and an owner who looked at me like a show pony instead of someone who could actually help lead the team—and Denver had a huge amount of space in their salary cap and a weak left side on their defensive line.

Not only that, but Denver was in not just a different division but also a different conference from the one I'd left. The one my brother now coached in.

And I really, really didn't want to have to play my asshole brother twice a year for the rest of my career—hence the running of the mouth.

One interview over some drinks, and I got a little too comfortable with the woman on the other side of the table. It wasn't like she'd tricked me; the mic was sitting right in between us, plain as fucking day, and because we'd spent the previous fifteen minutes laughing about something completely unrelated to the interview, my guard was down.

"So your brother will be coaching your divisional rival now. How's that gonna feel? You two haven't gotten along in years."

And she'd asked it so smoothly, like we were just talking as best friends.

"It'll feel like a fucking root canal," I'd said offhandedly. "With no numbing shot."

"That bad?"

"Worse."

She hummed. "I have a sister like that. We fought like cats and dogs growing up because we were only a year apart and constantly in each other's business. Was it like that with the famous King twins when you were still at home?"

A derisive laugh slipped past my lips before I could stop it. "No. Growing up, we were inseparable, even though we were complete opposites. Always competitive, of course. But most brothers are."

The rift had crept up slowly. Unnoticeable at first. Healthy competition through high school was honed into something sharper in college. Less comfortable. If he showed up to the weight room an hour before he was supposed to be there, I started showing up two hours before.

If I did conditioning six days a week, he started doing it seven.

Everyone around us fed into that competitive streak—starting most innocently with our father, then our coaches and our teammates. If the saying was true, that iron sharpened iron, then my brother and I were made of something even harder than that.

The difference was, everyone saw him as the disciplined one, despite the fact that I was toe to toe with him the entire time.

Not that there weren't times I'd made regrettable choices, but no matter how I changed, my brother and I were firmly cast in our respective roles, and there seemed to be no changing that.

"Can you do that"—she motioned to her temples—"twin-telepathy thing?"

Briefly, I arched an eyebrow. "I don't think I'd want to read my brother's mind even if I could."

The thought of being privy to Barrett's thoughts made me shudder. It was probably all spreadsheets and statistics and to-do lists, and so fucking regimented that I'd lose my grip on my sanity after about ten minutes.

He'd probably say the same of me. But if we *had* been able to read each other's minds, maybe we'd still be speaking now, I thought with a tight swallow.

Falling in love with the same woman had a tendency to split even the closest of brothers apart.

Difference was, my brother married her. Had a couple of kids with her. Had the unfortunate task of discovering she was a narcissistic attention-seeker who'd thought the eldest King brother could do a better job of tending to her emotional needs.

When he didn't, after years of coming second to his demanding job as a head coach and deciding the tedium of motherhood wasn't for her, Rachel attempted to come back to me.

Even though she was wearing a see-through bra to showcase her latest, very successful surgical enhancement, a thong so delicate it would snap with very little effort, and those thigh-high garter things I had a particular weakness for, I slammed the door to my penthouse in her stunned face after hustling her out of the kitchen.

Less than a minute later, a brisk knock had me yanking it back open, expecting to find Rachel.

And I did. But my brother was right next to her.

"Didn't expect to see my wife getting into the elevator on your floor, Griffin," Barrett said in a low, dangerous voice. Behind him, Rachel crossed her arms tightly across her chest and slicked her tongue over her teeth.

"You might want to keep a tracking device on her," I said, leaning my shoulder against the doorframe. "But I'm guessing you won't like what you find if you do."

Rachel stepped forward, eyes blazing. "You son of a bitch."

I whistled. "That's not nice. You weren't calling me names when you tried to undress in my kitchen."

"Fuck you, Griffin." She cut a look over to her husband. "Expect papers from my lawyer, asshole."

Then she stormed off in a whirl of long, dark hair and trench coat tails, and the ding of the elevator echoed down the hallway toward my penthouse.

I couldn't help but laugh, rubbing a hand over my neck while my brother stood there glaring at me.

"Is everything a fucking joke to you?"

I arched an eyebrow. "No, not really."

"How long was she here?" Barrett asked.

Did you sleep with my wife? He couldn't say the words. Even unsaid, they sliced straight through my chest.

How did we get here? That was the thing I wanted to ask. How had my life ended up in a place where my brother entertained even the slightest notion that I would sleep with his wife?

Stubborn King pride kept both our mouths shut, and briefly, I wondered if his stomach churned with unease like mine, a bitter by-product of keeping those important questions buried deep.

"Does it matter?" I asked with a deceptively casual tilt of my head. "She showed up at my house in nothing but a coat and some tacky lingerie, and you think it matters if she was here for five minutes or fifteen?"

Barrett sighed heavily, and I felt a quick, bright flash of pity.

"Less than two minutes," I said, crossing my arms over my chest. His brow furrowed as he studied my face. When he didn't say anything, I let out a dry laugh. "You don't believe me, do you?"

"I don't know what I believe anymore, Griffin." Barrett shook his head, swiping a hand over his mouth. "You always do this, you know? See something shiny and exciting and fun, and you don't think about the fucking consequences. Do you know how many times I saved your ass in high school because Coach wanted to kick you off the team for screwing around on the weekends? How close you came to losing your scholarship in college if I hadn't stepped in and begged them to give you a second chance?"

Anger flared hot, and I kept my arms crossed. "I'll make sure to send you a gift basket tomorrow for my entire career. Thanks, brother."

"Don't put words in my mouth, Griffin. You just don't think things through. Like letting her in here in the first place. What did you think was gonna happen?"

"Now it's *my* fault that she showed up on my doorstep? That's rich."

"No, it's not." He looked so fucking tired as he shook his head again. "But she showed up here because she knew you'd be the only other person who might hate me as much as she does. Can you blame me for not believing either of you?"

Before I could say anything else, Barrett turned and left, and in his wake, I felt the cold shift of that rift between us. But this time, it was irreparable. Irrevocably broken.

My jaw tightened dangerously at the memory, the pressure building up underneath my cheekbones as I pressed my teeth together.

"The King brothers aren't inseparable now, though," the journalist said easily. "But he's certainly making a statement by taking this job, isn't he?"

With a snort, I tossed back the rest of my drink and sighed.

Barrett King never backed down from a challenge. Neither did I. That's what made us so dangerous at our respective jobs. Dangerous to each other too.

"Every game we play against each other will be dissected by millions of people, and I have no desire to live underneath that kind of scrutiny, like a fucking bug trapped under the glass."

"Ahhh, so should we be on the lookout for news of a transfer?" she asked lightly, like she hadn't just baited the absolute hell out of me.

I didn't pay attention to the look on her face, staring down instead at the melting ice in my highball glass. Maybe if I *had* looked up, I'd have seen that sharp-eyed interest that covered every journalist's face when they got a big, juicy bite on a story.

"My brother is obnoxious when he wins, because he always prepares as if there's no other possible outcome," I said, only the slightest tinge of bitterness coloring my tone. "And hopefully, he'll be a very ungracious loser in his new divisional team, whoever he goes up against. I can't wait to see it." The moment the words came out, I pinched my eyes shut. "Shit, I shouldn't have said that."

But what I didn't say was *Can you keep that off the record?*

She merely hummed, sitting back in her seat and studying me openly. "You two certainly generate enough headlines to keep us busy all year round, don't you?"

I quirked an eyebrow. "You asking him about me too?"

This particular reporter was enough of a professional that she merely answered with a small sphinxlike smile. "You know I can't kiss and tell, Griffin."

I leaned in, holding her relentless eye contact. "Kissing my brother would be like sucking face with a dead body. He has no sense of humor."

Her wineglass immediately went in front of her face, and if she smiled at what I'd said, it was well hidden. After a long sip, she set it down. "Off the record, I will say this—you are definitely the fun one of the King twins," she whispered, moving in closer so I could hear her clearly.

I sat back in my chair and gave her a smooth smile, the kind that showed my dimple. "Of course I am. My brother wouldn't know fun if someone shoved it up his ass."

Her delighted laughter had my smile growing wider.

Until the moment her article hit the internet, the entire thing had felt so innocent. Like I could've been sitting with a teammate or a buddy who knew exactly why my older-by-two-minutes brother drove me up a fucking wall. Like she just wanted to commiserate about some slightly complicated family dynamics over a drink.

Oh, we'd commiserated all right. Right up until the article ran, front and fucking center in the biggest sports publication in the world. Sound bites from that tiny mic sitting right in the middle of the table were blasted everywhere. The one about kissing a dead body was a particular social media favorite. Women and men made countless videos saying they'd happily compare, if the King twins were down for sharing.

My uptight, type-A, militantly disciplined brother came out smelling like fucking roses, and I was the single playboy asshole who couldn't keep his mouth shut.

Now I was commiserating with my damn self about my agent-induced exile while the entire fan base currently obsessed with my brother was calling—quite loudly and quite insistently—for my head on a metaphorical platter.

Reminiscing about the interview wasn't going to help. I pinched the bridge of my nose and sat up on the sprawling couch, eyes focused on the distant line of the mountains. In my hand, my phone dinged again with another message from my agent.

Steven: Go for a walk on the property, it'll clear your mind. Head into Welling Springs and get something to eat, there's some great little restaurants.

Me: So the good people of this town can tar and feather me because they're probably obsessed with my brother too?

Steven: Please. If anyone approaches you, I'll pay you a thousand dollars. They don't care around there, that's what makes it a nice place to visit. I bring clients out to that house all the time and no one has ever bothered us.

Me: You've never brought ME here before.

Steven: Because you've always said no.

My brow furrowed. I had a vague memory of Steven asking more than once if I wanted to spend a weekend with him and his family after they'd bought this place.

Instead of answering—because I still felt an uncomfortable wash of embarrassment over the fact that I was already bored—I set my phone aside and wandered over to the large folding sliders that opened up onto the massive back patio in front of the pool.

He told me people would filter in and out, tending to the landscaping and the pool. An assistant had already dropped off enough preprepared food to last me the next week, but the thought of heating up a large dish just for myself sounded like fucking torture.

The surface of the pool glittered underneath the bright sun, and I decided I would swim laps later, try to expel some of this pent-up energy making me feel like I was stuck in a cage.

But first—food.

Exiting my car with sunglasses covering my face, I gave a quick look around to see if anyone was watching. The small stretch of a downtown was fairly quiet, with only a few people meandering down the sidewalks.

Less than five thousand people, he'd told me. Enough that there were some good food options, a handful of shops, a library, and schools. Standing at the curb where I'd parked, I glanced down the street in both directions and decided to head into the closest restaurant.

The sign hanging over the door was a sleek brown-and-white logo featuring a coffee bean and a steaming cup, and the smell of baked goods wafted from the open door as I approached.

There were bowls of water for passing dogs, and tied up next to the propped-open door was a beast of a dog, with a sleek bluish-gray coat and the perked ears and bright eyes of a pit bull–type mix. His tongue hung out the side of his massive mouth, and he glanced up at me with a slight tilt of his head.

Bruiser, his ID tag read. Attached to the light-green collar was a handwritten note: *I'm friendly and love head-scratches. Please don't feed me, though, even if I beg.*

"No muffins for you, huh, buddy?" I said, bending down to scratch the top of his head.

With a groan, he leaned into my touch, that panting tongue still unrolled. He looked like he was smiling.

Giving Bruiser a final pat, I slid my sunglasses onto the top of my head and entered the coffee shop with a glance around the inside. It was filled with overstuffed furniture, grouped together in a way that you could easily sit and spend hours there comfortably.

An elderly couple sat in two chairs, splitting a blueberry muffin, steaming cups of tea sitting in front of them. A young guy sitting at a high-top table had headphones on, typing away on his sticker-covered laptop, oblivious to my entrance. In the back corner, a petite woman sat by herself, her messy blond hair hiding her features as she bent to read something in her hands.

At the back of the shop were two teenage girls, and they both eyed me as I strolled in, hands tucked into my pockets. When I gave them a friendly smile, they giggled, and I approached the long gleaming counter and studied the neat rows of confections underneath the domed glass.

"Morning. Can I start a drink for you?" a woman behind the counter asked. She had two tiny gold hoops through one nostril, heavy winged eyeliner, and bright-blue hair tied up in a knot on the top of her head. Her arms were wrapped in intricate black tattoos. She was probably midtwenties, with the kind of sharp, striking features that made her very interesting to look at. Long legs too.

God, I hadn't had sex in months.

The end of the last season had been particularly brutal, my body too tired for me to even think about finding someone who was okay with casual. But I wasn't tired now. I was very *not* tired. And I was very, very bored. Maybe a tattooed, blue-haired local would want to help me break in the pool.

Leaning a hip against the counter, I gave her a slow once-over. "Everything looks delicious. What do you recommend?"

She arched an eyebrow. "Personally, I always get a dark roast over ice. One sugar and a splash of cream so it's not too bitter."

Crossing my arms over my chest was a strategic choice, and she noted the change in my stance with a slight narrowing of her eyes.

"I don't like it when things are too sweet either," I said in a low voice, keeping my eyes on hers. "I could go for . . . whatever you like."

Briefly, her lips pursed. "Interesting," she mused.

"Yeah?" My eyes traced her face. "I love the blue. It's bold."

Setting her hands on the counter, she leaned in, and I found myself slightly mesmerized. "My wife likes it too," she said smoothly.

Suitably chastened, I cleared my throat and straightened. "Right. A large iced coffee, and two of those blueberry muffins, please."

With a quiet snort, she started on the drink, scooping ice into a plastic cup. "The raspberry are better," she said easily. "Just brought those out of the oven, so they might still be warm."

"Wouldn't you know—a warm muffin is my favorite thing in the world," I said, giving her a friendly smile.

She rolled her eyes, lips fighting a smile, pulling the tray from the case. "I bet it is. For here or to go?"

"Here, I think." If I went back to that house too soon, I'd start climbing the freaking walls. What had Steven said? Go for a walk or something?

Nodding, she set the muffins on a plate, then added a lid onto my iced coffee. "Cream and sugar are on the counter over there," she said, tilting her head toward the back of the shop, where the blond woman sat at the table closest to the back entrance.

"Thanks." But her back was already turned. Definitely not a football fan.

Blowing out a slow breath, I glanced around the shop, but it didn't seem like anyone was paying me much attention. Before I slid my wallet back into my pocket, I glanced down at the counter. The tip jar next to the register had a few singles in it, and while her back was still turned, I slipped a fifty inside.

Balancing my plate of muffins and my coffee, I wandered back to the counter to fix my drink, my eyes snagging on the woman sitting by herself.

Her hair had blocked most of her face when I walked in, but when I set my coffee down, she was staring directly at me. Or rather, staring directly at my hands.

She was a tiny thing, her petite frame covered in a simple ivory blouse, with a collar buttoned up past her collarbone, and black pants that hugged her legs and ended high on her waist. But it was her eyes that had me narrowing mine.

Something about those eyes—dark silvery gray and huge in her face, surrounded by thick, dark lashes—tugged at something in the back of my mind.

I knew her.

How the hell did I know her?

She must have noticed I was staring, because she finally yanked her gaze off my hands and up to my face. Her mouth fell open slightly, and without realizing what I was doing, my lips curled into a pleased little smile.

Oh yes. I knew her. Hadn't seen her in years, but I could see the hints of her younger self in the more refined features in front of me.

Briefly, I turned away and added a splash of cream and snagged two packets of sugar for my coffee. When I turned back, she had her gaze firmly locked on the table. I walked closer, gesturing with my plate of muffins to the empty seat across from her. "Anyone sitting here?"

If she recognized me, I couldn't read it in her face. She rolled her lips together for a moment, sucked in a short breath through her nose, then shook her head in a quick jerky motion.

Setting the plate of muffins on the table halfway in between me and her came first, then the coffee in front of my chair. I took a seat, easing my long legs out while I studied her.

"Good morning, Ruby Tate," I told her.

She blinked a few times, but I tilted my head when there was no shock or surprise or . . . much of anything. Her cheeks flushed a pretty pink, and the slender column of her throat worked on a swallow. At the notch in the base of that throat, I could see her pulse flutter wildly.

I took a slow sip of my coffee and watched her. Her mouth was wide, almost too wide for her face, but something about her features was . . . nice. Not too perfect. I liked that they weren't perfect. "Imagine my surprise at seeing you here. After so many years."

The slightest pinch in her brow was the only reaction she gave me.

She'd been a quiet kid—a little prickly, in fact. In the back of my head, a memory sprang up: her climbing into the tree that straddled our backyard and hers, watching my brother and me play football or soccer or whatever it was we were training for at the time—all big gray eyes and a serious expression, like she could never quite figure out what the fuck we were doing, why we were so loud and boisterous.

I blew out a slow breath, crossing my arms as I sat back in my chair. "Do you not recognize me?"

Her pink lips finally fell open, then snapped shut again. Her eyes pinched shut, and based on the minute movement of her mouth, she was counting breaths.

Waiting while she reached ten was as close to meditating as I'd ever come, because for those ten seconds, I wasn't thinking about anything else.

Not my brother. Not my new team. Not the inevitable end of my career because my body was so fucking tired that each season got harder and harder to complete.

Under her breath, she muttered something like *This is not happening, this is not happening.*

My smile spread. I'd never been met with this particular reaction before.

Why was this so fun?

Her eyes fluttered open, landing unerringly on me. "I recognize you," she said quietly. With a smile playing around my lips, I watched her gather her composure. She wasn't doing a very good job. "But I didn't expect you, Griffin King."

"But you know it's me and not my brother. Well done." I held up my coffee in salute. "Our parents can't even tell us apart half the time."

That was bullshit, but she didn't call me on it.

Instead, she eyed me warily. "I always found it easy. Your brother never smiled."

"Still doesn't. I'm much more pleasant to be around, trust me."

Ruby ignored that, which was probably wise. Her fingers were long and graceful, tipped with sensibly trimmed nails in a clear gloss, and at the moment, they were shredding the absolute hell out of a napkin.

"Want one of these muffins?" I asked, pushing the plate closer to her.

Instead of answering, Ruby stared over at me, a slight furrow in her brow.

I broke off a piece of the sugar-topped confection, moaning slightly when it melted in my mouth. "Fuck, that's good," I said, my voice a pleased rumble.

She did that nervous-swallowing thing again, another soft flush of pink blooming over her cheeks.

"This feels like a monumentally bad idea, Griffin," she said carefully.

My eyebrows shot up. "It's breakfast, Ruby." I smiled, and her eyes darted to the dimple buried in my three-day-old stubble. "Granted, when I partake of a morning meal with a beautiful woman, we've usually enjoyed other activities leading up to it . . . but I digress."

Trembling hands came up to cover her face, and her entire frame slumped as she sighed. "No. No, no, no. I can't do this," she muttered.

"Can't do what?" Consider me officially fascinated.

Oh, and fascination was dangerous, wasn't it?

She dropped her hands, motioning wildly between us. "This."

Swallowing another large bite of the muffin, I eyed her as I licked a leftover crumb off my bottom lip. Those big dove-gray eyes tracked the movement. "Why's that?"

After a short exhale, she crumpled up the decimated napkin and smoothed her hands out on the table. Her eyes locked on mine, and over the sudden jump in my pulse, I realized just how very incredibly, wildly not bored I was.

"Well . . . when I hired an escort, I didn't expect it to be the former neighbor boy."

Chapter Three

RUBY

I could count on one hand the times that I'd wished for the ground to open up and swallow me whole. Something catastrophic and devastating, and oh, I'd welcome it with open arms right about now.

Do you recognize me? he'd asked. Please.

If I hadn't been halfway to dying from mortification, I would've snorted. The moment I saw that man's profile, saw him flirting shamelessly with Blake, I knew exactly who he was.

Like I didn't spend half my childhood completely obsessed with the King twins. Watching them play, watching them fight, watching them do anything, really. Watching them grow taller and stronger and somehow—always, impossibly—more and more handsome with every year that passed.

They were like some strange alien species—with a different language and different way of interacting with each other. They would shove each other, wrestle, yell, swear, come up sweaty and angry after playing a game, and the next day be completely fine.

In my own home, everything was quiet and contained, perfectly precise because that's how my parents did things. There weren't messes to be picked up or yelling matches between siblings, because, hello, no siblings to be had for me.

Watching Griffin and Barrett always made me feel a bit like a kid at the zoo, nose pressed to the glass, watching the lions roam their habitat.

My parents moved us away to Fort Collins when I was fifteen—a far cry from Michigan, where I'd grown up—but those two boys were cemented in my brain. Every kid has a formative moment, a book or a movie or a crush that makes you realize just exactly how powerful hormones are.

It was the King twins for me.

Over the edge of my book, I'd study them—the beautifully proportioned bodies, the strong jaws and the long limbs, the natural grace that seemed marrow deep. And I felt things when I did.

Pounding pulse.

Rapid heart rate.

Sweaty palms.

When one of them looked at me? I felt it all over, tingling skin and prickling heat.

And here he sat, the man with the beautiful smile. So, so much bigger than he had been the last time I saw him.

A sharp pang lanced my chest, and I rubbed carefully at my sternum, firmly assuring myself that I was fine.

Griffin blinked, his face completely frozen at my announcement, but he recovered swiftly, leaning back in his chair and studying me with such intensity that I felt it like a lightning bolt.

My God, he was gorgeous.

What would he look like naked? My face was flaming, because now I was looking at the size of his hands and, through the screaming static in my brain, thinking about the proportions of hand size and feet size to . . . other body parts' sizes, and I felt a little faint.

He'd look incredible, wouldn't he?

Not that I'd ever know.

I'd paid *so much* money for this meeting, and not once did I consider that I'd actually be attracted to the person they sent. I figured it would be like having a really good teacher who didn't smell bad and had clean teeth and could teach me things in a way that I'd be able to understand. Filter out my emotions because of how horribly they got in the way whenever I attempted . . . this.

"Hiring an escort is no small decision," he said smoothly, crossing his massive arms over his chest. My eyes lingered briefly on the curve of his biceps, the way they strained the black T-shirt. How ridiculous. No one should have arms that big. "I'd love to hear more, Ruby."

There was a purring quality to his voice. Like the lion at the zoo—powerful and big and dangerous—staring at me from his seat, just waiting for me to move too quickly. My whole body wanted to bolt, but some screaming instinct told me to hold still, because if I turned my back, he'd sink those giant canines into a soft, unprotected part of me and drag me someplace dark and quiet.

This is what happens when you act impulsively, I thought, with a wild, shrieking quality to the voice in my head.

"No, it wasn't a small decision," I said coolly, like my insides weren't shaking like a freaking leaf. "But I'd rather hear how you ended up in your job."

If there was a ranking system for the type of men in the world, he was at the top of the food chain. The size and strength of his body were just one piece of what put him there. His face was another. I'd watched him at the counter, flirting smoothly with Blake, recovering even more smoothly when she told him about her wife.

A pheromone surrounded him like a cloud, so very potent that I could feel the weakness in my knees even though I was sitting. Not just because he smelled good or because he had such physically pleasing features—a strong jaw and a straight nose, heavily lashed eyes in a golden-hazel color, and muscles stacked along his tall frame in a way that made my throat go dry.

Under any other circumstance, I'd hardly be able to make eye contact with a man like him. But God, I was so sick of that instinct to run. Sick of holding up the heaviest sort of armor when I didn't. After so many years, I wasn't even sure how much protection it offered.

The worst sort of feelings still lingered—loneliness, more than anything. It hurt in a way other emotions didn't, because it wasn't sharp or quick. It lingered, like a bruise that kept getting pushed, so it could never really heal.

Maybe I could set down that armor with him, though.

He wouldn't laugh at me, and he wouldn't tease.

There was a reason I'd called in a professional.

Your date will be in a black T-shirt, black pants, black-and-wood watch, tall with dark hair. Sit in the back of the restaurant, where the two of you can have some privacy.

That's what the email had said.

Griffin leaned in, and I fought the urge to back away. The eye contact was almost dizzying, something I could feel curling pleasantly in my stomach, lifting the hairs on the back of my neck.

"I love what I do," he said. "Always lining up against different people. I love the challenge of trying to figure them out. Keeps me incredibly fit. Every day is a little different." He paused, eyes raking over my face while his lips curled into a sinful smile that I felt down to my toes. "Though my body is completely wrecked by the time I've put in a lot of hours."

Attempting to swallow was pointless because my throat felt like it was packed with sand.

"Wr-wrecked?" I whispered. Looking for an outlet for my useless surge of energy, I plucked mindlessly at the button at the base of my throat. The thought of Griffin wrecking things—with his body or otherwise—made me feel a little fuzzy in the general area of my brain. "I didn't think . . . I wasn't aware that those lines got crossed. Unless you're . . . unless you . . ."

That smile deepened as my voice gave out. He hummed, low in his throat. "Oh, I cross a lot of lines, Ruby." His big, blunt fingers pulled off another piece of muffin, and he popped it into his mouth while his eyes stayed firmly on mine. The line of his jaw worked while he chewed, and I found myself watching the play of muscles underneath the stubble. "Tell me more about why you're here, little birdy. Isn't that what we used to call you?"

I huffed a laugh. "You came up with it. I hated that nickname."

Griffin smiled widely, a flash of white teeth and the dimple making my pulse skitter dangerously.

"Because you were always up in that tree, with your big eyes, reading your books all quiet and sweet." He licked at his bottom lip. How was it that that tiny flash of tongue and the lingering eye contact could make my skin so abnormally hot? God, he was good at this. No wonder he cost a fortune. "Tell me why you're here. I want to know quite badly."

My forehead furrowed briefly. "Well . . . I had to fill out the intake form, and it was quite thorough—"

"Griffin King?"

Griffin looked over at the guy who'd spoken, but his eyes darted back to mine, holding steadily. "Yeah, that's me."

Oh gawd, was he a *famous* escort?

Kill me. Just . . . kill me now.

"Oh, wow, do you mind if I grab a picture? You're a legend, man. I saw you play in New York twice last year. Absolute beast on the field. I'll be devastated when you retire."

My head reared back, skin prickling as I caught the guilty expression flash over Griffin's face. With my mouth hanging open, my heart racing, I let out a strangled sound.

"Wait, are you Ruby?" At the question, I blinked up—and up—at another tall, good-looking man. Wearing a black shirt. With a black-and-wood watch. He was no longer staring at my tablemate with bright, interested eyes, because his attention had shifted to me. "I'm sorry I'm late; it took me longer to get here than I thought."

"I—" It was hard to talk over the roaring of my pulse. Griffin rolled his lips together, a pleading expression filling his golden eyes. "You're not . . . you're—" My voice broke off, pathetically quiet, and my heart hammered so hard that I felt like my ribs might break.

"Ruby and I knew each other as kids," Griffin said, briefly breaking the chest-crushing eye contact to give our newest arrival a friendly smile. "I couldn't help but stop and say hi when I saw her."

Maybe the earth didn't swallow me whole, but how desperately I wanted it to. *Embarrassment* wasn't a strong enough word for what I felt.

This word looked like standing naked on a stage, the bright, hot lights aimed right at me, all the seats filled with clown-like smiles and the kind of nasty laughter that embedded itself in your ears.

The two men stared back at me—one justifiably confused, one looking very apologetic, and quite irrationally, I felt the urge to punch the latter of the two. Hard. I'd never wanted to punch anyone in my entire unremarkable life, but I was ready to break that streak for Griffin Freaking King.

Except I'd probably break my hand on his stupid face.

A mortifying crawl of tears made my nose burn and my throat agonizingly tight.

Griffin assessed the new arrival with a sharp eye. "Thought prostitution was illegal in Colorado."

"That's why I'm a licensed escort," the other said smoothly. "When I'm outside of Las Vegas, at least." Then he winked at me, and my stomach bottomed out.

Griffin eased out of his chair, unfolding his body to his staggering height. Holy hell, he had to be six five. He was an entire foot taller than me.

The other gentleman cleared his throat. Maybe the height difference was getting to him too.

Somehow that made it even worse. A metaphorical pissing match between two strangers.

What was I thinking?

I'd never be able to get over this debilitating anxiety when it came to men. Because of crap like this—when they sat at tables they weren't supposed to sit at, when they showed up in towns they weren't supposed to be in, and when they looked like he looked: criminally, heartbreakingly good.

I stood from the table so fast that my chair clattered backward. "I'm sorry, I—" My eyes pinched shut, and I started clawing at the high neck of my shirt. "I have to go."

The newest arrival held his hand out in a soothing gesture. "No, please. I'd still love to meet with you, see how I can help."

With my fist tight around my shirt, I stared at him. He was nice looking. Tall and wiry. Well dressed. Blue eyes. His lips were a little thin, and he had a baby face. All in all, he was quite unassuming. If I passed him on the street, I wouldn't have looked twice.

There was no hammering pulse, no goose bumps and hairs lifting on the back of the neck.

Maybe he'd be safe. Easy.

He was a professional. Maybe I could tell him the things that terrified me and what I wanted to accomplish from this.

How desperately I wanted to move through this thirtieth year of my life and not feel so achingly alone. Like I could do something about all the ways I'd lived scared.

But the thought of trying to come back from this, to recover from how I felt in that very moment, made me want to hide for, oh, about six months.

Yes. A locked closet sounded great right about now.

"I can't," I said, voice clipped and hard. "I have to go."

"Ruby, I'm sorry, I—" Griffin held out his hand like he was about to grab my arm. I stumbled back so fast I almost fell into another table.

"Don't you dare apologize to me right now," I said fiercely. "In fact, don't say another word to me, Griffin."

Then I turned and fled, fumbling with Bruiser's leash where I'd hooked him up, and once he was clear, I dashed off toward the library.

Chapter Four

GRIFFIN

"Shit," I muttered, watching helplessly as Ruby pushed through the door of the coffee shop.

"You think she's coming back, bro?"

Bro? I gave him a dry look.

The new guy's eyes widened when he took in our matching outfits, eyebrows arching in sudden comprehension. "Ahhh . . ."

"Where'd you travel in from?" I asked, watching through the floor-to-ceiling windows as Ruby walked briskly across the street and disappeared between two buildings. Her shoulders were pulled up tight by her ears, and her short legs moved way more quickly than I thought possible for someone of her height.

"Vegas," he answered. He blew out a short breath. "It's not, uh, illegal there. You know . . ."

My mouth flattened. The thought of Ruby Tate paying for a prostitute made my brain melt.

I gave him as friendly a smile as I could manage. "I'd head back to your hotel for the time being. I'm gonna go talk to her." Slapping a hand on his shoulder, I was mildly gratified to see him flinch. "She'll get in touch if she needs you."

"Oh, I think she needed something, considering how much she was paying me to fly over here and show her a few things. None of the really fun things, of course. Can't engage in those outside of a few very specific places back home. If she wanted to for free, though . . ." His eyebrows bounced. "Wouldn't have been a hardship. I love it when they're tiny like that. You know what I mean?"

As I pulled in a slow breath, I imagined the headlines if I broke this guy's ribs in a quaint little coffee shop in the middle of fucking nowhere, Colorado. My agent would probably drop me. Sponsors sure as hell wouldn't be happy. My brother would shake his head, feeling perfectly settled on his moral high ground as the Good Brother. In fact, I might get arrested, unless I could get him to swing first.

That should be easy enough, actually. If I had any talent in this life, it was pushing the right buttons to really piss people off.

And it wasn't like I had to break all his ribs. Maybe like, four. He could live with four broken ribs, right?

"Yeah?" I asked, and the quietly dangerous tone of my voice sharpened his gaze. "Maybe you should forget you came here." I took a step closer, extremely fucking gratified when he had to tilt his head up. "Forget you met her, in fact. I think you're better off, *bro*."

Instead of backing away, though, he lifted his eyes to mine. "You her keeper?"

I loved guys like this. Who thought they could intimidate me. I straightened to my full height—six five—and met that look of his head-on with one of my own. The kind of look I saved for when I lined up on the field before a snap. When I stared down the offensive line and imagined tearing through every fucking body they had lined up against me. The kind I saved for the quarterback right before I took his ass to the ground.

His throat worked on a nervous swallow.

"I'm an old friend," I said steadily. "And I promise you, that's so much fucking worse for you right now."

He snorted. "Whatever you say, dude." With a haughty sniff, he brushed his hands down the front of his shirt and angled his head toward the counter. "Nice meeting you," he said, sarcasm a little too heavy for my taste.

I walked over to the counter, and the woman with the blue hair arched her eyebrow. "Need another muffin?" she asked.

"Do you know where Ruby lives?"

Her eyes flattened immediately. "You're off your rocker if you think I'm gonna tell you that."

Blowing out a frustrated breath, I looked in the direction of where she ran. "Fair enough."

"She works at the library," Mr. Prostitute answered from behind me.

My jaw tightened as I turned. "What's that?"

He was studying the baked goods. "The library in town. She had to supply some information to my employer."

The blue-hair behind the counter muttered something that sounded decidedly unfriendly, but it wasn't clear enough for me to understand. But she stopped me with a wave of her hand, putting one of the blueberry muffins into a to-go bag. "I don't think Ruby ate breakfast," she said. "Bring her this if you find her. Can't have her going hungry before work."

Ten seconds later, I was jogging across the street in the direction she'd fled. The narrow alley between the two-story brick buildings was clean, leading straight through to the next block. Through the alley, there was a long stretch of empty land on the other side—a weeping willow tree and tall grasses, bright groupings of wildflowers, and a small creek cutting through the middle of the land as it meandered toward a one-story brick building wrapped with windows.

Everything about this place was quiet and clean and peaceful, except for the way my brain reacted when I caught sight of an ivory blouse and messy golden waves on a wooden bench. She was staring at the weeping willow tree. Next to her was the big dog from outside the bakery.

Her hand rested on the back of his neck, idly scratching his short fur. When you get older, you stop thinking about your childhood, don't you? Unless something very specific happens. A song that pulls you back. Or you see something that triggers a memory. I'd gone years without thinking of Ruby Tate. A lot of them too.

I couldn't even say that we'd known her well, but she was always there.

There wasn't even a lingering sadness when I'd heard that she and her parents had moved away when we were in high school. Once or twice, I'd glanced up into that oak tree that straddled her yard and mine, at the empty spot where she used to sit.

Approaching quietly, I tried to figure out what the hell my endgame was here.

There was only one place in my entire life where I could read people well, and that was on the field. I didn't have practice consoling a kid or a spouse or a girlfriend. There was no navigating personal relationships once I got home from work.

Wasn't that how I'd ended up here? It was all the outside shit that got me twisted up. The constantly seeking something shiny and new and exciting so that the quiet at home didn't make me feel like I was drowning.

I knew how to play the game. I knew how to prep for those games— in the weight room and on the field and in studying film.

I knew how to be a good teammate. All my friends did the same job as me. Most of them had families to go to when they walked out the facility doors. Some were single like me. Those were the guys I partied with, traveled with.

I knew how to do that too. The moment I was on my own, separate from that big part of my life, there was no one who relied on me. It left me reeling now, as I approached where Ruby sat.

Don't fuck it up, I thought. That was about the best pep talk I could muster. *Just . . . don't fuck it up.*

When I neared the bench, Ruby's frame went visibly stiff, her hands moving to her lap as her dog popped up on four legs to greet me.

"Careful," she said airily, in complete contradiction with the tension visible in every inch of her body. "He's really mean and overprotective. He might bite."

"No kidding."

"Yup. One word from me, and you're toast."

I whistled low. "Hope you aren't thinking about saying that word right now."

Bruiser tilted his head as he stared me down, and for a split second, I wondered if she was being serious. Nah. She wasn't serious. Even though she didn't turn her head, Ruby eyed me from her spot on the bench, gnawing on her bottom lip and looking ten times warier than her dog did. There was no tail for him to wag—his was docked—but his entire butt wiggled back and forth when I came a step closer.

I kept my arms loose by my sides, and Bruiser wiggled sideways against my legs, nudging my free hand with his big ol' head. "Yeah, he looks vicious."

Ruby didn't say anything, simply kept her head straight forward, but her eyes kept cutting over to me and her dog.

"Hey, Bruiser," I murmured. "You're not gonna eat me, are you?" His response to that was a happy groan as my fingers dug into the spot right behind his ears. Ruby scoffed quietly, and the annoyed sound made me grin. "You love me."

"How do you know his . . ." She snapped her gaze forward. "Never mind."

"Bruiser and I met outside the bakery." I smiled as he licked my fingertips. "He's definitely happier to see me than you are."

Her brow furrowed slightly. "Of course he is. He's a dog, and his critical thinking skills are lacking because you taste like muffins."

"Nah, I think he's a great judge of character."

"You *would* think that."

I fished around in the bag and pulled off a piece from the top of the blueberry muffin. "May I?"

Her answer was a tiny roll of her eyes, but her chin dipped a fraction of an inch.

"Bruiser, sit." His butt kept wiggling. "Sit. Gotta do something good to earn it, buddy. Otherwise, the next thing I know, you'll be chomping my face off because she said the scary word."

Ruby pinched the bridge of her nose, sighing heavily.

The massive pink tongue hanging out the side of his mouth made me smile, but his butt went nowhere close to the ground.

"Bruiser, wiggle your butt," I commanded. That he did epically, so I tossed the chunk of muffin in the air. His mouth opened wide, and the muffin bounced off the side of his snout. Ruby rolled her lips together to hide a smile, and we both watched as he snuffled the piece off the ground.

Since she wasn't commanding her dog to eat me, and she had yet to tell me to get the fuck away from her, I decided to risk it. There was enough space on the bench that I could sit and my shoulder wouldn't brush hers, so I set down the bakery bag first, allowing it to serve as a buffer between us. Ruby eyed it as if it were a bomb.

"That's from, uh, the blue-hair."

Ruby dropped her chin to her chest briefly. "Blake," she said. "She owns the shop. She's always . . . always making sure I eat something when I come in for my morning tea."

I nodded slowly. "Good to have people like that."

Instead of answering, Ruby reached into the bag and broke off part of the muffin, chewing quietly while I stared at the small creek. Tall grasses lined its banks; rocks covered in soft green algae popped out of the slowly moving water as it wound its way around a bend and toward the large brick building next to us. In front of the building was a deep-green sign with white letters—the library where she worked, apparently.

Ruby brushed the sugar crystals off her hands, and in my peripheral vision, I saw her lick a few crumbs off her bottom lip.

"How long have you lived here?" I asked.

"I thought about punching you in the bakery," she said instead of answering.

My head reared back, my mouth fighting a smile. "Yeah? I bet you've got a mean right hook, Tate."

"I wouldn't know. I've never hit anyone in my life."

I whistled. "You're missing out. Very few things in life feel as good as whaling on someone who really deserves it."

"So you're admitting you deserved it? I'm shocked at the self-awareness."

Her dry tone had me grinning. "Maybe a little."

"There would be a certain poetic justice to you being my first. First boy who teased me about how I was always reading." She turned her knees to the side, facing me with big, earnest eyes. "You made me think you were him."

"Actually, you assumed," I told her, wagging a finger in the air. "I never once told you that I was an escort. You have to admit, it's not something that comes up much in polite conversation. Naturally, I was curious why a pretty thing like you would need to hire someone to . . ."

Even though her cheeks flushed pink again, her eyebrows arched slowly. "To what?"

"Anything." I held her gaze. "He wasn't exactly very forthcoming with me after your sudden exit."

Ruby faced forward again, blinking rapidly, her chest rising and falling on short breaths. There was a slight wrinkle in the high neck of her blouse from where she'd crumpled it in her fist.

"I am not talking about this with you."

As I watched, her eyes pinched shut, a furrow appearing in between her brows that shouldn't have been cute but was.

Ruby, in fact, was cute. Very cute.

While she sat there, I studied her slightly off-balance features objectively. Her mouth was a little wide, her eyes a little big. Her nose was cute and small, and her cheekbones were high.

But everything about her worked, somehow—this small, pretty woman who used to hide in trees and watch me and my brother play.

"Okay." I sat quietly, taking in a deep breath. The air was clean and fresh and sweet, and I wasn't sure how much of what I was smelling was the trees and the grass, and how much was Ruby.

Glancing briefly in her direction, I noticed her eyes were open again, and she was staring at the creek too. In front of us, some children ran across the open field, pulling off their shoes to wade into the creek. Her face softened as she watched them. They clutched buckets in their hands and immediately started scooping up water.

"How does one go about hiring someone like him? I should've gotten his name. You never know when you'll need an escort."

Ruby didn't answer right away; only the slightest bend to her eyebrows even let me know that she'd heard me.

"I literally just said I wasn't going to talk about this with you."

"Oh, mine was a rhetorical question." I waved my hand in front of us. "Just putting it out into the universe in case *someone* wanted to talk about it."

"Someone doesn't," she snapped.

On the grass in front of us, Bruiser rolled onto his back, wiggling around with a contented groan.

I slowly stretched my arm out along the back of the bench, careful to keep my fingers from touching her shoulders, which she kept locked with tension. "I'm an excellent listener, Ruby."

"Most professional athletes are. I bet you have that listed right at the top of your personal strengths, don't you? 'Listens well to the problems of others'?"

"Ah, so you do know who I am now."

She motioned to her phone, sitting on the bench next to the bakery bag. "Not really. Thought about googling you but decided that would just make it worse." She plucked at another piece of muffin and ate it. "Your brother play too?"

"Nope. Not anymore. He got injured a few years ago and retired. He's a coach now."

"Seems like he'd be a good coach. He was always so smart."

Of course she'd say that. Everyone knew Barrett was the Smart One. My jaw tightened briefly, but she didn't seem to notice.

"People say he's great, but I think my head would explode if I tried complimenting him."

Her eyes shifted to the side of my face, but I kept my gaze forward. "Why? I remember the two of you being so close."

I'd smiled a few times at Ruby Tate, but this one was different. Tight with tension. Filled with uncomfortable subtext. "When we were younger, we were. Not anymore."

"That's sad," she said. "I always wished I had a sibling. Even if it was someone to fight with on occasion. It's better than feeling alone."

Oh, and wasn't that an interesting little clue?

"You feeling lonely, little birdy? That why you're paying for dates?"

"I wasn't 'paying for dates,'" she answered through gritted teeth. "Do you know how embarrassing this is? I haven't seen you in fifteen years, and you're here now. Today of all days."

Instead of answering, I pushed my tongue against the inside of my cheek.

Ruby let out a heavy sigh. "You're not going to leave me be until I tell you, are you?"

"Unlikely. I'm here on vacation for a couple weeks, and I'm bored out of my absolute mind."

She blinked over at me. "Vacation? Here?"

I hummed. "My agent has a house just outside of town. He grounded me because I've been causing more trouble than he prefers."

"And you're bored," she said cautiously. "How long have you been here?"

"About thirty-six hours." Ruby blinked again. "Anyway," I continued, "tell me all your deep, dark secrets, Ruby Tate."

She rolled her eyes. "They're not deep, dark secrets, it's just . . . mildly embarrassing."

"Who better to tell than someone you haven't seen in fifteen or so years and will be out of your life in a couple weeks?"

"Won't you be out of my life after this conversation?"

"Nah. I'll probably come visit you at the library, because now I know where you'll be every day."

She blew out a slow breath. "Great," she muttered.

I nudged her gently with a press of my hand to her shoulder. "Come on," I coaxed. "You know you want to unload on someone."

"I don't know anything of the sort."

"Ruby," I said. My low, pleading tone made her neck turn that same pink shade as her cheeks, and I briefly wondered how far down her chest that color went. "Please?"

"You're relentless," she whispered, pinching the bridge of her nose again. I wanted to assure her that it was common for me to have that effect on people. "You'd be the worst person to talk to about this."

"I'm the perfect person." I shifted closer on the bench. "Think about it: I don't know anyone here, I'm so fucking bored I could scream, and this is the most entertaining thing that's happened to me in a while."

She cut me a scathing look. "I am not here to be your entertainment, Griffin."

I held up my hand. "You know what I mean. I'm safe," I said. "Harmless as a puppy."

She snorted. "You look it. A six-five, two-hundred-and-fifty-pound puppy."

"You can't hold my height against me, it's hardly fair."

"You are exactly the kind of man who makes speaking to men impossible."

"What's impossible about me? I brought you baked goods. Your dog loves me," I pointed out.

Said dog chose that moment to flop back over onto his stomach and start licking his privates. Ruby shook her head and sighed. "You don't know what it's like for us normal people."

"You think athletes aren't normal people?"

"No," she answered dryly.

I clucked my tongue. "So judgy. Dealing with men is easy, birdy. I promise."

"You would say that, because you probably have a dozen groupies lined up outside the locker room after a game and you just point to one and they trot right after you."

"Ouch. I'm a little more discriminating than that."

"Are you?"

"Yes." I laid a hand on my chest. "I always talk to them first. Pointing comes later, once I've made them do a little song and dance for me."

The horrified look on Ruby's face had me bursting out laughing, and she smacked me in the chest. Hard. "Not funny."

"Sort of funny," I said, still smiling.

Her eyes darted over to my face, and she shook her head. "I need to go to work."

"Aww, come on. You can sit with an old friend for a little while longer, can't you? I'll join story time at the library or something. I bet even I could understand those picture books."

"No." She stood, smoothing her hands down the front of her trim black pants. Her dog bounded to his feet, accepting some head-scratches from his owner.

"He goes to work with you?"

"Most days."

"The dog is allowed in there but I'm not?"

"The dog isn't going to pester me all day." She sighed. "Besides, he's a certified therapy dog. We use him to help kids who struggle with reading."

I eyed the animal, with his giant tongue hanging out his mouth. "He can read? What kind of dog is this?"

Ruby's eyes closed briefly, like she was praying for patience. "The kids like to sit with the dogs. Makes it easier to read out loud."

"No kidding. No wonder he's outranked me." I stretched my arms over my head. "When do you open tomorrow? I'll come in for some reading material. As long as they don't have too many big words."

She sighed. Again. "Goodbye, Griffin. I hope you enjoy the rest of your vacation."

Ruby executed a sharp pivot, and with her beast of a dog by her side, she marched toward the library, and I watched her until she disappeared.

"Huh."

That was interesting.

I was very, very interested in what was going on here.

Since I had nowhere to be, I sat on the bench for a while longer, staring at the creek, then stood, whistling as I walked back to my car.

Chapter Five

RUBY

At a pretty pivotal point in my life, I'd learned a few lessons that would take years to undo. The first being that any sort of unknown could be made less scary with copious amounts of research. My browser history was probably in some sort of FBI database, for all I knew, especially the last couple months.

There was nothing to be done about that, though. Hiring and vetting an escort required a few private browsers, and no one had shown up to arrest me yet, so I was assuming that I was still safe from legal prosecution.

When I got to work the next day, there was an email waiting for me from the escort agency. If I wanted, I could reschedule a meeting with Jimmy (now that I knew his name, I'd decided there was no worry of sexual attraction to someone named Jimmy with thin lips and a baby face). But even though he would be the monumentally safer choice than trying to wade into the dating pool—shudder—I couldn't bring myself to do it just yet.

The day was still young.

If I didn't reschedule, Jimmy's brief visit would go down as a very expensive mistake that I had no intention of making again.

"How was the meeting with the hooker yesterday?"

There was no need to glance up from my computer screen, because Lauren was the only person in the world who'd ask me that. "He's not a hooker, Lo, he's an escort."

"An escort who also gets paid to have sex at his fancy brothel in Vegas, yeah?"

With a sigh, I closed out the browser. My search history had my cheeks going warm, and I prayed Lauren didn't notice. "Whether he does or doesn't is not my problem. I didn't hire him for sex, I hired him for . . ."

"Nonsexual sexual training?" she supplied helpfully.

I gave her a dry look. "Yes."

"God, when I was in high school, we learned everything from *Cosmo*." She plopped down in the chair opposite my desk. "They had the best articles. The day I learned about Reverse Cowgirl was the day my life changed."

Lauren wasn't that much older, but on days like this, it felt like she had decades more experience. She also had no filter, a healthy sex drive, and the determination to do her very best to bring me into the same hormonal space she occupied happily. "I don't think a magazine can fix me, Lo."

I smiled, but it was tight at the edges. In fact, I'd felt tight and edgy ever since walking away from that bench, leaving Griffin King sprawled on it like it was a freaking throne.

Because I had a healthy sense of vanity, I had managed not to look back until I'd cleared the library doors, finally allowing myself a peek around the corner to see what he'd do.

For a few minutes, he sat there, staring at the creek, that big, muscled arm still stretched along the back of the bench. Then he stood, unfolding his body with the kind of unhurried grace that you couldn't fake. That was a man who was comfortable in his skin, and I watched him walk away with a pinprick of foreboding digging into the back of my mind.

The research started immediately.

For as much as I'd watched those boys when I was younger, I had never really thought about looking them up. Why would I?

But the moment my search engine caught wind of their names, I sat at that computer with my jaw hanging open. Apparently this was the stuff I missed when I delegated the periodicals section to Kenny.

The King brothers weren't just talented, and they weren't just successful—they were famous. Article after article had my eyes widening.

> Griffin King: The Next Defensive MVP? Behind His Quest to Break the Offensive Streak

> Barrett King Retires at 28: The Hidden Dark Side of the League's Head-Injury Problem

> The Brain vs. the Brawn: The Biggest Showdown in Football Happens This Weekend. Which King Brother Will Come Out on Top?

> Marital woes overshadow Barrett King's triumphant second year of coaching. Is his playboy brother part of the problem? Our body language expert dissects their tense on-field exchange.

> Sexiest player in the league? Griffin King breaks down why he's not sure marriage is in the cards.

That last article came with a few photographs—practically indecent photographs that answered at least one of my questions.

Griffin—as one might imagine, if they wanted to imagine such a thing—looked incredible naked. The first photo, bigger than the other two, featured him standing in a dimly lit locker room, holding a football over his groin. The rest was skin. Skin and honed muscles and a dangerously attractive facial expression that had me pressing my thighs together.

Honestly, his body should've been in a museum somewhere.

The bend of muscles under flawless golden skin, curves over his shoulders, stacked squares on his stomach and the mouthwatering cut of the V-shaped muscles below his abs, the impossibly rounded biceps and the veins roping along his forearm where his big hand held the ball—it was all just a bit much, if you asked me.

Probably why I stared at it a little too long, but that was completely irrelevant.

"Whatcha staring at?" Lo asked, leaning closer to my desk.

I snapped the laptop shut. "Nothing. Just doing some research."

She arched an eyebrow. "So . . . the hooker."

"Could you say that just a little louder?" I hissed, looking frantically past the door of my office. It was, quite blessedly, empty. "The *escort* is probably back at his hotel. It didn't . . . the meeting didn't happen. Someone I knew from when I was younger showed up, and I got all . . ." I waved my hands next to my head.

Lo smiled. "I hate when that happens."

"It threw me off," I admitted. "Then I really started thinking about how it looked that I was hiring someone to help me build my confidence around men. Who needs that?"

"You don't," she said easily. "Many people live very happily without romantic companionship. It's only a problem if it bothers you."

Did it?

There was no one presuming on my time. If I wanted to lie in bed and watch Jane Austen movies all weekend? No one could stop me. If I wanted to read for days or go out to eat with friends and live on cereal for a week straight or . . . or . . .

The thoughts fizzled there.

Yes. It bothered me.

When I lay alone in my bed, nothing but the sound of my own heart to distract me from my thoughts, I wanted to know how it felt. All of it. The sweet parts and the simple parts and the dirty parts too.

I didn't need it all the time, mind you. The thought of man sounds and smells and . . . everything in my house made my nose wrinkle. He could stay in his own place, thank you very much. It was about possessing the knowledge. A reference point for comparison.

No, I couldn't hold it in my grasp forever; I couldn't lock it in a box for safekeeping. But it would still be mine. Those experiences and memories couldn't be taken away by anyone, no matter what.

If I closed my eyes and thought about what knowledge looked like, it was a tidy stack of shiny gold coins that locked together. Like building blocks. The more of those coins in your possession, the more valuable they became. It was a cumulative thing, each one building upon the one before. In my head, I wanted those coins to build something big and grand and beautiful that I could study and admire.

Right now, there was nothing but a flimsy deck of cards instead—at least when it came to this particular subject of study. A gentle breeze would knock it right over, and there was nothing I could do about that.

Slumping at my desk, I covered my face with my hands. "I'm not cut out for this. For any of it. I'm just going to die alone in my little house. I'll probably get some cats and learn how to knit and bake myself cupcakes because there's no one around me to eat them."

She clucked her tongue. "Well, aren't we one giant cliché, huh? First, Bruiser would be terrified of those cats, and you don't like them anyway."

"I don't. They freak me out."

Bruiser lifted his head from where he lay at my feet, letting out a commiserating groan as he flopped onto his side to get comfortable. Lauren smiled.

"You tried knitting once, and you got very angry."

I sighed. "I did. Making all those little loops made me want to stab someone." I gave her a meaningful look. "But I couldn't because I live alone."

Lauren rounded my desk, giving me a consoling pat on the back. "You'll get it figured out, shorty."

At the nickname, I leveled a glare in her direction. All it managed to do was make her laugh, which said more about my glare than it did Lauren.

Before she left my office, she snapped her fingers. "Oh, I got a call from the city offices while you were doing story hour earlier."

Immediately, I sat up in my chair. "And?"

Her face bent in a grimace. "Not good news. The property will start taking offers in the next couple weeks. Sheila told me there are two real estate developers interested."

"Damn it," I whispered, disappointment anchoring somewhere deep in my belly. On the far wall of my office were all the renders I'd had drawn up to present to the board of directors. They loved them. But, as always, it wasn't a matter of them liking my ideas; it was a matter of money.

For years, I'd been planning what we could do to the land surrounding the library once it went up for sale. The old man who'd owned it had passed away a few months earlier, and it took a while for his kids to decide what they wanted to do. I'd reached out more than once, telling them about the nature path, the butterfly garden, how we could highlight Colorado artists with small sculptures and interactive features for kids and families.

Make it something memorable and wonderful. A legacy that would outlive me, that was for sure.

It was the kind of thing that kids remembered as they got older, that they wanted to bring their kids back to. I thought of the two little boys with their buckets, searching for minnows in the creek, and it took everything in me to swallow my disappointment.

Lauren gave me a tiny wink. "Not over yet. We'll raise a lot of money from the fair next week."

"I know we will." I conjured a smile, but based on the slight arch to Lo's eyebrow, it wasn't a very believable one.

Kenny—one of our college-age employees—popped his head into my office. "Ruby? There's someone out here asking for you."

There was a feverish look in his eyes that had me narrowing mine. "Who?"

"You wouldn't believe me if I told you," he said gravely.

Lauren brushed past him and looked out into the main area of the library, her mouth falling open. "Is that . . . Griffin King?" she whispered. "Do you know Griffin King?"

Son of a biscuit. My eyes pinched shut, and I took a deep breath. I should've known he wouldn't just go away.

Still seated at my desk, I couldn't see out into the library, so I stood and glanced through the windows lining the side of my office. When I caught sight of him, a nervous swirling kicked off in my stomach, seeping out through all four limbs, making my fingertips tingle.

It wasn't even fair.

People shouldn't look like him and be able to just . . . walk around for anyone to see. This was a library, for crying out loud.

Today, he was wearing a sinfully tight white T-shirt and a black hat turned backward on his head. His long, thick legs were covered in dark joggers that hugged his tree-trunk thighs.

"Sort of," I hedged. "When I was younger, he and his family lived in the house behind mine."

Lauren clutched my arm. "Is that . . . is *that* the Griffin from when you were younger?"

"Yes."

Her eyes widened. "And you didn't know he was Griffin King?"

I held my hands up helplessly. "I don't watch TV. I hate social media."

My explanations must not have impressed her, because she continued to stare at me like I'd personally injured her. "*That's* who you saw before the hooker showed up?"

Kenny's eyes widened. "The what?"

I pinched Lauren's side, and she winced. "There were no hookers," I said firmly. "Ignore her, please."

Based on the look on Kenny's face, he was fairly unconvinced he could manage that. "Eh, what do you want me to tell him?"

I ran a hand through my hair, sighing heavily. "I'll handle him."

"Oh, please do," Lauren breathed. "I'd handle him so hard if he were here for me."

Crossing my arms, I turned and pinned her with a thoroughly unamused look. "Don't you have something to do, Lo?"

"Not that's more important than this."

"Go. Shoo," I told her, pushing her down the hallway. "There's a cart of books that need to be shelved."

As she walked away, she muttered underneath her breath about how I was the worst boss in the world. Pinching the bridge of my nose, I took a moment to try to steady my breathing.

Impossible, but worth a try at least.

My pulse was racing, and I wondered if it would echo through the quiet space when I joined him. Griffin had his hands tucked into his pockets, studying one of the displays in the middle of the room. I'd worked on it a few days earlier, highlighting some spicy summer reads.

And now he was standing in front of them, reaching to pick up the one on the top of a pile. His lips hooked up in a smirk as he read the back cover. That book was about a priest and his very forbidden love affair with a young woman, and I had to tear my eyes away before I lost the nerve to walk up to him.

From everything I'd found, Griffin was an actual, legitimate celebrity. Famous for his feud with his brother, for his talent on the field, and even more than that, for his string of casual relationships off the field.

He'd dated models and actresses, a couple of singers. All stunningly beautiful, none of them around for very long.

With a tight jaw, I looked down at the blouse that buttoned up to the bottom of my throat, with a lace collar that I'd always liked. The pencil skirt was probably half a size too big, but that never really bothered me too much.

I wasn't curvy, and I wasn't beautiful. I was just me. And even if I was okay with that, it was still hard to wrap my mind around someone like him showing up for someone like me. Maybe I was on the small side of a B cup and I didn't have the kind of curves that men tripped over, but I was smart and kind and friendly.

Sort of. Once you got to know me.

It felt insane to have any type of interaction with him—didn't matter if it was casual or friendly. There was a hierarchy of people in the world, whether we wanted to admit it or not. Like Maslow's Hierarchy of Needs, except that three-sided figure represented the mental structure of how each person viewed the world.

That ranking system looked different to every person. Some placed tech giants and billionaires at the top; others, esteemed politicians or activists. Some worshipped people like Griffin—uniquely talented in something physical, a sport that gathered millions around a field or a television every week to cheer for something larger than themselves.

My own pyramid was a little different. I revered the thinkers and the doers, the people who made a direct impact on their world, even if it was done quietly, with a spine of steel. But no matter whose hierarchy we were looking at, my own place likely came well beneath his, and we both knew it.

My hand toyed with the button under the lace, and I felt myself tug all that heavy armor into place. When I was a teenager, my dad always used to say I was like a feral cat, swiping at anyone who tried to help but melting when the right person came along.

There'd be no melting for Griffin, so I blew out a harsh breath, notched my chin up, and marched toward him.

"What are you doing here?" I asked.

He took his sweet-ass time setting the book down, and when he did, there was a teasing glint in his eye that made me instantly wary.

"Good morning, Ruby." His gaze tracked down the front of my body and settled back on my face a moment later. "You look lovely in that color."

This wasn't fair. A simple compliment, and the skin on my upper body was now registering a thousand degrees.

And he did it with a twinkle in his eyes and a grin hovering on the edges of his perfect mouth.

Ass.

"You have to leave."

The words came out with only the slightest tinge of panic, because something about Griffin made me feel very, very panicky, indeed. Like if I stayed around him too long, all the edges of my carefully constructed world would start peeling away.

And I wasn't entirely sure I wanted to see what was underneath.

With unhurried strides, he walked around the table, picking up a fantasy novel I hadn't had a chance to read yet. "Now, that is not the friendliest greeting, is it? I've been up since dawn waiting for the library to open."

I plucked the book from his hand. "You have not."

Griffin ignored me, selecting a cowboy romance with a gorgeous red cover. He flipped through some of the pages, eyebrows popping high at whatever he saw. His eyes flicked to mine. "You read all these books, birdy?"

My cheeks felt hot, but I held his gaze. "Not all of them, but some. It's part of the job to know what people are looking for, and right now, they want spicy romance."

"I think I might check this one out," he said, holding the book up. "Not much of a reader, but I could make an exception."

Holding his gaze, I pointed at the cover. "You want to read that book?"

"Oh yeah," he answered in a rumbling voice that I felt down to my toes. "Imagine all the things I could learn."

With a tiny wink, he tucked the book under his arm and ambled off toward the stacks in the back of the library, whistling low and quiet. Mouth agape, I watched him go. Lauren waved her arms frantically, and when I cut her a look, she mouthed, *What are you doing, go!*

Narrowing my eyes in a fierce glare did nothing to my friend, because she simply jabbed her finger in the air in Griffin's general direction.

The man in question paused and glanced over his shoulder. "You need to come with me, otherwise I'll be wandering aimlessly for hours. Unless you'd like to see my face around every corner. For your entire day."

When I leveled my glare in his direction, his smile simply grew, a deep, enticing dimple appearing in the dark stubble on his knife-sharp jaw.

What an ass.

"No." I crossed my arms. "You are perfectly capable of finding books on your own."

Behind me, Lauren hissed my name, but I ignored her.

I mean . . . fine, I was being a little snippy, but I couldn't help it.

This was exactly the way he was as a kid too. Nosy and pushy and always teasing me.

He glanced around the building, eyes narrowed in thought. "You got any picture books on how to get better at football? I bet my new coach would be happy if I started reading one of those."

The way my brow furrowed, I just knew I was popping some new wrinkles, courtesy of this freaking man. "You have a new coach?"

He hummed. "Just transferred to Denver. Signing the contract any day now. That's why I couldn't come visit until today, because my agent and I had to hammer out a few last details. Did I not mention that?"

Tha-thunk.

That was the sound of my heart dropping into the pit of my stomach.

"You did not," I said faintly. Oh God, he'd practically be local. Okay, fine. Not local. But within driving distance.

Freaking great.

"Five minutes," I told him. "You have me for five minutes, and then I need to get back to work."

"No, she doesn't. Her schedule's wide open," Lauren called out. Kenny's eyes widened. Someone from the other side of the library shushed her.

"See, now that's helpful," Griffin pointed out. "Thank you . . ."

"Lauren," she supplied graciously.

I rolled my eyes at the simpering smile on her face. Kenny looked like he was gonna pass out.

Griffin smiled oh so charmingly. "Lauren. You are a gem." Then he locked his gaze on mine and spread his arm out. "After you. I am your humble student, Miss Tate."

I was definitely going to punch him before this was over.

Chapter Six

RUBY

Trying to follow him was astronomically unfair. His legs were twice as long as mine, and I huffed loudly as I trotted off to where he'd disappeared down one of the nonfiction aisles. Lauren let out a satisfied sigh as I started walking, and I covertly flipped her my middle finger because there were no other patrons in my sight line.

The sound of her laugh was the last thing I heard before I caught up with Griffin, standing in the middle of the aisle, his head tilted to the side as he studied the spines in front of him.

"Ooh, not sure this is the right place for me."

"No, it wouldn't be."

"Should we go one aisle over?" He tapped his finger on a book. "Never mind. I think I need this one too."

When he pulled it from the shelf, I sighed quietly through my nose, just barely holding back the eye roll that threatened.

"*The Art of Seduction*," he read quietly, gaze narrowed thoughtfully as he read the back cover. "'Twenty-four maneuvers will guide readers through the seduction process, providing cunning, amoral instructions for and analysis of this fascinating, all-pervasive form of power.'" He whistled under his breath. "Yowza. And you keep this baby out for anyone to pick up? Seems dangerous."

I snatched the book out of his hand, just like I had the other, and tucked it back into its place, my cheeks flaming. "What do you want? I know you're not here for books."

"Speak for yourself," he murmured, leaning closer to me to grab the book back and tuck it underneath his arm. His arm brushed against mine, and the heat of his bicep seared through my shirt. The rolling muscle was the size of a python, for crying out loud.

I dug deep, letting out a slow, measured exhale.

By the time I opened my eyes, he was studying my face in a way that made my belly swoop weightlessly.

"No," I said firmly.

Griffin blinked. "What? I didn't say anything."

"You're looking at me funny."

"Are you always so prickly when a man tries to converse with you?"

"Yes," I answered in a grim tone.

"Ah. Hence the escort."

I huffed, trying to move past him, but he easily sidestepped, blocking my path from the aisle. It was quite irritating how I had to crane my neck to look up at him.

Griffin clicked his tongue. "See, now *you're* looking at *me* funny."

There was a moment where I considered lying, but honestly, my filter was just gone with how he loomed over me.

"It's annoying how tall you are," I told him.

"People have found me annoying for much less than that, so I can understand. Besides, you're pocket-size. It's cute." Then he patted the top of my head. Like I was a child.

I smacked his hand away, and he had the audacity to chuckle. Before I could speak, he grabbed the black-and-pink book again. "You read this?"

"Not yet."

"Maybe you should." He flipped idly through the pages, his eyebrows rising in interest at whatever he saw. "Maybe it would help you with . . . whatever . . ."

The way his voice trailed off, like he could drop breadcrumbs and I'd follow along, finally unleashed the eye roll I'd kept on such a tight leash.

Inexplicably, his smile grew, and I found myself tugging lightly on the hem of my pastel-blue cardigan to make sure it lay smoothly on my hips. Underneath it was my favorite silk blouse of the same color.

And now, thanks to him, I'd think of Griffin every time I put it on. *"You look lovely in that color."*

A sharp clearing of my throat effectively snipped the memory of his voice from my mind.

"I have a professional for 'whatever,'" I reminded him.

His eyebrows shot up. "You're still going to use him? He was a tool."

"You cannot possibly know that. You spoke to him for less than five minutes."

"Yeah, I can. I have amazing douchebag radar." He tapped the side of his temple. "Believe me, it was going off loud and clear after you bolted."

I tilted my head. "I bolted because you deceived me."

Griffin's big hand lay over his chest, and my eyes flicked briefly to the veins roping the back of that hand. *"Deception* is a very strong word, birdy. If he hadn't shown up, I would have told you the truth."

"Easy to say now." One of our regulars wandered down the aisle, and I smiled in her direction when she stopped to peruse some book at the end of the row we shared.

Griffin nudged my shoulder with his arm and angled his head one aisle over. We walked around in silence, but I decided to add in another row between us and anyone else, just to have a buffer.

He paused to study the books in this aisle. "World War Two?" he asked.

I nodded. "Some great ones in here, if you like history."

"Only history I usually pay attention to is in the film room," he answered, still studying the spines. His gaze lingered on a couple, but he didn't pick up anything else.

It was easier, it seemed, for him to tease me when the topic was something he felt like he could joke about. A tell if I'd ever seen one.

"How long is your vacation?" I asked.

He sighed heavily. "Two and a half weeks."

A reluctant grin tugged at my lips. "Sounds like a hardship. I can see why you're so upset."

"I already worked out for three hours this morning." His focus stayed firmly on the books, and I watched, with involuntary fascination, to see which ones seemed to snag his interest. "I played solitaire for another hour. My brain will rot if I don't find something to do."

"Your brain will not rot from having a relaxing vacation."

"Easy for you to say," he tossed back, leaning his big shoulder against the bookshelf and staring down at me again. "Does this mean I can't come hang out with you at work?"

"Not a chance."

He grinned widely, and there was an answering flare of heat so bright behind my chest bone that I tore my eyes away from his face.

"Here," I said, pulling a book down from the shelf in front of me. "Add this to your pile."

"*Against All Odds*," he read. "What's this one about?"

I took a small step closer and tapped the front cover, a clean, musky scent coming from Griffin that had me dipping my head slightly. "It follows four men through the war and after. They were in the same unit." His eyes met mine. "One of them was a former football player. He was the first American to win every award for valor."

"Brave man," he said, sliding his hand under the book, his fingers brushing lightly against my own. "You think I'll learn something from him?"

I snapped my arm away once the book was in his grasp, my fingers tingling ominously. "We can always learn something from the things we read or watch or listen to. But we have to be open to it, willing to apply it to our lives."

He hummed, flipping through the pages. "Three books, huh? Maybe I can finish them before the season starts."

The self-deprecating comments weren't lost on me, and I found myself studying his facial expression now, allowing myself the slightest of risks that he might notice too.

"If you like it, I can recommend some others. I'm sure you'll finish them in no time."

Griffin transferred the books under his arm into his hands, then straightened to his full height, his eyes moving over my face. "When you seeing him again?"

I blinked. "Tonight, I think. He suggested drinks so we can . . . talk."

"Just drinks?"

I nodded slowly. "I don't really drink, though, so it will probably be a short meeting."

Griffin glanced over my shoulder, down the aisle, and I could practically see the wheels turning in his head. When his gaze met mine again, decisiveness was bright in his eyes.

It was almost unbearable, how attractive it was on him.

"Come to my place afterwards," he said, voice low and urgent.

"What? No."

"Why not?" He leaned his shoulder against the bookshelf again, biting down briefly on his bottom lip. "Let me show my appreciation for the book recommendations."

"I only recommended one of them; if the other two are terrible, it's not my fault."

His brief grin was devastating, and I felt it tug at the hairs on the back of my neck. "Then let me thank you for one book recommendation. I'll make you some dinner. I'm a terrible cook, it'll be fun."

Suspicion had my eyes narrowing. "You're not trying to sleep with me, are you?"

Griffin's face went blank with shock. "What? No. I'm just trying to catch up with an old friend, that's all."

"'Old *friend*?" I asked skeptically.

"Fine. An old . . . neighbor. Former neighbor," he corrected. "You're definitely not old."

Wearily, I rubbed at my forehead. "I feel old. Don't you?"

"Sure as fuck ain't feeling any younger." He leaned in, and I got a whiff of that scent again. Sandalwood; crisp, clean air; something . . . spicy and wonderful. "Come on," he urged. "My agent's house is obnoxious, and I haven't been able to show it off to anyone."

I glanced at the front of the library and saw Kenny practically falling off his chair trying to watch us. My eyes fell closed and I sighed.

"Think of what a good story it will be." He spoke closer to my ear this time, and the rough, gravelly sound of it yanked goose bumps along the lengths of my arms, and boy, did I curse their existence.

It was so easy for someone like him.

There was the height and the smile and the stubble.

The jaw.

Don't even get me started on the muscles. When you added in his weekly paycheck, it was enough to curse the heavens for discriminatory practices against the rest of us.

Maybe it wouldn't be so bad to go to his place, just so that I had a legitimate excuse if the drinks were a disaster. I was the world's worst liar. My right eye always did this little twitching thing that was impossible to miss.

"And you won't ask about my drinks with Jimmy?"

Griffin's mouth fell open. "His name is Jimmy? What kind of hooker name is that?"

"He's not a hooker," I hissed. "Keep your voice down."

He recovered quickly. "Fine, fine. I won't ask about Jimmy."

The disgust with which he said the name made me fight back a smile. He caught it, a grin of his own spreading.

"Just dinner," I said.

Griffin held up one hand. "I'll be as innocent as a nun."

I snorted. Loudly.

And someone from the row behind us shushed me.

Griffin leaned in. "You're a terrible influence, aren't you, birdy? I should probably go so you don't ruin my reputation around town."

He walked off whistling, and I covered my face with my hands, letting out a small groan.

Chapter Seven

RUBY

Half my wardrobe was piled on my bed, and when I tossed another cardigan set behind me, the sound of Bruiser's whine had me glancing over my shoulder. The sleeve was hooked on Bruiser's ear, and when he batted ineffectually at the sweater to dislodge it from his face, I exhaled a quiet laugh.

"Sorry," I told him, unhooking the shirt. I kissed his snout, laughing a little when he tried to lick my chin as I pulled back. "I wish there was a guide for stuff like this. *What to wear when meeting a potential dating coach slash escort.*"

He tilted his head.

With a sigh, I sank onto the bed, scratching the spot behind his ears that he liked so much.

What was I *doing*? Of course it was hard to find clothes to wear, because the thought of sitting at a table with Jimmy the escort made me want to puke.

I had to, though. If I chickened out of this, I'd always wonder. Wonder if maybe a few practice dates with someone who did this for a living would be enough to snap me out of my funk. Bolster my confidence, as Lauren kept preaching.

Confidence. Everyone made it sound so easy, didn't they? Like self-love was a switch in the back of your mind, scuttling all the neurons into submission with a neat flip into the on position.

Yeah right. Maybe the people capable of that were part of the small minority destined to make us mere mortals feel like crap because our switch was broken and our brain didn't want to fall in step. I was proud of so much that I'd accomplished. And yes, while I had regrets about this one part of my life, I didn't feel the need to alter my personality or try to act like someone else. I *did* love myself. Most of me, anyway.

That felt more normal. More universal. That each of us stood in front of the mirror and could list a bunch of things that we liked and appreciated, and just did our best not to let the other stuff screw up our mood.

Jimmy, unless he was an actual miracle worker, wouldn't be able to make my brain do anything. Wasn't that depressing? I was the only one who could overcome my own hangups. The key was finding someone who made me feel comfortable being myself while I did.

And I was pretty freaking sure there wasn't a single article of clothing in my closet that had those magical powers either.

"Up you go," I told Bruiser. He wiggled his butt. "Unless you grow some opposable thumbs, the only way you can help me is by not laying on half my wardrobe."

I swear he could understand me, because Bruiser hopped off the bed and stretched with a groan, then circled until he found a comfortable spot on the ground.

As I started the arduous process of hanging up all the clothes I'd torn down from the closet, I decided in the end that the clothes I'd worn to work would be just fine for professional drinks with . . . the professional whatever-he-was.

"You look lovely in that color."

Heat crawled up my neck into my cheeks, and I blocked the man's voice from my head. I didn't even want to think his name lest he find out somehow. Wouldn't that make his ego quiver with glee? Knowing that I was thinking about what he'd said when I was getting ready to go out with another man.

I bet Griffin was one of those people who could stare in the mirror and not find a single flaw on his wretchedly perfect body. One of those people who'd flipped the self-love switch on when he was a child, and the blasted thing never turned off.

In the bathroom, I brushed my hair, added a little blush, and swiped on an extra coat of mascara, then shrugged. "Good enough, I think."

My phone rang as I tightened the cap on my mascara, and the sight of my mom's name had me smiling a little.

"Hey, world travelers," I said after accepting the call. "Where are we today?"

"Portugal," my mom answered. "We were in Spain a couple days ago, and it was wonderful. The architecture is absolutely divine."

"Did you tell her we were in Spain?" my dad's voice boomed in the background.

"I just did, Carl, didn't you hear me say it?"

"No, I can't hear anything with this shower on. Did you tell her we're in Portugal?"

"Carl," my mom sighed. "Either come in and talk to her, or just take your shower."

I shook my head, hitting the speakerphone button so I could clean up my bathroom counter. The mirror hinged open to reveal the medicine cabinet, and I slid the mascara into its spot, then set the hair spray next to it. My prescriptions went to the right of that, and while I listened to my parents' good-natured bickering, I straightened everything into place.

"Mom," I interrupted. "I only have about five minutes before I need to be out the door."

"Sorry, honey. How's work going this week? Any news on the land?"

"No." With the mirror closed, I took one last look at my reflection and flipped off the lights as I walked out. "We've got one more fundraiser, though. I'm hoping that'll do it."

"Well, let us know what happens." She paused, covering the phone speaker, muffling her voice while she said something to my dad. "You taking care of yourself? You're not staying up too late or anything, are you? You know how important sleep is."

"Oh, should I not be going to raves until dawn? Might have to cancel my plans for tonight."

Mom clucked her tongue. "I know. You've always been so responsible, but it's harder than I thought, being away."

Responsible. There was that word again. My own personal cross to bear.

I swallowed around the lump in my throat. "If it makes you feel better, Lauren is pestering me to an adequate degree every day in your absence. I'm drinking my water and exercising and taking all my vitamins and medicine, and eating my vegetables and getting nine hours of sleep every night." I slipped my feet into my shoes by the door. "Should I send you my blood pressure readings too?"

"All right," she said. "I'll stop."

No wonder I was slightly neurotic. It was literally in the genes. "It's okay, Mom. I know you guys worry." I hitched my purse strap over my shoulder and patted Bruiser before I walked out the door. "I'm fine. I will be fine until you get home from your trip, which you should be enjoying because you've earned it."

"We are, I promise. I'll send you some pictures." The sound of my car door had her pausing. "Where are you off to? Going to see Lauren?"

"No," I said lightly. "I'm having drinks with a hooker, and then dinner with a professional athlete afterwards."

She sighed. "Funny."

Mom couldn't see it, but my smile was grim. "I have my moments. Tell Dad I love him, okay?"

If the phone call from my parents was good for anything, it was that I hardly had any time to allow nerves a foothold in my stomach before

I arrived at the address that Jimmy had emailed me. He was staying at a hotel in Fort Collins, which felt much safer than having him stay in town, and he'd picked a place about halfway in between. That also felt safer, because the thought of Lauren or Kenny walking through the door while I went on my bought-and-paid-for date with a sex worker made my brain explode.

Maybe, just maybe, you shouldn't be doing this, then, an obnoxious voice hissed in the back of my mind. The voice sounded an awful lot like myself, and I blew out a harsh breath as I parked my car and walked briskly through the front doors, hand clutching my purse strap like it was the sole thing keeping me anchored to the ground.

Jimmy was waiting at a small table in a darkened corner of the room, and he stood with a friendly smile when I approached. Tonight, he was dressed in a deep-navy suit, his white oxford with two buttons left undone at the top, no tie.

Elegant. Understated.

To my utter relief, he did not look anything like a hooker.

"Thank you," I told him when he pushed my chair in after I took a seat. His hands brushed over my shoulders before he settled into his own chair. Jimmy's knee nudged mine under the table, and when he didn't move it away, I adjusted my legs.

He merely smiled, eyes tracing my face. "I'm glad you came, Ruby. It would've been a shame if we'd missed the opportunity to get to know each other better."

A shame. Uh-huh.

More like a waste of my money—but sure, we'll go with shame.

Here I sat in a romantic restaurant, with sleek lights and flickering candles, velvet couches and tasteful music, and all I could think was that it would be a *shame* if I left skid marks on the floor from sprinting out the front door so fast.

I managed to nod, opening my mouth to reply, but the server approached before I could answer. I ordered a sweet tea and passed on appetizers. Jimmy had a lowball glass in front of him, filled with something clear and bubbly, a lime wedge floating in the ice.

When we were alone again, I fidgeted with the napkin on the table in front of me.

"I'm still not sure this is a great idea," I admitted to him. "I don't normally act on impulse, but my friend was . . . persuasive."

He smiled. "Those are the best kinds of friends to have."

The thought of Lauren had me relaxing a touch. Lord, if she were here, she'd smack me on the back of the head and tell me to get my money's worth.

But what would that entail? I thought about the seduction book Griffin had checked out from the library and tried to swallow a nervous burst of laughter, settling on a conspicuous clearing of my throat instead.

Jimmy leaned forward, clasping his hands lightly on the table. His eyes locked on mine, and it caused a slightly unpleasant pitching motion in my stomach, like I was dangling off the side of a boat. "Now, tell me how I can help you, Ruby."

There was another pause in the conversation when my sweet tea arrived, and I took a grateful sip, because gawd, my throat felt like it was lined with sandpaper. My fingers were cold and tingly, and underneath the table, my foot tapped restlessly. Turned out fake dates that one paid for weren't actually less nerve-racking than real dates.

Lauren was the only person I'd ever explained this to. Griffin, to his credit, almost got me to admit why I'd done it. Almost. Five more minutes with his relentless charm and obnoxious good looks, and I might have caved, and I wasn't sure he'd ever let me live that down. But now? Allowing myself a moment of vulnerability sounded like actual hell. I didn't want to tell this man jack crap, and that was a much bigger problem than I was willing to face at the moment.

I cleared my throat again. "Maybe it would be more beneficial for you to tell me how you typically proceed with a client."

"Of course," he answered. His eyes were unwavering, and under normal circumstances, I might have found it comforting that he seemed so sure. Instead, I felt like a bug pinned to a corkboard, ready to be dissected. "Sometimes my job is as simple as providing company at an event where a client doesn't want to show up alone. I've attended weddings, family reunions, school reunions, because the thought of arriving by themselves is more than they can bear."

He took a slow sip of his drink, then set it down on the table with a quiet click.

"Other clients want more"—he paused with a meaningful tilt of his head—"in-depth work. They're trying to overcome a mental block or need help gaining confidence. In or out of the bedroom."

In-depth work in or out of the bedroom. Swear to high heaven, if this guy started giving me escort acronyms for the types of services he provided, I was going to set the land speed record back to my car. If he started saying things like, *We could build a meaningful friendship*, or *I can imagine very entertaining ways to pass the time*, I'd lose it.

It was the chin, I decided.

If there'd been no Griffin at the bakery yesterday, I think I would've found Jimmy cute. But now, all I could see was a weak chin that needed some stubble. The longer I stared at his chin—because it was better than trying to meet that unrelenting eye contact—the more I found myself surprisingly at peace with the money I'd just wasted.

"Jimmy?" I said quietly.

He grinned a crooked grin. Probably thought it was very appealing too. "Yes, Ruby?"

"Thank you for the drink. And for flying down here. But I can't do this."

His mouth fell open, brow furrowing in a brief pinch, but he recovered quickly. "Wait, just like that?"

It was amazing how something as simple as making the decision made me feel a thousand times lighter. "Just like that," I told him, feeling a little bit like I'd flipped a different sort of switch in my head.

There was no comfort level with this guy, and no matter what we did—what *in-depth work* he was capable of—it wouldn't appear like magic.

As I said my goodbyes, got back in the car, and entered the address from Griffin into my phone, a tight band of tension unlocked from around my chest.

That was a form of comfort, right? Knowing where I was headed . . . and something invisible eased inside me. I chewed on my bottom lip as I drove, brain racing with possibilities.

Chapter Eight

GRIFFIN

It wasn't until an alarm was screaming at me in the kitchen that I realized how much time had passed.

"Shit." I snapped the book shut and tossed it onto the couch, jogging into the kitchen when I saw wisps of smoke billowing from the oven. "Shit, shit, shit."

Why had I burned my dinner?

Because I was reading. In a million years, no one would ever believe me.

Reaching up, I punched a button on the exhaust fan set inside the massive vent hood. I fumbled with some of the smaller drawers on each side of the stove until I found the oven mitts. My eyes were watering from the smoke even before I wrenched open the door, and it poured out in a billowing wave.

"Oh, fuck me," I groaned. The pork tenderloin—perfectly tied and dressed with fancy-looking herbs—was charred to a blackened crisp but not actually on fire, thank God. It was the juice and oil surrounding the meat on the baking tray that smoked ominously.

The smoke alarm in the family room went off shortly after the pork came out of the oven, and I started pressing any button I could reach in hopes that something magical would happen.

"How do you turn off?" I growled. "You shouldn't need a PhD to operate this thing."

My big thumbs accidentally started the broiler, and then finally, finally, hit the correct button on the stupid little screen.

With a glorious beep, the oven turned off. I waved the oven mitts over the baking pan, dissipating some of the smoke, then did the same thing in front of the smoke alarm in the kitchen.

"God, this better not have the fire department showing up at the house," I muttered.

Almost immediately, my phone started ringing. I was still in the midst of waving the oven mitts around to shut the stupid alarms up, and the sight of Steven's name on my home screen made me wince.

A text came through. Then another. Then another. Each consecutive chime on my phone managed to sound angrier than the one before. Setting my jaw, I jogged over to the large walk-in pantry and pulled out the broom tucked into the corner. After settling my weight carefully onto a dining chair, I waved the broom in front of the family room smoke alarm, wafting the air back and forth until it cleared enough that the screaming noise stopped.

I blew out a hard sigh and tossed the broom onto the floor, then yanked open the folding doors so that some fresh air could clear out the remainder of the smoke. Hands on my hips, I glanced down with a frown. I must've gotten some of the oil from the pork on the mitts and then on my shirt.

With the brimstone-and-fire smell finally easing in the room, I peeled my ruined shirt off and tossed it toward the hallway that led to the laundry room.

Still had to figure out how to use that.

At home, things like laundry were always taken care of by my housekeeper, Eileen—a glorious, matronly woman from Scotland to whom I paid a small fortune to keep me fed and my house clean. I was also paying her a large fortune to move with me to Denver, a move made easier by the fact that her only son had moved to Colorado five years earlier, and the only reason she stayed in New York was because of how much I paid her.

Just as I was going to change into a new shirt and then reassure Steven that I was not, in fact, burning his house down, the doorbell rang, and I winced again.

It was either the Welling Springs Fire Department or Ruby. It was a toss-up of which option was less intimidating. I'd look like an idiot either way, but at least with the fire department, I stood a chance of recovery. With Ruby? Not so much.

A glance through the front window showed not big red fire trucks, but a nondescript white sedan.

As I jogged to the door, I couldn't help but grin as I pictured her horrified face when I'd asked her over for dinner. In fact, I'd never met a woman less impressed with me in my entire life.

Not sure what it said about my mental state that I was so fucking excited by that. And as I pulled open the door to greet her, that smile died immediately when I caught a glimpse of her face.

"What's wrong?"

Her eyes were glued on my chest. "Why are you shirtless?"

She said *shirtless* with such disgust and horror that, for a split second, I felt the need to cover my chest with the oven mitts. Then I remembered that I'd been voted Best NFL Body three years in a row and took a deep breath, flexing my abs a little as I adjusted my stance.

"Oh." I glanced down. "I kinda burned our dinner and got some oil splattered on my shirt in the process of trying not to burn the house down."

She blinked. "Okay." Her eyes rose to mine. "Can you go put a shirt on, please?"

"Your wish is my command, birdy."

She rolled her eyes.

With a laugh, I backed up, opening the door to let her into the house. Quietly, she entered, eyes wide as she took in the open living, dining, and kitchen areas.

"Not bad, right?"

Ruby sighed heavily as she preceded me into the room. My eyes surreptitiously tracked over her clothing choice for drinks with Jimmy the hooker. Same outfit she'd worn earlier at work, and even with a slightly too-big skirt, she still managed to fit neatly into the category of librarian fetish, if that was someone's kink.

Not mine, of course. But . . . someone's.

Before I found a clean shirt in my room, I snagged my phone from the counter and told her to make herself comfortable. The sight of Steven's texts had me grinning.

Steven: WHY ARE THE SMOKE ALARMS GOING OFF

Steven: Your ass is so fired if you burn my house down

Steven: So help me, Griffin, if you wreck all that furniture my wife spent six months buying, it'll take a year for the cops to find your body.

Steven: CALL ME RIGHT NOW, you dick

Me: Relax. My dinner got a little crispy in the oven. All clear. No couches were harmed in the process of me cooking. I just got a little distracted.

Steven: Were you having sex in my house? Don't tell me where.

Me: I was not. I was reading a WW2 book, actually.

Steven: Funny. Just have the housekeeper change the sheets before you leave, okay?

I rolled my eyes and plugged my phone in by the nightstand in the guest bedroom I'd claimed as my own. Steven told me to take any room I liked, but the thought of sleeping in the bed where he screwed his wife gave me the serious ick.

With a clean white T-shirt tugged over my torso, I walked back down the hallway and found Ruby standing by the folding slider doors, her hands clasped in front of her as she stared out at the sprawling view behind the house. The mountains were a dark brownish green in the distance, the acres of grass a lush emerald color that almost didn't look real. Just beyond the patio, with its rectangular firepit surrounded by white Adirondacks, the pool glittered underneath the setting sun.

"It smells like a bonfire in here," she commented, her eyes staying out on the backyard.

"Sorry about that. I might be able to scrounge up a frozen pizza or something if you're still hungry after your . . ." Her eyes snapped to me when I paused, but I recovered quickly. "Prior engagement, of which I will not be making inquiries."

She hummed, her hands clasped so tightly that I could see the whites of her knuckles.

"You know why I burned our dinner?"

"Difficulty reading the instructions?"

I whistled. "Touché. But no." I wandered over to the couch and picked up the book she'd selected, holding it aloft. Her eyes lit up instantly, and I saw the moment she tried to shutter it. "This is a great book. I lost track of time."

"Really?"

"God, you sound so skeptical. I did go to college, you know. I can read."

She arched an eyebrow. "You told me you needed a picture book about football."

"My sense of humor is somewhat dry, with a healthy side dose of self-deprecation. It has a tendency to get me in trouble."

Ruby's eyes flicked over my covered chest. "I found an article about you climbing a bell tower in college while drunk and naked."

"I have vague recollections of that."

She rolled her eyes. "My point is that I think you can get into trouble all on your own, without the help of your sense of humor."

I nodded sagely. "It is one of my strengths. Not one anyone else recognizes, though."

"It seldom happens that way." Her gaze tracked around the room, lingering on the pricey artwork decorating the walls. "What we view as our best traits don't usually end up being our most memorable."

"Now that's an interesting distinction." I leaned on the back of the couch and watched her. "But I'm not sure if that's true for me."

"How's that?"

I spread my arms out. "Tell me, Ruby, how do you view me? After a couple exchanges. What would you say I'm like as a person?"

The graceful line of her throat worked on a swallow, but there was a surprising lack of hesitation when she answered. "Handsome. Athletically gifted. A player . . ." She paused, holding up her hand when I opened my mouth to say something. "And not the kind who plays a game for a living."

"I think most people would agree with you," I said easily. "What else? No need to bite your tongue on my account."

Her chin notched up a stubborn inch. "Someone who doesn't take life very seriously."

"Ding, ding." I tapped my nose. "You always were a smart cookie, weren't you?"

"If I recall, you preferred the term *nerdy birdy*."

Shame crawled up my chest despite my best effort to quash it, and I pushed my tongue against the side of my cheek. "Well, that's not a very nice thing to call the neighbor girl," I managed.

Her answering smile was wry. "Don't worry, I was hardly crying myself to sleep. I pretty much just ignored you."

"From your daily perch, watching me and my brother? How'd that go?"

"Oh, I wasn't watching you, Griffin," she said. She tilted her head as her eyes met mine, and what I saw there had my head rearing back in surprise. "I was mainly watching him."

With a frown, I rubbed at the back of my neck. "Of course you were."

Ruby shook her head and wandered into the kitchen, her fingers trailing along the edge of the first of two islands anchoring the room. When she reached the charred remains of the pork, her nose wrinkled, and I found that I liked how clearly I could read her facial expressions.

"I'm a little shocked," she said, eyes still on the burned dinner.

"I have that effect on people. You'll get used to my overwhelming presence eventually."

Her eyes closed, and after a tiny shake of her head, she opened them again. "I'm shocked that you haven't asked about my drinks."

I blinked. "Because I promised you I wouldn't."

"So you're not curious?"

I set my hands on my hips. "Is this a trick? When I told you I wouldn't ask, I meant it."

Ruby sighed, clearly flustered, and she smoothed her hands down the front of her blouse, which buttoned all the way up to her neck. She had a habit of fidgeting with her shirt when she was nervous.

"No, I'm not playing games. I promise." Her cheekbones were tinged a soft pink, and she couldn't make eye contact for a moment. "I'm . . . I'm nervous."

"Why? It's just me. You've never worried about impressing me before."

"Quite true." She blew out a slow breath, tucking a stray strand of hair behind her ears. "When I was getting ready tonight, my friend told me to pick the outfit where I felt the sexiest. The most confident." She gestured at her outfit. "And this was the best I could come up with. It sounds pathetic to say this out loud, but I couldn't imagine one moment in my life where I ever felt anything close to those things. You told me today that I looked lovely in it."

"You do," I said cautiously. "If someone asked for a librarian fetish, this would be it."

Her eyes pinched shut briefly. "It would not."

I pursed my lips, glancing down at her shoes. "You're right. You'd need some fishnet stockings and higher heels—but it's not without appeal, trust me."

Her chest rose and fell on a deep breath. "I don't want to look like someone's fetish come to life, Griffin."

"I feel like I'm doomed to piss you off in the course of this conversation," I said carefully.

"Just say it. Whatever it is."

"What *do* you want, then?" I asked.

Her eyes snapped to mine, determination blazing hot behind the cool gray. "I want *you* to be the one to teach me how to do this."

With my heart hammering behind my ribs, I tilted my head and took a step closer. "Teach you what, exactly?"

"Teach me how to make a man want me."

Chapter Nine

GRIFFIN

I blinked.

Then blinked again.

She'd spoken English, to be sure, but I felt like my brain was moving at a glacial pace, because there's no way Ruby Tate would've asked me to do . . . that.

"I'm sorry, what?" I swiped a hand over my mouth. "You want me to what?"

"Never mind, this was a terrible idea." With a furious shake of her head, Ruby started to brush past me, headed back in the direction of the door.

Gently, I hooked my hand in the crook of her elbow and steered her back around to face me. "Easy, birdy, I don't have nearly enough information for you to say anything of the sort."

Her cheeks were bright pink, and she couldn't hold eye contact, just tiny little darts up and then down, landing anywhere in the house except on my face.

"Sit," I commanded. But like, nicely. Not in a dick-ish sort of way.

Ruby did as I asked, easing herself onto the overstuffed couch that my agent was ready to threaten me over. She propped her elbows on her thighs and sank her head into her hands, shoulders moving on a deep, rib-inhaling sigh.

God, what happened during those drinks?

Who was this strange little woman?

In the kitchen, I poured some very expensive wine into two very expensive-looking wine goblets and walked them back to the couch just as Ruby dropped her hands and studied me with big, wary eyes.

"I've never met anyone who looks at me like you do," I told her, taking a seat but leaving a cushion empty in between us.

She took the wine with a slight furrow in her brow. "Like what?"

"Like you're terrified of what I'm going to do next."

"That's because I am," she said, sniffing the wine before taking a tiny sip.

"How's the wine?"

"Drier than I expected, but I don't mind. Dry red is about all I drink."

I took a sip and grimaced. "Yes, I can see why. I love my alcohol to taste like ashy, wet cardboard too."

She sighed quietly, then set the wineglass down. "I don't think any sort of alcohol will help right now, but thank you."

"Talk," I instructed firmly. "I'm going to need more explanation, Ruby Tate."

"No, it was silly and impulsive."

"Two words I'd wager no one would ever use to describe you," I said.

She tilted her head. "No, you're right."

"With the addition of this most unexpected question, am I allowed to ask about your drinks with Jimmy the hooker?"

"He's not a—" Then she stopped, pinched her eyes shut for a moment, drawing herself upright and clenching her hands in her lap. When her eyes opened again, the decisiveness was clear and bright. "Yes, you're allowed to ask."

"Oh, goodie." I took another large swallow of the wine and decided to set it down by hers, because it tasted like there was actual dirt lining my throat. "How were your drinks with our friend James? I can't call him Jimmy anymore; it's too easy."

"Can I redirect your line of questioning a little?"

I swept my hand between us in a magnanimous gesture. "By all means."

"Maybe you could ask why I hired . . . James."

I nodded slowly. "I could do that. You're going to answer honestly if I do?"

Ruby nodded as well. Shorter and jerkier than mine, but enough so that I believed her.

"Okay. Why did you hire an escort, Ruby?"

She took a deep breath and finally met my gaze evenly. "I didn't hire him for sex."

"Excellent, because that's incredibly illegal and I don't think you'd last long in jail." Then I assessed her with a shrewd look. "Actually, I take that back. You'd probably go in there and have all those women wrapped around your little finger on day one."

Her reaction made me realize just how often Ruby sighed in my presence.

It was a lot.

"Oh yeah," I continued. "You'd be holding court by the end of the first week. Ruling with an iron fist. No mercy. They'd be bending over backwards to be in your favor."

"Are you done yet?"

I narrowed my eyes. "Hang on. Let me picture you in orange."

Ruby started to get up, and I laughed, asking her to wait. She froze, that wariness back in her eyes. Holding up my finger, I paused for a second, then nodded. "Okay. Now I'm done."

"I'm thrilled to hear that." Seeing one of her eyebrows arched imperiously, I had to fight to hide a grin. Picking on her was fun. More fun than I'd had in a while. "I hired him for confidence. Take me on a few practice dates. Teach me what to do when you want something . . . specific from a man. And then he was going to talk me through those specific things," she answered delicately.

Sitting back on the couch, I extended an arm, much like I'd done on the bench. "Like sex."

"Sort of," she hedged. "I don't . . . I don't have much experience, and what experience I do have isn't good."

Her eyes met mine, and hell if I didn't feel it like a lightning bolt down my spine.

Arm dropping off the back of the couch, I leaned forward and kept my gaze steady on hers. "Someone hurt you, birdy?" I asked quietly, steadily, no hint of the violent reaction churning and thrashing under the surface. "You can tell me who."

I might not have given any outward hints, but there was a flicker in her eyes that told me she heard it anyway.

"Not physically," she answered. "You can stow the caveman reaction for the time being."

Hands clenched in tight fists, I managed to sit back again. "I can understand wanting more experience, in that case."

She nodded. "I need someone to make me . . . sexier. More worldly. Help me get enough confidence where I don't feel like I'll jump out of my skin if someone touches me."

"And you think I can help you with that?" I asked in a rough voice.

After a visible swallow, Ruby nodded again, more slowly this time. "When I was out with . . ."

"Jimmy James the hooker," I finished.

She gave me a long look, but the edges of her mouth curled up slightly. "James. I didn't feel comfortable. Not even a little. He tried to talk to me and ask me questions, and I could tell he was smooth and used to being charming with women, but . . ." Her shoulders shook slightly.

"But he gave you the ick."

Ruby blinked. "Yes. He did."

I nodded gravely. "You can't ignore the ick when it happens. There's no overcoming that with the opposite sex."

She leaned forward, urgency lighting her eyes. "I *always* feel like that, Griffin."

My brows lowered. "Always?"

Then she paused, sucking in a sharp breath. "Except with you, much to my surprise." Her tongue darted out to wet her lips. "I'm not attracted to you, don't worry. It's nothing like that."

"Nothing?" I asked with a slight grin.

"No. You are not even remotely my type."

"Please, don't feel like you need to spare my ego."

"Your ego will be just fine no matter what I ask of you," she said confidently.

I blew out a slow breath. "And that is?"

"I'm asking you to help nerdy birdy, who only knew how to watch the boy she crushed on from up on a tree branch."

Her eyes. Holy shit. I couldn't look away, but the brutal vulnerability in her face made me want to shift backward or something. Hide from what I was seeing there.

"Sometimes I think I'm still stuck in that tree."

It was that discomfort in the face of her naked emotions that pushed me to say what I said next.

"God, I wish you'd had better taste than to crush on my brother. This is really killing the vibe for me." I motioned to my face. "I look exactly like him. Didn't you have a little crush on me too?"

"No. You annoyed me too much."

"Gee, thanks."

She leaned forward again, like she couldn't help herself. "Don't you see? That's what makes this perfect. You're safe. You need something to do while you're here, and in two weeks you'll be gone."

I wasn't even sure Ruby knew what she was asking of me. It felt huge. Massive. World altering. And the weight of it felt like more than I could carry for someone like her.

Ask me to steal a football from someone to win a game? I'm your fucking man.

Take some almost-naked pictures for a magazine cover? Not a problem.

I could do a whole lot of things well, with money and pressure coming from all angles. But for some reason, this quiet, tiny woman asking me to help her was terrifying, because for the first time, she was looking up at me like I was something—someone—important.

Before saying anything, I studied her for a moment. "I'm not sure I'm the best person for this."

"Why not? You know what men want, you know women . . . ," she said. "Lots of women."

"Not lots," I muttered. "A healthy amount for a single, moderately attractive man—"

"Professional athlete who makes millions of dollars a year," she supplied. "You're confident. You wouldn't be doing this for money, so there's no legal gray area. And most importantly . . ." She locked eyes with me in such a way that I actually felt a little breathless. "You won't fall in love with me."

I reared back, my head spinning. "That's the most important thing?"

"Yes."

"Aren't you doing all this so you can fall in love?" I asked, almost violently curious despite my best efforts. "Isn't that what you'd want from all this?"

Ruby shook her head. "No. I have no interest in love."

"Really?"

The skepticism in my tone had her crossing her arms. "You don't believe me?"

"No, I just . . . I'm shocked, is all." My gaze tracked over her face, and sure enough, she looked really fucking serious. "Most women—"

She held up her hand. "Please stop right there. Any time a man starts a sentence with 'most women,' he's probably wildly off base with whatever is going to come out of his mouth."

I shifted slightly in my seat. "Not wildly. I thought my imagined harem of women and the feminine understanding that brings is why you wanted my help."

Ruby ignored me. "Besides, I am not most women."

"That is abundantly clear."

By the look on her face, she didn't appreciate my dry tone. I chuckled under my breath. "Sorry. Okay, so you don't want love, you just want . . ."

"I want to know what it all feels like," she said quietly. "My hope is that experiencing something, even for a short time, is enough to satisfy the part of me that feels like I'm missing out. It doesn't mean I need it forever."

Every once in a while, someone unwittingly hits on a truth you can't really put a name to yourself.

That's how I felt about everything.

I hated missing out on things. Experiences or parties or trips. That's why feeling stuck in one place, feeling chained down, brought out the worst side of me. Why I accepted stupid dares like climbing a bell tower while I was drunk and naked because my friends didn't think I would. When that feeling curled around my insides, I stopped thinking about what might happen next. Because if I ignored it, if I shoved it down, I felt like a little kid who pressed his nose to the window but wasn't allowed out.

Was that how Ruby felt? If she saw a couple together?

Like she was separate. Kept apart. Maybe it was something in her own brain that held her back, or whatever had happened to her in the past. But I hated the idea that she did.

For whatever reason, whatever part of my teenage years involved her sitting quietly in the background, I hated the idea that Ruby Tate felt like less in any single way.

There it was.

The spike of interest, the spiraling sensation of challenge that wrapped itself around my spine. Ignoring this offer was all but impossible, now that I'd gotten a glimpse of what she'd been hiding. It was too delicious. Too intriguing to pass up.

Teach her how to make a man want her?

Let's fucking go. I'd have the single men of Colorado falling at her fucking feet before I packed my bags.

I leaned forward in the same way she had, and to my surprise, she held her ground. "So that means you won't fall in love with me either, yeah?" She opened her mouth to speak, and I gently laid a finger over her lips. Her head snapped back, and I brushed my finger over my thumb, where my skin still tingled from the softness of her bottom lip. "I'm extremely lovable, so you might want to think this over."

She rolled her eyes. "I think I'm safe."

"Lessons," I said slowly. "You're going to do whatever I say, and we'll get you ready for your Librarians Gone Wild phase by the end of the two weeks, huh?"

"If you ever call it that again, I will slap you."

"Kinky, but not my thing, birdy." I stood from the couch and set my hands on my hips. Warily, she stood as well. "I'm usually the one who likes to do the spanking, but we can talk about those things later, once we've gotten to know each other better."

Her cheeks were flame red. "That is not what I need to learn from you."

"I'm always open to renegotiating," I said generously.

Ruby sniffed. "Regardless. I think we can still be friendly and professional. I just . . . I just need some guidance, is all. A friend would tell me I'm not doing anything wrong and I shouldn't change who I am, but . . . maybe I need someone who's willing to use a firmer hand." The words dangled in the air, and the moment she realized what she'd said, Ruby pinched her eyes shut. "Do not make a spanking joke; you know that's not what I meant."

"I am aware, yes," I said magnanimously.

She sighed. "So you'll help me?"

Stroking my jaw as I studied her, I didn't even attempt to stifle the bright flame of interest. A game plan started forming in my head before I could stop it. I stuck my hand out between us. With a deep breath, she placed her much smaller hand in mine, and a grin immediately spread over my face. This was going to be fun.

"Ruby, you just got yourself a teacher."

Chapter Ten

Ruby

Bam, bam, bam.

Groaning into my pillow, I curled onto my side and pried my eyes open, wondering why the sun was hardly in the sky and someone was using a jackhammer somewhere in my house.

Bam, bam, bam.

"Bruiser, attack," I moaned.

The dog in question, sprawled out next to me just like he was every night, also groaned, sliding off the bed inelegantly and shaking off the sleep before ambling down the hallway to check on the commotion.

If someone ever tried to break into my house, that dog would probably sleep through it. The click of Bruiser's nails on the hardwood started tapping quickly, and he gave an excited whine as he danced around.

Staring up at the ceiling, I let out a heavy sigh. The clock on my nightstand told me it was 6:45 a.m., and that was much, much too early on my day off.

Instead of another knock, the phone on my bedside table dinged with a text, and I rolled over to a sitting position as I yawned.

"Coming," I called out. My bleary eyes narrowed as the text came into focus. "Oh, you've got to be kidding me."

Griffin: Let me in, birdy. I've got muffins and coffee.

With a huff, I flung off the covers, dumping my phone somewhere in the pile of blankets before I ripped a cardigan off the back of my bedroom door. I slipped my arms in as I walked down the hallway, pulling my hair out from the neck of the sweater before wrapping the fuzzy material tight around my upper body.

Bruiser's nose was pressed to the door, his butt wiggling in excitement, and when I yanked the door open, he sprang out to greet Griffin.

The man in question laughed as my dog ran in excited circles around his legs. "Good morning, pup. Did you miss me?"

I slicked my tongue over my teeth and waited—very patiently, I might add—for any sort of explanation as to why he was at my home before seven in the morning.

At my home looking fresh and wide awake and like he'd just hopped off a magazine cover. His long legs were covered in black joggers, his upper body in a fitted white T-shirt bearing the Denver logo. A black cap tugged low over his face made him look slightly mysterious, tiptoeing over the line of disreputable with the heavy stubble coating his jaw.

"If this is your idea of teaching me anything, I'm ready to renegotiate."

When he looked up, his eyes widened slightly, running over my sleep-crazy hair and the cardigan, lingering slightly on my bare legs. "Good morning, sunshine. That's quite a sweater."

It was criminal, really, his ability to keep me off-balance.

In truth, the sweater was a ghastly thing—three sizes too big, made from a fuzzy purple yarn that no one should be wearing in public. "Lauren made it for me," I explained unnecessarily. "She went through a phase a few years back. Tried to get me to join along, but knitting isn't my thing."

"No?"

I shook my head. "It makes me feel violent, actually."

He whistled. "Then by all means, make sure you don't do it when I'm around."

I smiled tightly. "You seem to bring out that side of me all by yourself. Now, what are you doing here?"

He held up the familiar bakery bag. "Blake says good morning and gives her apologies for being out of blueberries, but she's expecting a delivery today."

With a sigh, I stepped back to let him in. "How did you know where I lived?"

Griffin waltzed into my house, ducking slightly so he didn't whack his head on the doorframe. "We have this amazing newfangled thing called the internet now. You should try it." He passed me the bag, setting down the drink carrier on the antique credenza against the wall to the right of my front door. "It's cute in here. Very homey."

"Thanks."

"Do your parents live in town too?" he asked, studying the family pictures on the wall—trips we'd taken together when I was in high school. He tapped on the frame of a painting of an indigo bunting perched on the branch of an aspen tree. "This is pretty."

"Thank you. And no, um, they live in Fort Collins, which isn't far. But at the moment, they're on a cruise around the world."

His eyebrows shot up. "No shit? That's cool."

I nodded. "They retired a few years ago but never really got to celebrate. So . . . I told them there was no time like the present."

"Huh. How long will they be gone?"

"About five months, I think. They left eight weeks ago."

After he finished perusing the room, his eyes shifted back to me. I felt naked, and tugging ineffectually on the hem of the sweater didn't help, because then my sleep T-shirt was exposed. He noticed, of course, his sharp golden eyes resting on the faded words underneath when the cardigan fell open.

RUN LIKE MR. COLLINS IS PROPOSING.

"I don't get it," he said, gesturing to the shirt.

"*Pride and Prejudice* joke," I explained, my cheeks likely a bright, candy-apple red because my legs were bare, my hair was a disaster after disjointed dreams featuring the King twins in various stages of undress, and I wasn't wearing a bra. Not that he'd be able to notice. That was the beautiful thing about a B cup. Still, I crossed my arms tightly across my chest just in case. "Why are you here, Griffin? The sun's barely out."

"I need to look at your closet. I'm doing a clothing inventory."

The words came out of his mouth clearly enough, but I stared at him for what felt like a solid minute before I started laughing. He didn't find it quite as funny, and when I didn't stow the laughter quickly enough, he gave Bruiser a quick scratch on the head and started down the hallway.

"Hey," I called out. "You can't just wander around my house."

He ducked his head into the guest room, which I'd turned into a reading room because no one ever visited me. "Treadmill in the library, eh?"

"Yeah, um, I try to walk a couple miles every day, and I hate being cold, so in the winter I use that."

Griffin made a humming noise. "Didn't peg you for a runner."

"I'm not a runner," I said patiently. "I said I *walk* every day. You have terrible listening skills."

After a quick peek into the only bathroom in the house—which I'd recently repainted a soft, soothing bluish gray—he glanced over his shoulder. "Pretty color," he said.

"Oh. Thank you."

"Reminds me of your eyes." Then he brushed past me, ignoring the fact that my mouth had fallen open. No one had ever told me my eyes were pretty before.

Gray never seemed all that exciting to me. When I was young, I longed for green eyes or blue eyes or a deep chocolaty brown. Something rich and decadent and beautiful.

Also three words no one would ever use to describe me.

Wrenching a hand through my hair, I snagged a ponytail holder from the bathroom counter and attempted to wrangle the bird's nest into submission while I stared at the broad expanse of Griffin's back. He'd set his hands on his hips while he stared into my bedroom.

"God, it's like a tomb in here," he said, striding in and pulling open the light-blocking curtains.

"I like a dark room for sleeping." Defensiveness had my voice a little short, and it did nothing except make him smile. "It's important for your health to get good sleep every night."

"Hmmm." He glanced over his shoulder, eyebrow raised. "What time do you go to bed every night, birdy?"

"Nine thirty," I told him. "Ten at the latest."

He grinned. "Me too."

"Yeah right."

"During the season, I have to," he explained, idly scratching his stomach over the expensive-looking cotton of his shirt. "Need my beauty sleep as much as the next person."

Before he wandered over to the closet, he eyed the mess of blankets on my queen-size bed with a slight grin. "You're a violent sleeper, aren't you?"

"You'll have to ask Bruiser," I said, tugging the blankets up over the pillows and smoothing them out. The dog was sitting in between us, his ears perked high at the sound of his name. "He's never complained before, though."

"No, I expect he wouldn't," Griffin said distractedly, flipping through the matching hangers. "You own a shocking amount of black and white, young lady."

My chin rose an inch. "They're timeless."

After pulling out one of my many pencil skirts, he tilted his head. "You have six of these."

"Observant, aren't you?"

The dimple in his cheek flashed when he grinned; the fact that I'd even noticed made me astronomically pissy. "I need to eat something. Don't go through my underwear drawer, okay?"

"No promises," he called out. "Which drawer is that, just so I know?"

"Second one down. Don't open it," I warned.

The raspberry muffin was delicious, and I shoved half of it in my mouth while I wandered into the kitchen to boil some water for my single cup of tea in the morning.

"I got you a coffee." His voice traveled down the hallway as I filled the kettle.

"I saw that, thank you. But, um, I don't drink coffee. I try to limit my caffeine intake, so I usually just have a cup of tea."

"You hardly ever drink, you go to bed early. Walk two miles a day. Don't drink coffee. Men are off the table. Does Ruby Tate have any vices? Oh, hang on, I just figured it out." His frame filled the doorway, arms full of cardigans. "You have seventeen cardigans in varying shades of white and black. Seventeen!"

I exhaled slowly through puffed-out cheeks. "What's wrong with that? I know what I like to wear."

"You have one in blue. You were wearing it the other day when I was at the library."

Since I was leaning over to make sure the flames were at the right height on the burner, he couldn't see me grimace. "I was."

"Do you feel good when you wear it?"

With a tight jaw, I nodded.

"So why don't you own more clothes like that?"

Crossing my arms tight across my chest, I finally whirled to face him. "Because when I purchase clothes, it's utilitarian. Will they cover my body? Will they keep me warm in a freezing-cold library? I'm literally never thinking about the opposite sex when I go shopping."

Griffin pursed his lips slightly, studying me from head to toe. My hand gripped the eggplant-purple cardigan, just to make sure he didn't get an accidental glimpse of nipple underneath my shirt.

Note to self: sleep in a sports bra while Griffin is in town.

"I think I've got this figured out," he said.

"Have you?"

Despite my dry tone, he nodded. "Now, while that water's heating, come show me your three favorite outfits. Not to feel sexy or attract attention, but your favorites for when you want to dress nicely."

Sighing heavily, I followed him down the hallway, acutely aware that he filled so much space in my tiny little house. My room felt like it had shrunk down by half.

Instead of dwelling on that, or how it felt having him loom behind me while I studied my closet (honestly, it was obnoxious how much smaller I was than him), I gave my closet a cursory scan, then picked the first three things that came to mind.

A black sheath dress I'd had for the better part of a decade—my go-to for funerals or fancier events. I'd been known to wear it to weddings too.

A black-and-white tweed pencil skirt that I paired with different blouses.

And the light-blue set he'd seen me in.

Griffin did his best to hang the cardigans back in place, and afterward, he turned to the dresser and pulled open the top drawer.

"Hey."

He whistled. "This was not purchased to be utilitarian." Dangling on his finger was the single nicest piece of lingerie I owned. The bra was a delicate lace design in a deep, rich blue color, and it came with a pair of matching high-cut bikini panties.

I snatched it out of his hand. "It was a gift. I've never actually worn it." His eyes stayed locked on the bra in my hand, and I pushed past him to shove it back in the drawer.

"Now that's a fucking shame. Who gave it to you?"

"My friend Lauren," I said. "She's . . . very pushy sometimes." My cheeks flushed. "She bought me a monstrous dildo for my birthday last month."

Griffin's eyes sparkled like he was laughing, but his mouth stayed remarkably even. "No kidding."

"I made her take it home with her."

He clicked his tongue in disappointment. "Why would you do something like that?"

Instead of answering him honestly—that I was slightly terrified the thing would eat me alive—I said, "I was afraid Bruiser would think it's a chew toy."

"I think I'd get along with Lauren."

"That's why you're never allowed to hang out with her." Griffin laughed. Such an easy, rich sound. Ignoring the way it raised the hair on the back of my neck, I clasped my hands in front of me. "Now what? You going to donate all my clothes? Burn them in a ceremonial bonfire?"

"Nah." He clapped his hands together. "We're going shopping."

The blood drained from my face. "We are not."

Griffin's gaze swept over me. "You gonna pass out, birdy?"

"I hate shopping," I said miserably.

"This wouldn't be normal shopping, though. I can call in a few favors, we'll have the place to ourselves—"

"So everyone in there will know I'm naked behind a curtain and fawn all over me? No thank you." I shuddered lightly, because that felt like emotional trauma waiting to happen. "There's a reason we have the internet, and it's so we never, ever have to set foot in a clothing store ever again."

"Really? You don't want your own *Pretty Woman* shopping montage in an upscale boutique? Most women—" His voice cut off when I narrowed my eyes. "Right. No sweeping generalizations about the opposite sex. Got it."

My shoulders deflated. "It's a generous thought, Griffin. I just can't."

"You are a terrible student so far," he observed.

I pushed my tongue into my cheek, holding his gaze unflinchingly. If that man wanted to get me into a mall or something equally horrid, he'd have to *pay* me.

There was no hiding his disappointment when he sighed, but to his credit, he didn't try to argue. His pointer finger tapped over his lips, a considering look on his face.

Griffin studied me head to toe again, this time his gaze lingering on my legs. "Do you mind taking off the sweater, just for a moment?"

My hand gripped it tighter. "Why?"

"Research."

With that cryptic word hanging between us, Griffin watched me carefully as my hand eased its grip on the fuzzy purple and I let it slide off my shoulders, tossing it on the bed. With the knitted armor gone, I was left in some inexcusably short shorts, all but invisible underneath the oversize T-shirt.

With a tilt of his head, he took a step closer. The spicy, crisp scent of him filled my head, and I tried to hide a slow inhale as he came a bit too close for comfort.

Griffin lifted both hands and reached out, stopping just shy of touching my ribs when I tensed. "If I put my hands right here," he said quietly, "I could almost wrap them around you completely, couldn't I?"

Every inch of my skin buzzed with invisible currents. He was right. If he grabbed me around the waist, if he stretched his palms out around my rib cage, his massive hands would cover so much of my body.

The thing about strength is that it's intoxicating to be around when you're someone not in possession. Even if you're normally not impressed by such a thing, and I wasn't. Griffin was in possession of mind-boggling strength. His frame—so overwhelmingly large compared to my own—carried a massive amount of power, barely leashed, in the muscles he'd spent his life honing to resemble his own sort of weapon. And right now, he was being so careful not to let that weapon be something that scared me.

Because I was small. And rather weak, at least in comparison.

Strength, in this strangely charged moment, looked like outstretched hands that could crush bones and do even more damage to someone's heart.

Not mine, of course. Someone's.

My eyes felt like they weighed a thousand pounds when I tried to lift my gaze to his. "Trust me, I've heard enough in my life that curves are what make a woman sexy. I know I don't have that." Gritty sand coated my throat when I tried to talk next. "Like trying to fuck a corpse," I said evenly, although the words hurt coming up.

His brow furrowed immediately, eyes darkening. "Someone said that to you?" There was a dangerous timbre to his voice. An invisible pitch that he probably wasn't even aware of. A growling edge that crept into those five words.

That edge felt like a balm over a scar that I'd carried for years, something meant to heal and soothe the cracked, angry edges. Almost like he'd sliced open some hidden side of himself for the sole purpose of making me feel better. It would be so easy to sink into his protective streak if I allowed myself to.

Breaking the intensity was a necessity, so I cleared my throat, turning to pull the cardigan off the bed. "It's a general thought among most men, I'd wager. Am I allowed to put this back on now?"

Before I could wrap it around my shoulders, Griffin took yet another step closer. I backed up slightly, my calves hitting the edge of my bed.

"Most men would never, ever say that to you. Wouldn't think it either. Not in a million years. And if someone did"—he dipped his head, and I couldn't look away—"then he's a fucking moron who doesn't deserve to breathe the same air as you."

There was a horrid burn at the back of my eyes, and I looked down at the ground, where his much larger feet were bracketed around mine.

Shame felt like a sticky, oily cloak stuck to freshly washed skin, and if you tried to pluck it off, it simply left behind a black residue that wasn't easily wiped away. There was shame behind so many emotional reactions, wasn't there? Even if I hadn't been the one to say it, I still felt the slightest hint of that shame simply by being the one who'd inspired it.

It was so fucked up. Wrong. Unfair.

But it was still there, no matter how much I wished otherwise. Another switch I couldn't flip, stuck in the wrong position for far longer than I'd ever wanted it to be.

"I should get ready," I told him. "I have a doctor's appointment in Denver, so I need to be out the door by eight thirty."

Griffin was quiet for a moment; then he slowly backed up. Some of the pressure eased around my rib cage, and I sucked in a sharp breath through my nose.

"When will you be back?" he asked.

"Not before two. I have a couple places I'd like to stop while I'm downtown."

"Got any plans tonight?" he asked.

"Oh yeah, big ones."

His eyebrows rose fractionally.

"You asked what my vices are," I said, gesturing back toward the big, comfy couch in my family room. "I plan to sit right there and watch period romance movies until I fall asleep. And it's how I always end my days off, so I don't want to hear a word out of you."

Griffin notched his fingers to his temple in a mock salute. "Can I come back after dinner?"

"Why?"

Oh, the way he grinned in answer—it was devastating, and I fought the urge to place a hand over my stomach to calm the rioting burst of nerves at the sight of it.

"Do you trust me?"

No.

Yes.

Sort of.

The indecision must have played out over my face, because he laughed quietly under his breath. "Trust me," he said firmly. "I'll be back later."

Chapter Eleven

GRIFFIN

The second time Ruby opened the door for me at her house, she looked a lot less pissed off.

"This is progress," I told her as I walked past, ducking my head as I entered.

"What is? What are all those bags?"

"You're not looking at me with that cute little homicidal glint in your eyes like you did this morning."

Ruby smiled sweetly. "There's still plenty of day left for that to happen."

I booped her nose. "How true, my little student."

She swatted at my hand. "If you keep doing that, I'm going to tell Bruiser to eat you."

"Mmm-kay."

Ruby frowned. "Seriously, what's in the bags? They look expensive."

Instead of answering that, because they were expensive, I simply held them out to her. "Off you go."

Her brow furrowed, doing that cute little wrinkle thing. "Off I go, where?"

"You may have deprived me of the shopping montage, but I *will* get a private fashion show."

Ruby's mouth hung open. "A . . . what?"

I tilted my head down the hall. "Black bag first. I handed them to you in order of how I'd like to see them." The way her eyes narrowed had me grinning. "Oooh, you were right. I spoke too soon. There's the look I was waiting for." Gently, I curled my hands around her shoulders and turned her in the direction of her bedroom. "Come on now. This will be painless, I promise."

"Not for you," she muttered.

I laughed as she stalked off, wondering not for the first time how the hell I'd ended up here. Earlier that morning, my ass had popped out of bed, eager to start the day.

"There are clothes in here," Ruby said.

I whistled. "You are quick today."

Her head poked out of the bedroom door. "You bought me clothes? Where?"

I picked up the top book on a stack in her family room, studying the creased spine. *Persuasion* by Jane Austen. "Fort Collins."

She huffed, disappearing behind the door. I could hear the muffled sound of her clothes being removed, and I gritted my teeth for a moment, unwillingly imagining her peeling off a shirt to reveal that deep-blue lace bra.

"And you're aware of the best places to shop in Fort Collins how?"

I set the book down and picked up another. *Frankenstein* by Mary Shelley. Underneath that was a book of poetry with intricate gold designs on the cover. "My agent's wife gave me the name of her favorite boutique."

"So you just waltzed right in, huh? I can only imagine the looks on the other shoppers' faces."

One of the poems caught my eye, but I looked up from the book. "Oh, no one else was there. They closed down for an extended lunch so I could shop with just the manager's help. Her card's in there if you want to go in."

The rustling sound of a bag came down the hallway as Ruby found the card. She made a dry laughing noise. "She wrote her cell phone number on here and said, 'Call me anytime you're in town.'"

I grinned. "Did she, now?"

Ruby muttered something under her breath.

"How's it going in there?" I asked, flipping back to the poem I'd noticed.

I missed her response as I read through the pages about yearning and aching, seeking something to fill all those empty places we all seemed to feel.

Ruby cleared her throat, and I snapped the book shut, my lips spreading in an easy smile.

It was on the tip of my tongue to tell her she looked fucking gorgeous, but I waited, not wanting to make her uncomfortable. "Well . . . how did I do?"

The dress fit her perfectly, a more tailored fit than anything I'd seen her wear yet, and she smoothed her hands over the delicate floral embroidering along the front. It was a pale–sky blue dress with a collared neck and fitted design. The cap sleeves were lace—the manager had assured me it would balance out a petite figure nicely—and Ruby's eyes were huge, looking bluer than they ever had before when she looked up at me.

"I love it," she said simply.

"Good." My voice sounded gruff, and she must have heard it, too, because she pulled her eyes away from mine and looked down at the ground. "Could you see yourself wearing this on a nice date?"

Ruby tucked a strand of hair behind her ear and inhaled slowly before she raised her head again. Her answering nod was serious and slow.

"How much was it?" she asked. "I don't usually spend a lot on clothes."

"Why don't you try on the next two, and we'll talk about that later."

She pursed her lips, clearly gearing up to argue, but thought better of it after seeing my face.

Like I'd take a fucking penny for those clothes.

Out of the corner of my eye, I watched her walk back to her bedroom, then glance quickly over her shoulder, our gazes locking briefly before she fully closed the door. I breathed out slowly through my nose while I waited.

A muffled bark came from the kitchen, and when I walked through, I found Bruiser waiting patiently by the back slider. At the sight of me, he jumped up on the door, splaying his front paws on the glass and wiggling his body back and forth in an excited little dance.

Upon entering the house, he circled me immediately, leaning up against my legs for a scratch. "You're the worst guard dog in the world, you know that?"

His response was to let his pink tongue loll out his mouth while I patted the side of his belly firmly.

Ruby entered the kitchen in a deep wine–colored cocktail dress with a halter neckline and a flirty skirt that ended above her knees. This one showed her shoulders and a hint of clavicle—one of the sexiest and most underrated bones in the human body, if you asked me—and I made a low noise of satisfaction deep in my throat.

"I was right," I murmured, circling her where she stood in the middle of the room.

"About what?" she asked, voice slightly above a whisper.

"That color is perfect for you."

She shifted to the side just as I came up behind her, and I tilted my head. "What is it?"

"Nothing, I just . . . I couldn't get the zipper done up all the way in the back. It's fine."

"No, no. We need to make sure it fits," I said, easing closer. She'd been able to pull the gold zipper up to her shoulder blades, and even though the glimpse of skin was brief—flawless, pale skin with a smattering of tiny freckles on either side of the delicate bumps of her spine—my throat went dry all the same. There was a tiny eye hook at the top of the halter, and I brushed her hair out of the way before using my other hand to tug the zipper into place.

Ruby had gone still as a statue, so perfectly unmoving that I wasn't even sure she was breathing. Odd—I was having a hard time pulling air into my own lungs while I fastened the eye hook shut so that the dress fit properly.

"Let's see," I instructed, willing my voice to work properly.

It wasn't Ruby, per se. It couldn't be. There was no universe in which pulling up a zipper, covering a woman's body with a dress, would turn me on. But there I was, half-hard in her kitchen because of a glimpse of her back.

Slowly, she turned, and my eyes dragged over the fit of the dress.

"Perfect," I whispered. "You look beautiful. Do you feel it?"

Her inhale was shaky, and I found myself breathless, waiting for a response. I wanted her to feel beautiful. To feel desirable. But mostly, I still wanted her to feel like Ruby.

"I-I'm going to try on something else," she said, her eyes flickering slightly as she stared up into my face.

She moved past me, and I was able to suck in a breath. Before she walked into her room, I called her name. "The blue bag next. Save the black bag for work tomorrow."

"What about the gray-striped bag?" she asked.

With a small hum, I conjured up the image of what was waiting inside that one. "Save that one for a special occasion."

Her brow furrowed, but she nodded, disappearing behind the door.

When she was out of sight, I blew out a harsh breath and rubbed the back of my neck. Bruiser was sitting at my feet, watching me with knowing eyes.

"Listen, buddy, my intentions are pure." His head tilted, and there was an unconvinced twitch to his ears that I didn't like. "Did you see that dress? Anyone would get turned on, okay? Don't act like you've never gotten an inconvenient boner."

While she was changing again, I helped myself to a glass of ice water and rooted through her pantry until I found a bag of microwave popcorn. It was popping furiously when she appeared again.

Becks, the boutique manager with a keen sense of fashion and a fierce desire for me to call her again, had taken my final challenge to heart.

The lounge set was pure decadence—long, flowing pants in ivory and a matching turtleneck top that was slightly cropped, showing a hint of her toned stomach. The entire thing looked sleek and expensive on her.

"What is this?" she asked, gesturing to the last outfit with a hint of a smile on her face.

"I told her I wanted something comfortable. Sexy without being over the top, and expensive. So you felt like you were doing something naughty just by wearing it."

Ruby's cheeks held a hint of pink. "She did very well. I've never owned anything made out of cashmere." She ran a hand over the overly long sleeves. "I don't know when I'd actually wear it, though."

"For a night just like this one," I told her. "Where you've got a man in your house, and you want to teach him all about the old-timey romance movies you love."

"It's a period movie," she corrected. At my confused expression, Ruby shook her head, tucking a strand of hair behind her ear with a slightly self-conscious laugh. Then she saw the popcorn in the microwave and the giant bowl waiting on the counter.

"Oh no, you're not," she said, eyes widening.

"Yes, I am. You've got a date for movie night tonight, birdy. I hope you don't mind sharing your popcorn."

Ten minutes later, we were on the couch, my legs stretched out on the matching plush leather ottoman. Ruby was tucked into the corner, the popcorn bowl on her lap and Bruiser parked right in front of her, his eyes locked on the prize.

"How about this one?" I asked, flipping through some of the choices she'd had queued up. *Persuasion.* Same title as one of the books on the stack.

"I just watched that last week," she said.

I kept scrolling and saw another version of the same movie, and I cut her a sidelong glance.

"They're very different," she replied primly.

With a grin, I reached over and took a handful of popcorn.

"Ah, here we go." I clicked on *Pride & Prejudice.* "I choose this one."

Looking over at me, she raised her eyebrows doubtfully. "You seriously want to watch this with me."

"Fuck yeah. You can make me smarter. Teach me all about pride and prejudice in the olden days." I swallowed some popcorn and glanced sideways. "Is it sexy?"

She snorted. "Because it's you asking, I'm going to say no. But *I* think there are very sexy parts," she said.

"Such as?"

"You'll have to wait and see."

I settled back into the couch and tossed a couple of kernels at Bruiser. They bounced off his face, and he inhaled them off the ground while Ruby laughed quietly.

As the movie started, Bruiser stuck his front paws on the couch to the left of Ruby and whined.

"Oh, Bruiser," she sighed. She glanced over at me. "Sorry, he likes this corner the best."

I patted the cushion between us. "Come on over, birdy. I don't bite."

Ruby scooted sideways, tucking one leg underneath her, and it brought her knee to a resting spot against my thigh. Her eyes landed on that spot, and then she straightened her leg out.

With a sigh, I reached forward and put her leg back where it was. "Get comfy. It's movie night."

It took a few minutes, but eventually, with the delicate music in the background as the movie began, Ruby slowly relaxed.

Taking pity on me, she turned on the captions because I couldn't understand a fucking word they were saying in their English accents.

"What does that mean?" I whispered. "Why are they freaking out over these two guys?"

She tilted the popcorn bowl toward me. "Because the most important thing back then, especially for young women in a home with no male heir, was to secure a decent marriage. These two men are rich and unmarried, and that means every single woman in the area will be hoping for an engagement."

I snorted. "Damn. These guys don't have to do anything but show up and flash their bank accounts."

"Basically."

Over the next hour, I learned a lot about the precarious reputation of women. The disparity between Mr. Darcy (who didn't seem like such a bad guy to me; I wouldn't want to show up at a party with everyone staring at me like that either) and Lizzie (who was hot in a smart, mouthy kind of way).

"Fuck me," I whispered when he asked her a question about pride. "That's a big deal, right?"

Ruby gave me a thoughtful look. "Yes. First time he's letting down the mask with her. He wouldn't be engaging like this if he wasn't a little bit interested. Even if he didn't want to be yet, he can't seem to help it."

We reached for a bite of popcorn at the same time, our fingers brushing. Hers yanked back more quickly than mine, and I risked a glance out of the corner of my eye.

It felt like middle school, when you're sitting next to your crush in a movie theater, holding your hand out at an awkward angle and hoping they'd take the bait—butterflies exploding in your stomach when they did.

Ruby had fully relaxed by this point, her arm up against mine and her knee completely resting on my thigh. The scene ended, and we both sat, raptly watching as Darcy reached out and helped her into the carriage. Lizzie's stunned look had me glancing over at Ruby for a moment, and fuck if she didn't have the sweetest smile on her face.

Then Darcy pulled back, flexed his hand, and Ruby sighed decadently.

I grabbed the remote and hit pause. "Hang on a second."

"What?"

I gestured to the TV. "What the fuck was that?"

"The hand flex," she answered seriously. "He grabbed her hand. They weren't wearing gloves."

For a moment, I did nothing but stare. "They weren't wearing gloves?"

She edged forward in her seat, face more animated than I'd ever seen. God, was she always this fucking cute? I did a quick mental tally of concussions, because repetitive head injuries were the only plausible reason I hadn't noticed right away.

"Back then, skin-to-skin touching almost never happened outside of a dance, courting, or an engagement, and even then, it would've been considered scandalous." Her eyes were glittering in the darkened room, and I found myself with a dry throat again, slightly desperate to know what she was going to say next. "Him touching her like that would've felt . . ." Her voice lowered to a throaty whisper. "Electric." Then she smiled, biting down on her bottom lip as she did. It took everything in me to tear my gaze away from her mouth. "Just from holding her hand. Can you imagine?"

No. But fuck if I didn't want to.

"Show me," I told her in a rough, quiet voice, shifting the popcorn from her lap and easing my hand onto my thigh, just next to where her knee rested against it. My pulse hammered in my ears as she stared down at my hand. "If I were your date, a real one, and you were watching this—what would you do? Would you show me?"

The graceful line of her throat worked on a swallow, but she didn't shut down. "I don't know," she whispered. "I've never had a man here for a movie date. Are we renegotiating to account for hand-holding?"

Yes. Please, dear God, yes.

"If you want." My chin rose in a slight dare, and she saw it. Ruby tightened her jaw and stared down at my hand, where the pinkie was a fraction of an inch from the soft cashmere covering her legs.

"For practice," she said. "Right?"

I nodded, because fuck, I would've agreed to anything. I didn't know what power this movie had, but I wanted her to hold my hand more than anything in the entire fucking world. My heartbeat hammered in my chest when she slid her hand over the top of mine, just a whisper of a touch at first.

Scared to move too quickly, I let her drag her nails over my knuckles, over and back, before I turned my hand over, my palm facing hers now. The hair on my arms lifted at her gentle, curious exploration, and I clenched my jaw while I watched. Her hand was so much smaller. If she stretched her fingers out over mine, I would've been able to bend at the top knuckle easily, without her needing to remove her hand.

The skin on her fingers was impossibly soft when she danced her fingertips over the calluses on my palms. "This is from playing?" she asked.

I managed a nod. "Mostly from lifting, but . . . yeah."

She blinked slowly, staring down at our hands as she continued the delicate, torturous touches, and she eased her fingers in between mine. "And men would like something like this?" she asked. "It wouldn't seem . . . stupid? Too innocent?"

God, I couldn't even answer, because I felt like my voice might crack over the screaming sexual tension locking down my entire body. I shook my head and cleared my throat. "No. It's not stupid."

Even though I should've let her do it, and my head was swimming dangerously from this not-too-innocent, not-too-stupid moment, I curled my fingers up and around hers, pressing our palms together firmly.

Simply because I wanted to hold her hand.

Ruby glanced up at me, her eyes big in her face, and then she smiled. A real smile too. With the flash of a dimple in her cheek and a tiny spread of laugh lines bracketing her mouth when she did.

"Wanna start the movie again?" she asked.

I nodded, fumbling with my other hand to find the right button on the remote. The music started back up, and we stayed like that, hand in hand, side by side in the dark.

I knew two things right in that moment:

Ruby Tate was so much sexier than she realized.

And I was completely fucked.

Chapter Twelve

GRIFFIN

"Don't go anywhere, folks. After commercial break, we're going to talk about the King twins."

"Are we? I thought we'd talked about them enough last week. What are they up to now?"

"Barrett King has been working nonstop, no surprise there. *Preparation* is the man's middle name. But Griffin King hasn't been spotted anywhere around the team facilities in New York since his interview went viral—and we're going to break down all the gossip about where he might be, if the rumors are true that he's hunting for another team in order to avoid big brother." The podcaster paused. "Stay tuned."

Fuck. I punched the power button on the stereo in my car.

Because I was driving aimlessly, I wasn't paying attention to where I'd turned until the library came into view. In the back of the parking lot, I saw Ruby's car. Without thinking about it too heavily, I pulled into a spot, exhaling before I exited the vehicle and walked over to the bench where she and I had sat on that first day.

My phone rang with a video call about three seconds later, and with the assumption that Steven had heard the same clip, I didn't even bother looking at the screen when I picked it up.

"I know, you're pissed at me."

"I probably should be, especially if the rumors are true and you just signed with my team without telling me, you dick."

At the sound of Marcus Henderson's voice, I did a double take at the face filling the screen. We'd played at Oregon together, even though I graduated a couple years before him. His hair was longer, the reddish-blond beard around his face scruffier than I'd ever seen it. "Does that mean you're actually going to start catching the ball well enough that you don't need a stronger defense?"

His laugh was deep and rich. "I'll see what I can do. So it's true, then?"

I scratched the side of my face. "Yeah. Ink's not dry on the contract, but I go in next week to sign. You gonna talk shit about me in the locker room before I get there?"

"Yeah right. You're a fucking legend." He tipped his head back and howled. "I'm throwing a party for you once you're in town. How long has it been, man?"

"Not long enough. The last time you took me out for drinks—after I played you in Denver a few years ago—I was hungover for a week, and Steven threatened to fire both of us if we ever did that again." I grimaced. "I still can't touch tequila after that night."

He laughed. "Oh yeah. Remember those twins I took home?"

"I'm surprised *you* do," I said dryly. "You could hardly see straight."

"Text me when you're in next week. I want a repeat."

"No way. I'm getting too old for that shit." I narrowed my eyes at the screen. "What are you doing with your hair right now? You look like a fucking Viking."

Marcus stroked a tattooed hand over his beard. "Chicks dig this; you have no idea."

"Why? You look feral."

He grinned unrepentantly. "Exactly."

"Still an animal, Henderson."

"Like you didn't sleep with just as many women as I did in college."

"In college," I pointed out, laying a hand on my chest. "I've grown. I've matured."

"So if I asked you to streak through training camp, you'd say no?"

"I did that one time, asshole. We were nineteen."

He laughed. "Remember Coach's face?"

"Yes," I answered grimly. "I also remember that was strike one of my three."

Marcus's face turned thoughtful. "What was strike two?"

We remembered at the same time. "His office," we said in unison.

Marcus laughed. "He was cleaning glitter out of his files for weeks."

"I can't believe I stayed friends with you after all that. Why did I always get in trouble for your shitty ideas?"

"First, because I am excellent company. And second, because I was smart enough to let you have the spotlight." He wagged his finger in the air. "You and your competitive streak. Even if it was just to set yourself apart from Barrett, it worked out very well for me."

I snorted. "Yeah, because I always took the blame."

"What a good friend, always wanting to come in first with the big impression."

"Not anymore," I said. "I'll happily concede that spot to you. I'm an adult, Marcus. You should try it."

"Fuck off, you mean to tell me you've turned into Barrett?" He snorted. "I know better than that. He's got a stick up his ass so far I can't believe it hasn't come out of his mouth yet."

It was odd talking to someone who still saw you as a very specific version of yourself. It wasn't like I'd changed a lot, but I *had* changed. It was subtle, something that had happened day by day, but it seemed— especially recently—that no one but me had noticed.

Marcus leaned in toward the screen. "I see a whole lot of nature behind you. Where the hell are you right now?"

"Staying at Steven's place outside Fort Collins."

"No you're fucking not. You're that close? Shit, Griffin, I can be there before dinner." The background behind the phone was a blur, and only half of Marcus's face appeared on the screen as he walked through his house. "He's never invited me there, and I live in Denver. That prick."

Before I could respond, the door to the library opened, the sun glinting off the glass, and I was smiling before I knew what was happening.

"I have plans tonight," I told him, eyes lingering on the cut of her wide-leg pants as she walked and the pale-pink silk blouse that tied primly around her neck. Oh yeah. This was definitely her naughty-librarian look, but I decided it was best for my health if I didn't tell her that.

"What the hell are you doing at his place? Is he there with you?"

"Nah. He grounded me so I wouldn't piss anyone else off before the contract is signed in Denver."

"Did he? Steven never messes around when he's got money on the line."

"Fuck off," I said without any heat. "How about you? Still living in that stupid apartment?"

"The penthouse downtown? Yeah, asshole, I am. Chicks dig this too. They like all the glass windows, if you catch my drift."

"Remind me not to touch anything if I come over."

He laughed. "Oh, come on. When can we get together?"

Ruby set her hands on her hips and stared down at me, tapping her foot impatiently. I merely pointed at the phone, giving her an apologetic smile.

"Wait," Marcus said. "Isn't it your birthday soon?"

I gave him an incredulous look. "How the hell do you remember that?"

"Because I almost got alcohol poisoning the night you turned twenty-one."

"That sounds like something that happens to you weekly. I don't think you can blame me."

"I'll do that as long as I can." He notched his chin up. "Someone there with you? You keep looking at something."

"An old friend," I told him, eyes locked on Ruby, who crossed her arms and sighed heavily.

He made a knowing noise. "You going to introduce me? You know I enjoy making new friends."

"Not a chance in hell."

"Why not? If she's your friend, I can guarantee she'll like me. I'm definitely better looking, and I'm a hell of a lot more fun."

"She's way too smart for the likes of either one of us."

Ruby's eyes locked with mine, then quickly darted away.

He snorted. "Which means she's hot and you don't want me to know it."

If I admitted it out loud—because Ruby looked pretty fucking good today—she'd never believe me. She'd think it was for show. Instead, I merely smiled. "Use your imagination. I think I'll keep her to myself for now."

Ruby's cheeks flared pink, and I had a sudden spike of interest under my ribs, wondering how far down her neck and chest that soft sunrise color might spread.

"Tell you what," I said. "How about you come out to Steven's place for my birthday. Bring a couple guys from the team. We can keep it low-key."

Marcus perked up. "For real? You'd let me throw my Welcome to Denver rager at Steven's house?"

I rolled my eyes. "No one's trashing anything. I said we could hang out here, dickwad. Use your listening ears. I told you, I don't party like that anymore."

"Yeah right. Everyone says that until I show up."

"Think that sounds like a you problem, Marcus. No rager. No groupies. No drugs."

He pouted. "No women? Not even some nice ones?"

"They're all nice to you," I drawled.

"Fuck, are they. Come on, what if a couple of the guys have girlfriends? You gonna make me say no to them? I'm encouraging healthy monogamy by letting them come along."

I snorted. "Sure you are. Listen, I gotta go. I'll text you next week, okay?"

He leaned in, making an obnoxious kissing sound at the camera. "I miss you already," he crooned.

"Fucking hell," I muttered, disconnecting the call before smiling up at Ruby. "Sorry about that. He's the worst."

"Another football player, I presume?"

I nodded. "We played in college together. He heard rumors that I was getting traded to Denver. Marcus Henderson?"

She shrugged. "I don't pay attention to any sports, really. Is he good?"

"Unfortunately." I grinned. "He's got a minor drinking problem in the offseason, but once the games start, he's an absolute terror on the field." I paused, tilting my head to drink her in. "Look at you."

She set her hands on her hips and stared down at me. "How do these clothes fit perfectly? I've been shopping for myself since I was fifteen, and the stuff I pick out never fits this well. When I walked in this morning, Lauren almost passed out."

"I bet she did." I tilted my head the other direction, studying the way the pants hugged her hips and backside. Ruby might be small, but no matter what she said about having no curves, she sure as hell had some. She just wasn't used to displaying them properly. "I showed the woman helping me," I said, holding up my hands like I'd done at the house the morning before, when I almost curved them around her ribs to measure. "We made a pretty good approximation, don't you think?"

The line of her throat worked on a swallow. "Yes."

I leaned in to whisper, "Plus, I looked at your sizes once I finished counting all your cardigans."

She pinched the bridge of her nose, and my gaze traveled over the curve of her waist, around her hips and backside.

"Stop looking at my ass," she commanded.

"There's no helping it, birdy. It looks excellent in those pants," I said smugly. "And you can't tell me you don't feel good wearing clothes that fit you a little bit better, right? Feel powerful. Confident."

She huffed, taking a seat next to me on the bench. "I wish I was a more proficient liar, because your ego will be out of control once I admit the truth."

I nudged her gently with my shoulder. "Say it, Ruby. You know you want to."

The sidelong look she gave me was full of exasperation. But underneath it, there was a tiny spark of affection, and fuck if that didn't make me want to puff out my chest. "Fine. The clothes are amazing. I almost wore that white lounge set to work just because it's the most comfortable thing I've ever owned."

"And you look incredible in it," I told her.

Ruby's forehead wrinkled slightly. Compliments, I'd decided, made her very uncomfortable.

"What exactly are we achieving, though?" she asked. "The clothes and the movie night—and you stalking me outside my place of employment. I thought you were going to tell me what to do. Give me homework or a checklist or something."

"I'm going to ignore the stalking accusation because you don't own this bench." I also ignored her heavy sigh. "We're accomplishing the first important few steps."

"Which are . . . ? You bolted so fast after the movie last night I wasn't sure exactly what was happening."

"Oh, I didn't bolt. I just needed to rush home to download the full Jane Austen catalog. I have a feeling she could teach me a few things."

"Undoubtedly," she answered in a dry tone. "Pass her along to Marcus while you're at it."

"Way too many big words for that man."

Ruby exhaled a quiet laugh.

"I watched *Persuasion* this morning."

Her head whipped in my direction. "You did not."

"Her dad is a total dick. At first I wasn't sure I liked Wentworth, but I have to give the guy credit—he always loved her, didn't he?" Ruby's mouth fell open. I reached over and gently closed it using the tip of my finger. "We're building confidence," I told her. "Without that, nothing else will work. Last night, we stayed in your space, doing something you like, because you'll naturally feel more comfortable. How would you have felt if I'd forced you to go shopping and then took you to a club?"

"Like I'd need heavy psychotropic medication," she answered without hesitating.

"Exactly. And I bet you felt like a badass when you walked into work this morning, didn't you?"

She shifted uncomfortably. "I wouldn't use that word exactly," she hedged. After a moment, she cut her eyes to mine. "But I did feel good. Taller or something."

"Bingo. That's what we're looking for."

"I had a meeting with the library trustees this morning." A pretty blue bird fluttered in front of us, landing on the sloped banks leading down to the creek. Ruby's eyes tracked its movements. "Someone commented afterwards that I was a bit more . . . forceful than they're used to."

"Attagirl. Anyone on that board you want to sleep with?"

Ruby managed to tear her gaze away from the bird long enough to give me a dry look.

I held up my hands. "Just doing my duty. Making sure we're not missing any opportunities."

"I haven't had an opportunity in this town in years," she said.

"Why do I find that hard to believe?"

Ruby was quiet for a moment. "People get used to seeing you in a certain light. Even if you change, their perception stays the same." Her eyes darted over to mine. "It's hard to overcome that, don't you think?"

It was hard to swallow because it echoed so much of what I'd thought when talking to Marcus. When talking to *everyone*. I gave her a jerky nod. "Yeah. I do."

"Why'd you come to hang out here?" she asked. "I was half expecting you to be waiting at the front doors when I unlocked them this morning."

"It's a beautiful spot. And don't worry, I had every intention of coming in to pester you about what we're doing later tonight once I was done with my phone call. I had a couple ideas, if you're open."

"I can't do anything tonight, unfortunately."

"Why not?"

Did I sound pouty? I felt it. I must have, because Ruby smiled begrudgingly, gesturing to the library. "We're holding a community event tonight. I was going to attend and help out, but . . ."

At the way her voice trailed off, I thought something was wrong. But when I glanced over, she was staring at me. "What?" Her smile started small, then grew. That dimple appeared in her cheek, and fuck me if it wasn't adorable. "What?" I asked again, more suspicious this time. "Why are you looking at me like that?"

"You're coming with me," she said.

"I thought I was the pushy one in this relationship."

"You are. I'm not being pushy. I'm being confident."

"What's the event?"

"Oh, I'm not telling you." She patted my arm. "Trust me, it'll fit into your 'important first few steps' plan perfectly."

Chapter Thirteen

RUBY

"Everyone, you have five minutes before we show our partners what we've been working on. Five minutes," the instructor reminded us.

Brow furrowed as I studied what was in front of me, I paused to select a new brush, then dipped it into the white paint for some extra shading. When I glanced up over the top of my canvas, I had to dig my teeth into my bottom lip to keep from laughing out loud.

Griffin was frowning at his painting, muttering something under his breath. The woman wandering around the room stopped behind him to set her hand on his shoulder and give him some encouragement.

"Maybe you could try some of that," she said. "Fill in some of the negative space around her head."

He fixed his dubious facial expression on the canvas, then on me. "Do you think that will help?"

Her pause was telling, and I lost my battle, laughing into the back of my hand.

Griffin looked up, eyes locked on me, and he arched an eyebrow slowly. "What are you laughing at, birdy? For all I know, you're just as bad at this as I am."

"You're right, I might be," I said lightly, ducking in to sweep the skinny brush along the edge of his face. Then I picked up a damp sponge to create the texture I wanted. He watched me warily, then glanced back at his artwork with a sigh.

"I can't believe you roped me into this," he muttered.

Confidence building, as it turned out, was forcing the big athlete to do a craft with me and another thirty people from town. We'd transformed the inside of the library into a painting studio with long tables set up parallel to each other, every attendee supplied with an easel and a canvas, a stack of brushes in various shapes and sizes, and a palette of acrylic paint.

After seeing some videos on social media, Lauren had the brilliant idea to set up an evening at the library—Paint Your Partner Night. The assignment was simple: to paint the likeness of the person sitting across from you, be it friend or significant other, and once you were both done, show your paintings off for all to see.

We'd brought in Melanie, an art teacher from Fort Collins, who agreed to help out, and the library charged a set fee to cover our costs for the supplies and allow for some small fundraising to help us replace some of the items in the children's playroom.

Griffin had been recognized by one couple, but they did nothing more than wave excitedly when they saw him from across the room, and he gave a friendly nod in return. So far, no one had asked for his picture or autograph, and it made me wonder how much longer that would be the case when news got out that he'd signed with Denver.

Celebrity was a strange thing, and it was hard for me to picture him in that role, even knowing what I knew now. Again tonight, he was dressed simply—a light-blue long-sleeve T-shirt, pushed up to expose his muscular forearms, and dark jeans that hugged his tree-trunk thighs. After work, I'd changed, knowing what we'd be doing.

When he saw my shirt, he smirked—an ornate logo with the words PEMBERLEY & DERBYSHIRE—and I felt a zing of pride that he recognized the reference.

He did not smirk, however, when he realized what we'd be doing.

"I suck at painting," he whispered fiercely, lowering his head to speak close to my ear.

I patted his forearm. "We're not here to win any awards, Griffin. It's just for fun."

He snorted. "Please. Everything's a competition for guys like me."

He took the unspoken challenge seriously. For the first fifteen minutes, he rebuffed any attempt at conversation.

"Quit trying to distract me," he said, leaning in closer to study my face. "It won't work, Tate."

I couldn't help but laugh. "I'm on your team; why would I want to distract you?"

"Because you want to do better than me."

"Oh, I'm not worried about that." I dunked a brush into my cup of water and let it rest, finding a smaller brush to work on the shape of his eyes with.

"You paint a lot in your spare time?" he asked.

"No." The options I had to make his eye color were lacking, but adding another dab of yellow ochre helped make the brown a bit warmer. "I dabbled a little after college. I was sick for a while and needed a lot of rest. Even when you love reading, you need to find new hobbies that allow you to sit for long periods."

"Painting, huh?"

I nodded. "I liked painting birds and landscapes. Never practiced much with people, so for all you know, this might be terrible."

"God, I hope so." He tucked his tongue between his teeth while he dabbed a few colors together, blue and white and black, until they formed a silvery bluish gray. "There. I think I got the color right," he said, looking at my eyes once more.

"Too much blue," I replied lightly after glancing at the color he'd created.

His brows dipped into a V. "No it's not." He pointed his paintbrush at me. "See? You're trying to mess me up. Knock it off."

Eventually, he relaxed, and we talked a little bit about where his parents were—they'd retired to Arizona shortly before his brother took his coaching job. He skirted conversation about Barrett, and even though I found myself curious about what had happened there, I respected the fact that we were still in public, and he may not want to talk about it in a place where there was a risk of being overheard.

He asked how I'd gotten into my own job, and I talked a bit about college, how my parents had encouraged me to follow library science. His time in school was so different from mine; he'd spent years at the very center of the college experience, revered by thousands for his athletic ability, with his schoolwork coming in a distant second.

But even so, he never laughed at me. Never teased when I told him that I'd never lived in the dorms. Never attended a college party. He simply listened, assuring me that I'd probably saved myself from the inevitable pain of many hangovers as a result of my choices.

He was good at that, I realized. At taking me for exactly who I was. Not once had Griffin ever made me feel embarrassed for whatever life experiences I'd had—or not had, as the case was.

The time moved quickly, and no part of it felt like either one of us were forced to be there, and not for the first time, I wondered why I couldn't feel this kind of ease with someone else.

It didn't hurt, of course, that he was so attractive. For the better part of an hour, in the midst of fairly surface conversation, it was my job to study the details of his face, just like he was doing in return.

There was no lingering eye contact or anything like that, but I focused on the line of his nose, the curve of his lips, the sharp cut of his jaw, trying to get the shading of the stubble just right. Griffin perpetually looked like he needed to shave.

My hands shook slightly when I thought about what it would feel like scratching against the skin on my palm.

"Do you have to shave every day?" I found myself asking.

Griffin let out a small grunt of concession. "Pain in the ass, but yes. Two days is about all I can stretch it before I get annoyed."

"Why not just grow a full beard? You could pull it off."

His eyes sparkled at the unintentional compliment. "Well, if my lady wishes it, maybe I'll try."

"Oh, stop it," I said smoothly, even though my heart thudded painfully at *my lady*.

Occasionally, Melanie would come around and give us tips, laughing easily with different couples as they bemoaned their lack of artistic skill.

When the time ran down on the clock, she clapped her hands. "All right, everyone! Let's take a minute to clean up our stations and prepare to show our partners what we've been working on. Kenny, one of our friendly librarians, will be filming some of the reveals, so please raise your hand if you're comfortable being shown on the library's social media channel."

Griffin and I locked eyes but kept our hands down. He winked, and my stomach swooped dangerously.

"You're going down, birdy," he said as couples to our right and left showed their artwork to each other, dissolving into hysterics at what the other person had painted.

Suddenly, I felt a bright burst of shyness. "What if we . . . don't show it now?"

His brow furrowed. "What do you mean?"

"I don't want everyone to see," I told him. "Maybe we could wait until they're gone or . . . do it out in the parking lot or something."

Griffin nodded, eyes serious. "I see. You're embarrassed because I'm about to kick your ass in a painting competition."

"Yup, that's it," I replied lightly, then set my canvas to the side, making sure he wasn't looking at it. Griffin held my gaze and did the same with his.

Without being asked, Griffin helped Kenny, Melanie, and me clean up as people filtered out of the library. Almost all of them asked for a repeat of the event, and I promised we'd do our best.

"Come back for the fair this weekend," I told the sweet elderly couple who had just finished cleaning up their mess. "We're holding it in the high school parking lot; it should be a ton of fun."

The couple smiled. "We will. Our grandkids have been talking about it all month."

Griffin was carrying a stack of chairs under his arm, twice the amount Kenny was struggling with. "You're doing a fair?"

I nodded, tossing the palettes and disposable tablecloths into a large trash bag. "Fundraiser for the library."

"Maybe I should come," he said. "You could practice fluttering your eyelashes and being very impressed while I lose all my money on the games trying to get you a stuffed animal bigger than your dog. Men love that shit."

"Fluttering eyelashes and fake enthusiasm? If that's what you're teaching me, I'm screwed."

"You have no idea, birdy." He flashed me a quick grin. "Still sounds fun, doesn't it?"

"It's not that big of a deal." My cheeks were warm, imagining him there in the swarms of people. "Besides, I know you're trying to keep a low profile."

"It's a huge deal," Kenny interjected, walking past us to deposit his chairs against the wall. "She spearheaded the Welling Springs 5K last year, and the town T-shirt sale, and the spaghetti dinner, but we needed one more fundraiser." Kenny ignored my pointed glare and kept talking. "There's a reason she never goes out, and it's because she's been working sixty hours a week for the last two years to get enough money to buy the land next to the library."

I pinched my eyes shut, and when I peeled them open, I settled another lethal look in Kenny's direction. He merely smiled.

Griffin's brows shot up. "The land with the creek and the willow tree?"

I nodded slowly. "It's going up for sale soon, and . . . I thought maybe we could purchase it before that would happen, but the family who owns it wants to see how much they can get for it." I shrugged one shoulder. "Can't blame them, I guess."

Melanie interrupted to ask me a question, and I was relieved. Griffin quietly went about his work, helping Kenny take down the tables and stack the remainder of the chairs. Every once in a while, my eyes would snag on the way his arms bulged when he lifted something.

I cleared my throat and moved my canvas into my office, leaning it up against the side of my desk. When I exited, Melanie was standing by Griffin. "I'm so sorry to do this, but would you mind if I grab a selfie? My son is a huge fan," she said with an apologetic smile. "He'd never forgive me if I didn't ask."

"No problem." He leaned in toward her, setting his hand on her shoulder while she snapped a picture. "Maybe just . . . don't post it on social media, at least not for a couple of days, if that's okay with you?"

"Of course," she said. Her eyes were bright and her cheeks slightly flushed, a far cry from the composed woman who'd run the evening without a single hint that she knew who he was.

Griffin lifted his chin in my direction. "You have any paper?"

I nodded, darting back into my office to grab a pen and an index card. Griffin took it, leaning over the counter. "What's your son's name?"

"Bryan," she said. "Thank you so much. I can't even tell you what this will mean to him."

Griffin scrawled out a quick note, then signed his name—a big, bold signature—and handed it to Melanie with a smile. "Tell him his mom is really cool."

"I will," she breathed. "Thank you again. This was amazing." Melanie gave me a brief hug. "You call me anytime if you need help with something like this."

"Thank you," I told her. "We will."

Griffin approached, his arm brushing against my shoulder as we watched her leave the library with quick, excited steps. Before she went out the door, she had her son on the phone.

"Bryan? You won't believe what just happened . . ."

The door swung shut behind her, and I glanced up at him. "That was nice."

He grunted. "Don't tell anyone. They won't believe you, anyway."

I rolled my eyes. Kenny walked past us, his messenger bag over his shoulder. "You okay to lock up?"

With a nod, I hitched my thumb at Griffin. "He's my bodyguard tonight since Bruiser isn't here."

Griffin cut me a sideways look. "If Bruiser is my competition, that doesn't say much about me."

Kenny smiled. "All right. Good night, guys."

It felt different when he left, leaving me and Griffin in the quiet of the library. The whole building seemed to pulse with it—the utter stillness. For the first time all night, the first time since he'd bulldozed back into my life, I felt an overwhelming wave of nerves, something fidgety coating my skin as I risked a glance up at him.

"Well?" I asked quietly. "You ready?"

Griffin gestured to my office, where he knew I'd set my canvas. His was resting against the wall near where we stood, and he picked it up in one hand and followed me. My office was lit with only the small lamp on my desk, and because the sun had already set, there wasn't much of a view out the windows along the far wall.

But he stood in front of them anyway, humming in understanding. "That's how you saw me so quickly earlier."

"It's my favorite view," I told him, settling a hip onto my desk and staring out into the dark, where I could see a shadowed glimpse of the bench and the weeping willow tree, the branches dancing lightly in the breeze. "And I hope it stays just like that."

"When does the land go up for sale?" he asked, wandering over to the other side of my office to study the framed renders of what we'd planned should the land become ours.

"Soon. Probably next week," I told him. "There's an important place in any town for development, of course. It's good for the economy when a city gets new restaurants and shopping and nice places to live.

But I want this library to serve a different purpose. People come here for the sense of community it brings, as much as they do for the books. Like tonight," I said. "We've known all those people for years. Watched them get married, have kids—some of them bring in their grandkids to get books now. And I love the idea that they can stay and play outside too. Watch for birds and butterflies, go for a walk, play with some interactive art."

I sighed, fighting a tug of defeat that it might not happen. "That land could be a legacy that's just as important as any of the books inside this building, and I want to know we're using that land as something good for this town. Someday, we'll all be gone, but that beautiful place could still be here, you know? Proof that we did something good."

Even now, well past my school years, I wanted to have something to show for all the work we'd done. It wasn't a test hanging on a fridge or a project to be admired, but I wanted to know that someday when I was gone, there'd be something *good* left behind.

Griffin had gone still listening to me, his eyes tracing my face. "Why do you look so sad?"

My nose was burning from the press of tears, and I pulled in a sharp breath to will it away. "I'm not sad, I'm . . . frustrated, I guess. There's only so much I can do."

He leaned a shoulder against the wall. "Sounds like you're doing it."

"I suppose."

Griffin cleared his throat, tapping the edge of his canvas with two fingers. "I know what'll make you feel better."

"What's that?"

"Me kicking your ass in a painting competition."

I laughed. "It's not a competition."

"Says you," he answered on an exhale. "I'd say that, too, if I knew I was outmatched."

With a roll of my eyes, I grabbed my canvas. "Fine. Are we showing them at the same time?"

"Oh no. Ladies first."

"Okay." I shrugged, sucking my bottom lip into my mouth as I turned the canvas around.

Griffin didn't move.

Then he blinked.

Then he leaned closer to the canvas, snatching it out of my hands.

"The fuck . . . ," he whispered. His eyes locked with mine. "Why didn't you tell me you're like, fucking Picasso?"

My eyebrows arched. "Because I'm not?"

"This is good." His head reared back as he studied the painting with almost frantic eye movements. "Holy shit, Ruby, this is really fucking good."

Clasping my hands in front of me, I cleared my throat. "Thank you."

His jaw hung open. "I'm keeping this. I'm framing it and keeping it and it's going up at my house whenever I buy one."

I laughed. "You are not." Standing from the desk, I tried to take the canvas back, and he snapped it out of reach. I set my hands on my hips. "You are not framing that at your house."

"Says who? It's my house. This is the best thing I've ever seen."

"Of course you'd say that. It's your face."

He kept his gaze locked on the canvas. "I do not look like this in real life."

"Don't be ridiculous. I painted you as I see you."

"I don't think I'm this hot, birdy." Griffin turned the canvas around so it was next to his face. "Tell the truth. You made me hotter."

My face burned at the insinuation. For a moment, I tried to study the image objectively—golden-brown eyes straight to the front; the way his hair curled, slightly too long over his ears; the hard line of his jaw and the crooked smirk I'd given his mouth—but all I could see was him. "I think it looks like you."

He blew a raspberry. "Whatever you say."

I drew in a deep breath. "Okay, your turn. Let me see."

"No fucking way." He picked up his canvas. "This is going into the garbage."

With a gasp, I marched forward. "It is not. You show me right now."

Griffin shook his head, ruthlessly swatting at my hand when I tried to take the canvas from him. I huffed, setting my hands on my hips again. "You're ten times bigger than me; this isn't fair."

He clicked his tongue. "Tough shit. Life isn't fair, cupcake."

I was two seconds away from stomping my foot when I had an idea. It was Griffin's idea, really. Something he'd said to me on my very own couch, just before he held his hand out to me and offered himself up as the world's sexiest hand-holding partner.

What would I do if this were a real date?

Courage was something I could hold in my hand. Something I could see and feel and touch. A canvas with bright colors, painting a man with a sharp jaw and a beautiful smile and big, big hands that were so warm and rough when they curled around my own.

Bravery was something different, of course. It was the absence of fear when you stepped into a precarious situation.

Maybe that wasn't me all the time. But it was tonight.

And it wasn't because he'd bought me pretty clothes or checked out my ass like it was something worth staring at. It was because he'd let me hold his hand and made me feel good in that seemingly insignificant snippet of time. Worthy of that small piece of affection and normalcy.

I took a deep breath and stepped forward, laying my hands on his chest. Griffin went still as a stone the moment I touched him. The heat from his skin seeped through his shirt like it wasn't there.

"Please," I whispered, taking one step closer. "Please show me."

A muscle twitched in his jaw. "What are you doing?"

My tongue darted out to lick at my suddenly dry lips, and my stomach flipped weightlessly when his eyes tracked the movement. "You asked me last night what I'd do if this was a real date, right?"

With slightly narrowed eyes, Griffin nodded. "That's what you're doing now?"

"I guess." My voice shook a little as I spoke. Underneath the thin layer of his shirt, it was just muscle. We all had them, right? It shouldn't have felt so shocking. But his muscles were different. Firm, hard, and hot, and my whole body went up in flames at the feel of them. My fingers spread out wide, covering a paltry amount of his pectorals. "Please show me, Griffin."

He exhaled a quiet laugh, blinking slowly as he stared over my shoulder for a moment. "You're a little too good at this already."

I bit down on my bottom lip when a smile threatened. "Is that a yes?"

"I'm gonna regret this," he groaned, shifting the canvas out from under his arm and handing it over to me.

There was a stunned beat of silence while I tried to figure out what the hell I was looking at.

I didn't want to laugh, but honest to God, I couldn't help it.

My face was huge, my eyes too small, and there were no whites to be seen around the bluish gray he'd created. Tiny lines for my eyelashes and monstrously huge lips in a bright red. My hair was made from yellow sticks protruding from my head, and he'd forgotten to paint my nose.

"Oh my gosh," I wheezed.

Griffin crossed his arms, shifting his weight. "Okay, get it out."

"Griffin . . ." I wiped at tears, my stomach seizing from how hard I was laughing. "This is terrible. Do you think I look like this?"

His hands rose and fell helplessly. "Obviously not, but . . . I can't . . . How am I supposed to just look at you and paint what I see?"

After another moment, I was able to suck in a deep breath and calm myself. A little. With a last glimpse at his attempt, I set it down on the floor and faced him. His cheeks were flushed pink, but his gaze stayed steady on mine.

"I love it," I told him.

"You do not."

"I do. I'm keeping it forever. Framing it in my house."

Griffin growled under his breath, a playful sound of exasperation that sent my pulse skyrocketing. He stepped forward, his hand raised like he was going to reach for me, then stopped.

Without thinking, I gripped his wrist before he could pull his hand away. "What were you going to do?"

He inhaled through his nose, studying my face through heated eyes. "Not sure I should tell you that, birdy."

"What if we renegotiate so you can?" I said in a rush.

Everything about this felt real and crisp and vivid, and I didn't want it to end. I wanted to feel more of it, bask in this perfect little moment and let it play out so I could remember it someday.

"You really want that?"

God, his voice. There was desire in that rough-edged voice, and it was stamped all over his face. I wasn't sure when it had happened, but it was heady. Dangerous. And oh, I wanted more.

Dazedly, I nodded, my hand still tight around his thick wrist. Griffin stepped forward, backing me up against the desk, his hands sliding easily around my hips as he boosted me up onto the surface. My legs split open, and he crowded into me, cradling my jaw with both big, calloused hands.

My head spun from the sudden, overwhelming proximity of his large body.

He dipped his head to run his nose against mine. "I was going to touch your face like this," he said in a low, fierce voice. "Tell you how beautiful you look when you laugh. That you should do it every day. Every fucking day."

A helpless whimper crawled up the back of my throat, and his hands slid back into my hair, where his fingers tightened.

"That's a nice little sound, Ruby," he whispered. "What else can I do to make more of those?"

My hands curled helplessly into the front of his shirt, and I tilted my chin up, drowning in this thick pulse of desire that felt like fireworks all over my skin. I didn't want it to end. *Let it be real,* I begged quietly in my head. And I said the most terrifying thing I could imagine, words I could never take back once they were out, but I refused to let the fear hold me back.

Not tonight. Not with him.

"You could kiss me," I whispered back.

He rolled his forehead against mine, sucking in a sharp breath. "You gonna let me? You gonna beg me for it if I hold out much longer? Tell me you want this, baby."

That unthinking nickname flipped a switch under my skin. It wasn't a holdover from our childhood, something cute and sweet and innocent. It was tossed out in the heat of the moment, falling off his tongue because he couldn't stop himself.

Tell him I wanted this? Easiest thing I'd ever done.

"Griffin, please—"

The word was barely out when Griffin slanted his mouth over mine—a skillful, bold first kiss. Nothing like I'd expected, which was what made it so achingly perfect. It wasn't tentative and innocent. It was sex in a kiss. The kind that made for sweaty skin and whispered dirty words.

And when his slick, hot tongue teased the line of my lips, I opened immediately, throwing my arms around his big shoulders and holding on for dear life.

The man could kiss. If there was anything he was better at than this, I'd explode before I ever got the chance to experience it.

His arms moved down my back, gathering me closer to him as his lips worked in a devastating push and pull over mine. He sucked at my bottom lip, soothing it with his tongue afterward. That tongue moved back into my mouth, tangling with my own until my back arched, pressing my aching breasts into his chest.

When I dug my hands into the thick length of his hair and tightened my fingers, he groaned, the sound reverberating deep through my bones as I lost myself in that kiss. Lost myself in Griffin.

How easily I could let him carry me away completely. When did this happen? When did he become the safest man I knew? The only one I trusted with this kind of mindless desire, this frantic, clawing desperation.

His hips rolled against my center, and I gasped, throwing my head back as I registered the hard, hot, *big* length of him.

"Oh," I exhaled.

"For you, baby," he murmured against my throat, then dragged his teeth against the line of my neck.

For me.

There was no faking this, no polite veneer over the way his hands clutched my body to his. All this . . . for *me*. God, the way it made my mind spin and spin and spin.

Being wanted by Griffin was power unleashed, my skin sparking with invisible bits of magic. There was a reason this was addicting, why desire became a trembling sort of craving that couldn't be ignored.

He wanted me. There was proof hard against my body, and even if it was just for this moment, I wanted him too. More than I'd wanted anyone in my entire life—to a senseless, illogical degree.

It wasn't really senseless, though. I could pull threads of logic in every single step that got us here, with his mouth on mine and his arms curled tight around my frame in a way that made me feel . . . everything. I felt everything with him, and it was perfect.

It was a loss of control that I welcomed because handing it to him felt like the only conclusion I could possibly reach. Griffin sucked at the sensitive skin underneath my ear, licking along my jaw until he took my mouth again in another searing kiss. It didn't matter that I wasn't entirely sure what to do, that the steps of this dance were unfamiliar to me, because he masterfully led me through each kiss, each twist of his tongue around mine.

His hands dove into my hair again, tilting my head so that the angle of the kiss changed into something luxurious and decadent. Our kisses slowed, deepened. Burrowing farther into his arms kept me from trembling, and it was the heat of his body that had me sighing softly as he changed the angle again with a deep, rumbling groan. The way his hands mapped out my body, along my back and waist, up over my shoulder to cup the base of my neck, using his thumbs to lift my chin into another kiss.

There were too many clothes in between us, and a restless sort of energy built and built in my fingertips, desperate to tear at whatever separated us. This was a possession, a not-so-simple kiss from the absolute last person I should be touching.

He slid one big palm around to cup my breast, his thumb circling around my impossibly hard tip. "You feel incredible."

I couldn't breathe. It felt so good I couldn't breathe.

Then his hand settled over my sternum—and a bright throb of panic made my eyes snap open. "Wait," I gasped.

Immediately, Griffin pulled back, his eyes searching my face while he pulled his hands off me. "Too much?"

I settled my hands over my chest and took a few deep breaths, willing myself to calm down. "Maybe," I whispered.

"I'm sorry," he said. Griffin ducked his head down. "I'm sorry."

"No." I cupped his face and pulled his forehead down to mine, letting them rest together while we struggled to catch our breath. "Don't be sorry. That was . . ." I shook my head. "That was incredible."

He gave me a tiny smile. "I'll paint you a thousand pictures if that's the way you want to thank me."

I exhaled a laugh. "Please don't."

Griffin's smile widened, and he stepped back from the desk, holding his hand out to help me down. "If that were a real date, that would've been a hell of a way to end it."

Something about his words made my bones ache, and I forced a smile.

I wish it was real, I thought. *Don't you?*

But I couldn't force the words out. They wouldn't budge from where they were anchored in my throat. Saying them would change everything, and for the briefest of moments, I felt naive and silly for even thinking them.

"It would," I replied softly.

He waited patiently while I turned off the lights in the library, then locked the doors. As he walked me to my car, neither of us said anything, and I had a sinking feeling we'd just wrecked something that couldn't be fixed easily.

"Well, when should we get together next?" he asked. "Maybe do a practice date at my place and you can show me all your newfound skills? I'll flutter my eyelashes and everything."

A breathy laugh escaped before I could stop it. His charm was effortless, and instead of being annoyed by it like I had been at the beginning, it threatened to reel me in. The lights in the parking lot cast a filmy, mysterious air around us, and with the way he stood, his hands tucked in his pockets—just out of reach—it lent an air of innocence to this entire exchange.

Ironic, given that only a few minutes earlier, I'd been two seconds away from stripping naked on my desk, the devastating side effect of Griffin King's ability to kiss me stupid.

Leaning against my car, I gave him an apologetic smile. "I'll be really busy the next couple days with the fair. I'm not sure I can get away easily."

Griffin nodded. "Make sure you still get your beauty sleep. It's good for your health, I hear."

"I will," I promised. "Don't get too bored."

"Oh, I have plenty to keep me busy. *Sense and Sensibility* tomorrow night."

A shocked laugh fell from my lips. He was joking, right?

He had to be.

He gave me a dangerous smile and told me good night, watching while I hooked myself into my seat and started the car. After I'd pulled out of my spot, I glimpsed in the rearview mirror and saw him standing there, hands still tucked into his pockets and watching as I drove away.

Chapter Fourteen

GRIFFIN

For his many faults, Steven had a great fucking home gym. I'd spent hours a day in that thing, and I didn't want to think too deeply on the fact that I felt like a mopey little puppy with Ruby not having time for me for a couple of days.

The harder part of my workout happened at dawn, when I spent an hour on upper body, followed by mobility work, because the older I got, the less flexible I was, and when you're chasing down quarterbacks every week, you want to be flexible enough to get sacked by an O-lineman and not feel like death afterward.

After a call with my new head coach and the Denver GM, the team sent a chopper to the closest private airfield and a sleek black car to drive me out to the team headquarters to sign my contract—smiling at the flashing cameras and providing a few sound bites that would make the rounds on every sports show for the next few weeks. The whole time I fielded questions, I found myself wondering what Ruby was doing. If she'd see any of this.

God, I was like a kid on the playground who wanted a cute girl to pay attention to him. One kiss and a little groping, and I was a fucking wreck.

By the time I returned to the house, my stomach was growling loudly. I flipped on the TV to hear what press had come out of the news, and when they took too long talking about baseball, I turned the screen off and made a sandwich before heading outside.

I sat out on the back patio with my book and a quick lunch, only coming inside because a crew showed up to do the lawn and weed around the landscaping beds. Two of the younger guys whispered to each other when they saw me sitting outside, and I gave them a small nod before disappearing back into the house for more low-impact exercise.

I'd already finished the World War Two book and moved on to the cowboy romance. Damn if that thing wasn't good, and I couldn't wait to tell Ruby about my favorite parts.

Brought a smile to my face just imagining it.

Steven had one of those self-propelled treadmills with a giant stand along the top. I could read easily if I wanted, but I wasn't in the mood—nor did I trust that I wouldn't get so distracted that I'd end up tripping over my own feet.

Instead of searching for music, I put on a movie and started a light jog.

Exercise always cleared my head, which was good because I spent more time working out than I did playing football, if I really thought about it. Today, it was clearing out all the thoughts of ill-advised kisses and the sounds Ruby made when I dug my hands into her hair.

The things I would've done to her if she'd asked . . .

I was never particularly good at restraint when an exciting opportunity presented itself, and Ruby looking up at me and asking me to kiss her was lethally effective at decimating my reserve.

Lips that were softer than I'd imagined.

Skin too.

Her body was firm and lithe, subtle curves that made my mouth water. It would've been so easy to press her back against that desk and see just how far we'd both be willing to go.

I glanced down between my legs and gave a stern look to my burgeoning hard-on.

"Knock it off," I muttered. "You're no help right now."

In the back of my head, I knew I should've regretted it, but I really fucking didn't. If I were a better man, less selfish, less driven by pleasure and enjoyment of things like kissing a beautiful woman in a dark room, I might've felt bad for it. If she'd been upset, if she'd slapped me for taking liberties—even ones that were offered—there might have been more of those feelings.

But even as she stopped me, her eyes were locked on my mouth.

I'd increased my speed on the treadmill without realizing it, now running at a fast clip, sweat gathering across my chest and back. I eased back, the machine adjusting automatically. The movie played on, and I'd hardly paid attention. I picked up the remote and backed it up until I recognized one of the scenes. My brow furrowed as the captions caught up, and I nodded when I finally figured out what was happening.

"What a dick," I whispered.

The door to the gym burst open, smacking hard on the wall, Marcus Henderson jumping into the room with a roar.

I jumped, losing my balance in the next heartbeat, and even though I reached for the bars on either side of the treadmill, my hand grasped at nothing but air and I toppled sideways, legs tangling as I fell to the floor.

With a groan, I pried my eyes open, and Marcus Henderson's face was right above me. He was grinning, one hand braced on his knee, the other holding his phone, which was also aimed at my face. "Dude, I'm so glad I was filming. This shit is gonna go viral."

"Give me your fucking phone," I said, pushing myself to a seated position. When I tried to reach for the phone, he pulled it out of my grasp. "You post that anywhere and you're dead to me."

He snickered, tapping on his screen a few times. "It'll be a great Welcome to Denver video. Everyone's gonna love it." Marcus eyed me where I sat. "You okay? Coach would skin me alive if I injured you before your first game."

Instead of answering, I got up to my knees and tried to swing at his junk with my fist, which made him jump back on a laugh.

"I'm fine," I told him. Once I was on my feet, I tested my ankles and knees, but they seemed all right. "No thanks to you, asshole. How did you get in here?"

He hitched a thumb over his shoulder. "You left the front door unlocked. Landscapers recognized me. Took a couple selfies, and they were happy." Marcus glanced around the gym, and his eyebrows rose in surprise. "This is a nice fucking gym, considering how out of shape Steven is."

"I think it's more for his wife than him," I said.

"Ah. That makes sense." He whistled. "She is hot."

The screen flashed with a scene change, and my eyes widened. I grabbed the remote off the treadmill and fumbled to turn it off but hit the wrong button. Marcus caught sight of the screen and whipped his arm out, snatching the remote from my hand.

"Hold the fucking phone, King," he said, cranking the volume up. "What is this?"

"You been drinking already today? It's a movie, dingbat."

Instead of taking the bait, his face split into a pleased smile, and I pushed my tongue into the side of my cheek while the Dashwood sisters consoled each other after all their relationship woes.

Slowly, Marcus pulled out his phone, aiming it at the TV, and I smacked it out of his hand before he could start filming. "Oh, come on," he laughed. "My followers will love this shit."

"By all means, blast it on the internet, then."

"You're watching a chick movie while you work out, Griffin," he said like I was slow to understand the gravity of the situation. A flick of his hand toward the TV and a meaningful lift to his eyebrows didn't help. "You'd get laid a hundred times over in a week if you put this out there."

I rolled my eyes. "I'm not trying to get laid, you idiot."

The words felt like rotten fruit coming out, because I was trying to accomplish *something* by watching these films, wasn't I?

Desperate moans, silky hair between my fingers, the warm, slight weight of her breast under my hand crashed into my brain before I could stop them.

Instead of lingering on that, I cleared my throat and grabbed the remote, punching the off button. "Sometimes it's good to expose ourselves to other sorts of entertainment. I've learned a lot about women by watching these movies. Do you know the kind of shit that was considered foreplay back then? Hand-holding. Dancing at a public ball when they hardly touched, and they had no privacy. Ever. It wasn't about anything physical, you know? Yeah, they're going for the rich guys because women had no power back then and they needed the protection of a secure marriage, but they still wanted someone who was kind and respectful and loyal."

The beat of silence was so thick I could hear my erratic pulse thundering in my ears.

He stared at me like I'd grown a second head. "Holy shit, I think I'm having a drug-induced hallucination."

"Are you high?" I asked incredulously.

"Well, no, but I have to be, right?" Then he waved a hand in front of his face. "No, I can see clearly. My vision isn't warped. Maybe I'm sleeping."

I smacked the back of his head. Hard.

"Ouch, you fucker." He smacked me back. "That hurt."

"It was supposed to. You're barging into my vacation and making fun of my movies; what do you expect me to do? Throw you a welcome party?"

"Yeah." He grinned. "I wanna raid the bar, man. Guaranteed Steven has some good shit. He'll forgive us, right?"

"Doubtful."

Marcus slung his arm over my shoulders and turned me toward the hallway leading back to the living area. "Let's find out."

Twenty minutes later, Marcus had emptied the cupboards of all the most expensive bottles of our agent's liquor, taking tiny sips of all of them. "Oh yeah, that's sexy," he groaned. "That's the winner."

It was a whiskey, by the looks of it, and he made his way to the kitchen to put a tiny bit of water into two lowball glasses. Then he added a generous amount of the whiskey, swirling a glass before handing it to me.

I took a small sip, humming as the warmth slid down my throat. "Good."

"Fucking great," he sighed, taking a seat on the couch and spreading an arm out. "You taking me out tonight?"

"Absolutely not."

He laughed. "Oh, come on. You used to be the fun King brother."

"I still am, believe it or not."

Marcus scratched the side of his beard and studied me thoughtfully. "Nothing to do with this friend you wouldn't show me, is it?"

Somehow, I kept my face even. "No. She's just a friend."

"Come on, she's hot, right? You can tell Uncle Marcus."

I swatted at his hand when he settled it on my shoulder. "You are so fucking creepy." I laughed.

He grinned. "She local?"

I nodded slowly. "We knew each other when we were kids. She had a crush on Barrett. Didn't know that until recently."

"Ahhh," he answered with a grave expression. "So she has shit taste in men."

My brain stalled around a vivid memory—the way she'd whimpered when I sucked lightly on her tongue—and I shifted uncomfortably in my seat.

"I suppose she does," I answered dryly. "How long you staying around?"

He shrugged. "Might crash here tonight if that's okay. Then I can get drunk with my friend."

I shook my head. "How the hell do you function during the season, Marcus?"

"God only knows," he replied seriously.

My phone rang with an incoming video call, and even though she'd never once called me, my heart gave a ridiculous jolt at the thought that it might be Ruby. Instead, I narrowed my eyes when I saw the name. "No swearing when I answer, okay?"

Marcus notched his fingers to his temple. "Yes, sir."

Before I answered, I set the drink off to the side so it was out of view, then hit the button to connect the call. "Holy crap, is it my favorite niece and nephew?"

Their faces filled the screen, so much older looking than the last time I'd seen them at my parents'. Maggie hogged the screen, and Bryce rolled his eyes, pushing her face with the flat of his hand.

"Bryce, stop touching me," she hissed. "I'll hide your Xbox again."

Her brother finally got some space on the screen and grinned. "Hi, Uncle Griffin."

"Hey, bud. Hey, Maggie. How you guys doing?" I eyed them carefully. "Your dad know you're calling me?"

Bryce shrugged. "He's at work; he won't care what we're doing."

Marcus gave me a meaningful look from his seat on the couch.

"Okay," I said. "So what's up? What are my two favorite kids up to?"

Maggie smiled. She was missing a couple of teeth. "Thanks for the birthday present, Uncle Griffin. I loved it."

My eyebrows shot up. "Did you? I thought you were way too young to have your own camera, but Miss Eileen said you were ready for the responsibility."

She giggled, holding up the pink instant camera. "Did you see it before she wrapped it? It's pink. I love pink."

"Who says I didn't wrap it myself? I'm offended, Maggie Moo."

Maggie rolled her eyes. "It was way too pretty, I know you didn't."

"You're right. But I did pick it out all by myself."

"And the karaoke machine?" she asked, eyes bright.

"Miss Eileen picked that out. She said her granddaughter loves it."

Bryce shoved his face in. "She's awful, Uncle Griffin. You should hear her."

"I am not," his sister hissed. "At least I can carry a tune, you ass—"

"Okay, okay," I interjected. "No swearing, young lady. Where's your nanny?"

"She quit," Maggie said happily. "Dad hasn't hired a new one yet. The housekeeper is kinda deaf, so she can't hear anything we're doing. It's awesome."

I shook my head. "What did you guys do to the nanny this time?"

Bryce wore a devious smile. "Nothing."

"Yeah right. Like I believe that."

He and Maggie shared a grin. "Not our fault she couldn't hack it," he said. "Besides, I'm *eleven*. I'm way too old to need a babysitter—"

"I'm ten; that's too old too," Maggie interrupted.

Bryce scoffed. "You're still a baby. You sleep with stuffies and a blankie."

Her cheeks went red. "So? You cried the last time it stormed."

"I did not. Besides, the lightning was right outside my room. It almost electrocuted me."

She rolled her eyes.

"Good grief, you two argue like this all day?" I asked.

"No," Maggie answered.

"Yes," Bryce said at the exact same time.

Maggie pushed her brother's head to the side. "Can we come visit you, Uncle Griffin? We haven't seen you in two years, not since you visited Grandma and Grandpa's while we were there."

God, these kids. An ache formed under my chest before I could stop it. "I'd love that, Maggie Moo, but it's not up to me if you can come. I'm not sure your dad would want you to stay with me. But let me know the next time you're going to Arizona, and I'll see if it works in my schedule, okay?"

Her eyes brightened—they were dark brown, just like her mom's, and that simply intensified the ache. Neither of them really looked like her, which was a fucking gift. Any reminder of her was like a high-pitched whine you couldn't get rid of. It's not like my brother was my favorite person, either, but at least he wasn't a raging narcissist who'd bailed on their kids.

"Okay!" she exclaimed. "I'll ask Dad."

I blew out a slow breath. Not what I meant, but okay.

Bryce said something under his breath, and Maggie nodded. "We gotta go, Uncle Griffin. We'll talk to you soon, okay?"

"Love you guys."

"Love you too," they said in unison.

The call disconnected, and I sighed heavily.

Marcus shook his head. "He still won't let you see the kids?"

"Can't blame him," I said. "I'm not exactly his favorite person."

Marcus snorted. "I wonder why. You told the entire world he had a stick up his ass."

"Yup," I answered grimly. "Not my best moment."

"Doesn't mean it's not true," he pointed out. "Remember when Coach Haskins sat the two of us down junior year and said he'd have kicked us out if Barrett hadn't vouched for us?"

I glared at my friend. "Yes. What's your point?"

He shrugged. "I don't know. Just that maybe that stick up his ass has some occasional merit."

Of course it did. That's why I was reminded of it constantly. Any other brother might have turned that situation—him stepping in to save my ass when I did something stupid—into a bonding moment.

Hey, I believe in you. Get your act together and prove everyone wrong. I'm on your side.

Oh no. That's not what Barrett did. Instead, I got hit with something entirely different.

Get your shit together, Griffin. You keep this up, and all you'll do is embarrass our family.

What he meant was I'd embarrassed *him*. Mr. Perfect. Ice Man, who showed no weakness. Never took a wrong step. Never messed up.

The world slotted us into roles when we got drafted—the Brain and the Brawn. I got my shit together in college, all right, and when draft day came, it was my name they called first. He smiled for the cameras, of course. But for a moment, we locked eyes, and I felt that unhealthy, hot zing of competition again. Turned out the very best kind of motivation was that of a younger brother who was sick of always being looked at second.

The last year of college ball, I played each game like a man possessed. My stats were insane, bringing me into the Heisman conversation, despite the rarity of a defensive player hoisting that trophy. Until the off-field stuff started causing bigger issues between us, widening the rift until I couldn't see the other side, I thought maybe—just maybe—my brother would come to me and say, *Hey . . . you did it. I'm proud of you.*

The screwups needed that validation just as much, if not more, than the perfect kids. I may not have acted like it, and a few years earlier, I wouldn't have admitted that even with a knife to my throat. But I could now.

Contrary to popular belief, I didn't hate my brother. That was too strong a word. Every once in a while, I'd see something that would remind me of growing up in Michigan: A song we used to listen to while we drove to school. The first snow of the year and how he'd always reminded me to bring my gloves and hat to school so I wouldn't catch cold.

Despite the fact that I didn't hate him, it wasn't possible to imagine a world where we could coexist peacefully either. In his mind, I was always the screwup. The one who needed saving. Who needed a sermon. And in mine, he was the obnoxiously perfect brother whom everyone compared me to. The ideal I could never quite meet, no matter what records I broke, what awards I won.

Except to Marcus, of course.

Marcus never expected me to be like Barrett, so I couldn't even be pissed at him for saying it. No matter how it would stick like glue in my throat, I might be willing to admit that yes, occasionally, my brother had positive things to contribute to the world.

But I still kicked my foot out at Marcus, catching him square in the side of his thigh. He swore, and I laughed.

"That's probably gonna bruise," he muttered, rubbing at the spot. In his other hand, he scrolled on his phone. "Hey, I was trying to find something to do around here, and it says there's a fair tomorrow. I fucking love fairs. Wanna go?"

"You think we won't stick out like a sore thumb at a small-town fair?"

"No one will even notice it's us," he said.

"Uh-huh." I eyed the dozens of tattoos covering his arms, the reddish-blond hair tied off his face, and the big beard. Marcus was even taller than me, an absolute monster at six six. "I'm sure you'll blend right in."

"Is that a yes?"

I stared at my friend, then picked up the whiskey, trying to imagine him anywhere in Ruby's vicinity. Maybe she'd be so busy I wouldn't even see her. I nodded. "Yeah, we can go."

"Sweet." He eased his long legs out onto the ottoman in front of him. "What should we do the rest of the night?"

I picked up the remote. "You can do whatever you want. I'm watching the rest of my movie."

"Fuck you, no you're not."

"Yes, I am." I raised my eyebrows. "If you like the end of this one, I'll show you *Pride and Prejudice*."

Marcus knocked back the rest of the whiskey, pinching his eyes shut. "I think I'm trapped in a nightmare."

"You'll love it." I chucked a pillow at him. "There's a hand flex."

He caught it and wedged it behind his head. "Whatever you say, King. Whatever you say."

Chapter Fifteen

RUBY

Under normal circumstances, a fair atmosphere would be considered the ultimate form of punishment for me. It was crowded and loud and germy, and it smelled like deep-fried food.

But that particular fair, on that particular evening, felt just on the right side of magical.

Shrieks of laughter filled the air, whooping from various rides, ebbing and flowing on a slow loop as the machines whipped people through the air on swings, whirling teacups, and kiddie rides. We'd invested a lot into this fundraiser, opting for a larger up-front cost with the possibility of a higher reward, knowing that the promise of community fun might sway people to be a little bit more generous.

The weather was perfect all day, the sun staying behind just enough intermittent cloud cover that no one got too hot, no one got sunburned, even though the temps were in the midseventies. Instead of doing an all-day event, we'd opened the fairgrounds at two and were able to manage the volunteer list so that everyone was in their designated spot for a couple of hours on each rotation. The gates would close at nine, and with a few hours left to go, I was more than ready to crawl into bed, but as one of the chairs of the event, I'd been moving all day, making sure everyone had what they needed.

"We're almost out of cinnamon sugar, Ruby," Lauren called.

"On it."

After visiting the second funnel cake stand on the opposite side of the high school parking lot, I heaved a bag onto the counter next to the deep fryer.

"More sugar than a small country should consume, but here you go." She leaned over to kiss my cheek soundly. "Bless you."

Because no one needed anything at that moment, I watched her deftly pour out more dough to create the lacy design of fried goodness for the next person in line, a towering lumberjack of a guy with red hair and a big beard, his massive arms covered in ink.

"God, that looks fucking delicious," he said, leaning in to watch her.

She met his gaze and winked. "Cakes won't be bad either."

His eyebrows shot up, appraising her frankly. "I like a woman with confidence."

"Do you?" Using the tongs, she flipped the funnel cake, nodding with satisfaction at the even brown color before she slid a plate next to the fryer. After shaking off the excess oil, she set it on the plate and eyed him. "What's your pleasure? Cinnamon sugar or powdered sugar?"

He licked his bottom lip—an undeniably naughty lick too—and even though it wasn't directed at me, my face heated nonetheless. "Your phone number would be even sweeter."

Watching them from the side, I managed to hide my smile. Not that it mattered anyway; neither one of them paid me an ounce of heed.

Lauren laughed. "You're too young for me, but I'm flattered."

His brow lowered. "I'm thirty. You can't be more than . . ." He paused, eyeing her carefully, and I held my breath for what he said next. "Thirty-eight."

Lauren and I traded a quick look. She'd just turned thirty-nine.

"Close enough, cowboy." Even though he hadn't specified, she added a liberal amount of cinnamon sugar to his funnel cake, then handed the plate over the counter. "If you're not my age or within five years, you've hardly begun to learn what to do with a woman. I don't waste my time on the young ones."

With a dazed expression on his face, he accepted the funnel cake, looking at her like she'd just handed him a check for a million dollars. "*What* is your name?"

She shook her head. "Nothing you need to know."

"Lauren," I told him helpfully. She glanced over her shoulder, narrowing her eyes dangerously. I smiled sweetly. "That's payback for my birthday present," I told her.

The big beast of a man took a massive, wolfish bite of the funnel cake, staring at her unabashedly while his jaw worked. Then he swiped at his muzzle to clear the cinnamon sugar and leaned in again. "Lauren, I could have you screaming my name in five languages by the time I'm finished with you."

I was in the middle of sipping some water, and I slapped a hand over my mouth, just barely managing to stem the flow of it out my nose.

Lauren laughed in delight, accepting his money and giving him change with a good-natured shake of her head. "You're confident, I'll give you that."

"It's well earned. I promise."

"You might as well find someone else to entertain you. My ex-husband was just like you, and I'm not in the mood to soothe your ego because I didn't rip my panties off at the sight of your smile." She grinned. "And unless you get me screaming your name in *six* languages, I'm not all that impressed. I can do that myself, honey."

His jaw fell open. "Woman, if you don't give me your phone number, I might actually die."

Watching them was like a master class in unhinged flirtation, and not for the first time that day, I found myself missing Griffin. The way he was helping me was subtle. Less, maybe, than what I'd assumed when I first asked for his assistance, but already I could imagine his commentary on what I was witnessing.

Lauren rolled her eyes dramatically, shooing him off to the side. "I promise you won't. Off you go. There are other people who need funnel cake too."

Despite the fact that she was rushing him off, I knew my friend. Her cheeks were flushed, her brown eyes bright. And for the last six months, she'd been bemoaning her dry spell but wasn't ready to jump back on the dating apps.

"I have her number," I heard myself say.

The guy's face lit up.

Lauren's mouth popped open. "You wouldn't dare."

"Wouldn't I?" I asked, narrowing my eyes in her direction.

"Fuck a duck," she muttered under her breath.

"You are a great friend," he said, sidling up next to me on the side of the booth.

"I tell her this all the time." I pulled up my phone and scrolled to her contact, angling the screen so that he could copy the number into his own device. Lauren was muttering under her breath as she made the next funnel cake, but it wasn't lost on me that she didn't tell me no.

He stuck his hand out once he was done saving her number. "Marcus Henderson," he said, loudly enough that Lauren could hear.

Her movements slowed, her eyes widening incrementally, and I gave her a brief curious look as I returned the firm shake. "Ruby Tate. It's nice to meet you."

"You know, I had to convince my friend to come tonight, and I am so glad."

"I'm sure Lauren is too."

She fixed me with a fierce glare, which I ignored. "What did you say your name was?" Lauren asked slowly.

He held her gaze, finishing off the last bit of his funnel cake. "You heard me."

The sexual tension was thick, and I cleared my throat. "Well, I think I'll leave you two to it," I said breezily.

Kenny came jogging up, halting my departure. "We have a slight problem. Our next two volunteers for the dunk tank can't come. It was the mayor and the chief of police. They were going to be our biggest draws for tickets for that game."

I blew out a short, harsh breath. "Okay. What happened?"

"Mayor Briggs is sick, and the chief had an emergency. Not sure what."

Mind racing, I wiped a hand over my forehead. "Okay, um . . . We can figure this out. We need people who will bring in a lot of tickets."

"Marcus can do it," Lauren said smoothly.

My eyebrows shot up, gaze darting over to the man in question. "Pardon?"

Marcus was grinning at Lauren, his eyes practically shining. "Can I?"

"Oh yes. Didn't you say you had to convince your friend to come with you? Assuming you two are coworkers," she added meaningfully.

"I am so lost," I whispered.

Kenny seemed to notice who we were talking to, his eyes widening. "Holy shit."

My head swiveled in his direction. "What's wrong with you?"

Kenny's mouth dropped open, and he pointed weakly at Marcus.

Marcus nodded slowly. "We *are* coworkers. And I think I'll agree to that—on one condition." He gripped the side of the booth and stared down my friend. "You go out with me after the fair is done tonight."

My eyes bounced between them. "What is going on right now? Why do we want Marcus to do the dunk tank? Who's your friend?"

Marcus never took his eyes off Lauren. "He's at the booth next door. Wasting all his money on some rigged shooting game because he saw a stuffed bird and said he needed to win it for a friend."

Angling myself for a better view, I looked past Marcus at the shooting game, a surprised squeak coming from my mouth before I could stop it.

Griffin freaking King stood with a BB gun against his shoulder, his unwavering focus aimed at the small metal targets as they shuffled back and forth. He was wearing a fitted white T-shirt and black athletic shorts today, which hugged the curves of his ass in a way that made it genuinely hard to look at anything else.

"You're . . ." I blinked. Blinked again. "You're on the team with Griffin?"

He nodded. "You know him?"

Lauren laughed. I swallowed hard. "Uh-huh."

Marcus's eyes sharpened. "You're the friend."

My gaze was not willing to be parted from the sight of Griffin handing over another fistful of cash so he could start the game again. Even from this distance, I could hear the *plink, plink, plink* of the small metal balls hitting the rusty targets. "I . . . Sure. Yes. I'm his friend."

"Interesting," he said smoothly. "We might need to trade some stories, young lady. He said you knew him when he was young. Was he horrible? You can tell me."

Griffin finally got the last of the targets down, smiling at the small smattering of applause that came from the crowd gathered around him. He handed the gun back to the volunteer and pointed at one of the stuffed animals hanging from the ceiling of the booth.

After a nod to the volunteer, he tucked the massive plush under his arm, and my heart thudded erratically when he turned in our direction. Our eyes locked, and his smile deepened.

Oh boy.

This was not good.

Everything in me screamed to run in the opposite direction, but some primal part of my brain kept me rooted in place because he'd won something for me. He did exactly as he said he would and wasted all his money to win some ridiculous prize as a show of . . . what, exactly? Chivalry? Ego? Effortless charm because he knew it would make me melt?

Marcus sidled up next to me, easing his arm around my shoulders. "I met your friend, despite all your best efforts to the contrary."

Griffin rolled his eyes, knocking Marcus's hand off my shoulder. Then he produced the stuffed bird—a large scarlet cardinal with an enormous fluffy plume on the top of its head—from underneath his arm. "For you," he said. "I told you I'd get you one."

"You did indeed." I clutched the bird to my chest, wondering if it managed to cover the pounding of my heart.

Honestly, this was absurd.

Marcus perked up. "Lauren, I can get you an even bigger bird," he promised.

She ignored him, serving up another funnel cake with a friendly smile. "Save your efforts for other activities, Henderson. I'm still not convinced."

"Oh yeah." Marcus smacked Griffin in the chest. "We're doing the dunk tank."

Griffin cocked an eyebrow. "What, now?"

"If we do the dunk tank and raise a fuck ton of money, Lauren will go out with me tonight." Then he pointed at me. "And your good friend Ruby will be really happy. Don't you want to make Ruby happy?"

Griffin's eyes leveled on mine. "Always."

The flutter in the pit of my stomach was beyond ridiculous, and I quashed it ruthlessly.

I'd quash those little jerks if it was the last thing I did on this *earth*.

"Then it's settled," Marcus said, clapping his hands, the sharp snap of sound pulling me out of my mental self-flagellation. "Start spreading the word that the good people of Welling Springs can dunk the shit out of the two hottest Denver players."

Lauren snickered. "Most humble too."

He fixed her with a heated stare. "Just wait, sugar. I can back it up."

"Oh boy," I sighed. "I'm not so sure about this." My eyes found Griffin's again. "Didn't you want to keep a low profile on this visit?"

"Yup." Then he smiled. "Don't you need to raise a lot of money?"

I let out a slow exhale, then nodded. "Land goes up for sale next week. We can put in an offer on Tuesday."

With a wry lift to his brow, he gestured past the booth into the screaming chaos of the fair. "Lead the way, birdy." Then he leaned down to speak close to my ear. "Don't pretend like you're not excited to watch me get wet for a good cause."

A shiver danced down my spine, and the jerk noticed, laying his hand lightly on the lower part of my back as we walked. I sighed dramatically, but the annoyance was thin, a wobbly smoke screen for the real culprit—weak-kneed, head-spinning desire. Under his breath, he chuckled, and the two men followed me and Kenny as we led them through the crowd.

Word of their presence, as intended, spread like actual wildfire. Crowds edged their way toward the dunk tanks, which was the game closest to the school building, lines forming immediately.

Kids bounced up and down with unrestrained glee, their parents angling for a look at the two players with just as much excitement on their faces.

When it was time for Marcus and Griffin to climb up into the tanks and take their spots on the seated planks, Griffin toed off his shoes and socks, then handed me his phone, wallet, and keys for safekeeping. "You owe me for this one, birdy," he said in a low, skin-tingling voice just next to my ear.

Marcus pointed at me as he climbed the stairs. "Is she the reason we were watching that *Sense and What's-It-Called* movie last night?"

My head snapped toward him. "*Sense and Sensibility?*"

"That's the one." He shook his head. "That fucking Willoughby," he said. "He did Marianne dirty."

Using the tip of his finger against my chin, Griffin exhaled a quiet laugh as he pressed my mouth closed. "All right, birdy. Let's make some money."

Somehow, I snapped myself out of it, handing the microphone to one of our more gregarious library trustees, who was serving as emcee. She was hardly needed, though, because Marcus and Griffin worked the crowd effortlessly.

They talked trash with whoever approached to try to dunk them, always with a smile and a well-meant joke when the attempt failed.

The kids all missed, but they told them to come back to the tank after their turn for a selfie, and they obliged each and every one. It took a bit longer to get through the line, but it made for a fun, buoyant atmosphere.

I stood to the side, filming some videos as they ribbed the crowd and posed for pictures, signing occasional shirts and hats with a Sharpie that Kenny provided. Everyone who walked away from them wore the kind of smile that was undeniably contagious.

Yes, they played a game for a living, but the unbridled joy they delivered to every person was a tangible, sweet thing that had an ache blooming in my chest. Maybe money couldn't buy happiness, but these two were incredibly adept at creating it in their wake.

In turn, it meant the longer I filmed what they were doing, the longer I watched the ease with which he made kids smile and laugh, the less effective my quashing abilities became. The flutters were growing into something dangerous.

The first to get dunked was Marcus. The high school's star baseball pitcher lined up for him, delivering a rocket to the center of the target, and as the crowd erupted, Marcus fell into the freezing-cold water with a yell. He emerged with a roar, arms raised and his T-shirt plastered to his chest and stomach.

Griffin waved me over during a break between people in his line, leaning down from his seat on the top of the tank. "How pissed do you think he'll be when I come out of this dry as a bone?"

I rolled my eyes. "You won't. I'll dunk you myself if that happens."

"Oh yeah? You got a secret talent for pitching, too, birdy?"

"If you think I won't walk straight up to the button and hit it just to prove a point, you don't know me at all."

He tipped his head back and laughed, and good Lord, what was it about an exposed throat on this man that had me pressing my knees together?

With a steadying breath, I moved off to the side so the next person could throw, and my eyes stubbornly stayed glued to the curve of his biceps when he lifted his cupped hands to his mouth to heckle the group of girls who were up next.

The first girl, with red hair and a big smile, had terrible aim; she came closer to hitting me than the target. The second girl, with a high blond ponytail and sharp blue eyes, was a little closer. And the third girl—tall and thin, with coiled braids hanging to her waist and dark, toned arms—stepped up with the composure of a major-league pitcher.

Griffin shifted nervously on the plank. "Nah, she's not gonna get it," he called out, trying his best to derail her.

It didn't work. She whirled her arm around, delivering a ruthless pitch, hitting the target square in the center, and he disappeared into the water to the absolute delight of the crowd. I was still laughing when his head emerged.

Water dripped off the chiseled planes of his face, and his eyes were locked on me. "You think this is funny?"

"Yes."

His hands curled around the edge of the tank, and with his foot on the middle rung of the ladder, Griffin hauled himself out in a great rush of water, landing gracefully onto the ground. When he whirled to me, I let out a squeak, trying to dart behind Kenny when I caught the predatory glint in his eye.

It didn't help.

And have you ever imagined the most perfect male specimen you've ever laid eyes on—in soaking-wet clothes that cling to every visible muscle—rushing toward you?

It's potent. Paralyzing. And really, unfortunately attractive.

Escaping a dripping-wet male is harder than you'd think. Mainly because my feet were anchored to the ground for a solid two seconds longer than they should have been.

Before I could whirl in the opposite direction, Griffin scooped me up in a bear hug, absolutely soaking the entire front of my body.

"Oh, you ass," I said in between helpless peals of laughter. "It's so cold."

With his arm banded around my waist, my feet dangled helplessly off the ground. My hands settled lightly on the curves of his shoulders, and I tried to catch my breath as he stared up at me, a sinful grin stretching his lips and his eyes dancing. "You think this is cold, I should dump you in that tank," he threatened in a silky voice.

"You wouldn't dare," I whispered.

His gaze moved to my mouth. "Maybe not."

Kenny cleared his throat. "Um, Ruby? Is he getting back in?"

Pushing briefly on Griffin's shoulders was all it took, and he set me back down. When I glanced at the front of my shirt, I gasped, my hands flying to cover my chest. My light-pink T-shirt was completely transparent.

I fixed Griffin with a glare, and he winced. "Sorry. Didn't think about that."

His shirt was no better. Through the white material, I saw the dusky circles of his nipples and each pronounced ridge on his pecs and his abdominals. The veins on his arms stood out against his golden-tan skin, and he plucked at his shirt with a short laugh. "Guess I didn't choose the right color either."

"I didn't bring any extra clothes," I moaned.

"I have a shirt in my car," Griffin said. "It'll be huge, but it's yours if you want it."

I gave him a distracted nod. "That would be great. I have the keys to the school; I can change in the bathrooms."

Griffin told the crowd he'd be back in about five minutes, and Marcus led the line in some earsplitting, good-natured jeers, proclaiming that no one could dunk him while Griffin chickened out for a few minutes. Griffin darted forward, slapping the button, and Marcus fell into the tank while the crowd cheered.

We were both laughing, his arm warm where my shoulder brushed against it as we walked.

I kept my arms crossed over my chest, staying behind the booths and games so that we could remain out of sight—him so that we didn't get stopped, me because I wasn't trying to win any wet T-shirt competitions. Since the sun had gone down, there was a chill in the air I hadn't felt all day, and I shivered. Griffin laid a hand on my back, and the warmth of his palm had my eyes falling closed.

"I'll be right back," he said, jogging off toward the parking lot.

After I wrestled with the key, the door to the high school opened with a creak, and I waited just inside, leaning against a cinder block wall until Griffin approached with some dry clothes in hand. I fixed a smile on my face and pushed open the door for him.

"Thank you," I said. "I wouldn't feel comfortable walking around like this."

He handed me the shirt, lifting his chin in a nod. "Go ahead, I'll wait."

My hands tightened around the soft cotton, and it served as an effective visual shield to my see-through shirt. "You don't have to do that."

"Not gonna leave you alone in here, Ruby."

I sighed quietly, slightly relieved by that. "Okay."

"Where's the bathroom?"

"Just around the corner." I swallowed tightly, the absolute stillness in the big, empty building reminding me of us being together in my office. Maybe me and Griffin and empty buildings should be avoided at all costs, because there was something sinful about it, the warm pulse of temptation filling in the space between each breath.

He walked a few steps with me, and I kept his T-shirt pressed against my chest, lest he get an eyeful of nipple. It was distracting enough seeing his.

Instead of going all the way into the bathroom, I simply walked around the corner of the cinder block wall until I was out of sight, peeling my wet shirt off and tossing it onto the ground, where it hit with an audible slap. The sound was loud enough that I winced, because immediately following was a sharp inhale from Griffin.

It was all so unbearably and unintentionally sexy.

I was holding the shirt so tightly that my fists trembled. Even though my bra was damp, too, the warmth from his shirt—probably from sitting in a hot car—was practically narcotic. It smelled like him too.

Instead of quashing anything, I sucked in a deep, fortifying breath and let the flutters go wherever they wanted.

"I wish I was the type of person who knew how to take advantage of these moments," I said, the words out before I could stop them. In truth, I didn't want to stop them.

I didn't want to stop whatever this feeling was, because it was powerful, sleek and strong and addicting.

"What moments?" he asked, voice just around the corner from where I stood.

With my eyes pinched shut and my forehead pressed against the cool cinder block, I let out a shaky exhale. "Moments of opportunity. I've never really known what to do with them. And this is . . . this is one of them, isn't it?"

"God, Ruby," he groaned. "It is."

The sound of his voice, rough and desperate and so very, very close, made me tremble all over.

Everything was getting jumbled in my head—what we were doing, what we shouldn't be doing, and what I wanted to do. None of it was clear anymore, and somehow, in all that confusion, the only thing that seemed straightforward was that I wanted him.

"Griffin," I whispered, not even sure if he could hear me.

"Look at you," he whispered.

I froze, head snapping up as he caged me in completely. The heat of him—tall and broad and impossibly warm—swamped my entire frame, even though he wasn't actually touching me yet.

Yet.

My eyes fluttered shut, my breath coming in embarrassingly loud pants as I waited for the *yet* to turn into something else. It was a word filled with so much promise, wasn't it? A vow of action that hung thick in the air between us.

With his hands braced on the wall on either side of my head, Griffin inhaled slowly, his nose brushing over the crown of my hair, his chest lightly brushing against my naked back.

For a few seconds—impossibly long and delicious—we stood there, simply breathing in the moment and letting it expand into something else. If he was waiting for me to pull away, he'd be waiting a long time.

"Please," I whispered.

Griffin let out a rumbling groan, his hands curling into fists on the wall. One dropped down, and I stilled, the anticipation yanking goose bumps on my arms while I tried to guess where he'd touch me first.

My back.

The brush of one finger along my spine, like he was closing a zipper, following it all the way up, up, up, dancing over the clasp of my bra until he reached the base of my skull. For a brief, breathless moment, his hand curled possessively around my neck, his nose dragging along the edge of my ear while he held me anchored in place.

It was that firm hold that had me melting, forehead resting against the wall again. His hands coasted over my skin, one down my shoulder and along the length of my arm, the other following the line of my back until he ghosted his fingertips over the curve of my ribs.

"Tell me to stop," he whispered, his mouth brushing over my shoulder, laying soft kisses over the side of my neck.

I was holding his shirt so tight to my chest that I feared my fingers might snap, and no matter how badly my more rational brain screamed that I should do exactly that, my throat lost the ability to make sound, my tongue the capability of forming speech.

No, I didn't want to tell him to stop.

And it was the first time in my life where I wanted to ignore all those responsible thoughts and good-girl tendencies and let this moment fray at all my usual impulses, my typical responses.

When I didn't say anything, Griffin eased himself against me, his towering height and absurd muscles against my back in a way that had me pushing my hips against his.

He was hard.

So hard. And holy shit, so big.

His hands curled around the sides of my hips, tugging me back against him more firmly. "That's it," he groaned. "That's how much I want you, baby."

My eyelids fluttered shut at the nickname, that these mindless moments were the only time he allowed it to slip. I wanted to do so many things: Grip his wrist and push it down beneath the waistband of my shorts. Push it up and feel the blunt tips of his fingers pluck at my aching nipples.

I just wanted him to touch me, wanted to allow this moment to unspool into something bigger than both of us. Bigger than him and me and the whole blissful world that we'd constructed the last week. We were the only ones who existed in it, and I found a selfish satisfaction in that.

No one knew we were here. No one knew it was like this between us.

That he did this to me, and I did this to him.

Griffin licked at the line of my neck, nosing at my jaw until my head turned in his direction. His hips rocked against me, and he dipped at the knees, his hardness rolling between my backside in a way that had me whimpering helplessly.

The sound had him swearing into my skin, his hands demanding that I turn in his arms with firm, sure movements. The moment I did, he slid those hands underneath my ass and boosted me up against the wall, pressing me into place with his unyielding strength. My legs wrapped around his waist, my hands still clutching that shirt trapped uselessly against the wall of his chest while Griffin slanted his mouth over mine.

Chapter Sixteen

GRIFFIN

Keeping your own strength under control is surprisingly difficult when you're used to allowing your impulses free rein. On the field, it was my job to unleash it, to hit harder, run faster, to cause disruption by ripping into someone else's space.

The foundation of my success was knowing exactly when to allow myself to tap into that ruthless energy that I kept locked inside. Never before had I worried that it might spill over into an interaction with a woman.

What a stupid, dry word for what this was.

It wasn't an interaction—it was a revelation. And if I wasn't careful, if I didn't tighten my grip on my own control, I'd end up fucking Ruby straight through the concrete wall and leave us covered in rubble at the end. A sharp-toothed, clawing voice inside my head screamed with the need for it, to touch her more and kiss her harder and give us both more, more, more.

And even then, I had a feeling it wouldn't be enough.

Echoing through the empty hallway was nothing but the sound of me kissing Ruby.

She made the sweetest little noises as I sucked her tongue into my mouth, spearing my hand into her silky hair while I rolled my hips along her center. Only the thinnest scraps of material separated us—her cotton shorts, whatever might be underneath them, and my own athletic shorts.

The impulse was anchored tight around my spine, impossible to ignore.

Take her. Take her. Take her.

She'd be soft and wet and sweet—so very, very tight too. My head spun at the thought, all the blood rushing between my legs, where it pooled into one angry hard-on.

Our kisses were fierce and sloppy, clacking teeth and hot, wet tongues, a dirtier version of how we'd kissed in her office. That kiss had been testing something new. My hands moved more carefully, my restraint perilously in charge.

This was an entirely different beast. It wasn't unknown, and God, was it better because of it.

It was impossible to imagine any universe where kissing her wasn't vital. Where it wasn't the single most significant use of my time. Her hands, still trapped between us, grappled at my shirt, fisting the cotton tightly to hold me in place. Like I was going fucking anywhere.

I'd live there with her if she asked. I'd kiss her and touch her and make her mindless and screaming in the dark for as long as she'd let me, because Ruby Tate in my arms was better than anything I'd ever felt.

Would she let me do that?

I broke my mouth away from hers and sucked at her neck, coasting my hand down her back to fill my palms with her backside underneath her shorts as she writhed against me. Ruby gasped when I bit down on the slope of her shoulder, then dragged my nose up the edge of her jaw.

My hand on her ass directed her movements, and I pulled my head back, watched her eyes go hazy as she found the right rhythm.

Even though I hadn't done it since I was a teenager, I was going to come in my shorts if I watched her like that for too much longer, and fuck if that didn't sound like a sacrifice I was willing to make. The thought of her using me for anything sounded like my patriotic duty at this point.

I was doing this for America.

The rocking motion of her hips had my eyes fluttering shut, my jaw tightening as I gritted my teeth. I sucked her bottom lip into my mouth, and she groaned when I released it.

"That's it, baby," I whispered. "That feeling good?"

"Y-yes," she said in a stuttering voice thick with desire. "I can't . . . I can't do this myself."

I hummed, sucking the soft skin of her earlobe into my mouth, relishing the shocked hiss that sprang from her lips. Her body jerked against my own. "You want help?"

Frantically, she nodded. "Yes. Yes."

My hand moved between us, hooking my fingers into her shorts and the soft elastic of her panties, pulling them aside while I slanted my mouth over hers in a deep, searching kiss. Her hands clutched the back of my head while we devoured each other. When her fingers tightened in my hair, that sharp bite of pain pulled a helpless groan that escaped into her mouth. She swallowed the sound, rocking her hips in a slow, rolling movement.

I pushed my chest back a fraction, making room for my arm between us as I slid one finger in between her legs.

Her head snapped back, a loud, drawn-out moan leaving her lips, and the sound was so fucking good, so delicious and unrestrained, that I wanted to hear it for the rest of my life.

Then I added a second finger, whispering naughty things against her bare shoulder as she took me easily.

"Feels so good," I told her. "Fucking perfect, Ruby."

The words didn't surprise me, because she felt it around my fingers as they slid easily between her legs, as she rocked herself to orgasm on nothing but my hand. But what did shock me was how easily I'd allowed myself to say them.

Neither of us was pretending; there were no false words or forced interactions. This was tiptoeing right up against the flame and hoping we didn't get burned. Her especially, because I was the one leaving soon, but there was a part of me that worried I'd feel so much more than I let on once this was done.

Only once had I felt like this about a woman, someone I thought I'd loved and would've destroyed my life for if she'd have let me. Instead, I was the one destroyed—and Ruby wasn't anything like her.

This was different. The feel of it, of her, rattled the cage of everything I'd built around myself the last few years. Ruby was pure and good and kind. She was naive and straightforward, and she had no idea what she was missing out on.

God, how I'd show her if she let me.

"Close," she whimpered. Around my fingers, she fluttered. Her head dropped back against the wall as she keened, and I angled my fingers, using my palm against her as she rocked. Disjointed, whispered pleas fell from her lips, and the moment she broke apart, it was the most beautiful fucking thing I'd ever seen.

Her body jerked in my arms, shuddering through what seemed to be a really great orgasm, and I kissed her through it, swallowing her sounds with swipes of my tongue into her mouth. The tension bled from her frame, but I was able to hold her easily with one arm banded underneath her ass while I slowly worked her through the aftershocks, finally easing my fingers out from between her legs.

Surreptitiously, I wiped them on my shorts before I smoothed my palm around her waist. Her skin was so soft. I wanted to kiss her everywhere. I briefly wondered if I could ask to do just that. Take her home and strip her of all her clothes and kiss every fucking inch of her body, see which parts she liked my mouth on best.

"Oh, wow," she breathed against my lips. "Can we do that again?"

I laughed, devouring every detail of her expression, a soft, tender feeling growing big and scary under my ribs. "Liked that, did you?"

She hummed, her gaze drowsy as it lingered over my face. Her hand cradled my jaw, her thumb tracing the bottom edge of my lip, and I nipped at her finger, sucking it briefly into my mouth and biting down on the fleshy pad with my teeth.

Her smile was fucking incandescent, and maybe it was some hidden poetic side of me coming out, but I felt it echo in my chest. Felt it soak into my bones.

Because I wanted to, I leaned forward to kiss her again, a little bit sweeter this time. I held her face with my other hand and let my fingers trace over the line of her cheekbone and jaw while we kissed lazily.

She wasn't pulling back this time, and even though this wasn't the place to take whatever this was any further, I wasn't in a rush to disappear either. I just wanted more.

How much would she be willing to give me? This cagey little bird who held herself so separate, held herself back. My fingers moved from her face, coasting over her shoulder to trace the line of her arm as she smiled softly, her eyes closed.

"Don't fall asleep like that," I teased.

Her lips lifted at the edges and she hummed. "No promises. I don't even remember my name right now."

"Ahhh. The best side effect of a really good orgasm." I fitted her bottom lip between mine and sucked lightly, applying the same treatment to the top lip. Her tongue snuck out to brush the seam of my mouth, and I opened with a low groan, tilting my head to allow her to deepen the kiss. Everything was slower now, but still, my restraint was holding on by a single fraying thread.

Ruby rocked her hips restlessly, her eyes flying open when she felt how hard I still was. "Oh."

I grinned. *"Oh."*

She huffed, but her mouth spread in a happy smile. "You can't go out like that. You'll scare the children."

"You gonna help me with it, birdy?" I nipped at her lips. "Use your hand and let me make you a little messy?"

Her exhale was shaky, her eyes direct. "Do you want that?"

"Oh, I want all sorts of things," I told her, keeping my tone light. My fingers tightened on the curve of her waist, pressing for a moment against the line of her ribs under the skin. "More than anything, I want you in a bed, pretty girl."

Her eyes searched mine. "Really?"

I rocked my hips against her, and her eyes fluttered shut. "That feel real to you?"

Ruby swallowed audibly, tilting her head back again. "Griffin, it feels amazing."

That was all it took; I couldn't imagine setting her back down. There was no letting her go. Maybe a bed was overrated. Maybe half-clothed wall sex was exactly what we needed in our lives. There was plenty of time for beds later.

I dipped my head down to suck at her shoulder again, tonguing the strap of her bra. I dragged my nose along her clavicle, inhaling the sweet, soft scent of her until I encountered the balled-up shirt of mine still trapped between us.

I smiled, reaching up carefully to pull it aside so I could lick along the line of her bra.

As I tugged on the edge of the shirt, Ruby's entire body froze, just as my eyes locked in on the center of her chest.

When they did, there was a sharp crack of silence, a resounding vacuum of noiseless shock as the air was sucked from the building.

"What the fuck?" I breathed, my head rearing back as I stared slack-jawed at the rough-edged, pinkish-white scar that ran down the entire length of her sternum. It had to be close to six inches long, given where it started and where it disappeared under her bra. My entire chest was caving in. "What happened to you?"

Ruby pushed at my chest, untangling her legs from around my waist. "Put me down," she said, frantically trying to create space between our bodies. "Oh God. I'm sorry. Please put me down."

"Why are you sorry?" I held my hands out, wanting to soothe her obvious agitation but unsure if she'd welcome my touch. "Ruby, what is that?"

Her whole body was trembling, her hands again clutching the shirt. "I have to go."

"No, wait," I said, reaching out and laying a gentle hand on her arm. She froze. "Please just tell me something. *Anything.*"

Ruby was sucking in short, panting breaths, her cheeks splotched with red and her eyes filled with tears. One slipped down her cheek as she fumbled with the shirt, and I almost fell to my knees.

"What do you need?" I asked quietly. God, I was glad my voice was quiet, because everything inside me shook with a tremendous force, and it felt like there was no outlet for the frantic thoughts racing through my head.

"The shirt," she said in a halting voice. "I can't . . . I can't get it."

I stepped forward and pulled it carefully from her shaking hands, finding the neck hole and easing it over her head. She shoved her arms through the sleeves, her eyes pinched shut but her breath coming a little bit easier once the oversize shirt swamped her frame.

Backing away to give her space, I swiped a hand over my mouth and tried to find words.

When she opened her eyes, I felt the pain and embarrassment in them like she was screaming it into the room. But when she spoke, it was hardly above a whisper. "It's my heart." Absently, her hand rubbed at the line of the scar. I couldn't get the image of it out of my head. "I . . . I had heart transplant surgery about four years ago."

"What?" My brow furrowed. "Why? Why didn't you say anything?"

Another tear dashed down her cheek, and she scrubbed at it with an angry swipe of her hand. "I don't owe anyone that information," she said fiercely. "This was supposed to be fun, simple, easy, right?"

I held my hands up. "You're right. You don't owe anyone that." I swallowed, mind racing while I searched for the right thing to say. "That's why you stopped us the other night, isn't it?"

She was crying openly now, not even trying to stop the tears coursing down her face. Ruby gave a jerky nod. "You don't know what it's like," she whispered.

"Did you think I'd care that you have a scar?"

Her chest heaved, her eyes tortured. "Do you know what the last man told me who saw that? How he reacted when I pulled my shirt off? I'd warned him before I slept with him, and he still looked at me with disgust. *Disgust*, Griffin."

My jaw was tight and my chest hot with ineffectual anger. "The corpse comment," I said raggedly.

"'Can't you cover it?'" she whispered. "'It makes me feel like I just fucked a corpse.'"

"Holy fuck," I breathed, hanging my head down as my chest cracked wide open for this fucking woman.

She pressed her fingers to her mouth while she swallowed a sob. "Every time I think about someone looking at me or touching me, I hear him say it." Her eyes pinched shut. "I just want to forget it's there, and I can't, because when I tell someone it happened, everything changes."

"Ruby," I said helplessly, reaching out to touch her, then pulling my hands back out of an abundance of caution. "That guy was a fucking asshole."

Her eyes flashed. "I know that. But everyone treats you differently once they know. Like I'm fragile and I'm breakable. Like I can't . . . like I'm not normal." She shook her head, her cheeks now splotchy and red from crying, and each tear made me want to tear my own fucking heart out, if only it would make her feel better. "You will too," she whispered. "I can see the pity in your face."

"You had a fucking heart transplant, Ruby, and I found out about it two seconds ago—of course I feel bad." I speared my hands into my hair, shaking my head, desperately grasping for the reins on my control. The stark, obscene difference in why I needed it now was not lost on me. "It doesn't mean I can't handle it."

She shook her head. "This is my fault. I'm sorry for not telling you earlier. I should've told you as soon as I asked for your help."

It was on the tip of my tongue to agree, but I kept those words leashed by some sort of miraculous restraint. The truth was, I didn't know what she felt like, and I never would.

A heart transplant in her midtwenties? Fucking inconceivable. A million questions peppered my choppy thoughts, but I kept them banked.

Now wasn't the time. I just hoped she'd give me more of that.

"I need to get back out there," she said, voice heavy with resignation. "I, um, I won't go back to the tank with you, though. I should check on the other booths." She glanced at her watch and sighed. "We only have about an hour left."

She started turning away, and before I could stop myself, I reached out, wrapping my fingers lightly around her wrist.

"Ruby," I whispered, wanting to step closer and fold her up in my arms, wanting to hold her tight and take away everything inside her that made her sad, that made her hurt. Something in her face held me back, as effective as her hands, firm and unyielding, against my chest.

Her mouth curled into a sad smile, and she gently pulled out of my grasp. "It's okay, Griffin."

She disappeared around the corner, and I braced my hands against the wall, head hanging down.

No. No, it wasn't okay. I just didn't know what it meant.

Chapter Seventeen

GRIFFIN

"Bro." Marcus snapped his fingers.

I blinked. "Sorry, man. What'd you say?"

My friend grinned. "Said I'm heading out soon to meet up with Lauren. She asked me to meet her at a hotel room to talk, because she wasn't giving my 'manwhore ass' her home address." He rubbed his hands together. "I'm gonna have a good night."

With a laugh, I shook my head. "I hope she wants to tie you up and make you suffer."

"God, so do I," he sighed. "Tonight was fun."

I nodded.

He finished his drink, leaning back on the couch while I swirled my empty glass, watching the melting ice cubes clink against the crystal. "You good, Griff?"

I pinched my eyes shut and sighed heavily. "I don't know, man."

It was easier to put on the mask at the fair, with dozens of people watching and wanting that transactional exchange from me and Marcus. They got it in spades too. The line ended up snaking through the fair, we both got our asses dunked more than a dozen times, and Ruby's coworker Kenny kept selling tickets, beaming the entire time.

Ruby, however, never made her way back over to our game, and I knew that was intentional. No matter what I'd done all evening, I couldn't get her face out of my head.

It wasn't the shock over what I'd seen; it wasn't the embarrassment or the tears that kept playing over and over and over on a buzzing loop.

It was the fear.

She was genuinely scared of my reaction.

Carefully setting down the glass, I braced my elbows on the tops of my thighs and held my head in my hands, staring down at the rug. "I think I gotta go," I said quietly.

"Your friend," he said knowingly.

I raised my head and pinned him with a look. "Don't start. We just . . . we started a conversation that never got finished, and it was kinda heavy. I want to see if she's okay."

He pushed my phone across the coffee table. "Too bad they don't make a little contraption where you can like, send a message or call her or something."

My jaw tightened, and I slid my phone into my pocket. "No one asked for your input, smart-ass."

It wasn't like he was wrong. I could call. I could text. The end result would likely still be the same—she'd tell me she needed some space, but at least she'd know I was thinking about her. It just wasn't enough.

Maybe it was selfish, but sitting idle right now was unthinkable. Sending a text, making a phone call—it wasn't enough. From the moment I saw her again, there was something about Ruby that always, always had me wanting to do more. Be more. Be better, because she deserved that.

However the best version of me would act, that's the Griffin she'd get.

I stood from the couch and held my fist out to Marcus, and he tapped it with a grin. "Be safe," I told him. "I hope she makes you cry."

"Me too," he answered seriously.

Without overthinking what I was doing or what I was going to say, I hopped into my truck and found myself uncharacteristically nervous as I approached Ruby's house. It was the first time I'd arrived in the dark, and if there hadn't been any lights on—warm, inviting yellowy light spilling through the windows in the family room—I might have turned back.

I knocked briskly, then tucked my hands into my pockets as I stepped back from the door. Bruiser's face shoved the curtain aside in the window, and he let out a couple of happy barks, his whole body wiggling.

At least someone in the house would be happy to see me.

Ruby's face appeared in a small crack of the door, and it was immediately obvious she'd been crying.

"Hey," I said softly. "Can I come in?"

Resting her temple on the frame of the door, she stared at me for a second before eventually nodding and backing up, opening the door to let Bruiser through to greet me.

"Hey, buddy," I whispered, patting his side while he leaned against my legs. "Think you can let me in?"

Ruby clicked her tongue, and he bounded into the house. She was wearing the ivory lounge suit I'd bought her, and I couldn't stop myself from staring at the high neck with a lightning bolt of comprehension.

Her fingers plucked at it after noticing where my gaze had landed. "Yes," she said. "That's why I like high-neck shirts."

I cleared my throat, rocking slightly on my heels. "Makes sense."

Silence cloaked the room. I swiped a hand over my mouth while I stared at her—unsure of what I could ask, or shouldn't, or if she'd want to talk about it at all. When my hand dropped, I shook my head a little.

Ruby's eyes bounced between mine, and then she groaned. "This is exactly what I was afraid of. You're being weird. You don't know what to say or . . . or how to handle me."

"To be fair, I've never known how to handle you. You're terrifying."

She gave me a slightly narrow-eyed look that almost had me smiling.

"You are. Most women—" The narrow eyes turned into a full-on glare, and I exhaled a quiet laugh as I held up my hand in concession. "I won't finish that sentence, I promise."

"Thank you." Her eyes searched mine. "You really want to know? I thought this . . . us . . . was just a fun diversion for you."

"It was," I admitted hoarsely. "But we're friends, right?" Fuck if that word didn't feel wrong. But there wasn't another easy one to replace it. If there had been—a simple switch, something with fewer complications or strings attached—I would've used it.

She wasn't just my friend, not in any way I'd normally use that word, but I couldn't say that to her without a ripple effect.

"I guess," she answered after a brief hesitation.

"Why were you crying?" I asked.

Self-consciously, she swiped under her eyes, removing some lingering mascara. "I wasn't."

I gave her a look.

"Much," she conceded with a small shrug. "I don't know why, exactly. I haven't had to talk about this with anyone new in so long. Just brought up a lot of feelings, and it's always better to let that out than pretend like they don't exist and shove them away."

"Lauren knows?"

She nodded. "So does Kenny. My parents, obviously, but they're gone on their trip."

My brow furrowed. "You said they couldn't go right after they retired."

Her hand landed lightly on her chest and tapped. "This is why." She swallowed hard, eyes anywhere but on mine. "The couple of years after a heart transplant are . . . stressful."

Everything inside me felt heavy, like I was carrying a weight over every inch of every bone that held me up. Like my muscles were fatigued in a way that I wasn't used to. "I'd like to hear about it, if you want to tell me."

She gestured to the couch. "Sit. It feels even more awkward that we're just standing by the door, because all I keep thinking is that you're doing it so you can plan a quick exit."

"That might be true if I wasn't the one who showed up unannounced." I took a seat, finding her eyes as soon as I did. "I want to be here."

Ruby's face was sheepish, and her shoulders sank as she sighed. "I know you do." Then she pinched her eyes shut briefly, prying them open again as she clasped her hands together in her lap. "You can . . . you can ask me some questions, if you want."

"Only if you're comfortable talking about it." I held her gaze. "I'm curious. But I don't want you talking about anything that upsets you."

Ruby licked her lips and sat back in her corner of the couch, pulling a throw pillow into her lap and hugging it to her chest. Bruiser must've sensed that it wasn't cuddle time, because he flopped onto the floor next to the couch with a loud groan.

"I didn't know I was sick until just after college." She pulled at a tassel on the pillow. "We started some testing a few months before I graduated because I fainted a couple of times after I did a hard workout. I was lightheaded, had some palpitations. We didn't think it was serious," she said quietly.

"But it was."

She nodded. "Hypertrophic cardiomyopathy," Ruby said evenly. "It's a . . . thickening of the heart muscle. Eventually, it makes it hard for the heart to pump blood correctly."

I sat quietly while she talked by rote, listing off signs and symptoms, things she dismissed as common while, unbeknownst to her and her family, her heart was growing sluggish and hard. Her voice stayed steady and her eyes dry while she talked about all the different medications and treatments they'd tried. And how when they'd failed, at the age of twenty-five, she was a candidate for a heart transplant.

Time passed strangely while I sat and listened. It felt like hours. Minutes. Seconds. Days. My mind was curiously blank while she talked about the young woman who died in a car accident, a perfect match for her, and it was three days before her twenty-sixth birthday that they received a call telling her to come in for surgery.

Her hands relaxed at some point, easing their grip off the pillow, and consumed by a sudden urge to touch her, just a little, I reached forward slowly to pluck one of them off her lap so I could hold it in my own. Her eyes pinched shut when I held it up to my mouth and let her fingertips rest against my lips.

I didn't even really kiss them; I just laid them there so I could feel some part of her. Where my thumb held her wrist, I could feel the steady thrumming of her pulse, and the fragile *thump, thump, thump* made my throat feel impossibly thick.

When she spoke next, Ruby's voice wasn't even anymore. She lost the steadiness that had held her upright. Her chin wobbled, but she sucked in a deep breath through her nose.

"I didn't feel like a real human after my surgery," she whispered, eyes locked on her fingers against my mouth. "I felt like Frankenstein's monster. Carved up and pieced together and . . . terrifying. Everyone was looking at me like I should be relieved and happy, and I was, but . . ." Ruby exhaled shakily. "I didn't feel like myself for so long."

My eyes felt dry and hot and filled with sand, and I fought against a tide of restlessness, hearing her say something like that about herself— that she felt like a monster from a cautionary tale. The book on her table made sense now, and I made a mental note to try to read that one too.

"When did that change?" I asked, my voice rough from disuse. I kept her fingers in place, and she shivered slightly when my lips brushed her knuckles as I spoke.

From his perch on the floor, Bruiser whined, notching his big square jaw on the couch by his mistress's leg like he could sense her distress.

"It took almost three years. I was so focused on staying healthy. Walking every day. I was so strict with what I ate, drank, never went out—outside of work—because I was so afraid of getting sick." Ruby licked her bottom lip, carefully extracting her hand from mine to scratch at Bruiser's head. He settled, eyes eventually falling closed.

"And then I just wanted to live. Not anything crazy, like jumping out of an airplane. But normal things, you know? Like stay up all night talking to someone because the conversation is so good, and I forget to care about sleep. Or a really good one-night stand or going on a long drive in a beautiful convertible. Dance with someone in a club and not worry about people watching." She shrugged one shoulder lightly. "It all sounds so small, but it's big to me. And I was sick of not doing any of those things."

Fucking hell, I was going to cry, wasn't I? It was the list of simple things, all of which I'd taken for granted but now seemed like a fucking miracle. How thoroughly this woman had humbled me, without intention or forethought. I wasn't sure my life would ever quite look the same after this. After her.

"And you're okay now?"

She pulled in a slow breath, eyes locked on her dog. "I'll always be a little bit at risk," she answered carefully. "I take immunosuppressants to make sure my body doesn't reject the heart, but an infection would be much worse for me than anyone else with a normal immune system."

When her eyes finally lifted again, there was so much heartache there that I felt it like a tear down the middle of my chest. "About half the people who survive the first year after a transplant should live about thirteen years or so. Some live more. Some live less." She shrugged, like she wasn't talking about possibly fucking dying in her forties.

A shocked gust of air pushed from my lungs, and I leaned forward, bracing my elbows on my knees and sinking my head into my hands. "Holy shit, Ruby."

When I looked back up again, her lips—those beautiful soft, soft lips—were curled in a tiny little smile. "That's why I told you not to fall in love with me. I'm a terrible long-term bet."

The urge to bolt was so fucking strong.

Facing her—facing *this*—was a lot like being shoved off the side of a ship when I least expected it, and the thrashing for air only seemed to make it worse. Sucking in a deep breath helped, and I straightened my shoulders as I stared at her.

She fidgeted. "Say something."

Don't fuck it up. Don't fuck it up.

There had been so many situations in my life that I'd treated flippantly, that I hadn't held with care or respect, and if this became one of them, I'd never forgive myself. I'd never be able to look myself in the mirror again if I caused this woman more pain than she'd already experienced.

This wasn't a time to make a joke or pretend like the things she'd admitted to me weren't precious, because they were. The thought of this woman not feeling human—God, if it didn't break my fucking heart.

No, this was a moment for honesty. A moment to trade places with Ruby's stunning show of vulnerability, even though the mere thought clawed at my skin.

"I-I've never dealt with anything like this," I told her. "And it scares the shit out of me to say the wrong thing or make you feel worse." I shifted closer, easing my hands onto her knees where she'd crossed them on the couch. *Do something helpful, you idiot,* a voice battered at the back of my skull, and I spoke without really thinking it through. "What if . . . what if we renegotiate again?"

She inhaled slowly, eyes bouncing between mine. "To what?"

To what?

Great fucking question.

What would I want if this were me?

"I don't know, exactly. You don't need my help, Ruby. Not with anything. You're"—I shook my head—"you're so much better at this than you think." Carefully, I reached up and grasped her chin between my thumb and forefinger. "But I like you. You're smart *and* a smart-ass. You don't take any shit, and you're not fake or pretentious or pretending to be anything. I like spending time with you. Can we . . . be friends while I'm here?"

The word tasted like acid on my tongue. A couple of hours earlier, I'd learned what she felt like from the inside when she came, and wanted to tattoo the sounds she made onto my subconscious—but sure . . . friends worked too. I could bend my second head into submission if it was the last thing I did.

He'd be pissed. But I'd gotten used to people being pissed at me. My dick could get in line.

Ruby's forehead did that delicate little wrinkling thing it did when she was thinking really hard. After a slight hesitation, she spoke. "Is that what you want? To be friends?"

Fear gripped me instantly, because no, it really fucking wasn't. Even sitting here, I had to fight an overwhelming urge not to touch her as she talked, or tuck her up against my chest and listen to her breathe, just to assure myself that she was okay.

Was that how you acted with friends? For a moment, I tried to imagine tucking Marcus's big-ass body up against my chest, and I grimaced. "No."

She sucked in a breath as she nodded slightly. "No?"

"I want . . ." I looked down at my hands and stretched out my fingers, then curled them into tight fists, needing that anchor of tension because I felt so fucking powerless.

Ruby took pity on me, easing one of her hands over mine.

"I've talked a lot tonight, Griffin. Maybe if you told me what you're feeling about all this, it might help us figure out where to go next."

I wiped at my mouth and studied her while my thoughts attempted to untangle themselves. "We almost had sex tonight. And then I found out you almost died. That's . . . that's a lot. I'm not sure *how* I feel."

With those big gray eyes fixed steadily on me, my hands started sweating a little bit. How ridiculous. I didn't have sweaty palms when I was in the divisional championship. Maybe that was my problem.

If something this big happened out on the field, I'd know exactly what to do. I'd know how to process some big, earth-trembling change without blinking. I'd listen to my gut and trust my training, but this entire thing with Ruby—from the very beginning—had me feeling so incredibly out of my element.

"I'm scared to hurt you," I blurted. "Like . . . even sitting here, I have this crazy fucking feeling in my chest." I rapped lightly at the space over my heart and just let the words come out without second thought. "Like I should be gentle." I tilted my head while my hands reached out, carefully tucking a strand of her hair behind her ear. "Tender. Cover you with a blanket or carry you to bed and make sure you're sleeping. Warm up soup or something. I don't really know why, because in general, I think soup is a giant fucking waste of a meal."

Her eyes went soft. "Do you?"

"Yes. No one's full after soup. Not unless you eat an entire loaf of bread with it."

"But you want to feed me soup," she clarified.

"Yes." I shook my head. "I don't fucking know—you're staring at me with those big eyes and I can't think straight."

"Sorry." But she smiled a crooked little smile, and I felt a jump in my pulse at the sight of it. God, if I wouldn't hurt someone just to see this woman smile. "That's a lie, actually. I'm not sorry."

"I think that's because you enjoy torturing me."

"Everyone needs hobbies, Griffin," she said solemnly.

With a slight roll of my eyes, I sat back on the couch and stretched my arm to the side, easing my legs apart while I tried to figure out what to say next.

"Does that tenderness scare you?" she asked quietly.

"Yes."

My gruff answer didn't seem to deter her. If anything, she looked more and more certain the longer this nonsensical little therapy session went on.

Ruby sucked in a deep breath and moved, shifting to brace one knee on the couch as she rose up. Her hands settled onto my shoulders, and she swung her other leg over my lap and settled her slight weight on top of me, looking down into my shocked face with a stunning sort of resolve.

"What are you doing?" I barked, keeping my hands straight out. But when I tell you the urge to *tenderly* grab her ass was strong . . . I mean it.

"We can't be friends," she stated. "Not after the last couple of days. To your point, we almost had sex, though I'd amend that to say we never would've gone any further because the unsanitary nature of a bathroom is the least sexy thing I can imagine."

I arched an eyebrow, ignoring the way my hard-on grew underneath her as she settled herself more fully on top of me. "I think you found it sexy enough, birdy."

She let out a lofty sigh. "Fine. It's a moot point because we stopped anyway."

"And you relocated to my lap, why?"

"Because I wanted to." Her own eyebrow arched, and I had a feeling it looked so much more imperious than mine. "And I've found, in this new phase of my life, that when I want to do something because I think it will feel good, I'm going to follow that impulse." Ruby huffed. "Isn't that your fault? You encouraged all this."

"I'm very good at encouraging a lot of stupid shit; it doesn't mean you should keep doing it."

Ruby watched her hands as she trailed them down the front of my chest and anchored them over my abs, her eyes going a little hazy, and I had to fight the urge to rock up into her.

How had we gotten here this fast?

"I don't want to be treated like glass," she whispered. Her finger smoothed out over my ribs as they expanded on a deep breath. "And I enjoy feeling like I have autonomy over my body. Over the things that feel good. I never thought that would happen for me again."

"That makes sense," I rasped. Her fingers started inching up underneath my shirt, and my head spun when the edge of her fingernails lightly danced over the line of hair that split my abs and disappeared down into my shorts.

"*You* feel good, Griffin." Her eyes were so direct there was no looking anywhere else but at her. "And more importantly, you make *me* feel good. That's not a small thing."

"So you don't want to be friends," I said. She shook her head, tracing her finger just underneath the waistband of my shorts. An inch lower and she'd find a very big surprise waiting for her. With a frown, I plucked her hands away from my stomach. "Fuck, I can't think straight when you do that."

"That's the plan," she said gravely. "Because . . . I'd like to approach an alternative negotiation for the rest of your time here."

"What?"

Her eyes bounced between mine, and I found myself holding my breath. "We're friends . . . who do other things too."

My voice sounded like I'd swallowed rusty blades when I spoke, because "other things" opened up the floodgates of really good mental images. "Like what kind of things? And please feel free to be specific."

She exhaled a small laugh. "You can still teach me things, Griffin." Ruby leaned forward, sliding her hands up the sides of my neck and into my hair, rolling her forehead against mine. It shifted her hips over mine in a way that about had my eyes crossing. My hands clenched into fists, arms dropping onto the cushions next to me, muscles shaking from the need to touch her. "I want you to keep making me feel good." Her nose nudged mine. Her breath smelled like sweet tea. "And I want to do the same to you."

Never in my entire life had I held back in a moment like this one. A woman I wanted—pretty and smart and funny—was sitting on my lap, rubbing herself all over me like I was the greatest thing since sliced fucking bread, and I was keeping my hands off.

My head fell back and I took a deep breath. "God, Ruby, I don't know. You deserve someone better than me for stuff like this. Someone who can give you all the forever shit."

With a grip firm enough to shock me, she grabbed my face with both hands, forcing me to look at her. "I'm not looking for forever, Griffin. Listen to me. I don't want to make promises to anyone that I am physically not able to keep. I'll . . . I'll never get pregnant. I can't imagine allowing someone to fall in love with me, marry me, when I have no idea what the rest of my life looks like." Her voice shook slightly, and I felt a strange, terrifying wave of emotion push up against my ribs. "But I trust you, and you can show me things that I want to know. Do you know how important that is? I want to own this for myself."

The easy thing to do would've been to slide my hands around her hips and lean forward to slant my mouth over hers. Push up underneath her shirt and palm her breasts, suck on her tongue and work my way down a sweet little list of things to make her feel fucking incredible.

But for the first time in my life, I felt a whisper of caution slicing through all those things we both wanted.

Careful, it said. *Careful with this one. She's special.*

It didn't mean Ruby didn't know what she wanted or that she didn't deserve to take ownership of all those things she was talking about. Lord knew I'd done the same over the years with women who were clear on what the score was, who knew that forever wasn't in my repertoire either.

With gritted teeth and a hiss of pleasure when she shifted slightly over top of me, I pulled my head back and finally used my hands to cup her face in return. My thumbs brushed over her cheekbones, and triumph surged behind her eyes.

"Take tonight," I told her. "Rest tomorrow. And I'll come over Sunday morning." She opened her mouth to argue, but I laid my finger over her lips. "Please. Today was a lot. I'm not saying no, because you are so fucking tempting—you don't even know."

Ruby melted. "Really?"

"Do you feel me right now?" I growled.

"Yes." Her voice was hardly above a whisper, and I felt it like a bat to the head.

"Take tomorrow and think about what you're asking for." I tangled my fingers in her hair, cupping the back of her head while she leaned into my grasp. "I don't want you to regret anything with me, baby. That would kill me."

Ruby simply sat there and watched me for a few long moments, then finally nodded. "Okay. But I won't change my mind."

I laughed quietly. "You're allowed to, though. That's the point."

Ruby sighed, easing herself off me, and with a pointed look at my lap, she arched her eyebrow. "Would *he* let me change my mind, though?"

With a wince, I stood, adjusting the obnoxious asshole behind the flimsy material of my athletic shorts and boxer briefs. "Don't you worry about him," I said.

Ruby walked me to the door, pausing before she opened it. I didn't move, either, an obvious lingering between both of us. I knew what I wanted. Knew why I didn't want to leave.

I held my arms out. "Come here, birdy."

With a deep, relieved breath, she walked into my chest, wrapping her arms tightly around my middle. I smiled lightly, curling my arms around her back and settling my chin on the top of her head.

There was an element to Ruby, no matter how badly she wished it out of existence, that made her feel inherently breakable. The wrong twist of my hands, exerting muscles with too much force, and I could genuinely hurt her.

I'd sooner cut off my own arm.

"Thank you," she whispered into my chest.

I smoothed my hand up and down her back, an unexpected tightening in my throat as I felt her pressed against me in such an innocent way.

A world without Ruby Tate.

Fucking unfathomable.

And it had almost happened. It could have happened before I had a chance to see her again, to know what kind of person she was. It could have happened and my life would've kept right on spinning. The thought of it made me sick to my stomach. With burning eyes and a heavy chest, I pressed a soft kiss to the top of her head and then cleared my throat as I pulled back. "You're welcome."

"Sunday," she said.

I nodded, booping her nose with the tip of my finger. This time she smiled, and the sight of it lightened the weight behind my ribs. "Sunday," I promised.

Chapter Eighteen

Ruby

Me: I cannot believe I'm going to ask this, but how does this outfit look?

With a small shake of my head, I stepped back and snapped a picture of myself in the full-length mirror hanging on my bedroom wall, attaching it to the text I sent to Lauren.

Lauren: Look at you showing a baby glimpse of stomach! Hot. I need more details though. What's the purpose of the clothing in question?

Me: Function (going for a walk) and Seduction (I'll explain later)

Lauren: UMM NO, YOU WILL EXPLAIN NOW, YOUNG LADY

Me: Quit yelling at me.

Lauren: If you think I won't drive over right the fuck now . . .

Me: Fine. I think you're rubbing off on me.

Lauren: Explain.

Me: I propositioned Griffin with a friends with benefits situation after the fair, because I told him about my surgery when he accidentally saw my scar because he was trying to undress me in the bathroom of the school, and he was just so APPEALING in how he responded, I couldn't help myself. I was climbing into his LAP before I knew what was happening. He told me to take a day to think about it, but the extra time was unnecessary. My reasoning is entirely sound.

My phone was ringing before I could take my next breath, and I answered it on a laugh. "Good morning."

There were no words on the other end of the phone, just unintelligible squealing. On my bed, Bruiser tilted his head back and forth, whining slightly at the high-pitched noises he could hear. I scratched behind his ears and walked out of the room, giving one last glimpse to the crisscrossing straps of the white halter-style sports bra underneath the white mesh top.

The bra covered my scar, but the see-through cropped shirt over it, even though it was boxy and loose, showed more of me than had been shown . . . well . . . maybe ever.

"So the outfit is okay?" I asked dryly.

"Ruby," she gasped. "I am speechless. I am without speech."

I laughed, pulling aside the curtain in my front room to make sure Griffin wasn't here yet. "We don't have long. He's going to be here in a couple minutes."

"Did you have sex with Griffin?" she whisper-yelled.

"No. And he's not here, you know. He can't actually hear you."

The sound of a door closing came through the phone. "No, but Marcus is in my bedroom sleeping, so . . ."

My eyebrows shot up. "Still? I thought you weren't going to take him home?"

She laughed quietly. "He was too good not to, and I hate to admit that because I was convinced he'd be a lazy lay. But"—she whistled—"he was so damn eager to prove me wrong. I rode that man until his eyes crossed, and I'm pretty sure he's ready to tattoo my name on his ass after last night. At one point he came so hard, he shed a tear. I left him alone for a few hours yesterday just to prove a point, and he was feral by the time I walked in the door. My neighbors probably thought I was getting murdered because of the sounds coming out of my mouth." She paused. "And I'm pretty sure we broke my dining room table last night."

I blinked. "That thing was solid wood."

"I know," she sighed. "Epic, right? I had to keep him around for a bit after a performance like that."

"I guess so." It was hard not to feel naive, and slightly inferior, when I heard stories like that.

My internal temperature gauge, along with my pulse, spiked immediately when I tried to imagine me and Griffin breaking tables, screaming so loud that my neighbors could hear.

I waved a hand in front of my face and glanced down the street again.

"So . . . ," she drawled. "He handled the heart news well?" Lauren asked the question lightly enough, but we both knew it was a Big Friggin' Deal.

"He did. Really well, all things considered." I swallowed past a tight throat. "I feel so comfortable with him, you know? And we have . . . chemistry or whatever."

She snorted. "About time you figured that out."

"You think we do?"

"Honey, if you think I don't know how to spy on someone in the stacks without them noticing, you don't know me very well. Anyone standing within ten feet of the two of you noticed."

I winced. "Did Kenny?"

"Oh yeah. He sent me a text after the dunk tank on Friday night and it said, 'Hundred bucks those two will get married someday.'"

With a groan, I covered my face with one hand. "I don't want to get married, I just want—"

"Simultaneous orgasms and to make a man cry. That's what a lot of us want, honey."

"Apparently you've achieved it," I answered dryly.

She laughed. "The outfit is hot, Ruby. I may ask to borrow that shirt, actually."

Smoothing a hand down the shirt in question, I let out a quiet sigh. "Am I crazy for offering this?"

"Oh, let me think . . . you have one of the hottest football players in the world wrapped around your darling little finger, and he's in town just long enough to have your cosmos rearranged." She made a knowing little sound. "No, I don't think you're crazy. Be safe, of course, and make sure you tell him what you want."

"I almost printed off a checklist last night when I was doing research. I hardly know what I want." I sighed. "But some of them sounded *very* intimidating. Gags and fisting and spitting . . . it's all a bit confusing. Can't I just start with . . . I don't know . . . missionary?"

Lauren laughed. "You'll figure it out. If you're with him and something sounds . . . intriguing, just go for it. Men love it when a woman is up front about what they want." She cleared her throat. "Speaking of intriguing. I saw a story about Griffin cross my newsfeed his morning. I'll text you the link."

My phone pinged, and I opened it up, brow furrowing immediately. It was a grainy snap of Griffin by the dunk tank, cropped so that the fair didn't really show. He was next to a pretty coed, his shirt soaking wet.

Griffin King: Most Valuable Wet T-Shirt Contestant?
NFL's Favorite Bachelor Soaks Down with Fans

My stomach curled unpleasantly. "That's a gross misinterpretation of what he was doing," I scoffed. "It was for charity."

She sighed. "I know. I was standing three feet away when they took that picture. Griffin was completely polite, never laid a hand on her, even for the picture."

I chewed on my bottom lip, closing out the article after skimming a few lines about his offseason antics. Yeah. His antics were basically Debauching Ruby Tate, but that didn't make for a very good headline.

The sound of a purring car engine came down my street, but I didn't look because I knew it wasn't Griffin's truck.

A sharp burst of a car horn had me pulling the curtain aside again, and my jaw practically unhinged when I did. "Lauren, I gotta go."

"Have fun! Use a condom!"

I hung up on her and blew out a sharp breath, my eyes narrowing as I tucked my phone into the side pocket of my leggings. There was one thing clear as day right now: I was never telling Griffin King anything ever again.

I yanked open the door. "What is that?"

He crossed his arms, a smug grin gracing his stupidly handsome face. "A convertible. You said you wanted to ride in one."

Despite my very best efforts, my stomach did this swoopy little flutter thing. I pinched the bridge of my nose. Quashing was an absolute waste of my time at this point. "Please tell me you didn't buy a brand-new car because I said that."

The vehicle in question was sexy, and that was not a word I used lightly about an inanimate object. Sleek and low to the ground, it was painted a rich deep blue, the seats inside a sumptuous camel-colored leather. Even the knobs on the dashboard looked expensive. Like if I broke one, I'd need to take out a loan for the amount of money I made in a year.

He laid a hand to his chest. "Would I do something that impulsive, birdy?"

I gave him a look, and he chuckled under his breath.

Oh yeah. It was sexy. It looked fast. And if he bought it because of our conversation, I'd have to go scream into my pillow.

The type of screaming—frustration or feet-kicking excitement—was yet to be determined.

"Fear not. It's my agent's," he said, gently patting the hood. "After an exhaustive search, I accidentally found the keys in the mudroom, sent him a text, and promised to return it safely back into the garage when we were done with it."

Chewing furiously on my bottom lip as I leaned forward to study the interior, I let out a little whimper when my fingers brushed the leather. Like freaking butter. "He doesn't even know we have his car right now?"

"Based on the lack of response so far, I'd say no." Griffin stood up, laying his hand on my lower back and ushering me around to the passenger side. It was the oddest thing, but ever since I'd felt comfortable enough to climb into his lap—a momentary lapse of judgment that was still up for debate as to, one, the efficacy, and two, the ultimate outcome of my offer—there was a different sort of vibe when he touched me.

Him touching me did things. Even innocent touches. Like his hand to my lower back. It seemed physiologically impossible that the lower back was an erogenous zone, but the warm weight of his hand just above the hem of my workout leggings made me actually press my thighs together, a quick zap of energy that came out of nowhere, like it had a direct line to my nipples or something.

I cleared my throat, stepping back when he opened the passenger door and made a gallant gesture inside the gorgeous, lush interior. "I thought we were going for a walk," I told him, glancing up as he shut the door.

"We are." Griffin whistled as he rounded the hood. Somehow, he eased his long legs into the car as he took his seat.

"*Where* are we going for a walk?"

"Don't worry. You'll love it. It's beautiful. Top of the line."

"'Top of the line' for a walk?"

Griffin slid on a pair of mirrored aviator glasses and twisted his Denver hat backward on his head. With the scruff on his jaw and the slightly overlong hair along the back of his neck and over his ears, he looked far too appealing for his own good.

"Buckle up, birdy. We're gonna test the limits of this thing when we get on the highway."

My stomach jumped into my throat. "Why are we getting on the highway? Where are we going?"

Not that he would've answered anyway, because the man was clearly a sadist, but his phone rang and when he caught sight of the name on the screen, he let out a small hoot of laughter.

He punched a button on the dashboard to answer. "Steven, how are you feeling this morning?"

"If you get a single scratch on my wife's car, I'll drop your ass so fast."

My head whipped over to gawk at Griffin, but he was merely grinning. He leaned forward and pressed a button, the engine purring to life. Over the phone, his agent groaned.

"It'll be fine. Have I ever gotten in a car accident before?"

"You are a menace."

"A menace who just got you a nice paycheck. I paid for this car, Steven."

His agent scoffed. "You are so lucky they just paid you thirty-two million dollars, because that commission is the only reason I put up with your ass."

My eyes widened, the proverbial floor dropping out from underneath my feet, and I slowly swung my head back in his direction.

"You put up with me because you love me, Steven," he said, giving me a tiny wink when he caught the flabbergasted look on my face.

"All evidence to the contrary, King. I've got seven new gray hairs this week, just from you living at my house."

I sank down into the seat, pinching the bridge of my nose. Thirty-two *million dollars*. Just like a normal person, my ass. While my head was buzzing with shock, Griffin said something to his agent about how we'd be perfectly fine and there was nothing to worry about, and to the backdrop of Steven's creative use of swear words, he disconnected the phone call.

"You all right, birdy?"

"Thirty-two million dollars?" I squeaked.

He lifted a shoulder. "Not bad for two years, especially at my age. Denver really wanted me."

"That's for two years?" I groaned, covering my face with both hands. Griffin laughed warmly, tugging my hands down.

There was a fond look in his eye while he studied my face. "What's the matter? Because I know you better than to think that something like money would intimidate you."

"Of course it does." I gestured erratically. "I had this whole speech planned for our walk, and I was going to tell you why I still think my friends-with-benefits idea is highly logical, and now all I can think about is how I climbed into your lap and you make sixteen million dollars a year. No wonder women do a song and dance for you after games."

"I was kidding about that," he said dryly.

I sighed. "I know."

"I make more than sixteen mill, you know," he added. When my head angled toward him, he winked again. "Endorsements."

I blew out a slow breath and sank into my seat.

He eased the car forward, and I had to admit, the low hum of the engine was extremely appealing. The whole vehicle seemed to purr, and it dulled a bit of my embarrassment as the breeze ruffled the loose hairs by the side of my face. It was silly to be so bothered by it. Obviously he made millions. How many professional athletes didn't? Plus, he was on commercials.

During my rest the day before, when I was supposed to be thinking about whether I'd actually meant to proposition him, I'd found myself scrolling YouTube. A simple search of his name produced a mind-boggling number of videos. Game replays (which I didn't watch), highlight reels (which I did), feats of physical strength and prowess that made my skin feel tight and itchy and warm. The things he could make his body do defied any sort of logic I had within my grasp. Naturally, I had to watch those, um, a few times to make sure I could process them correctly.

He had commercials—for a shoe company and an athletic beverage. One cheesy campaign for an insurance company that made me laugh despite myself. I watched that a few times too.

Out of the corner of my eye, I watched the flex of muscles under the golden-tan skin on his forearm and felt my mouth go dry. When he glanced in my direction, I yanked my head around to look out my side of the car.

Griffin pressed down on the gas, and the corresponding roar of the engine, the whipping air around our faces, pulled a smile onto my face immediately. He zipped the car onto the highway, and I tipped my head back, allowing the sun to warm my face and the hypnotic swirling of air make me go weightless.

After only a couple of minutes, I lifted my arms up and stretched them into the air, almost like I was riding a roller coaster. Griffin turned his head to watch, a slow, devastating smile creasing his face.

"Faster?" he asked.

I nodded immediately.

He eased a hand over my leg; then, at the same moment his fingers curled possessively around my thigh, Griffin pressed down on the gas again. The car surged forward, and I laughed breathlessly.

It felt like flying.

There was a time after my surgery where a moment like this might've held a bittersweet edge. That it came at a devastating cost—years of my life, my health, someone else's life. But today, sitting in the sun with the breeze ripping through my hair, I simply let myself enjoy how good it felt.

I lowered my arms, then clasped Griffin's hand with my own and smiled over at him.

"Where are we going?" I yelled over the roar of the wind.

He pointed at the next highway sign. "Somewhere on that sign."

There were four cities listed; Fort Collins was one, Denver was another, so those were the most likely. But knowing him, he'd spring an overnight trip on me without hesitation.

I rolled my eyes. "Helpful."

Griffin squeezed my leg. "I do what I can."

As we drove for another twenty minutes, I mentally crossed off Fort Collins and decided to simply enjoy the journey. The Rocky Mountains off to the west were imposing under the sun, big and majestic against the blue Colorado sky, snow still visible on the highest of the peaks, variegated greens and browns spread out like a carpet over the base.

"You ever go hiking?" he asked, slowing the speed on the car enough that he didn't need to yell to be heard.

I shook my head. "Hiking mountains wasn't something I wanted to do *before* I had a hand-me-down heart. Looking at them is good enough for me."

"No hiking dates. Got it."

My cheeks were warm as I turned my head, fixing my attention outside the car. Something about the casual way he'd said that had my pulse sky-high. I closed my eyes, and instead of overthinking, I simply distilled all my thoughts into one singular direction.

What do you want, Ruby?

It was easy enough to answer, my gaze lingering again on his big body as he deftly handled the car, the way his hand held the top of the steering wheel and his other held my thigh.

We passed a sign for a rest area, and I squeezed his hand. "Are we on a time limit?" I asked.

"Not a firm one, why?"

I pointed at the sign, and he nodded easily. Behind the relative safety of my own sunglasses, I was able to study the hard lines of his profile. Those caused a tightening of my thighs, too, and another fluttering thing in my belly.

Lying in the dark of my room the night before—completely exhausted yet unable to sleep—I was able to logic myself through my wanton little display quite easily. It was effortless to do things like climb in Griffin's lap because he'd made the chemistry between us feel equally effortless. Speaking up and saying what I wanted, for the first time in my life, didn't feel like a hurdle to overcome. With him, I wasn't paralyzed with worst-case scenario outcomes because the noise in my head was muted, like he'd single-handedly conjured the loud wind to drown out everything except what I really needed to hear.

Griffin removed his hand from my leg to hold on to the steering wheel as he eased the car off the highway and down the slightly curved path to the parking lots. It was a parking-only rest area, and other than a few semis on the far side of the lot, we were the only car there.

"Park over by those trees," I told him, and with a nod, he obliged.

Once the car engine cut off, leaving just the sound of the highway behind us, both Griffin and I exited the vehicle. He tucked his hands into the pockets of his black joggers and joined me at the front of the car, where I attempted to fix my tangled mess of hair into a neater ponytail.

"You always have to stop this soon into a road trip? Remind me not to take you cross-country anytime soon."

I exhaled a short laugh, then pushed my sunglasses onto the top of my head. Griffin followed suit, anchoring his glasses on the top of his hat, glancing up at the towering grove of trees where we'd parked. There were no mountain views here, not where we were standing, but we did have privacy, and with no clear idea of where this jaunt was ending up, I needed privacy more than anything.

Griffin stretched his arms, groaning in a way that tugged at the hair on the back of my neck. His T-shirt lifted, a glimpse of his hard stomach making the fluttery things return. Belatedly, I realized he was watching me watch him, and the grin on his face had my cheeks burning hot.

"Like something you see?" he asked lazily, seating himself on the hood of the car and spreading his legs out slightly.

An invitation, based on the glint in his eye.

I raised my chin an inch. "Yes."

At my frank answer, his brows popped up. I let out a deep breath and moved between his spread legs. He closed them slightly, adding pressure to the outside of my thighs with his knees, and I swallowed against a dry throat.

"I took the day yesterday, like you asked," I said. I found myself staring at his hands where they rested on his thighs. Staring at the curl of his big fingers, remembering with vivid clarity what they felt like inside me.

"And?"

The rough edge to his voice had me pinching my eyes shut for a moment, only opening them again when I felt a bit steadier.

"Did you know that regular sex not only improves your blood circulation, but studies have shown that it can reduce the risk of heart disease in women by up to fifty percent?"

His firm, beautiful lips stayed in a straight line, but oh, the way his eyes smiled—I felt it like a lightning bolt.

"No kidding. Any other interesting tidbits?"

"It's a natural pain reliever too." I stood straighter, inching closer to him, allowing my hands to rest on his forearms, curling my fingers around the smooth skin and roped muscles there. "Orgasms release oxytocin and endorphins into your system. It can even help with menstrual cramps."

"Keep talking, birdy," he whispered, easing his hands forward until they slid up the backs of my thighs. "I'm surprisingly turned on by talk of blood circulation and menstrual cramps."

Even though he was teasing me, I licked slowly at my bottom lip, gratified when his pupils flared slightly. "You'd be good for my health, Griffin. Doesn't that sound nice?"

A deep hum came from the back of his throat, and I wanted to hear it against my ear. Wanted to hear it while he held my hands down on the bed and worked my body until I was screaming so loud the neighbors could hear. My head was dazed and spinning, standing in the bright sunshine, no one to see us but the trees, and his hands slowly coasting over my backside to tug me even closer. He adjusted his seat on the car, bringing his hard body flush with my center.

"Not sure anyone's ever said that to me before," he said, eyes full of wondrous heat.

When I'd gotten dressed that morning, I had thought about touching him. I had thought about watching when he tipped over the edge of control, like I had in the bathroom—shuddering and gasping in the circle of his arms.

I leaned forward and placed a featherlight kiss on his lips, and when I pulled back, he rested his forehead on mine, his hands gripping me firmly around my hips. The hard press of his thumb into the sensitive skin just underneath my hip bone had me hissing in a breath.

Prying my eyes open, I looked down at his lap, at the impressive bulge underneath his joggers, and I licked my lips again.

"Why the hell are you looking at me like that, baby?" he whispered, raw and rough through gritted teeth.

I lifted my head and remembered what Lauren had said before he picked me up.

If I wanted to . . . I should.

No matter what it was, and no matter how many times I might have talked myself out of it under normal circumstances.

"I owe you," I whispered back, tugging slightly on the waistband of his joggers with curled fingers that brushed against the heated skin of his stomach. "Let me."

"Fuck," he groaned, tipping his head back. "What if someone drives back here?"

I placed a light kiss at the front of his throat, where the hard wedge of his Adam's apple stood against his tan skin. He didn't stop me, though.

On the contrary, Griffin helped me tug his pants down just far enough that we might not get arrested for indecent exposure. He braced one hand on the car, adding a slight barrier for anyone who might approach from that side. From a distance, we'd look like a couple embracing.

"You really want this?" he asked. "With me, I mean."

I held his gaze unflinchingly. "Yes."

Griffin exhaled, the sound as unsteady as any I'd heard from him, and eventually he nodded. "Who am I to say no to Ruby Tate?" he asked, and then he dropped his mouth to my neck and sucked at the sensitive spot where my shoulder curved.

When he was free of the confines of his pants, it was a really good thing he wasn't looking at my face, because my eyes widened almost comically, my jaw hinging open.

If there was a part of my psyche still trapped in middle school, I would've run screaming from the sight of the absolute monster he was hiding in his pants. But considering the height and the big hands and the big feet . . . he was very, very proportional.

I almost let out a panicked laugh, but blew out a slow breath and focused instead on the heat of his skin as I started exploring.

Griffin was nosing against my neck, licking lightly at my skin, grunting softly as he helped me wrap my fingers around his length.

"Like that," he groaned. "You won't hurt me, baby."

I exhaled shakily, relishing the way he felt. Hard. So hard. Soft and smooth as I moved my hand. And beautiful, but I didn't dare say that out loud.

My fingers wouldn't touch as they wrapped around him, and there was something wildly intimidating about that, as was the way he tightened our intertwined grasp so much harder than I ever would've dared.

"What else do you want me to do?" I asked.

Griffin snaked his arm around my waist and brought us closer, fingers gripping my ribs under the mesh shirt, and with my hand between us, I worked him with small rolling motions of my wrist. When I tightened my grip, squeezing hard, he slanted his mouth over mine with a groan, his tongue seeking mine in a demanding sweep between my lips.

It felt so wicked, being kissed like this, with arguably the most beautiful penis in existence in my hand and Griffin King making helpless growling noises into my mouth.

I'd never felt wicked in thirty years on this earth, and wearing that mantle now scrambled something delicious in my brain. I don't know what cosmic intervention brought this man back into my life's path, but I wanted to send them a giant freaking thank-you basket.

I sucked lightly on his tongue, and he grunted into my mouth, pulling back from the kiss to tug at my wrist until my hand was up by his mouth. As he held my eyes, he licked a wide swath over my palm, and I gasped when he settled our joined hands around him again.

"That's it," he groaned.

"Tell me if this is good," I begged, words tumbling out unchecked. "What do you think about when you do it to yourself?"

His eyes fixed on mine, color rising in his cheeks. "Lately? I think about you on my lap, baby."

"Really?"

"Oh yeah," he groaned. "Wanna see that soon, pretty girl. Want to see you scream while I'm underneath you. Want to feel you fall apart when I'm inside you. Want that so fucking bad, even if I shouldn't."

The imagery, with his guttural, demanding voice narrating it, had me letting out a shaky breath. Maybe I was in over my head, but there was no way I was backing out of this now.

I wanted it. So I was going to do it.

I wanted *him*. So badly that I was trembling.

Our hands moved faster, and he sucked in a sharp breath. "Ruby," he growled, "that's it, baby."

Griffin tipped back his head as he let out a low groan and came over our joined fingers. I stared down in awe, watching while he slowed the movement of our hands and worked himself through the last pulses of his pleasure.

He let out a shocked laugh, staring at me like he'd never seen me before. "Holy shit, Ruby Tate. You just blew my fucking mind with that one."

I grinned, and he ducked down for a hot, searing kiss. When he pulled back, my head was spinning again.

"You're trouble, you know that?" he whispered. We kissed again, luxurious and slow. "You just keep making me want more."

The way he said it had me studying his face. At first, I couldn't even pinpoint what I'd heard. Reluctance, maybe, and a hint of resignation.

"I'm guessing you don't want me to return the favor while we're out here," he said, lips brushing mine softly.

Breathing out a laugh, I shook my head. "No. I just wanted to do that for you," I told him.

He hissed in a breath. "Baby, you keep saying stuff like that, and I'll have to give you one anyway."

My breath was coming in short pants. "It's okay, really."

Griffin kissed me again—lingering and dirty and the kind of kiss that started things, not ended them. His hand slipped underneath my shirt, and he pulled back to watch my face while he dragged his thumb over the front of my sports bra. "I bet I could slip my hand right between your legs and have you moaning without laying a single finger on your pretty little—"

I slapped my hand over his mouth, and his eyes twinkled. "Later," I told him. "Show me later. Now, maybe we should figure out how to clean each other up."

I held up the other hand with a wry arch of my eyebrow, and Griffin's muffled laugh behind my hand made me smile. He licked my palm, and I removed my hand with a scoff.

"Hold on," he said, sliding off the car and tugging his pants back into place. He popped the trunk and fished out his gym bag, jogging back around to the front of the car to cradle my hand in his while he cleaned it off with a small white towel.

"Well, that's handy," I said primly, because watching him clean his own mess off my fingers was giving me a slight out-of-body experience. "Didn't know you'd packed for a night out."

He laughed. "Oh, we're not gonna be gone overnight. We're going to the gym."

My brow furrowed. "What gym?"

Griffin kissed me again, smacking me firmly on the ass as he pulled away. "Team facilities. Team doctor and head trainer are meeting us there." With a wince, he glanced at his watch. "We'll be late at this point. I'm sure they won't mind."

My mouth hung open. "What?"

"Your fault," he said smoothly. "I did not have *hand job in the parking lot* on the itinerary, but I'll leave it up to you if you want to tell them that or not."

I fixed him with a glare, and he laughed again.

"Come on, birdy. We've got another forty-five minutes until we get there. You keep glaring at me like that, and we'll have another problem on our hands."

"You are impossible," I told him, sliding back into the car.

Griffin grinned, carefree and wind-blown and staggeringly handsome, as the car engine roared back to life. "Don't I know it, Ruby."

Chapter Nineteen

GRIFFIN

"You know what's interesting?"

Marcus's head popped up over my shoulder while I did bicep curls. With gritted teeth, I stepped away from him. "That you have a sudden obsession with being around me all the time? I'd pick a different word besides *interesting*."

He chuckled, taking a seat on the weight bench next to me while I finished my reps on that set. I set the bar down and rested my hands on my hips while my chest heaved on deep breaths. Across the room, Ruby stood with one of our head trainers. He was taking her through a weight routine that would be manageable for her with the equipment she had available, adjusting her form as she did some upper-arm reps.

They'd started with a review of what her existing routine was, and with our team physician listening in, they talked a bit about her history. Because I could tell she was a little embarrassed by all the attention, I'd excused myself to go through my offseason weight routine.

To my utter annoyance, Marcus was still sitting near me, his long legs stretched out in front of him and his arms crossed over his chest as he also watched Ruby.

"*Interesting* is the fact that you've confiscated our dear Steven's Fuck Me car and had a romantic little road trip to the team facilities—where you've never worked out—and your friend is also here getting special treatment."

There was no way I'd be lucky enough that a simple glare would get him off my fucking case, but I gave it a solid try. He did nothing except chuckle.

"She's got some . . . health issues," I replied lamely. "I wanted to help."

Marcus pursed his lips thoughtfully. "What kind?"

"Not my story to tell, dickwad. Go do your workout."

"Don't feel like it. Giving you shit is more exciting."

I rolled my eyes and unloaded the plates off the bar, setting them back onto the correct rack. "I'm surprised you were able to pry yourself away from Lauren long enough to come into work."

"Me too," he said seriously. "But you know what's even more interesting than the fact that she's here, or you're doing all these book-boyfriend things for her—"

"What?"

"Lauren told me about it. Anyway," he continued gamely, "it's the way that you're looking across the room right now."

My eyes snapped away from Ruby. "I'm not looking at her any certain way."

Marcus hummed. "You have this feral light in your eye," he said, easing his hand out in the air, like he was gesturing to an invisible board with all his notes on it. "Primitive, one might say. Or possessive."

Yeah, well, it was easy to start feeling possessive after she'd worked me into a mindless orgasm in the middle of a parking lot with nothing but her hand and the eager look in her big gray eyes. All these feelings were like a thorn splintering my chest, and I didn't quite know what to do about it.

"Henderson," someone barked from across the room.

"Oh, baby," my friend hooted. "I cannot wait to include you in this conversation. Davies, we need your opinion on something."

I straightened, immediately recognizing one of the Denver team captains—Liam Davies. He was one of the few Brits playing in the league, and he was an absolute beast on the field. His off-field reputation was just as intimidating, as Liam was well known for having no filter, no people skills, and a protective streak for the guys on his team.

We'd only met once, but I wasn't even sure he'd remember me.

Based on the glint in his eye, he did. One tattooed arm stretched out, and I clasped his hand in mine.

"Griffin, right?" he asked. At my nod, he sucked in a deep breath and gave me an appraising look from head to toe. "Welcome to Denver. We could use your help on the left side."

"That's what I hear," I told him. Despite my best efforts, my gaze wandered back to Ruby. She laughed at something the trainer said, then adjusted her stance when he touched her gently—professionally—on the backs of her arms.

"That your girl?" Liam asked.

My head snapped in his direction. "No."

"Yes," Marcus said at the same time.

Liam's already impressive glower deepened. "So she *is* your girl?"

"No."

"Yes," Marcus replied.

Turning slowly, I held his gaze before reaching up and yanking on his skin in the approximate location of his nipple.

He yelped, batting at my hand. "Ouch, you fucker, that hurts." Then he pointed a finger accusingly in my direction. "See? This is what I needed your help with. He's acting like she's not, but she is," he hissed quietly, like he was afraid Ruby could hear us fifty feet away. "And he's gonna do something stupid unless he figures it out."

"No I'm not," I hissed back. "We've . . . we've got an agreement."

Liam sighed heavily, pinching the bridge of his nose. "I'm going to regret this, but here goes." When he dropped his hand, his face was serious. "You think about her when you're not with her?"

I cleared my throat, crossing my arms tightly over my chest. "Sometimes."

All the time.

Liam nodded. "You worry about her?"

Before answering, I pushed my tongue into the side of my cheek. "Sometimes."

All the time.

God, I didn't even believe myself with how flimsy that sounded. I worried about her all the time now.

Liam's eyes sharpened. "What would you do right now if this redheaded twat—"

"Hey," Marcus said in an affronted tone.

"—walked over to her for a good snog."

Marcus leaned in, whispering, "I don't know what that is."

Liam didn't take his eyes off me. "Kissing, you nob. It means you try to kiss her. You all right with her having a go with one of your mates?"

My body went hot. Despite the fact that Marcus wouldn't, and he was ass-over-tit obsessed with Ruby's best friend, the thought of him attempting anything with her made me want to rip his balls off.

When I fixed my glare on his stupid face, Marcus held his hands up and scoffed. "I'm not actually going to do it, quit looking at me like that."

Liam smiled serenely, patting me on the shoulder with a truly impressive amount of condescension. "Right, then. She's your girl, even if you don't want to say it. Now, this is the important part—"

I sliced a hand through the air. "Hang on. I met you five minutes ago; why are you giving me relationship advice?"

"You'll get used to it," Marcus said. "We have no secrets in this locker room." He widened his eyes meaningfully. "And now that Liam has fixed all his rage issues and is blissfully pussy-whipped for his wife—" His words cut off in a choke when Liam snapped a hand out and covered Marcus's mouth.

"What have I said to you about mentioning any physical features on my wife's body?" Liam asked quietly.

After Liam dropped his hand, Marcus sighed, rolling his eyes up to the ceiling. "Sorry. I wasn't speaking about hers specifically; it was more of an observation of your general relationship status."

Eyes darting between them, I rubbed the back of my neck and wondered if it was too late to back out of this transfer. "You know, we really don't have to talk about this. Ruby and I are friends. We just . . . do other stuff too."

"That's a bunch of bollocks, and I'll tell you why," Liam said, fixing his attention back on me. "You can't do the other stuff without your feelings changing. They either change for the bad—where you start getting annoyed by all the stupid little shit they do and wonder why they breathe so loud and how come they can't just be a little different . . ." His voice dropped a touch. "Or they change for the good. And you get obsessed with all that little shit. Why does her hair shine in the sun? Why does she smell so good? Isn't it cute how she walks and how she laughs. Why can't she just be around you all the bloody time?"

My mouth went dry. "I don't think I want to have this conversation anymore."

"'Course you don't," Liam said evenly. "Because she's your girl and you haven't been able to admit it. You sleep with her yet?" When I shook my head, he gave me an assessing look. "What's she want out of this?"

"Nothing," I heard myself say. "Sh-she doesn't want a serious relationship. She just wants . . . she wants some experience because it's been hard for her to feel comfortable around men."

Marcus nodded, emitting a smarmy little hum that made me want to punch him. "Maybe Ruby's feelings are having good changes too."

He gave me a questioning look, and I shrugged miserably. "I don't fucking know, it's not like she's updating me afterward. She's so . . . logical, though. And decisive. I don't see her changing her mind easily. Not about this."

It felt really fucking grim to explain why, and it wasn't my story to tell.

Around us, a few other players laughed and chatted. Trainers filtered in and out. The clang of weights being racked and music filtering through the speakers was enough that I didn't worry about anyone overhearing us. The vibe in the weight room during the offseason was always pretty chill, save, of course, for our little corner of the room, where I was getting the shit scared out of me by a really terrifying Brit and the most relationship-dumb man in the entire universe.

Liam set his hand on my arm. "Listen to me. You sleep with her when you're feeling like this, and I promise you, it'll be a thousand times worse when it ends. Because if she's not feeling those good changes, then you're fucked."

"I am?"

"If she's not there with you? Yeah." He nodded. "Being in love like that is the worst fucking kind of purgatory, and I wouldn't wish it on my worst enemy."

"Aww, that's sweet," a soft voice came from behind me.

Liam's grouchy demeanor changed instantly, his eyes softening, mouth lifting into a hint of a smile. "Hello, wife. Obviously not true for us anymore."

A petite woman with curly blond hair sidled up to him, smiling at me and Marcus. Her hand twined around Liam's arm as he immediately turned into her, rubbing his palm over a visible baby bump under her shirt.

"I'm Zoe Davies," she said, holding out her hand. She had a friendly face and bright eyes, and on her ring finger was a glimmering diamond. I had a brief recollection of hearing their story during a piece on *SportsCenter*—they'd been named co-guardians of a little girl when one of their Denver teammates and his wife passed away. Liam and Zoe eventually got married, adopted the little girl shortly after, and were now expecting one of their own. "Please ignore any horrible advice my husband has given you."

Even though I was on the cusp of a sweaty, hand-clenching panic attack, I mustered a friendly smile. "Griffin King. He really is doing a terrible job of making me feel better."

"I'm being honest," Liam said, undeterred.

Zoe patted his chest. "You always are, honey."

"It's not easy navigating this shit for men like us," he continued, smacking Marcus on the chest when his attention wavered. "It's hard to feel our feelings sometimes, innit?"

"Oh yeah," Marcus said. "Big . . . big feelings over here."

Zoe smothered her smile, and I could not restrain my eye roll. "The only feelings you have are in your little head, Henderson."

Marcus flipped me off, which made Liam smile.

"We need to go," Zoe told Liam. "We have to pick up Mira from school."

Marcus perked up. "Little bit's in school now? How's she doing?"

"It's fucking awful," Liam barked. "We have to send her away every fucking day, and I have no idea if the little fucking prick boys are being mean to her, and it makes me want to punch something."

I glanced at Marcus. "I thought you said he fixed his rage issues."

"He did," Zoe and Marcus answered in unison.

"Right." I rocked back on my heels. "Well, nice to meet you both."

"I'll be in the car," she told Liam, patting his stomach before walking away.

Liam leaned in. "I mean it, King—you're fucked if her feelings aren't changing like yours. You better figure that out before anything big happens."

Marcus held up a hand. "Yeah, but what if she wants to have sex and then Griffin tells her no and can't really explain why? She'll feel like shit, and then he'll feel like shit because he made her feel bad about herself. Then she's got a complex because she thinks he doesn't want her, and he's left wondering for the rest of his miserable life what it would be like to have sex with her."

I groaned, covering my face with my hands.

Liam held up his hands. "I gotta go. Best of luck, mate."

"That's it?" I said, hands dropping ineffectually to my sides.

"Either that, or you just tell her you're in love with her and see where the chips fall." He shrugged. "Never know, it might not ruin your friendship." He slapped me on the back. "Cheers."

Marcus grinned. "Isn't he great? I fucking love that guy."

I sank down onto the weight bench and speared my hands into my hair. "I hate all of you right now."

"Cheer up, dude. If nothing else, you'll only be at Steven's house for a few more days, right? You won't have to see her anymore if you don't want to or if shit ends badly."

Marcus wandered off to start some weights, leaving me in the absolute misery of my thoughts. The day had felt so easy when I found the keys to Steven's car.

Surprise her with a convertible! Why not? It didn't mean anything. I was just doing something nice for a friend.

Except I wasn't. I wanted to make her happy more than I'd wanted anything in a long fucking time. Craved it, even.

I got high off the feeling of making her feel good.

Was I really falling in love with her? I scrubbed a hand over my face and watched her finish up another rep with the trainer. Her face was pink from exertion, but her eyes were bright and her smile . . . God, my chest turned over looking at her smile.

I was fucked.

No matter what her feelings were doing. No matter whether we slept together or not.

I was *fucked*.

For a teeny, tiny speck of a moment, I indulged myself in what might happen if I just told her. If I came clean. If we slept together and it was as good as I imagined it would be and I poured my heart out to her.

That's where my brain stalled. Where my imagination fizzled out.

There'd never been a time in my life, outside of the football field, where anyone relied on me for something big, something important. I'd never carried the weight of someone else's emotional well-being. And if I came clean to Ruby, that's what would happen.

If her feelings hadn't changed and she was more than ready to bid me adieu when my time in Welling Springs was over, I couldn't find myself—yet again—standing in front of someone important only to watch them walk away.

My jaw tightened uncomfortably, my brain looping around something Rachel had said to me the day she came over wearing Barrett's engagement ring. *"You're good for a few things, Griffin. Forever isn't one of them."*

Ruby wasn't Rachel. That much was clear.

But at the end of the day, I was still me, wasn't I?

If being myself came with a risk of hurting this person who'd become so important to me, then the best thing I could do was hold up my end of the bargain. I'd promised Ruby that I wouldn't fall in love with her, and as far as she'd know, I'd keep that promise.

With a sigh, I watched her smile again and rubbed at the pinching sensation in my chest, knowing I'd have to lie to myself, and her, in order to do it.

Chapter Twenty

RUBY

"I need to hit something," I announced as soon as Griffin opened the door.

"I'll volunteer as long as you don't break my jaw." He moved aside, tweaking the back of my ponytail. "I almost came to see you yesterday. I'm out of books. The cowboy one was steamy. I think I learned a few things."

The teasing joke went straight over my head. He was shirtless and I hardly noticed, and if that wasn't an indication of my foul mood, I don't know what was.

With a sigh, I brushed past him, about to sling my gym bag onto the couch when I stopped short. Marcus was sprawled out on one section, hand on his chest and his eyes glued to the TV. He was shirtless, too, but I really didn't care about that.

"Shhh," he said. "This is a really good part."

In theory, I knew what I was seeing, but I was wide-eyed and slack-jawed all the same.

"I know," Griffin said. "I'm shocked he's still here too. Can't figure out how to get rid of him."

"What the fuck?" I breathed.

"I'm trying to watch here!" Marcus yelled. "Do you mind?"

Griffin whistled. "She does swear when the situation warrants it. I like that more than I should."

"Shut up," Marcus hissed. "Go somewhere else. She just saved Rochester from the fire, and they're in their pajamas. If I miss something good, I'll never fucking forgive you."

Griffin wrapped a hand around my elbow and gently steered me down the hallway off the kitchen, leading us toward Steven's home gym. I lifted a hand and pointed dumbly back in the direction of the family room. "He's . . . he's watching *Jane Eyre.*"

"You've got us well and truly trained in finding period-appropriate seduction techniques, birdy. He views it as a learning opportunity now." Griffin smacked my ass and grinned when I let out an indignant squeak. "Oh, don't pretend like you don't love it." He crowded behind me as we walked, using my hips as handles to steer me into the room, dipping his head down to speak closer to my ear. "If you're a good girl and do all your exercises, I'll spank you in the shower after I clean all your sweat off."

Turning my head to look up into his face, I arched my brow haughtily. "I walked into the house saying I needed to hit something, and this feels like the best course of action?"

"Workout. Sweat. Shower. Naked spanking." He booped my nose. As much as I wanted to, I couldn't actually dredge up a shred of annoyance when he did it. "Can't think of many other things that would turn my frown upside down quite like that."

I rolled my eyes, but his mood was undeniably persuasive.

"Not even football?" I asked, easing myself onto the rubberized floor to go through some stretches.

Griffin joined me, his legs together in a straight line. Quite easily, he hinged forward at the hip and wrapped his hands around the bottom of his feet, bringing his head down while he groaned through the hamstring stretch. "Sometimes," he said. "I love playing the game, but all the other shit that comes with it can be pretty overpowering."

"Like what?"

"The press—they're the worst."

I hummed, taking the stretch deeper. "Lauren showed me an article from the fair. They totally skewed what you guys were doing."

He laughed. "Yeah, they love doing that."

My brow furrowed. "Doesn't that bother you? I got so mad, and it wasn't even about me."

Griffin shrugged, his face carefully blank. "Every once in a while, yeah. But trying to fight is like that guy with the rock going uphill. What do they call that?"

"Sisyphus," I answered. "Pushing the boulder up the hill. They'd call that a Sisyphean task."

"That's it. Not that I remember the story; I think I slept through that class a lot in college."

"It was a punishment," I said. "He was a horrible ruler. Sisyphus angered the gods by killing his guests as a show of power, and by cheating death. Once he was with Hades in the underworld, they cursed him to push a boulder up the side of a hill, only to have it slide back down every time it neared the top. He was doomed to repeat the same task for eternity as a consequence for his choices."

Griffin eased out of his stretch and gave me a thoughtful look. "Yeah. That. Sounds pretty fucking miserable, doesn't it? Doing the same thing over and over and never achieving what you want?"

"It does," I agreed quietly. To varying degrees, we all fought that battle. The literal definition of *insanity*—doing something the same way over and over and expecting different results. With Griffin, for the first time in my life, I was choosing a different course of action, something wildly out of character. And because of that deviation, because I broke a pattern formed by myself, I was finally getting the things I'd always wanted.

"I was like that in college," he said, eyes firmly trained on his hands where they wrapped around his feet as he bent his legs in another stretch. "Wanted one thing. Never acted in the way that would get me what I wanted, over and over and over, and I could never figure out why it wasn't working."

"What did you want?" I asked.

He let out a quiet breath. "Respect." His eyes landed on mine briefly, then moved away again. I opened my mouth to respond, but he kept talking. "I hate the league dynamics too. Constantly changing rules, even if they're for a good reason, affects how we train and how we've been playing for years." He sat up, crossing an arm over his chest and holding it down with his other, his eyes focused elsewhere. "My body can't recover like it used to either. I'm thirty-two, and most days after a game, I feel twenty years older than that."

I thought about all the times I'd changed the subject, unwilling to open up the neatly compartmentalized box where I'd kept the topic of my hand-me-down heart. Was it the healthiest way to go through life? Maybe not. But sometimes, it was also the only way you felt like you could move forward. Coping mechanisms came in a million different shapes and sizes, and I was the last person to judge what his were. I chewed briefly on my bottom lip, trying to decide how far I wanted to push.

Griffin had pushed me—gently, which still surprised me for the great big oaf he could be sometimes. He didn't bulldoze through my reserves; he simply listened and let me know how important it was that he didn't make anything worse. For a hard-to-define relationship, he'd stepped into that space in the absolute perfect way. Perfect for me, at least.

So I took a deep breath and held his gaze for a moment. "And you hate that your brother is there too."

His eyes stayed fixed on mine. "And I hate that my brother is there too." Griffin swallowed, his jaw flexing briefly. "Feels like pushing that fucking rock up the hill, you know? Everyone's waiting for it to fall right back down to the bottom."

"When's the last time you saw him?" I asked.

Griffin blinked. "A couple years ago. We played his team. They won by three points after a bullshit holding penalty set them up for a last-minute field goal, and I wasn't particularly gracious as a loser."

"And before that?"

The dry, unamused laugh Griffin let out had my brows lowering.

"Before that," he said slowly, "is not a very fun story." He nudged my foot with his own. "We only have a couple days left, birdy. My brother's ruined a lot of things, but I don't want him ruining this."

Right then.

It wasn't a harsh reply, but I chewed on my bottom lip, brain churning over the possibility that I'd overstepped while we moved through a couple more stretches in companionable silence. I moved into another position, noting the way his eyes tracked over my new sports bra. It was another high-necked number—I wasn't sure I'd ever feel comfortable putting my scar on display—but it left my back almost bare underneath a black mesh shirt, two straps crisscrossing in the middle of my spine.

Only a couple more days left, I thought, with a slight pang in my chest.

There were a dozen reasons why I should be thrilled at how this all had played out. More than that, even. And I still somehow found myself wanting.

I'm not ready, I wanted to yell, but I didn't.

Can't we have just a couple more days past that? I almost asked.

But I didn't do that either.

There's more to be learned here, I almost told him. Not just the sex, but other things too. Just once, I wanted to know what he looked like when he was sleeping. What his voice sounded like first thing in the morning. What the skin on his chest smelled like when he wasn't fresh out of the shower. It was more than those superficial details, if I was being honest.

What was he like during a game? Was he sad after a loss? Who took care of him when he was sick? What made him and his brother hate each other so much? Maybe if I knew those things, then I'd feel more at ease with his whirlwind presence in my life.

What a mark he'd left on me, and he wasn't even gone yet. A scar whose existence would be known only to me.

If I *knew* Griffin—the real, honest version of him, not what the press would have me believe—then I could make peace with only having him for a short time. Already he'd shown much more than he might have intended, and each glimpse simply amplified my desire for more.

More of everything, really.

I let out a slow breath, standing up and swinging my arms back and forth to loosen my back, then dropping my fingertips down to brush the floor. Griffin joined me, and it was my turn for lingering glances in the general vicinity of his chest and stomach too.

The smattering of dark-golden hair on his chest was somehow the most visually appealing thing I'd ever seen, because it matched the shade of the thin line of hair that split through the bottom of the stacked muscles on his stomach and disappeared beneath the waistband of his athletic shorts.

He clicked his tongue. "None of that, Miss Tate. We have work to do, and you'll not distract me with sex eyes."

Face hot, I blinked up. "I don't have sex eyes."

"You sure do." He ambled toward me, and I stumbled back, almost tripping on the weight bench behind me. With a laugh, Griffin wrapped an arm around my waist to keep me upright. His skin was warm on mine, and my fingers curled around the waistband of his shorts as he held me against his chest. "Now, why did you want to hit something?"

The playful mood burst like a pinprick, and my shoulders deflated in an instant. How easily I'd been able to forget, even just for a moment. That was his superpower, I realized. He helped me forget everything. When I lifted my face to his, he must have seen the gloss of tears in my eyes.

"Are you okay?" he asked, brow wrinkled in concern. He cupped my face in both hands, thumbs sweeping gently over my cheekbones. "What happened?"

I sighed. "We lost the land next door to the library. A developer from Fort Collins put in a much stronger offer, so the sellers accepted it."

"Shit. I'm sorry, birdy." His hands moved up and down my back, a motion meant to soothe, and it actually helped. Sort of. Lauren and I had already had our rage-texting earlier, and that certainly hadn't calmed me down. "How much more did he offer?"

I shrugged. "Not sure, exactly. We came in well above asking price."

"Want me to go break his kneecaps?"

I emitted a shaky laugh, then caught sight of his face and sobered. "Oh my gosh, Griffin, *no*."

He grinned, tugging me close for a hug. He was big, and warm, and with all those muscles up against my body, it was incredibly easy to succumb to the way my brain responded. We'd uncapped something between us, and even though the mood had swung wildly since I'd arrived at the house, I found myself melting into yet another shift.

My hands grazed the hot skin on his back, dipping beneath the waistband of his shorts to knead the hard muscle there. Griffin let out a low rumbling sound and nuzzled the side of my head, his hands tightening where they were wrapped around my waist. The edge of his fingers dug into my ribs, and I sucked in a sharp breath, dragging my nose along his chest, laying light kisses over his skin. It was like he flipped a light switch, all the bells and whistles screaming in the back of my head.

Prepare your vagina, they said, clear as day. *Because he is big and you are not, and if you keep half-naked hugging, then it's a fairly easy step toward sex on the gym floor.*

I would've done it too.

He smelled incredible like this, with no barrier between me and his flawless body. I reached the skin over his heart and kissed him there, a light brush of my tongue against his skin, and his hands tightened, one sliding up to anchor at the base of my neck, where he exerted just enough pressure that I looked up.

"You trying to start something again, baby?" he murmured, a feral glint to his eye that lit a spark deep in the pit of my belly. Heat coiled through my veins at the way he looked at me—because there was a heady sort of power in this interaction.

"N-no," I lied, but my hands traced over his stomach, and I thought about how it would be if I were anchoring them there, if I were on top of him, writhing in his lap like he'd said he wanted. Using that as my balance while he wrenched his hips up underneath me.

Griffin registered the change in my expression, his gaze heating as he stared at my mouth.

"Shit," he breathed, his hands pushing around my hips, filling his palms with my backside, and the impatient flex of his fingers had me pinching my eyes shut against the relentless wall of heat. This couldn't possibly be normal, right? How did people function in normal society— working and sleeping and eating and doing yard work and . . . doing taxes or whatever—when they could be doing this all the time? "Not yet," he said. "Workout first. You need to do more strength training, okay? It's good for you."

"So is sex."

At the pleading tone in my voice, he let out a pained laugh. "God, you're gonna be the end of me, aren't you?" He leaned down and kissed me with a low groan, and I rolled up to the balls of my feet to push closer while his tongue brushed lazily over mine.

"Is that a yes?" I asked against his mouth.

He hummed, cradling my face while he deepened the kiss. "Will it make you feel better, baby? If it made you smile, I'm pretty sure I'd do any fucking thing you asked."

This was so much bigger than anything we'd done, and yet I couldn't find a single shred of reservation. My lifelong role of the responsible girl was nothing but a wispy, insubstantial thing in the back of my mind.

Just as I began to nod, a pointed clearing of the throat came from the doorway. My eyes slammed shut.

"I really, really don't want to intrude," Marcus said.

I deflated into Griffin's chest, and he growled low in his throat. "What is it?"

"You, uh, got some visitors."

Griffin's head snapped up. "You didn't invite more people here, did you?"

Marcus held his hands up. "Trust me, if I was inviting people, it would not be two little kids who look like your brother." He tilted his head. "Or look like you, I guess."

"What?" Griffin yelled. He snatched a shirt from the weight bench and tugged it over his head, and I followed both of them back down the hallway, almost running into Griffin's back when he came to a dead halt in the kitchen.

"What are you two doing here?" he said incredulously.

"Uncle Griffin!"

I'd hardly peeked around him when two tall, gangly kids with the exact coloring of their dad and uncle threw themselves at Griffin.

He gathered them up in a tight hug. "Holy shit, how did you get here, and how the fuck did you know where this house was?"

The boy—he couldn't have been older than thirteen—hitched a thumb at his younger sister when Griffin released them. "You said you were at your agent's house outside of Fort Collins. She searched the sale records on the county website once she had his name."

My eyebrows popped up as the girl grinned devilishly. She had the exact same smile as Griffin and Barrett, and deep dimples on either side of her mouth.

"Maggie," Griffin said in a low warning tone. "How did you get plane tickets? Because I know your dad didn't agree to this."

She blinked innocently. "Those consent forms for an unaccompanied minor are incredibly easy to forge. Honestly, it's like they're not even trying."

Griffin swiped a hand over his mouth and stared at his niece and nephew. Marcus and I traded a quick, panicked look.

"He's gonna kill me for this," Griffin said. "Does he know where you are, Bryce?"

The boy shrugged. "I left a note in the kitchen. He'll figure it out when he gets home from work."

Griffin tipped his head back and stared at the ceiling, muttering things under his breath that none of us could understand. It was probably best for the kids that they couldn't.

Maggie glanced at me, tilting her head. "Who are you?"

Marcus cleared his throat. "Don't you want to know who I am?" he asked, laying a hand on his inked chest.

Maggie rolled her eyes. "I know who you are. I watch *SportsCenter* every morning."

"Nice," he said.

Griffin rubbed the back of his neck, looking a little bit like he might pass out.

"But she's new," Maggie said. "I know Uncle Griffin's single because it's all over the internet."

My mouth was dry as the freaking Sahara when I opened it to speak. "I—"

"She's my friend," Griffin said, "and you don't get to be nosy right now, young lady. You're in so much trouble."

"Technically, we're only in trouble once Dad catches us," she pointed out.

Marcus snickered. "I hope I have a kid like you someday."

Maggie beamed.

Her brother rolled his eyes. "Don't encourage her."

Griffin pulled out his phone. "As much as I don't want to do this, I have to call your dad."

"No!" both kids wailed.

Indecision was stamped all over Griffin's face as Maggie tugged on his arm. "Please," she begged. "He'll make us leave, and we haven't seen you in so long. Just . . . just send him a text and let him know we're okay and that you'd love to have us stay for a while. Please?"

Her chin started wobbling, and Griffin sighed, tugging her in for a hug. "I missed you, kid."

She flung her arms around his waist and lost her battle with her tears. "We missed you too."

My own eyes burned as I watched him extend an arm to a suspiciously red-eyed Bryce, and he joined them in the hug. Griffin sighed, kissing the tops of both of their heads, his eyes falling closed as the two kids cried softly in his arms.

Oh, this was dangerous.

Griffin showing sweet paternal energy was like a rallying cry for my ovaries, and I actually pressed a hand to my stomach to instruct those little jerks to calm down. Not once had I heard the ticking clock, or even a whisper of wanting to have kids. For years, I'd been so consumed with just . . . staying alive that procreating was so far off in the distance I couldn't even squint to see it.

But the sudden image of Griffin holding a baby almost knocked me down to my knees.

I pinched my eyes shut and turned toward the kitchen, bracing a hand on the counter until I could ruthlessly banish that picture into the depths of . . . I don't know . . . mental purgatory, where it belonged.

Marcus gently touched my arm. "I think I'm gonna go see what Lauren's up to," he whispered, with a quick glance at where Griffin was talking quietly to the two kids. "Give him a little space."

I nodded, wondering if I should do the same.

Marcus exited without fanfare, sneaking out down the hallway through the garage. Griffin straightened with the kids still holding him tight, eyes briefly locking on mine. He looked so lost. My hands itched to hug him. Hold him. Do something. Maybe this was why he always threatened violence when I was upset about something—because then he could do something to make it better. Make it go away.

In that moment, I would have done anything to give him an anchor. Make him feel safe, like he wasn't alone. It was the same thing he'd been doing for me this entire time. *What a dangerous game we're playing,* I thought. And yet, nothing could've dragged me away from him before our time was up. Nothing.

I'd take every minute, every second that he gave me, and soak up this sweet torture for as long as possible.

After a moment, Griffin told the kids to go check out the pool, and they ran off into the background with an excited whoop. He turned to me, blowing out a slow breath, that lost quality seeping back into his expression. "What the fuck?" he whispered.

I let out a small laugh. "So," I said. "Those are Barrett's kids."

He nodded, eyes flitting between me and them. A soft, adoring smile played around his mouth as he watched them, and it was so unbearably attractive that I almost screamed.

"They're so big. I haven't seen them in a couple years." Griffin pinched his eyes shut. "He's gonna kill me when he finds out they're here."

"Should I go? I can give you guys some time alone."

"No way," he said immediately. "If Barrett shows up, I'll need you to protect me."

Chapter Twenty-One

GRIFFIN

It took six hours and thirty-two minutes. Not too bad, considering he had to get home from the office, book a flight, land in Denver, and drive out to Welling Springs.

Bam, bam, bam!

"Griffin!" my brother's voice boomed through the door.

At the kitchen island, with plates full of pizza and sliced watermelon, Maggie and Bryce froze, eyes widening.

Ruby was in the bathroom, and I briefly considered hiding in there with her just to see how long it would take Barrett to sniff me out. I gave my niece and nephew a quick, encouraging nod but felt my face fall into a grimace the moment I turned toward the door.

I couldn't exactly remember when this started, but for as long as I could remember, being around my brother made me feel like the annoying little kid whom no one trusted with the big, important stuff. And no matter how much I wished it not to, my stomach curled tight with anxiety as I neared the door.

It wasn't even my fault, and I could feel my guard sliding up and locking into place when I flipped the dead bolt and yanked open the door.

For a moment, all we did was stare at each other. To the rest of the world, we looked exactly the same, but I never, ever felt like I was looking in a mirror when faced with Barrett. There was something different about his eyes to me, the way he never smiled. The set of his shoulders always made it seem like he was carrying the weight of the world.

Maybe he was. Single dad to two scarily intelligent kids with a knack for subterfuge, and an ex-wife who was as warm and cuddly as a snake.

His jaw flexed as we stared at each other for the first time in two years, and I opened my mouth to say something, but his eyes moved past my shoulder, where he saw his kids quietly sitting at the island.

"You two are in so much trouble," he started, striding into the house without a word to me.

My stomach sank into my feet a little, wishing I'd gotten Ruby out of the house before Barrett arrived. Last thing she needed was a visual reminder of the better, smarter, more responsible King brother.

Maggie ran to give her dad a hug, looking up at him with a pleading expression. "Please don't make us leave right away. We just wanted to see Uncle Griffin for a little while."

Bryce joined in, wringing his hands while his sister attempted the physical side of the emotional-manipulation attempt. "We've had so much fun today. We went swimming, and he played pool volleyball with us, and we played Chicken and Marco Polo and ordered pizza, and he said we can stay over tonight if you'd let us."

Barrett's eyes flashed to mine, anger flaring so hot that I almost couldn't breathe for a second.

"That's not his to promise," he said. "And you didn't even ask to see him," Barrett continued, voice raising slightly. "You don't forge paperwork and board a flight by yourself because you didn't ask me a question."

Maggie pulled back, her eyes full of their own fire. "Yes, I did. I asked after he sent me my birthday present." Barrett swiped a hand over his mouth, staring down at his daughter with tired-looking eyes. "You told me no."

Barrett dropped his hand. "I told you I couldn't talk about it right then. I was in the middle of—"

"The middle of work," Bryce chimed in. "You always are."

My brother let out a slow, steady breath. I'd heard the pundits say that his ability to keep his cool was one of his superpowers. That with a single disappointed look, he could have his players willing to play through broken bones if necessary. There was no need to yell or scream or indulge in any of the sideline antics so many coaches made famous.

In college, someone had nicknamed him Ice Man, and it stuck. Through the pros, into his coaching career. In the end, I think it was why Rachel picked him. His drive, coupled with the steely, immovable demeanor, made him look like the solid bet. Someone who'd never stray. Never leave. Never fuck up.

Apparently, that trait did not extend to being the perfect parent. The thought of it didn't bring me any joy, knowing there was one part of his life where he wasn't a superhero. God, maybe I was experiencing a quarter-life crisis of sudden emotional growth. Maybe my capability for understanding my brother was growing in direct correlation to being around Ruby.

Like I was becoming a better person by osmosis or something. She was literally breathing her goodness into me. She'd gloat when I told her, and I couldn't even blame her a single bit.

In the pulsing silence while my brother assessed his kids' face clearly trying to figure out how to extract them without causing damag I wondered what was taking Ruby so long. She'd keep me from doi something stupid.

"I really don't mind them staying," I heard myself say. "I'm ha to have them here. Even if it's just . . . until you leave tomorrow."

The kids perked up immediately, a chorus of "please, please, p' echoing through the kitchen. Barrett's head snapped in my dire his expression so fucking cold that I had to grit my teeth.

Something stupid like that, apparently.

"Kids, go play outside while I talk to your uncle," he said. It wasn't just the even tone of his voice that had me sucking in a sharp breath through my nose; it was the absolute chilling fury in his eyes.

"Can we get back in the pool?" Maggie asked. They were still wrapped in towels from earlier, their hair damp and their cheeks flushed from being out in the sun.

Barrett gave her a short nod, and they ran off without a single worry that I was probably about to get my ass reamed.

I slid my hands in my pockets and rocked back on my feet while they disappeared, cutting a quick glance down the hallway, but there was still no sign of Ruby.

"What the fuck are you playing at?" my brother asked, lethally quiet.

My eyes snapped to his. "I'm not playing at anything. What do you expect me to do when they show up here unannounced?" I held my arms out. "Turn them away?"

"I expect you not to undermine me right in front of them," he ground out. "If you had kids, you'd understand that what you just said made things ten times harder for me."

"I'm not trying to make things harder for you. I'm trying to spend some time with my niece and nephew." I exhaled harshly. "But that's an easy card for you to play, isn't it? I don't have a wife, I don't have kids, so it's always going to be my fault." I raised my eyebrows. "Right?"

His jaw hardened. "You have no idea what it's like to be responsible for anyone but yourself. And half the time, you can't even manage that without someone stepping in to fix things for you."

I emitted a dry laugh. "That's getting old, big brother. You haven't had to step in for me in years, and even when you did, I didn't ask you to. If you want to find a place to lay the blame, maybe you should look little closer to home."

"I won't apologize for working hard. I work the way I do for them. that I can provide them with the best possible life."

"Yeah, every workaholic says the same thing when their life falls apart because everyone around them is miserable." I held his gaze unflinchingly. "Like your wife was at the end, right?"

Or something stupid like that. Maybe emotional growth was a slow, subtle one, because the moment it rolled off the tongue, I had to bite down on the impulse to take it back.

He took a step toward me, hands curling into fists. "Speaking of easy cards to play, Griffin. Even you're smart enough to know what a crock of shit that is. Rachel created her own misery. Showing up at your place when she knew I was less than ten minutes behind her is a perfect example."

My jaw tightened, eyes narrowing as I tried to weigh the truth of that in his face.

Vaguely, I wondered what would happen if the two of us actually got into a fight. Barrett was strong. Same height. Same build. But I was the one still in the gym training for game day. When it came to sheer muscle mass, I had the edge on him, and he fucking knew it.

Barrett opened his mouth to say something else, but when the sound of quiet footsteps entered the room, his face went slack with shock.

I pinched my eyes shut, wishing I could magically make her disappear. Not because I didn't want her around—fuck, if anything, her presence might keep me from taking a swing—but neither did I want her witnessing this.

"Hi, Barrett," she said, hands clasped together in front of her. Ruby's hair was pulled up off her face from being in the pool, and even though we'd never seen her in a swimsuit as a teenager, there was no denying it was her. "It's good to see you."

His brow furrowed deeply. "Ruby Tate? What the hell are you doing here?"

Briefly, her eyes met mine, and there was a moment where I couldn't fight it even if I wanted to—my lips lifted in a badly timed smirk.

"I live here," she said, then pinched her eyes shut. "In town, I mean. Griffin and I . . . ran into each other when he first got here."

"And you're . . . what? Hanging out with him?" he asked incredulously.

A short laugh escaped my lips, and I swiped a hand over my mouth to try and stem it. She gave me a look meant to chasten, but instead it just added to the utter absurdity of the situation.

My entire life felt like a fucking soap opera sometimes, and this was just one more thing added to the list. I knew what my brother would see right now—I was the big, bad wolf and she was the innocent maiden waiting to be ravished.

She sent me a tiny glare at my poorly timed laugh but shifted her attention back to my brother. "Yes," she said evenly, raising her chin a notch. "I am."

Barrett looked between us, back and forth and back and forth, finally shaking his head like he couldn't believe what he was seeing. Then he tipped his head back and stared at the ceiling for a moment. "I feel like I'm in the fucking twilight zone right now."

I slicked my tongue over my teeth. "When are you leaving?"

He glanced out at his kids, playing happily on a giant flamingo float, and he sighed, wiping a hand over his face. "I'd take them right now if I thought they'd ever forgive me," he said tightly, cutting his eyes in my direction. "But you made sure I can't do that, didn't you?" Barrett shook his head. "You never think through the consequences of your actions. More concerned with being fun Griffin than anything—the mantra of your entire life, and the rest of us just have to deal with it."

I exhaled a harsh, dry laugh.

Ruby tilted her head. "How is this Griffin's fault?" she asked. "He didn't know they were showing up. As soon as they got here, he told them what they did was wrong."

"Don't worry about defending me, birdy," I told her. "He won't listen to a word of it."

Barrett licked his lips, giving her as friendly a look as he could manage, which wasn't saying much. "My brother and I need some privacy, Ruby, if you don't mind stepping outside."

"She is my guest," I said icily, stepping forward, chest expanding on a deep breath. "You don't ask her to go anywhere."

She set her hand on my arm, and the effect was immediate—like sweet, cool water poured over the frustrated heat that only my brother seemed skilled enough to ignite. "It's okay," she said. "I'll go outside with the kids." Then she paused and looked up into my face. "Unless you want me to stay."

My heart kicked at the back of my ribs in a single, uneven beat. I did want her to stay. Having her around made everything better, and that sent a coil of fear so quick down my spine, because the passage of time just went quicker and quicker every single day.

Ruby was the literal grains of sand sliding through my fingers. No matter how tightly I clenched my fist, there was no stopping the way she'd slip out of my grasp when all this was over.

"You can go," I said quietly. "This won't take long."

She gave me an encouraging smile, and with petty satisfaction, I saw it tighten uncomfortably at the edges when she shifted it toward Barrett.

The moment she was outside, wisely pulling the sliding doors shut behind her, my brother let out a disbelieving laugh. "Oh, wow, Griffin. That's . . . that's something even for you."

I crossed my arms over my chest and turned to face him. "Fuck off, Barrett. We're friends."

He pursed his lips. "Yeah, you've had a lot of those."

"Not like her."

At my tone—hard and cold, brimming with tightly leashed violence—his eyebrows popped up briefly. "She was always a nice kid. Smart. Quiet. Better than both of us, that's for sure."

He'd get no argument from me there. My eyes found her as he spoke, and the way she smiled at Maggie and Bryce made my chest feel tight. She eased into the water, immediately joining another round of Marco Polo.

She *was* better than me. In pretty much every way.

"Don't let her be another consequence of the shit you don't think through," my brother said quietly.

I thought about what Liam had said. What Marcus had said. And I thought about my own roller-coaster thoughts when it came to that woman and her big gray eyes. I did want her. I did have feelings that were changing. Good changes.

Big, scary, uncomfortable changes.

And while she was still in my orbit, there would be no walking away, no putting up invisible boundaries in some cut-rate attempt to protect myself. As long as Ruby wanted me, I was hers. And I still would be, even after she didn't.

I swallowed past the flimsy denial crowding my throat, tearing my eyes away from Ruby. "Anything else you'd like to lecture me on?"

He sighed, looking back out at his kids with a slight shake of his head. "I chartered a private flight to Arizona from here. We're gonna go visit Mom and Dad." His jaw flexed. "I'll change the flight to tomorrow and pick them up around ten. Make sure they've had breakfast."

My mouth popped open, but I snapped it shut. "Sure."

"No drinking while they're here," he said firmly.

"I won't," I promised. "Uh, Marcus Henderson has been crashing with me the last few nights, but I'll tell him he's gotta go back to Denver."

"The giant Viking frat boy from college that convinced you to throw a kegger in the college president's backyard?"

I winced. "That's the one."

"Fuck's sake," he muttered. "Yeah, I'd appreciate that."

In stunned silence, I watched my brother sigh heavily, the toll of all this clear on his face.

He caved. He was allowing space in his kids' lives for me, even if it was just this once. Fuck if I didn't feel a little bit like the Grinch, an unsteady punch to the heart that seemingly grew three sizes as I stared at the brother who'd never conceded a single inch for me in the last fifteen years.

Maybe I could concede an inch too.

"Happy birthday tomorrow, in case I forget to say it," I told him quietly.

His jaw flexed, eyes locking briefly on mine before he nodded.

"You too," he said, voice tight and rough with emotion.

Barrett went outside to tell the kids they could stay overnight, and beyond the sound of their excited screams, it was Ruby's triumphant grin aimed in my direction that caused a seismic fluttering inside my chest.

Fucked.

I was so fucked.

Chapter Twenty-Two

RUBY

"Oh my," I breathed, taking in the utter chaos in front of me. "What happened?"

Griffin was lying in the middle of the family room floor, legs out, arms on his chest as he stared up at the vaulted ceiling. "Maggie."

I slowly set down my bag on the floor and took in the carnage in the kitchen—mixing bowls; an undoubtedly cold stack of pancakes; two half-empty containers of eggs; a half-eaten, lopsided cake with blue frosting dripping sadly down the side.

Happ Birth was all that was left on the cake, written messily in a red gel frosting. Colored sprinkles coated the parts of the cake that hadn't been touched, and I swiped my finger through a glob of frosting on the cake plate and sucked it into my mouth while I turned in a slow circle.

"Is it your birthday today?" I asked.

From his spot on the floor, Griffin made a quiet grunt of assent. "I'm not moving. I'm staying here all day. That's what I want for my birthday present."

"Well, now I feel bad," I said. "I didn't know to get you a present."

"You can help me clean up the kitchen. It'll be the greatest gift anyone's ever given me."

I laughed, turning toward the dining room. My eyebrows shot up when I saw the table. Beads everywhere. Stacks of construction paper. Stickers. Glitter.

"They were here for like, twenty-four hours," I said incredulously.

Griffin sat up with a groan, rubbing a hand over a bleary-looking face. "I know. She found the crafting closet, and it was all over. They didn't want to go to bed because they only had one night, so I let them stay up until midnight thinking they'd sleep in a bit." He shook his head. "Nope. She was standing over me at six a.m. Scared the absolute shit out of me when she whispered my name, asking if she was allowed to make breakfast."

I smothered my grin, because he really did look exhausted. "Everything go okay when Barrett picked them up?"

Griffin yawned, giving his stomach a lazy scratch as he ambled into the kitchen to survey the damage. "He stayed outside, which is probably for the best. If he'd seen this, it would've just reinforced that whole Griffin-is-an-irresponsible-child mantra that makes up the cornerstone of his tidy, perfect little universe."

With a tight throat, I started picking up the mixing bowls and moving them to the sink, then turning on the hot water and adding soap so that they could soak for a little bit.

"Everyone's always looked at me a certain way," I said quietly, tossing the cold pancakes into the garbage. The eggshells went in right after. "I'm the responsible one. The quiet, smart one. I never got into trouble, but I also wasn't very noticeable either."

Griffin joined me in the kitchen, soaking a washcloth with hot, soapy water. He started wiping at the dried frosting on the gleaming counters, swiping up little piles of crumbs while he listened quietly.

"In high school, I was constantly picked on by the popular kids." In one of the drawers, I found aluminum foil and covered the cake, sliding the plate into an empty spot in the fridge. "Because I was too nerdy and too quiet and didn't party and no one asked me out."

Griffin's eyes were heavy on me as I closed the egg cartons and moved those to the fridge as well.

"I was one of those kids, wasn't I?" he asked quietly. "Before you moved."

My eyes fell shut, but instead of answering—because even if there was a good-natured angle to it, we both knew he was—I kept cleaning, busying my hands as I washed the bowls and stacked them next to the sink to dry.

"It didn't take me long to realize something," I continued. With the counters clean, Griffin went over to the dining table and started stacking the construction paper, his eyes still on me as we moved around each other in the big space.

"People's perception of others is always colored by their own issues. Their own insecurities. The things we see in other people—especially when it's a trait that we're secretly a little jealous of—twist around in our brain before we're even aware it's happened. It becomes an ugly thing to tease them about. Make them feel like they're doing something wrong, because we're sick with envy that we don't have just a little bit of that."

I joined him at the table, using a damp paper towel to pick up the glitter. My arm brushed his, but instead of lingering, I moved away again. "The kids who teased me about being a boring little bookworm—I saw them struggle in class. Saw them fight with exhausted teachers, when all they really wanted was respect." His eyes were fixed on mine when I glanced up, the space between us thick with tension. "I think they wanted to be a little bit more like me without having to give up the good parts of being themselves." I dumped the glitter-covered paper towel and turned in his direction. "Just like I gave you a hard time about being a player. Someone who made women line up to do a song and dance."

Griffin's movements slowed. "You wanted to be a little bit like that," he said.

After a slight hesitation, I nodded. "I was jealous of how easy it was for you."

His brow furrowed. "My brother isn't jealous of me."

"Isn't he?" I shrugged. "Look at the lengths his kids went to just to spend a single evening with you. He probably doesn't know how to be more like you any more than you know how to be like him."

It was like watching a wall lock into place behind his eyes. "I don't want to be like Barrett. He's cold and hard and impossible to soften."

"And he's respected," I said quietly. "Admired. Taken seriously."

The hard muscle in Griffin's jaw twitched as he gritted his teeth.

I dropped my eyes, stomach fluttering nervously at the change in subject. Anytime we'd tiptoed into the harder things, they were always mine. But seeing him yesterday, facing off with his brother, I saw something in Griffin's face that was entirely foreign.

Intimidation. The thought of this larger-than-life man being intimidated by anyone was impossible to reconcile, but it was there all the same.

Only until his brother requested that I leave the room; then there was a pulse of anger, of possession—like the release of a flash-bang into the enclosed space, momentarily disorienting me with the painful brightness and the staggering echo. It was the mention of me that brought Griffin back into himself, with the straightening of the shoulders and the puffing of his chest.

Not for the first time since we'd started whatever this was, I desperately wanted to pry back the layers of this man. If he'd let me, of course.

It seemed at every turn, this thing with Griffin was destined to challenge me. Force moments of bravery where before I might have hidden from the hard—allowing the thoughts of what could go wrong to dissuade me from acting.

I walked closer to him and pulled my phone from my back pocket, clicking on a link that I'd saved, and turned the screen around so he could see it. Confusion bent his brow as he carefully took the phone from my hand to bring it closer to his face. His mouth went slack with shock.

"What is this?"

I sucked in a breath, letting my shoulders rise and fall in a helpless shrug. "Figured you could let someone else push the rock up the hill for a little bit."

His eyes were fierce and bright when he tore them from the phone screen, locking onto mine for a breathless moment. "How did they get these pictures?"

I gently eased the phone out of his grasp and smiled at the headline of the article. Griffin curled his hands around my hips and stood behind me, resting his chin on the top of my head while I scrolled through the article, stopping at a picture of Griffin crouching in front of the dunk tank. In this one, he was surrounded by a group of first graders from the elementary school. His shirt was soaked from a recent trip into the tank, his smile wide and happy as the kids held up his number on their hands.

Underneath that one was a shot I'd snapped while he took a selfie with a tiny elderly woman who lived down the street from me. Her wrinkled hand cupped his face while she grinned, and the picture caught Griffin midlaugh.

The article talked about his appearance in a small town north of Denver, where he'd been spotted helping with various fundraising efforts for the local library. The last line made my eyes gloss over, and I carefully highlighted it, making sure he took the time to read it.

> Denver may have signed the younger King for much-needed power on the D-line, but from the looks of things, his superhero presence is being felt in far greater places than on the football field, making this one of the best roster moves we've seen in a while. Welcome to Colorado, Griffin. We hope you stay for a long time.

"It was you," he murmured. After I managed a short nod, throat tight and my eyes still filled with helpless tears, Griffin wrapped his arms around my waist and ducked his nose into my hair for a long inhale. "I think you're too good for me, birdy."

Slowly, I turned in his arms and cradled his jaw with my hand. "Says who?" His brow pinched briefly, but I laid my finger over his lips before he could answer. "I see you, Griffin. Not what people say about you or what you used to be. I see *you*, and I have never respected anyone in my life more."

His eyes held mine, and the thick line of his throat worked on a swallow. "I see you, too, Ruby Tate."

A soft, warm feeling spread through my chest—something good and wonderful and undeniably bittersweet. Was that the thing I'd been missing all this time? Not the sex or the affection or sharp snap of desire. It was that. Being known by someone intimately and trusting that they liked what they saw enough to stay. That was it, wasn't it?

Fear came in right on the heels of allowing myself to ask that question. Fear of losing it. Fear of losing him, even though I'd been the one to set the rules that kept us safe.

Don't fall in love with me, I'd told him. And there I stood, perilously close to doing exactly that.

"I know you do," I whispered.

There was more to be said, and admissions danced on the tip of my tongue, but I swallowed them down. Griffin rested his forehead on mine and breathed out, curling an arm around my shoulders as I tightened my grip on his shirt.

"Do I get a kiss for my birthday?" he asked, voice a pleased, deep grumble. His nose nudged mine, and with that simple question, the mood lightened in a heartbeat.

I nodded, pulling my head back to smile up at him. He hummed, tracing his thumb under my bottom lip. "Good girl."

A delicate shiver racked my frame, and his mouth widened in a grin. Before he could tease me about a praise kink—Lord, what straight-A student didn't have one of those—I pushed up on the balls of my feet and sealed my mouth over his. He took control of the kiss immediately, angling my head with a simple press of his hand under my jaw, his tongue slicking over mine as he let out a low, decadent groan.

Griffin pulled back, sneaking one more quick kiss, laughing quietly when my mouth followed his. "A kiss and some good press. Any other birthday surprises, baby?"

I pushed a smile onto my face and adopted a light tone. "I thought of asking you to give me a step-by-step tutorial in fellatio." I laid my hand carefully on his chest, and the flare of heat in his eyes melted every bit of tension I'd been holding in my body. "I'm a very good student," I whispered, giving an innocent flutter of my eyelashes.

"Yeah?" he murmured. "Feeling eager, are you?"

"A little. Though I'm not sure my gag reflex is adequately prepared. You're quite the overachiever in the size department," I said. After a low chuckle, Griffin leaned down and placed a light kiss across my lips, and my eyes fell closed.

"You are so good for my ego, birdy." His hand, which had been resting on my backside, snapped against my leggings in a sharp smack. "Let's finish cleaning up first; then we can talk about who owes who the next orgasm."

"Oh hell yeah, I'm right on time," Marcus crowed from the doorway. "Who's giving out orgasms?"

Griffin rolled his eyes. "You have the worst timing known to man."

Marcus held up his hands, each clutching an expensive-looking bottle of amber-colored alcohol. "On the contrary, I was blessed with a sixth sense of when my presence is absolutely vital."

Griffin gave a wry quirk to his eyebrow and backed away. I tried not to pout. With an amused tilt to his mouth, he turned to face his friend. "I thought you were Lauren's problem now."

Marcus sighed happily. "I am. She doesn't know it yet, but she's never getting rid of me."

"Oh boy," I muttered. "Can't wait to see how that plays out. She said she's never getting married again."

Marcus set the bottles down onto the island. "Who said anything about getting married? I'll just travel up here weekly to slake her unquenchable sexual desires. That woman can use me for the rest of her life if she wants to."

Griffin and I traded a look. "What does she do to you, exactly?" I asked cautiously.

Marcus patted my head. "Nothing I can talk about in polite company, birdy."

"Hey, that's my nickname for her." Griffin sounded so annoyed that I couldn't help but smile.

Marcus ignored him, tapping out a message and then tucking his phone away. "We have two hours, buddy."

"Before what?"

"Before your birthday party," Marcus replied. "A bunch of the guys are coming up. You told me I could invite them."

Griffin's eyes pinched shut. "Fucking fuck, I didn't think you'd actually do it."

"Oh yeah. DJ should be here in about an hour." He spread his hands out, narrowing his eyes as he stared into the family room. "We move those couches to the side, get rid of the coffee table, there's plenty of room for dancing."

"What? No. No DJ. No dance party. If you turn Steven's house into a club, he'll never forgive you."

"Please. This entire trip is an exercise in how far we can push that man before he finally drags his ass here from LA to stop us."

"I don't know," Griffin hedged. "I heard stories about that party you threw after the big game last year."

"Fucking epic," he said. "It won't be nearly that big. About half a dozen guys from the team." Then he grimaced. "And a couple girls."

"Marcus."

He held up his hands. "Girlfriends. A fiancée. Maybe even a wife. How crazy can the party get if we have a wife here?"

"But if *they* bring friends?" Griffin asked.

"I cannot control their social circles, mister."

Griffin muttered something under his breath, then pinched his nose. A smile lifted the corner of my mouth. Sometimes there really was no other alternative for a moment of spiraling loss of control. It was kinda nice to see it be him every once in a while.

Marcus held up one of the bottles by his face, then snapped a picture with his free hand, tongue hanging out. "I'll text Steven that right after the party starts." After setting down the bottle, he put his hands on his hips and turned a shrewd eye in my direction. "You're not wearing that for his birthday party, Ruby. We can do better."

I huffed, smoothing my shirt self-consciously. "Well, I didn't know I was coming to a party, Marcus. I came to work out."

"Oh, you'll get a workout," he promised. "You should see his dance moves once he gets a few shots in him." He tapped his wrist. "Clock's a-ticking. You have a few hours before the party's really going. Me and your man here will finish cleaning up, and I expect a full Cinderella moment when you come back."

Griffin gave me a searching look. "Is this okay? It'll be loud. And people-y."

The idea of walking alone into a party full of football players was normally the kind of thing that would make me lock myself in my room. It *would* be loud. And not just people-y, but big, athletic, confident, attractive people.

A whimper threatened to claw up my throat. And not the good kind, like when he'd had his hand between my legs.

He took a step closer, effectively blocking Marcus. "I can tell him no," he said, eyes on mine and voice low with intent. "We can watch the new version of *Emma* instead. I can't imagine it topping the Gwyneth version, but . . ."

Marcus, though he was out of my sight line, snorted loudly. "Yeah right. She was born for that role."

Griffin rounded on his friend. "Go away. You hijacked my vacation, and now you're stealing all my movies. Give me two fucking seconds to talk to her."

Miraculously, the man listened, although he grumbled the entire way out of the room.

Even though my stomach was tight with the sudden, blistering onset of nerves, and I was effectively waving goodbye to one of our last quiet nights before he left, there was an undeniable pull to want to prove to myself how far I'd come.

The fact that he would tell Marcus no—for me—triggered a rush of anticipation so thick that my heart gave an uneven thump.

"I'll be back later," I told him. "Don't have too much fun without me."

Chapter Twenty-Three

GRIFFIN

What a dumbass I was.

In hindsight, everything was perfectly clear. That was the horrible part of being able to recognize our mistakes after we'd made them.

It was all cumulative, of course. Each day of the last couple weeks was a small, seemingly insignificant building block to this moment. The party was in full swing when Ruby walked back in, and even though I'd plotted Marcus's demise several times while he helped me clean up the house, I couldn't fault any of the steps that had led us here.

The music was good—loud and sexy and throbbing through the center of my chest. The drinks were delicious, the laughter easy, as was the conversation. A bunch of the players were new to me, but everyone was kind and friendly, and I felt myself settle into the rhythm of this unwanted celebration.

The doors opened, and I swear to every deity in existence, there was a fucking spotlight—thick bright light aimed at the entrance—when she walked in.

Her eyes skimmed the crowd, anxiously looking for me, and I ducked past one of our linemen, unable to tear my gaze off her, soaking in the last of the dresses I'd bought for her. The unbearable pressure on my ribs didn't make any sense, but I decided I didn't care.

It was a white lace number, molded to her upper body and flaring out at her waist, the hem stopping at her upper thighs. The tiny black bow at the top of the neck made her look so prim and proper that my mouth watered because I couldn't help but wonder what she had on underneath. The base of the dress was a nude-colored slip, giving the illusion that she was naked under the white lace.

On her feet were wicked-looking black heels, and I blew out a slow breath as I eased through the crowd. The nerves on her face intensified when she couldn't find me in the kitchen, and for a moment, I thought she might back out of the house . . . but then she turned and saw me, a smile breaking open over her face as I approached.

A more polite man might have stopped at a respectable distance, but I wasn't polite.

Wasn't even close to anything of the sort. The ticking clock over our time left together, the music making my pulse throb, the sight of her in that dress, had me feeling something far more uncivilized.

I didn't say a word, simply stepped up against her, my hands skating down the length of her arms until our fingers wove together, and I dropped my nose into the crown of her hair and inhaled—deep and greedy.

"Happy birthday to me," I growled by her ear as I gathered her close against my chest. "You look incredible."

Ruby lifted her head, eyes wide in her face. Fuck, why did they look like that? Bigger. Sparklier. Like she wanted to eat me alive.

The feeling was very, very mutual.

Her lashes were darker than normal. Thicker too. There was something slick and shiny on her lips, and I dragged my thumb along the bottom edge. "You look beautiful tonight, Ruby Tate."

It was her eyes that smiled, her lips opening on a shaky exhale. "You told me to save this for a special occasion, didn't you?"

I grinned. "I can't believe I ever said you were a terrible student." Leaning down, I ran the edge of my nose against hers, placing a featherlight kiss against her lips. She tasted like cherries, and I hummed as I pulled away. "Want some cake?" I asked. "It's chocolate with raspberry filling."

"Maybe one piece," she said, eyes locking on my mouth. "I think I can allow for a few vices tonight."

It took everything in me not to sling her over my shoulder and march to the bedroom. I closed my eyes as I fumbled for restraint in a very public place, folded my fingers around hers, and led her into the kitchen. The introductions were quick and overwhelming, Ruby's eyes wide as I ran through everyone who was there. For as nervous as she'd looked walking in the door, those nerves didn't last long. After a few minutes, Ruby was chatting with a few of the wives, shyly catching my eye when one of them asked how long we'd been dating.

"We're . . . friends," she said, her fingers squeezing mine under the table, where I'd refused to let her go. She was eating her cake with one hand.

Leticia, one of the linemen's wives, eyed us. "Mm-hmm. I can see that. My husband and I were friends like that once too."

"Ruby used to live behind me when we were kids," I said. "She had a crush on my brother."

Leticia's eyebrows popped up. "Did she, now?"

"What can I say? I had terrible taste when I was younger," Ruby said. She licked a bit of chocolate frosting off her lip and caught my eye. "Now I actually know what—and who—is good for me."

There was no chance in hell I was letting this woman go tonight. Careless of who might see us or what they'd think, I leaned forward and snagged her mouth in a quick, searing kiss. "Careful, baby, I'll think you're staking a claim," I murmured against her lips.

Ruby exhaled a quiet laugh, her eyes falling shut while her forehead rested against mine. Everything about her made my head spin, and I didn't want it to stop. There was a disbelieving part of me still searching for a foothold in logic. Why was it like this? Why her? What was it about the two of us together that felt so fucking good?

For the first time in my life, the sense of rightness was unshakable, and that was the scariest thing imaginable. Showing her parts of myself that no one else saw, knowing that she appreciated them, felt like hanging myself off the edge of a cliff, and Ruby was the one capable of either tossing me off the side or helping me up and over into safety.

Maybe it was this short window of time. The ticking of a clock that I could practically hear in the background as I watched her pull away, cheeks flushed from our public display of affection. Leticia said something that made her laugh, and all I could hear was the roaring in my ears.

It sounded like her name. How long would it feel like this after she walked away?

After she returned to the cocoon she'd built, safely kept away from hurt. From hurting anyone else. The blood pumped quick and hot through my veins the longer I thought about it, about her alone every night, when I wouldn't be part of her life. Alone, because that was how she wanted it.

Leticia left the table, and Ruby pushed the plate away, only a few bites of the cake left. "I'm done," she proclaimed. "That half a piece will probably keep me up all night."

Staring at her profile, I felt my heart churn restlessly, a persistent itch at the back of my mind urging me to do something important. My mind raced over the things she'd told me, shifting through confessions like a deck of cards, and when the thumping pulse of the music broke through my thoughts, I found myself laser sharp with focus. I shifted, untangling my hand from hers so I could angle her chair toward me. I widened my legs around her chair and tugged her seat forward.

Her eyes widened, and I slid my hands along the silky-smooth skin on her thighs.

"Dance with me?" I asked, fingers trailing along the edge of her knees.

Ruby's chest rose and fell in sharp breaths, and her lips curled, in a sweet smile. "I'd love to."

Shifting my grip so that both of her hands were in one of mine, I stood and led her into the middle of the room, where the group of people dancing shifted to accommodate us. No one looked twice at us when I turned and settled Ruby's hands onto my chest. Her fingers danced up and over my shoulders, her eyes fixed on mine, her cheeks slightly flushed as I grinned down at her.

We began to move, one of my thighs slotted between hers as I guided the movement of her hips. Her smile was radiant in the dark room, and my hands moved restlessly over her body, the lithe line of her back impossible to resist as I banded an arm around her to drag her closer while the throbbing beat had our hips shifting back and forth.

Gripping her hand, I spun Ruby out and back, and her laughter, sweet and happy, caught somewhere under my ribs, and I wished I could fucking bottle it. We swayed for a few moments, her hands sliding over my chest, her gray eyes hazy as she surrendered to the music.

She was too far away. I slid my arm around her waist, anchoring her tight to my body while we danced. Her breasts were firm and warm against my front, and my throat went dry as I imagined what they'd look like. What they'd taste like under my tongue.

Sweet. She'd be so fucking sweet.

There was no resisting this woman, not for any reason that any sane, logical person could conjure, and I banished the slightest hint of it while we rolled together to the driving beat.

It didn't matter if I got hurt or was left feeling even the slightest pinch of disappointment, because Ruby knowing I wanted her was probably the most important thing I'd do for the rest of my life. The thought that she might ever doubt it made me want to scream.

I plucked one hand off my chest and twirled her around so that her back was against my front, and I wrapped an arm around her shoulders while I rolled my hips against her backside. My other hand curled tight around her hip, and I almost groaned when she arched her ass against my very prominent hard-on.

The fact that this woman had ever felt like she needed my help was fucking laughable. My hand, anchored on her hip, dipped lower, gathering the material of her skirt until my fingertips brushed the firm, warm skin on her thigh. She dropped her head back onto my chest, and I dipped down to speak next to her ear.

"You in this dress should be fucking illegal, birdy," I growled, licking along the edge of her ear. "Got me thinking about what's underneath it."

Her shaky sigh was noticeable only because of my arm banded around her frame, and from my mouth trailing along her temple, the pulled-back curls tickling my cheek. Ruby turned her head slightly, her hand clutching my arm as she arched her back.

With her big, sweet eyes aimed up at me, the trust I saw there was enough to break my heart. Then she licked her lips, slow and intentional, rolling up on her tiptoes as she turned in my arms. I clutched her backside as she tugged my head down toward her mouth.

"Nothing," she whispered, her lips brushing the shell of my ear.

The hair on the back of my neck lifted, my skin buzzing with a bright shock of desire, something that spiraled quick and fast. In a slight daze, I pulled back to meet her eyes.

There was a question there. A wicked request that I was helpless to deny.

"You sure, baby?" I asked, my hand curling gently around her throat, using the slightest pressure of my thumb to tilt her chin up. She swallowed, and the flare of heat in her eyes with my hand around her like that almost brought me to my knees from the bone-cracking shot of lust.

Ruby's tongue darted out and she licked at her bottom lip, then nodded slowly.

I dropped my head down, rolling my forehead against hers. Her hands clutched at my biceps, and I struggled to think clearly. We were in a house full of people, and I couldn't find it in myself to care. "The party," I said weakly, one last grasp at sanity. "It's a full fucking house, Ruby."

Her hands cradled my jaw, easing me back so that her gaze met mine. "Then you better not scream too loud."

I exhaled a shocked laugh, and God, my heart felt seven sizes too big in my chest. It almost spilled over into something maudlin and ridiculous, where I just wrapped her in my arms and asked her to let me hold her all night instead. Almost had me asking if sex could wait and I could simply kiss her for hours and hours and hours.

"Please," she whispered.

My forehead fell against hers again. "Anything," I told her. With every molecule in my worthless body, I meant it. I'd give her anything I was capable of giving. All she had to do was ask.

Clutching her hand behind my back, I turned and started weaving through the group of people, occasionally smiling and nodding at some of my teammates as we passed. Marcus lifted his hand as he came into view, and as soon as he was within reach, I gripped his shirt and tugged him closer.

"Don't come looking for us, and if you turn down that music, I'll break every bone in your body."

He grinned, giving me a crisp salute. "You got it, birthday boy."

The very best thing about Steven's house was that once you passed the main bedroom and his office, then went past the gym, another hallway branched out, leading to the extra bedrooms. I'd chosen the one at the end because it had a large slider overlooking the backyard and I liked the view of the mountains as the sun rose.

The sound from the party faded, and as soon as Ruby cleared the doorway, I slammed it shut, locking it with a decisive click, crowding her against the hard surface as her chest heaved on deep, panting breaths.

Our kiss was brutal, my hands gripping her ass as she tried to fucking climb me where we stood. I boosted her up against the door, my tongue licking into her hot mouth as her legs wound around my waist. My hands worked under her dress, and I groaned into her mouth when I found that she was, in fact, wearing nothing underneath.

"You wicked, wicked girl," I whispered against her lips, my nose brushing hers as I skimmed my fingers along the bare curve of her ass. She dropped her head against the door, writhing in my arms as I teased her with soft brushes of my fingertips. "You've been thinking about this, haven't you?"

"Yes," she moaned, sweet and impatient. "Please, Griffin. Don't make me wait."

With one arm banded around her ass, I latched my mouth onto hers and whirled around to deposit her carefully onto the bed. She was light enough that I didn't need to set her down when I braced my knee on the mattress and lowered my weight over hers.

Ruby's hands fumbled with the buttons on my shirt, and I paused the kiss to help her. Once half the buttons were undone, I ripped the shirt off and tossed it onto the floor.

Her pupils dilated as she stared at my chest, her fingers dancing over the newly uncovered muscles. "Look at you," she whispered. "I don't understand how you're real."

I let her look her fill, flexing my arms as I pulled at the buckle on my belt. "You want me to prove it to you?" She chewed briefly on her bottom lip as she nodded, shifting her hips on the bed, which worked the hem of her skirt high enough that my mouth started watering. "Good, because I finally found what I want for my birthday."

Anchoring my hands easily around her ribs, I pushed her higher onto the bed, then slid my palms down her thighs, letting my fingers curl into the warm flesh there, pressing her legs open with a slight pressure on her knees.

"You tell me if you want to stop, okay?" I said, easing myself down between her legs. I kissed the inside of her thigh, draping one and then the other over my shoulders as she nodded jerkily. "I mean it, Ruby. Any time. At any point. We stop if you don't want any more."

She raised her chin. "What if you want to stop?"

My eyes closed briefly, and I let out a low, dangerous chuckle. "Oh, baby, I won't be stopping us." I rucked her skirt above her waist, making sure she could see my eyes as I lowered my mouth toward her. "I want this too much."

If this was my only night to have Ruby Tate in my bed, I was going to tear her world apart with nothing but my tongue and fingers and lips. I was going to rip down any reservations that made her feel less than or not sexy or not good enough.

"Happy birthday to me," I said against the warm skin of her inner thigh.

Before she could say anything else, I pressed my hand onto her trembling stomach and locked my gaze with hers as I licked straight up her center, groaning at the taste of her.

She clutched my hair in both hands and moaned so loud that goose bumps sprang up on my arms.

New life goal: find every sound that this woman could possibly make with my mouth between her legs. Fuck the Super Bowl—this was the only thing I wanted to win for the rest of my life on this earth.

Through sweet little rocking motions, Ruby worked herself against my mouth, and I found very quickly that she liked it when I used my fingers along with slow, tongue-heavy kisses. Her moans turned to choppy, rib-shaking, gasping breaths, and her hands were so tight in my hair that I had to pinch my eyes shut, my own hips rocking against the mattress to seek relief.

What made her break, though—mouth wide open on a silent scream, her back arched helplessly—was a simple twist of my wrist and press of my fingers, my tongue soft and slick against her.

I watched her ride it out, her ribs rising and falling on shocked gulps of air. Sitting up on my haunches, I wiped my mouth on the side of her thigh and pushed my pants and boxer briefs off.

She watched me hungrily, still catching her breath as I wedged my hand underneath her body to find her zipper. When it loosened, Ruby helped me wiggle the dress up her body. Every inch of skin that was uncovered sent blood rushing between my legs.

Her breasts were high and firm. No more than a small handful, they were so sweet and pretty, and I let my fingers ghost over the hard tips as she shyly eased the dress over the top of her head. With the dress gone, her hair fell around her shoulders, and even after the muscle-melting relief of her orgasm, the nerves clearly returned in the pinch of her brow and in the way she bit down on her bottom lip.

I was quiet at first, gaze following the path of my hands over her body. The curve of her ribs, the dip in her belly, and the perfect little circle of her belly button. My hands skimmed the skin over her hips, and I let my fingers spread wide as I pushed them back up her midsection, my thumbs brushing gently at the bottom curve of her breasts.

Her scar was a long, thin line, and I let my fingers trace that, too, holding her eyes while I sat between her legs and took in the absolute fucking glory of her naked body.

"You're perfect," I whispered, spreading my hand over her chest, my fingers brushing over the curves of each breast. Ruby sucked in a sharp breath, sliding her hands up my arms to tug me down over her.

Our kisses weren't as rushed and furious as when we'd first come into the room. They were sweet and slow, luxuriating in each brush of her tongue on mine. A hundred years. I could kiss this woman for a hundred years, and it wouldn't be enough. A million days, a billion hours. Nothing short of forever felt like enough, and I found myself clutching her against me with a trembling sort of possessiveness that rocked me to my core. Her hands coasted over my shoulders as I rolled my hips between hers, allowing my hardness to drive her mindless again as I teased her.

For the first time, there was a slight shadow of nerves over what I was supposed to do next. The urge to make this perfect for her had my breath sawing in and out of my lungs while we kissed endlessly.

And there was that too . . .

I didn't want this to end. I didn't want to leave. Didn't want to leave *her*, more specifically. It was the type of fear that had me kissing her harder, clutching her more tightly in my arms, like it might imprint this moment somewhere permanent.

Maybe this was what forever felt like. Where the wanting of forever began.

In kisses that could never be deep enough or long enough. In exploring her body and finding it perfect for me. In the unexpected ache coiling tighter and tighter and tighter in my chest.

It wasn't just sex, and I didn't think it was for her either. I couldn't wipe away my past any more than I could erase hers, but I could give her everything she'd ever wanted. Could make her feel sexy and cherished and wanted, because God, she was all those things to me.

Her hand reached down to grip me, exactly the way I'd shown her in the parking lot, and I rolled my forehead against hers, hissing through gritted teeth.

"Later," I told her, then sucked her bottom lip into my mouth as I pulled her hand off me. I reached over into the nightstand and sat back on my heels while I opened a condom packet with my teeth. She watched with huge eyes as I rolled it on. "This might hurt, baby. Do you want to be on top? That might be easier."

Immediately, she shook her head, hands curling around my back, tugging me back down on top of her. "No. No, I want you on me."

My heart was fucking hers, and there was no way I could say it out loud. It was the one thing she'd made me promise, wasn't it? The only promise I'd broken.

I nodded, kissing her deeply again. Her thigh pressed high against my side, and I dipped my head down, pushing her breast up with my hand, licking a tight circle around the tip. She clutched my head and gasped.

I sucked the other one into my mouth, dragging my teeth over the hardened nipple. And oh, she liked that. Gently, I held her gaze and bit down on the bottom curve of her breast, sucking it into my mouth harder than I might have dared if my feelings were any less. It would leave a mark, and something primitive flared hot in my chest, roaring louder and louder to mark her more. To leave behind proof that I'd been here and that I'd had her, even if it was just once.

Ruby tugged me back up her chest, and I slanted my mouth over hers while she writhed helplessly underneath the weight of my body.

I took myself in hand and almost blacked out when I tried to press forward.

So hot. So very, impossibly tight.

I'd die. Right here, in between her legs. And I wanted it on my tombstone how I went out, because I'd never felt anything better than this.

She broke away from the kiss with a gasp. "Griffin," she moaned, wiggling her hips and trying to work me in farther.

"I know, sweetheart," I hissed, holding her still with a firm hand on her hip. "Let me do this, baby. I don't want to hurt you."

My hips rocked forward an inch. Then back.

In. Out. In and out again. Then again.

Each inch gained, I slid farther and farther into absolute heaven. Ruby couldn't stay still; she met my rhythm perfectly, working herself onto me as each shallow thrust brought me more fully inside.

The screaming impulse to snap my hips forward had me gritting my teeth, and that restless energy had me biting down on her bottom lip until she whimpered. My tongue licked into her mouth, my hands wrapped around her back to grip her shoulders for leverage.

Ruby wrenched her other hip up onto my side, widening her thighs, and I sank in, slick and effortless, like an anchor cutting through water, a groaning sound I'd never made before wrenched from the back of my throat. Helpless desire. Desperate wanting. A crude need to rut into her until we both blacked out from the force of what raced furiously through my veins.

I buried my head into the curve of her neck and felt the trembling of my hands as I held her tight. "You're so good."

We paused there, unmoving, as she acclimated. If I closed my eyes, it would be so easy to get lost in the slick, tight feel of her around me. My mouth nuzzled at her jaw, seeking her sweet lips, and Ruby sighed quietly as we kissed.

When the kisses turned sharper, fiercer, the licking of our tongues wilder, she rubbed her breasts against my chest. "Please, please, please," she chanted.

I propped my weight onto one elbow as I lifted up to watch her face while I slowly pulled back, pushed forward. Pulled back, then pushed forward. Her brow furrowed adorably at the steady drag of my body in and out of hers, and she bit down on her bottom lip when I ground against her when my hips met hers. Pulled back again, holding there until my pulse screamed, my body shook from the restraint it took to stay in place, teasing her that way.

She wriggled helplessly, and my eyes fluttered shut for a moment. When I opened them again, a flush was crawling up her neck into her cheeks.

"Tell me what you want, baby," I commanded. "I'll give it to you."

Eyes locked on mine, Ruby didn't even hesitate. "Harder."

She was perfect. So incredibly perfect. All the things I didn't know I wanted, and she was right fucking here for the taking.

"You sure?" I asked, tilting my head as I made a few shallow thrusts. She was already fluttering around me, her pulse visible at the base of her throat as she made a tortured keening noise.

"Griffin," she begged. "Please."

I gave my girl what she wanted. With a ruthless snap of my hips and a loud groan, I bottomed out in one thrust.

Heaven.

I'd never get over this. Never have anything better than her.

Ruby took everything I had for her, over and over and over, and with each pivot of my body, each roll of my hips, each rocking thrust that brought me against her again and again and again, she sobbed against my mouth as she told me it couldn't possibly get bigger, that it wasn't stopping, that it kept growing bigger and bigger.

She slapped a hand over her mouth to stem the sounds, and when I slid my hand down between her legs and pressed with my thumb, her back snapped in a powerful arch, and Ruby let out a muffled scream behind her fingers, tears streaking down her temples.

My own orgasm crashed over me, a blistering squeeze of painful pleasure that started at the base of my spine and split out in a wide burst. I yanked her hand away from her lips and grunted into her mouth as we kissed through it.

I didn't want us losing those noises because we were afraid of someone hearing; I wanted to take hers and give her my own. I wanted the whole fucking world to know that we were doing this to each other, because there was no way anyone else had ever experienced sex quite like this.

I hadn't, at least.

The truth of that—of how she'd changed me down to my marrow, carving her name somewhere deep and vital where I'd never be able to remove it—had me gathering her into my arms while we kissed in the dark.

And I knew, even as I felt the wild crash of her heart against me, I was never going to have her in the way I wanted.

Chapter Twenty-Four

RUBY

Fucking oxytocin.

Eventually, I'd blame that for everything. For the fact that waking up with my face pressed into the broad expanse of his chest had me imagining that this was heaven on earth. For the way his arm banded around my back, holding me against his side, was the most poignant and bittersweet of anchors.

Not the kind of anchor weighing me down, but keeping me in a safe, warm place, making sure I didn't float away into nothing. He was my gravity, and there was no denying it anymore.

After a brief trip into the bathroom to pee and clean up (no one needed a UTI), Griffin tugged me right back toward the bed. There was no time to worry about where I'd sleep or what might happen, because he slipped one of his T-shirts over my head and pulled me straight into his side with a contented grunt.

Sleeping next to him was like having a giant purring cat as my own personal pillow. He snored lightly, and I lay there in the weak predawn light, studying the line of his profile as my rib cage squeezed uncomfortably.

He smelled so good. Was so warm and solid. My hand was still settled on his stomach, where it rose and fell with his steady breaths. It said a lot, really, that my first thoughts after waking weren't about the sex itself, though that nipped straight on the heels of my more innocent musings.

Because the sex . . . oh, the sex.

World-scrambling, off-the-charts, I-might-never-walk-normal-again sex.

That was the real reason I was lying there, staring all moon-eyed at the line of his jaw and the curve of his lips and the stubble on his chin, and wondering beyond those physical features, why he was alone after all these years.

It didn't make sense, knowing the kind of man he was and how thoroughly he'd taken care of me. Taken care of me in ways that I hadn't even been able to articulate.

Careful not to wake him, I raised my hand and skimmed it lightly over the line of his bottom lip. My eyes burned with a sudden press of unshed tears because of how badly I wanted to kiss him again.

It was the oxytocin, I told myself. That powerful little chemical released in a sharp spike during orgasm, but more importantly, released during moments of affection. Even small ones like this. One of the things I'd found when I researched sex was how often people confused the flood of oxytocin with real, deep feelings about the person who'd unleashed it.

There was a natural order to that—viewing Griffin as a symbol of these new things I'd never felt before. Even if it seemed impossible now, I might have felt this with anyone.

Liar.

Filthy little liar who lies to herself.

The voice ripped through my head before I could stop it, and I slammed my eyes shut. In the wake of that whispered warning, I had a vicious memory of my parents sitting by my hospital bed with pinched faces, the perpetual exhaustion stamped on their features after years of worrying about me.

It didn't take much, with powerful chemicals seeping through all the cracks and crevices of my brain, to slide Griffin into that memory and feel the clench of my chest in return. To imagine him worrying and tired and parked in a hospital chair while I struggled to breathe easily or fought some simple infection that shouldn't sideline a woman of my age.

A tear slid down the side of my nose before I could stop it, and I wiped it away before it dropped to his chest.

I wouldn't feel this with anyone. But neither would I sentence him to living out a bleak future with a murky end date. Loss came in dozens of ways when you experienced what I had. Loss of a future. Loss of possibilities. Loss of physical strength and emotional bandwidth. Maybe I hadn't handled all those different kinds of loss perfectly, but neither would I allow selfishness to color my decision-making.

It was the cold truth of logic, something I could easily apply to this situation with the sleeping man at my side. I refused to see him be hurt. To see him sad. Letting him walk away without knowing how easily I'd fallen for him was the best gift I could give.

He slept on while I eased out of his embrace, and I breathed out slowly as I sat on the edge of the bed and speared my hands into my hair. My legs were bare, and I grimaced when I realized that I wasn't entirely sure where my underwear was.

I froze.

"Fucking oxytocin," I hissed quietly. I hadn't worn underwear. Lauren, in her infinite wisdom, had told me to show up with as few barriers as possible. Sure enough, we didn't have many. Not even a houseful of people, as it turns out. My face was hot as I remembered how his hands had played with the hem of my dress on the dance floor.

Past Me—driven by that very powerful, almost magical chemical force—had made some really questionable decisions.

Not that I was shaming myself for wanting sex with him. That would've been stupid and steeped in rampant misogyny, but it was more about doing things that weren't like me.

They were like me, though. It was me who had shown up at his party. Me who'd let him kiss me at the table, in plain view of everyone there. Me who'd slipped easily into his arms.

It was me . . . with Griffin. A side of myself I'd never known before, and damn it, I liked that version of Ruby Tate.

With a sigh, I tiptoed across the room and picked through the pile of clothes nearest the foot of the bed, exhaling in relief when I found my dress. Before I slipped his shirt off, I brought the neck up to my nose and inhaled deeply, my eyes rolling shut.

God, it wasn't fair.

When it was lying in a pile on the floor and I'd tugged my dress into place, I eyed that shirt briefly, wondering if I could steal it without him noticing. Just, you know, sleep in it every night until the scent disappeared.

I'd almost reached down to grab it when he shifted on the bed, emitting a low groan that had my thighs pressing together.

"No," he moaned in a raspy voice. "Why are you getting dressed? Come back into bed, birdy."

Pasting a small smile on my face, I turned. "I have to work today."

Griffin stretched his arms over his head, and my mouth watered at the way the sheets pooled around his waist. There was a distinct bulge underneath the sheet, and I tore my eyes away, blowing out a short, forceful puff of air.

"Work is overrated," he said, leaning up against the headboard and devouring me with those I'm-going-to-eat-you-alive eyes. "I think you should call in sick since it's my last day."

At the reminder, my eyes slammed shut. "What time do you have to be in Denver?"

"Doesn't matter too much," he answered. "Steven said his cleaners will get here around five, so I just need to be packed up before then.

Come on, birdy. Let's play hooky, and we can have a Jane Austen marathon. I'll even let you paint my picture again." He grinned—crooked and playful and so freaking attractive that I felt like bursting into tears.

A thick sob threatened to crawl up my throat, but I swallowed it down.

The suggestion was a nice one. A really nice one. But when it played out in my head, all I felt was sick to my stomach. Like playing house when I damn well knew that nothing was going to come from it.

Nothing was going to come from this. From us. The more I forgot that, the worse it would be.

His phone dinged on the nightstand, and he made a growling sound under his breath when he read the text. "Fucking Steven," he muttered.

"Something wrong?"

Griffin smacked his head against the headboard in a brief show of frustration, his jaw clearly tight. "He wants me at the facilities at ten. Shit. I need to hop in the shower. Marketing department wants me to do some social media stuff, and I had . . . I had something I wanted to do before I left."

"Oh." I wrung my hands together and fought the clammy sensation of panic as it dug its claws into my skin. This was it, then. My entire life felt like it had been upended, someone sneaking in when I wasn't looking and ransacking the perfect order of things. I'd say goodbye to him and try to figure out how to pick up the pieces.

Naive. So very, very naive.

Increasing the distance between our bodies wasn't erasing the powerful grip that the sex chemicals had on my brain. It was a helplessness that made me imagine myself getting sucked into a dangerous current in a dark-blue ocean. The kind that looked smooth and straight and was incredibly dangerous. My head was hardly above water, and no matter how hard I thrashed to get free, the allure of this man snaked me right back in, like a hook to my waist.

I gritted my teeth and pulled up my metaphorical big-girl panties.

It was just sex, and I was capable of leaving it that way. I'd better be, since the entire arrangement was my idea anyway. "Maybe that's for the best," I told him. "I have to get home and let Bruiser out."

Griffin nodded, his eyes flitting over my face. My back teeth were clenched tight, and the beginnings of a headache bloomed behind my eyes as I struggled to decide what a more experienced woman would say in a situation such as this. Someone who wasn't naive. Someone who was confident and clear about the stakes we'd laid at the beginning of all this. Someone who promised that the feelings would stay safe and out of harm's way.

"Last night was fun," I told him lightly. The words felt like lead coming out, reducing our incredible night to something so small and insignificant. Over and over, he'd reminded me that fun was what we had. Fun was what he could offer. But saying it felt like the worst sort of betrayal to how he'd actually made me feel. To what he'd become in my life. "Thank you."

Griffin's chin dropped to his chest, a muscle jumping in his jaw, and for a moment, I worried that I'd offended him.

"Fun," he said quietly. When he looked up, I almost lost my breath at the intensity I saw there.

Clutching the sheet around his waist, he prowled off the bed and strode toward me, not stopping until he was towering over me. Without the help of my heels, I had to tip my face up to look at him. At this proximity, the clean, spicy scent of his skin had my head swimming, and I fought the urge to sway into his chest, press my nose against his sternum and just breathe.

"That wasn't fun," he said in a low, dangerous voice.

I blinked a few times, my throat going tight. "It wasn't?"

His hand shot out and gripped the back of my neck, and the sheer possessiveness of it yanked the breath from my lungs. He dipped his head down, speaking against my mouth. "That was fucking phenomenal."

When he didn't kiss me, I exhaled shakily. Unmoving, he held there, his eyes locked on mine. "Don't think it's always like that, baby. Because I promise you, it's not."

My chest felt like it was going to explode, and I struggled to pull in a full breath. There was no possible way he could know what those words did to me, how thoroughly they wrecked me. Hollowed out the space between my ribs until the beat of my heart echoed against absolutely nothing.

Somehow, I managed a nod, my nose brushing against his as a tear slid down my cheek.

Not kissing him felt like a crime, so I cradled his jaw and pushed up on the balls of my feet to seal my mouth over his in a possessive kiss that came from somewhere deep inside me, someplace secret I'd never tapped into before this man. His hand tightened on the back of my neck, his jaw opening as he brushed his tongue over mine and let out a small, pleased grunt.

My arms tightened around his neck, and his arms banded around my waist to lift me up against his chest. I didn't even dare stop to breathe, thankful for the way he shared oxygen with me during that endless, searing, world-altering kiss.

He broke his mouth away from mine, resting his forehead against my own before carefully setting me back down. Griffin licked his bottom lip while he stared at me.

"You're right," I told him. "It wasn't fun. It was . . . it was perfect, Griffin. You were exactly what I needed."

For the briefest moment, there was a breathless sort of heartbreak in his eyes. I set my hand on my stomach and stared down at the ground, unable to look him in the face for much longer.

No.

There was no shying away from this.

No shying away from him and how fucking hard this was.

When I looked up, he looked like Griffin again. There was no lingering sadness, no unspoken thing, just a cocky curl to his delicious lips. With his mussed, golden-brown hair and the endless expanse of skin on display, he looked like sin incarnate. Temptation that I'd never move past. Never get over.

"Thank you," I told him again, carefully setting my hand on his bare chest as I swallowed against a dry throat. "I don't think you understand how much this meant to me."

"Anything for you, birdy." He curled his fingers around mine and squeezed. Griffin's smile softened into something more genuine, and my pheromone-drenched brain captured it like a photograph. I wanted to frame it. Paint it. Put it somewhere as a permanent reminder that I was the one who made him smile like that.

After a thick beat of silence, he let go of my hand, and I cleared my throat. "Well, if I find myself watching football this fall, I know who to text if I have any questions."

Griffin's eyes bounced between mine. "I hope you do." Then he held up a hand. "Oh, hang on."

With a rueful grin that made my chest clench, Griffin quickly reached down to grab his boxer briefs and tugged them up his legs, then tossed the sheet aside before he jogged around to the other side of the room. For the record, I did not stare at his ass when this was happening. Not really. When I dragged my eyes up from . . . certain areas, I felt my stomach flutter.

There, on the large solid-wood dresser, was a small stack of books. He stared down at them in his hands for a second, his back expanding on a deep breath before he walked toward me again. His crooked smile was almost my undoing as he extended the library books in my direction.

"Read them all," he said proudly. "Does this mean I'm smart like you now?"

I exhaled quietly, too small to be considered a laugh. "Which was your favorite?"

The thick line of Griffin's throat worked on a swallow, his eyes intent on mine. "The one you recommended. The World War Two book."

My lips tilted in a pleased smile. "Really?"

He nodded. "Really. The legacy we leave behind is important." His brow furrowed slightly. "You left one hell of a stamp on me, birdy. I hope you know that."

"You did too," I whispered.

For a moment, I worried that my body would reject my brain's command to leave. Simply refuse. I worried that the chemicals still coursing through my blood would protest anything except crawling back into bed with him and letting the day pass without any thought of the repercussions.

We still have things to learn! those chemicals screamed. *We haven't felt sweet and slow. We haven't experienced what his skin is like in the shower. Or how it feels to be on top of him.*

We should have started sooner, I thought with a quick spike of my pulse. *If we'd started right away, we would have had two weeks to enjoy each other's company.*

That was the thing, though, wasn't it? It would be so easy to create a list a mile long of all the ways I still wanted Griffin. It would never end. Not unless I was the one to end it before anything soured. Or worse.

With one last smile in his direction, my feet moved. So did my legs. And with the distinct knowledge that I'd lied deeply to myself to believe that I could get through this unscathed, I walked out of the room, then out of the house and into my car, with a numb sort of disconnect I'd never felt before. Not even after my surgery, when my whole body felt like it belonged to someone else.

With that thought, in the safety of my quiet car, I sank my head into my hands and cried.

Chapter Twenty-Five

Ruby

Bruiser was judging me. I was sure of it.

"Quit looking at me like that," I told him. His ears perked up when I ate another small mouthful of ice cream. "Yeah right, like I'm sharing with you. It's just a TV show, Bruiser. Millions of people watch this every day, all right? Concerned citizens who want to know the goings-on in the professional sports world."

He set his head down on his paws and groaned dramatically.

The commercial break ended, and I unmuted the TV. "If you've been living under a rock, welcome to the shock of the week coming out of the NFL. Griffin King—all pro-defensive end—signed a two-year, thirty-two-million-dollar deal in Denver." The commentator raised her eyebrows, looking knowingly at her cohost. "There were rumblings of this, of course. He was seen in Colorado before he signed his contract, but no one seemed to take that as a sure thing, did they?"

The other suit at the desk shook his head. "No. I talked to multiple sources who did not see this coming before Griffin signed his contract. Besides the eye-popping number on that bottom line—which brings him very close to being the highest-paid defensive end in league history—there are lots of rumblings throughout the league that Griffin really did take this deal to avoid going up against big brother a couple times a year in a divisional matchup."

His cohost smiled. "Can you imagine what holidays are like at the King house? I hope someone brings a referee to Christmas dinner."

"If I were to place a bet, I think I'd still put my money on Ice Man."

She made a disbelieving noise. "I don't know. Did you see him signing that contract? He was not the outgoing jokester we're used to seeing in Griffin. That looks like a man on a mission if I've ever seen one."

With melting ice cream dripping off my spoon, I stared wide-eyed at the following clip of Griffin sitting at a sprawling desk with the Denver logo directly behind him. His arms flexed as he signed his contract, and the journalist was right. When he looked up into the camera afterward, there was a fierce determination in his eyes.

My chest fluttered when his lips tilted in a subdued, slightly crooked smile as he shook the team owner's hand. He was wearing a Denver shirt, and briefly, I wondered when he'd taken care of all this. The sight of his stubbled, hard jaw was jarring, and when I got an X-rated memory of him wiping his mouth against my thigh, I had to set the bowl of ice cream down lest I spill it all over the couch.

Bruiser whined at the bowl's proximity to his nose. I rolled my eyes. "Oh, fine, go ahead."

Like a masochist, I watched the rest of the segment as they worked their way through a highlight reel of Griffin's years in New York.

It would get better, right?

There would come a day when the sight of his sweaty arms and the tightly leashed violence he was capable of on the field wouldn't trigger a tsunami of dangerous butterflies. I swear, they showed him sacking a quarterback, scooping up the ball, and running it into the end zone, and I almost had a little orgasm.

I speared my hands through my hair, then fumbled with the remote to punch the power button.

"Enough," I hissed.

And I did pretty well staying away from *SportsCenter* after that. Sort of.

Any time Lauren saw me checking the sports section of the newspaper over the next week, I decided that I could retire early if I got a dollar for every concerned look she sent my way. When she tried to ask me if I needed to talk anything out, I realized just what a phenomenal coping mechanism denial is.

"Nope," I said forcefully. "I'm just fine."

"Yeah, you look it," she mused, setting her chin on her hand while I stamped due dates onto cards with a mighty vengeance. The *bam* echoed through the library. A woman perusing the romance section gave me a concerned look. "You know, we don't actually use those cards for anything anymore. Everything's digital."

Bam.

Bam.

Bam.

I fixed her with a glare. "I'm aware."

She smiled sweetly. "Feeling the need to get a little angry energy out?"

"Nope."

Bam.

"It's completely natural to feel an emotional connection to someone when you have great physical chemistry with them."

"I know, Lauren. It's just . . . the stupid chemicals in my brain, and they'll pass." *Bam.* "I can get the same high from cuddling a puppy."

She tilted her head. "Mmm, I don't think you can." Then she patted my arm. "When you're ready to talk about it, I'll be here."

My eyes burned for a moment, and I watched her walk off, my shoulders slumping. With a groan, I ditched the stamp and walked back into my office. The walls were bare where I'd pulled the framed renders of the butterfly garden and sculpture walk down. That made my eyes burn too.

It was hard to feel like my life was too quiet again. Too empty. Because it wasn't empty, but at the moment, it felt like it. Eventually, I'd have to watch machinery dig through the dirt and cut down trees, and things would change again. The feeling of loss always came in waves, and it was important not to fight the ebb and flow.

Wanting that land to become something important—and seeing it become something else—sure felt like another one of my failures this week. Something I had thought I was capable of achieving, a fingerprint I could leave behind.

You left one hell of a stamp on me, birdy.

My stomach pinched, just like it did whenever I thought of him, and I took a deep breath, whirling toward my desk.

I sat down and opened my laptop, eyes snagging briefly on the bench facing the weeping willow tree. No more conversations there, for anyone. Not big ones or little ones, or life-changing ones, like the one I'd had with Griffin. There was a heaviness in my chest, and I set my hand there, closed my eyes, and took a few deep breaths.

For so many years, feeling pressure there had caused a sharp spike of anxiety, wondering what was wrong, wondering if something invisible was happening that they wouldn't be able to fix. I'd count my pulse and catalog my symptoms and send a note to my doctor making sure I didn't need to go in.

This wasn't anything a doctor could fix. So I took another deep breath, reminded myself that I was fine and I was an adult who could handle the end of a casual relationship that was never meant to be anything more. The days would pass, and my life would continue, whether I participated or not. Griffin's life would pass on a bigger stage, with more eyes watching, and I knew he wasn't sitting around moping. Neither would I.

With a false display of bravado, I notched my chin up and got back to work.

◆ ◆ ◆

GRIFFIN

"Quit moping."

I glared at Marcus, feeding another football into the JUGS machine. It zipped through the spinning wheels and shot toward him. He caught it with ease, tossing it off to the side, where a Denver staff member caught it and added it back into the bin I was pulling from.

"I'm not moping," I managed through gritted teeth. "I'm here helping you, aren't I?"

He caught another one, part of his pre-workout routine to catch two hundred and fifty balls before he touched any weights. Normally, one of the training staff helped him, but I was done with weights already and had an hour to kill before I met with the defensive-coaching staff.

"Why don't you just go back there? It can't be that far of a drive from your new place."

An hour and forty-two minutes, depending on the time of day. But I kept that little tidbit right the hell in my own brain.

"Go back for what? To borrow some library books?"

My neck felt hot at the satisfied gleam in his eyes, because it was more of an admission than I'd meant to make.

"Sure," he said easily, tossing the next ball away and setting up for the next catch. "Or for sex. Can't imagine she'd kick your ass out."

"Oh sure, I'm gonna do just that." I mimicked his stupid voice. "'Sup, girl, you want to keep being my easy side piece when I'm bored?"

He pointed a football in my direction. "I do not sound like that, and that's not what you'd be doing. You don't have to go back for sex. Go for a walk. Watch a movie. Tell her you want to fucking date her. Whatever, man. She liked you too."

His words caused a tight clench in my throat. "It doesn't matter if she liked me or not. She won't let herself get in any deeper with someone."

Marcus sighed. "That doesn't make sense. Why not?"

I jerked my chin at the employee, some bright-eyed kid whose name I didn't know. "Can you give us a minute?"

He nodded easily. "Sure thing."

Marcus motioned for another ball, and I fed one into the machine. "She had a heart transplant a few years ago."

His head reared back and he dropped his hands. The ball zipped straight into his stomach, and he doubled over with a loud groan. "Fucking hell, that hurt."

I rolled my eyes. "You're supposed to catch it, asshole."

Marcus straightened, rubbing at his stomach. "You're serious? About Ruby?"

After a deep breath, I nodded. He walked over and flipped off the machine. The whirring sound disappeared, and as serious as I'd ever seen him, Marcus listened while I explained what had happened.

His eyes were huge. "And she could just . . . reject the heart at any time?"

"Seems like it," I said lightly. More than once in the past week and a half, I'd found myself sitting up in the middle of the night, researching heart transplant survival rates on my phone. "There's a guy in Europe right now, he's lived like . . . forty years. Longest of any heart transplant recipient. He had the same condition as Ruby, actually. Got his new heart at seventeen."

Marcus perked up. "That's good, right?"

"Yeah." I swallowed around the rock wedged in my throat, but the fucker wouldn't budge. "Yeah, that's good."

His face filled with understanding. "That's why you were helping her with the weights and the training. Help her stay healthy."

I nodded.

"And she doesn't want to be a burden to anyone because she knows what a heavy load it is to carry," he continued.

My eyes narrowed. "Since when are you emotionally intelligent?"

"Are you kidding? I'm so good at this shit. Reading people is like, my fourth-best skill in life."

"I don't think I want to ask your top three."

Helpful man that he was, Marcus ticked them off on his fingers. "Playing football. Throwing parties. And cunnilingus." He smacked me on the shoulder. "I can give you pointers on all of the above."

"Please don't."

He laughed. "I know what'll make you feel better."

"Do you?" I asked with a disbelieving tilt of my head.

"I do. Find me in the team film room after your meeting."

About an hour later—my meeting complete and my head finally shifting back to football, where it belonged—I wound through the maze of hallways until I found the primary film room. Whenever we met as a team, it would be in here. At the front of the room was a giant projection screen, with a podium off to the side. The walls were emblazoned with the Denver logo, and big, cushy stadium-style seats in a deep-blue leather filled the rest of the room. They were big enough for a lineman to fit comfortably, and when I walked in, about thirty guys were talking and laughing, picking seats while Marcus tried to get control of the room.

"All right," he yelled. "Pick a fucking seat and get comfy." My eyebrows popped up at his tone, and he winked in my direction. "This is important, assholes. It's come to my attention in the last few weeks that I may have missed out on a very important seduction technique." Everyone groaned, but he held his hands up to restore order. "Our newest beast on defense, Mr. Griffin King, is the reason I've become aware of this giant misstep, and as an homage to him, I think it's time to pay it forward and teach the rest of your single asses about it as well."

Confusion rumbled around the room, and an O-lineman seated to my right held up his fist for a tap. I did, crossing my arms over my chest, because fuck if I didn't know what was coming next.

He clicked a button on the remote, and the opening credits of *Pride & Prejudice* filled the screen. I closed my eyes and swiped a hand over my mouth while the room echoed with a chorus of "what the fuck" and "what is this?"

"I fucking love this movie," the guy to my right whispered.

In surprise, I glanced over at him. "You do?"

"Hell yeah, man. Chicks love a sensitive guy."

Marcus stuck two fingers in his mouth and whistled, the chatter cutting off immediately. "You're gonna watch and you're gonna love it," he instructed, eyes looking a little crazy as he glanced around the room. "Anyone who doesn't has to sit in the ice bath for thirty minutes."

About an hour later, every guy in the room was glued to the screen, and from his spot at the podium, Marcus held up his hands and waited for the right moment. "Now watch . . . watch what he does here."

Darcy extended his hand and grabbed Elizabeth's, and I heard someone whisper, "Oh fuck yeah, he did that."

When he walked away, flexing his hand out, the guys went wild.

My laugh was loud, and hell if it didn't feel good after ten days of feeling like I had concrete blocks tied to my lungs. In my pocket, my phone buzzed, and with a smile still on my face, I pulled it out.

Steven: Emailed you the documents you need to sign. Everything's all settled. Want me to take care of this for you?

Me: That would be great, thank you.

Steven: I'll pick up the check tomorrow. Might stop by your new place and throw a rager and drive your car around the state.

Me: Have at it, buddy. I'll give you the keys myself.

Steven: Oh, I think it's the lack of permission that makes it more fun.

Before tucking my phone away, I pulled in a short breath and tapped on my photo app. The selfie of me and Ruby filled the screen, and my chest ached with a fierce pinch. For a few more seconds, I stared at it—at the lines of her face, the delicate slope of her nose, the long lashes around her gray eyes, and the wisps of golden hair sliding across her face—then let the phone go dark, sliding it back into my pocket so I could pretend like I was fine.

Chapter Twenty-Six

Ruby

Three weeks later

The knock on my office door was tentative—which meant it wasn't Lauren—and with the phone wedged between my ear and my shoulder, I whirled in my chair and waved whoever it was inside.

"That sounds amazing, Mom. Where do you guys go ashore next?"

"Edinburgh. Did you see my pictures on Facebook? I just uploaded everything from our stops in Scotland and Wales." She pulled the phone away and said something to my dad in a muffled voice. "Your dad says hi."

I managed a smile, a headache stemming from the tension I was holding at the base of my neck. "I didn't see the pictures, no, but I'll go check. I've been staying off the internet as much as possible."

Social media wasn't my favorite thing in the world to begin with—I'd had to reset a forgotten password just to be able to follow my parents' trip—but now my internet was effectively trained to serve me everything about Griffin. I'd seen more gossip-column articles in the last month of my life than in the previous ten years combined. Everything from recaps of his outings in Denver with teammates to the ice cream he was spotted buying at an upscale grocery store near the mansion he'd bought in Cherry Creek—a $2 million home with seven bedrooms, and maybe he was looking to fill it with a family? I clicked out of that one quickly.

I blinked, realizing my mom was still chatting about things they'd seen.

One of our library trustees was in my office doorway, a manila folder in her grip, and I held up my hand to ask her to wait. She nodded.

"Mom, I have to go. Have fun in Edinburgh. Have a beer for me," I told her.

"I will, honey. You're taking all your medicine? Working out?"

"Every day," I promised. "Even started doing some strength training about a month ago."

"Good! That's wonderful. Not too much, though?"

"Hard to say. I'll be so bulked up when you get back home you may not even recognize me."

She sighed. "All right. I'll leave you alone. Love you, Ruby."

I rubbed wearily at my forehead, quietly chastising myself because it was her love that caused her to worry. My mom was probably doing the same thing, reminding herself that when I used humor to deflect, it was because I didn't really know what else to say. "Love you, too," I told her quietly.

I hung up and aimed a smile in Carol's direction. "Sorry about that. How can I help you, Carol? I didn't expect to see you today."

She held up the manila folder. "Have something for you. I almost waited until the trustee meeting next week, but I decided you deserved to see it first."

Carol was a successful real estate agent, and she'd worked in the Welling Springs area for the last fifteen years. The last time we spoke was when she broke the news about losing the land. This time, though, she looked substantially happier.

I stood, holding my hand out for the folder as I moved in front of my desk, a quick whirl of nerves hitting my stomach at the excited glimmer in her eyes. There was nothing written on the folder, and I should have waited until I was seated again before I opened it.

For a long moment, all I could do was stare at the innocuous black ink printed on the pristine white paper.

My breath caught in my throat. "What is this?" I whispered.

Carol didn't answer.

Tears filled my eyes, and I blinked furiously to clear them. There was a lot of legal jargon on the paper in front of me, but I recognized the outline of the land like I was looking in the mirror. "Carol, this says we own the land . . . How . . . how is this possible?"

She smiled. "Because we do."

My hands were tingling, and I blindly sank back onto the surface of my desk, thankful that it was there as my knees gave out. "How?"

She shrugged lightly. "I got a call last week from the developer's agent. Someone approached them and gave them an offer they couldn't resist. It took some time for the deal to close, but it's ours, Ruby."

Shock had my head spinning, and I laid a hand over my chest, the pounding of my heart mimicking the racing thoughts as they split out into a million directions.

Carol took a seat and pinned me with a mischievous grin. "Someone likes you an awful lot, Ruby Tate."

My head snapped up. "What makes you say that?"

"They had one stipulation for the transfer of the land," she said.

"What was it?"

She handed me another paper. It was thick, with another render on it, one that I'd never seen. The weeping willow was there, and in the background was the bench. But in front of it was a drawing of a sign.

Ruby Tate Gardens and Nature Preserve.

"What the fuck?" I breathed.

Carol coughed, patting her chest as she recovered quickly.

I pinched my eyes shut. "Sorry."

"Quite all right, dear. That's why I'm showing you now."

Suspicion took root, coiling up through the dirt and pushing up into the sun, but there was an almost violent urge to rip it out and not let it grow any further.

He wouldn't. Would he?

Even thinking it made me feel insane. Like my ego had grown ten sizes in the last month. I was still staring at the render long after Carol left and when Lauren wandered into my office. Numbly, I handed her the paper and chewed my bottom lip as I watched her eyes widen until they seemed to take up half her face.

"Ruby," she said slowly. "Did Griffin King spend millions of dollars to buy a chunk of land because he knew you wanted it?"

I covered my face with both hands. "I don't know. It feels crazy to even think it."

"Holy shit, you have a magic hoo-hah, don't you?"

Face flaming, I smacked her on the arm as she cackled. Kenny walked past my office, his cheeks suspiciously red, and I knew he'd heard her.

"I don't have a magic hoo-hah," I hissed. "Stop talking so loud."

"You did something right," she said, eyeing me with interest. "You told me it was really good, but I'm getting the distinct feeling that you're withholding some pertinent information."

Sitting was no good, not with all the energy crackling through my veins, so I paced my office restlessly while I thought. "There's no information on the deed about the sale itself, and I could probably do some digging at the city office, but I don't know if the closing documents are even filed yet."

She closed the folder and slid it across the surface of my desk. "Epic, Ruby. This is completely epic. I could call Marcus and see if he knows anything."

"No," I said instantly. "I don't want anyone else involved in this. And I didn't think you were talking to him anymore."

Lauren sighed airily. "Who was I kidding? I might even be willing to go on a real date with this one. He called me last night and gave me the best phone sex of my life; then he talked to me until I was almost asleep." Her cheeks were flushed pink, and I found myself smiling at how flustered she seemed. "He's still a total caveman, but . . . he's all right."

"I'm happy for you," I told her. She tried to wave it off, but I gripped her hand and wouldn't let her look away. "I really am."

Lauren cleared her throat primly. "Thank you. Not that anything is going to come from it, but . . . thank you." She arched an eyebrow. "I think you should just call Griffin and ask."

"No way. Because if it's not him, I look like a code-red-level stalker for assuming that it was."

"How many other people do you know who could afford this?"

I set my jaw, patently refusing to respond because we both knew what my answer would be.

"He won't think you're a stalker," she replied gently.

"Yes, he will. Think about all the crazy he has to deal with on a regular basis. I saw an article the other day about these twin girls— they're not even girls, I think they were twenty-two. *Hot* twenty-two-year-olds. They make like, six figures every month on that website, you know, the fan one." Lauren bit down on her smile but didn't interrupt. "They each got a tattoo of Griffin and his brother on their asses because they're so convinced that they're destined to marry them." I shook my head. "There's no way I'm entering into that particular competition."

"Okay, fine. Then you figure out if it's him before you call."

"How am I going to do that? What if the buyer showed up with a briefcase full of cash and there's no paper trail for who bought it?"

Lauren stood with a sigh and tapped the folder. "Then it's a good thing you're a librarian, huh? If we excel at anything, it's research." She paused before disappearing through the door. "And mind-blowing sex, apparently."

I dropped my head in my hands and sighed, my eyes still locked on the image of that sign. I'd done enough work on my mental health in the last five years to recognize exactly what held me back.

Fear. Absolute mind-numbing, action-paralyzing fear.

If it wasn't him, I would be disappointed.

And if it was . . .

My eyes pinched shut while I played through that. But I couldn't see a single outcome where we made sense, or where I'd ever want to risk bringing that man—with his big, wonderful, solid, stable, loving heart—into the life that I was destined to live.

But if it was him, then I had to thank him. It was the least I could do.

After a moment, I picked up my phone and called the city offices. "Hey, it's Ruby. I need you to do me a favor."

Chapter Twenty-Seven

GRIFFIN

A week later

I knew it was coming. Her first text came through just as I'd sprawled out on the new loungers in my backyard. Didn't even know what it said, and I was already smiling, heart turning over happily in my chest.

Ruby: Hi.

Me: Hi.

Three little text bubbles danced across the screen, and instead of leading her into conversation, I simply wedged a hand behind my head and waited to see how she was going to handle this.

Ruby: Are you busy right now?

Me: Terribly.

Ruby: Oh. We can talk later.

Biting down on my grin, I snapped a picture of my legs in the lounger, the pool and trees and grass beyond it. I sent it without anything else.

Ruby: Looks rough. I'm out of practice feeling sorry for you, but I might be able to conjure something up.

Me: You should. I'm all alone. No one to play Marco Polo with.

Ruby: You cheat at that game anyway, so I wouldn't play even if I was there.

Me: Just because you're the loudest swimmer in eastern Colorado doesn't make me a cheater. I have excellent senses, you know.

Ruby: Whatever helps you sleep at night.

Me: If you were here, huh? Is this your way of saying you want to come for a visit? I've got six extra bedrooms.

Ruby: If you're trying to elicit sympathy, I'd work on your approach.

Me: Trust me, I know better than to try. That's why I like you, birdy. You keep me humble.

The text bubbles appeared again. Then disappeared. It happened two more times, and I exhaled slowly while I waited. Then my phone vibrated with an incoming call, and I sat up so fast I almost dropped my phone.

"Hey."

At the breathless sound of my voice, I winced. Fuck's sake, it sounded like I'd just sprinted a mile before picking up.

"Hi. I hope it's okay that I'm calling."

My eyes slammed shut, an immediate tightening in my throat at the sound of her voice. Fuck, I'd missed her. It was on the tip of my tongue to tell her that, but I held back. For now.

"Yeah, birdy," I said, my voice rough and quiet. "It's good to hear your voice."

"You too." She sucked in a quick breath, and I could see her face so clearly in my head. Could imagine that little furrow in her brow. "I, um, I practiced what I was going to say, and now that I'm actually talking to you, I feel like I'm going to burst into tears."

The tremble at the end of her sentence had me smiling softly. "What's going to make you cry, sweetheart?"

The endearment slipped out, and I swiped a hand over my face while my heart hammered wildly in my chest.

"You," she whispered, voice thick with emotion. "Griffin, I . . . I don't even know what to say. When I think about how much you must have spent . . ."

I bit down on my grin. "I'm sure I don't know what you're talking about."

"Griffin," she admonished. "I found the name of the shell company that bought the land and traced it back to you."

"Did you?" I murmured. "I might need to do a better job hiding my tracks."

"You bought the land for me," she said quietly, and I could hear the tears. "I can't believe you'd do that."

I'd do so much more, I almost told her. Instead, I said, "It would've been a fucking shame to lose that view from your office."

On the other end of the phone, she was quiet. "That simple, huh?"

No.

Not even close.

"Nothing about my life feels simple," I admitted tiredly. The sun had gone down enough that I could finally see bright little specks of stars in the midnight-blue sky. Wouldn't it have been nice to have her there with me? "But that decision did, if you can believe it."

She inhaled shakily. "Thank you. It's . . . it's the nicest thing anyone's ever done for me."

"Did it make you smile when they told you?"

"Yes. I swore in front of the library trustee when she showed me the paperwork."

I laughed. "Worth every penny, then."

"Why did you do it, Griffin?" she asked. "And don't say it's because of my office view."

The fact that she wouldn't let me off the hook had me smiling, a hand rubbing absently over my chest. She'd never make anything easy, and there was something about that that made me so fucking happy.

Before I answered, I swallowed. "There's a big tree in my backyard," I said. "It's got the same kind of branches like the one that was in between our yards growing up." Instead of giving me shit about the slight shift in direction, Ruby just listened quietly. "I'd looked at a couple houses before I saw this one, and I don't know—when I saw it . . . I just felt like it was a sign."

"Of what?"

Even during this eternal month without her in my life, Ruby was pushing me. In the way we should be pushed when there's something in our life we've been too scared to do. My throat was crowded with a hundred things unsaid, and I forced the answer out past all the others.

"That maybe it's not too late to be a little bit like the people I admire," I admitted in a thick, emotion-roughened voice. "That I can see the things about them and try to do what they'd do without losing the good parts of myself."

"Must be quite a tree to remind you of that."

"*You* remind me to do that, Ruby." I sat up and ran a hand through my hair. "I kept thinking about that weeping willow tree that you loved and those little kids in the creek, and I knew what you'd do if you had the money. You wouldn't even think twice about doing it for one of your friends."

Ruby sniffed, crying quietly on the other end of the phone.

"Don't cry, birdy," I urged. "It's fucking killing me."

"Sorry," she said in a tear-thick voice. "I wish I could give you a hug to thank you."

I dropped my head back and exhaled a harsh puff of air, arms aching to wrap tight around her. "I wish you could too."

"Will you come see it when it's all done?" she asked tentatively. "We've already commissioned a few local artists for sculptures, and a landscaper is working up final plans for the butterfly garden."

I smiled. "Couldn't keep me away."

"Okay." She sighed. "Great."

"You've been good?"

Ruby hummed quietly. "Busy. We were able to take all the money we raised to buy the land and put it into improvements around the library. We're renovating the kids' section and adding some new private study rooms."

"That's great."

"What about you? You start training camp soon, right?"

My eyebrows popped up. "Look at you, with the correct verbiage. Someone learning a little bit about football since I left?"

"Maybe," she answered primly. "*SportsCenter* is very informative. They love to talk about you."

I snorted. "They sure do."

"They talk a lot about Barrett too." She paused. "About your rivalry."

"That's also true."

Ruby blew out a harsh breath, and I braced myself for what was coming next. It was only a matter of time before she asked.

"What happened between you two?" she asked. "If I'm allowed to ask."

I smiled. "I'm impressed you made it this long without forcing me to tell you."

Ruby scoffed. "Like I could force you to do anything."

"Oh, you'd be surprised, sweetheart." I winced at the thick beat of silence that followed. Every time one of her nicknames slipped past my lips, it felt like I was screaming at her: *I have Big Feelings for you and I don't know what to do about it.* "It's not a pretty story. You sure you want to hear it?"

"Yes."

She sounded so eager that I laughed. "All right," I murmured, settling back into my chair. "I'll jump past all the regular brotherly competition as we grew up. You saw a lot of that."

"But you still loved each other," she said, so completely sure that I had to smile.

"We did." It hurt to admit that out loud. "I don't blame my dad; he leaned into that competition to motivate us, and fucking hell, it worked. He beats himself up for it now, but it's not his fault. We've both told him that. In high school, we were both starters, both getting heavily recruited by Division I schools, and the fun in our competition just . . . slowly chipped away. He was still getting straight A's. I was skipping classes with my friends, phoning in my grades, and God, it pissed him off that I was still getting the same interest he was. It pissed *me* off that he thought I should be doing exactly what he did, that he thought he was the one who had it figured out, so I kinda . . . rebelled, I guess. You think I'm a screwup? You think I can't have fun and still be a better player than you? Fucking watch."

My throat was a little dry, so I took a sip of my drink, staring up at the stars. "In college, though, things turned again. We ended up at Oregon; the athletic department really made a big push to have both King brothers because they thought we could transform their program on both sides of the ball."

This was where the story got harder to say out loud, and in my pause, Ruby asked, "And did you?"

"Yeah," I said gruffly. "Won our conference title two years in a row. Made it to the championship both times too. Lost it our junior year. Won it our senior year." I let out a dry laugh. "Almost wasn't at the last game, though."

"Why not?"

"The longer we played together, the worse our rivalry got. He was . . . fuck, he was revered by coaching staff. Professors. Everyone. Spent an ungodly amount of time watching film, preparing for the games, was on the dean's list every fucking semester. I was going to parties on the weekends, and I was a legend on campus. The kind everyone thinks of when it comes to an athlete. Revered for a completely different reason, by total strangers who constantly reminded me how fun I was. How impressive, because I could do all that and still dominate on the field. I hate how much I lived for all that approval." I swallowed hard. "But I took it too far. Did stupid shit, over and over and over, to prove exactly how different we were."

"What happened?" she asked quietly.

"I almost got kicked out after my junior year." I clenched my jaw, imagined her face if she were sitting next to me. "They were going to take away my scholarship, boot me from the team. I got arrested for indecent exposure for climbing up the outside of this famous building on campus—naked as the day I was born."

Ruby exhaled a soft, shocked laugh. "Of course you did," she murmured, and if it weren't for the blatant affection in her voice, I might not have kept talking. "But they didn't kick you out?"

"Because of Barrett."

"Ah."

I smiled a grim smile. "He went to the disciplinary board and convinced them to let me stay. Vouched for me, as his brother. Said the team needed me if we wanted to win, and he'd personally make sure I didn't screw up any more if they gave me one more chance."

She hummed in understanding. "And they listened to him?"

"Yeah. All he said when he came to my apartment to tell me he'd done that was, 'Why do you think I have to work so hard? So I'm the one they'll take seriously when shit like this happens. And as long as you're around, it will keep happening.'"

"Oh, Griffin," she sighed. "He never even gave you a chance to change, did he?"

"Just wait," I added lightly. "Story time isn't over yet, birdy. It gets better." I wanted to knock back a strong drink, but I took another sip of my water instead. "We both stayed in Oregon that summer instead of going home, but we kept out of each other's way as much as possible. While I was out one night, I met this girl. Rachel. She was beautiful. Smart. Driven. We didn't have anything serious, but at the time, I thought . . . this is exactly the kind of woman who'd make me want a real relationship."

"Rachel," she said slowly. "Didn't your brother . . ."

"Marry her?" I said in a dry tone. "He did."

"*Oh.*"

"Yeah," I sighed. "We weren't aware she was dating both of us at the same time. Then . . . she got pregnant with Bryce. We hadn't slept together in over a month by that point. I went on a trip with Marcus to visit his family, was busy when I got home, so she knew it was Barrett's. She came clean to both of us after that. They got engaged because my brother, of course, stepped up to do the right thing and take care of her. Barrett and I stopped talking when they got married."

There was a telling beat of silence—thick and loaded—while she took that in. Her brow was probably pinched, eyes big in her face. If she were in front of me, I'd smooth my thumb in that space between her eyebrows and tell her not to worry.

"Isn't he divorced now?"

"He is. Lucky guy. She's a fucking snake."

"So why don't you talk now? If she's out of the picture."

I managed a tight grin, thankful she couldn't see. "Because the night he asked for a divorce, she showed up at my apartment in New York, and he followed her. Found her coming out of my place not long after she showed up."

"Oh." She cleared her throat. "D-did you—"

"No. But he assumed we did. Couldn't bring himself to actually ask."

"Didn't you tell him? I can't believe he'd think that." Her indignation came through the phone like a heat wave, and I had to smile. Still defending me, even when I didn't deserve it.

"I told him she wasn't there more than a few minutes." I swallowed, staring up at the stars, brighter now in the ink-black sky. "And I guess that wasn't enough of a denial to him."

"He didn't believe you?"

"Why would he? All Barrett ever saw me as was the fuckup little brother who skated by on luck and a big personality."

"That is not true," she said hotly. "You're . . . you're so talented, Griffin. And smart and kind and funny."

"You gonna fight my battles for me, birdy?"

"*Yes.* He's not being fair."

"No, he wasn't," I admitted. The next words came out slower, like I had to tear them from my throat. "But . . . sometimes I can't help but wonder if I would've reacted any differently if I was him."

She paused. "What do you mean?"

I swiped a hand over my mouth and tried to figure out how to say all the things looping through my brain. "I'm just as stubborn as he is, you know? I acted out, made childish decisions, pushed his buttons when I could've just . . . backed off. I was so focused on not being him that it became this mask I was wearing, you know? Dropping it got harder and harder the older I got."

"You weren't wearing a mask with me," she said, and I smiled at how certain she sounded.

"No, I wasn't."

Ruby sucked in a breath. "So . . . what would happen if you told your brother that? He was wrong too. He judged you unfairly, and he owes you an apology for that. But maybe . . . maybe you could take the first step, if you wanted to try and fix things."

I laid a hand on my chest and did nothing more than breathe. When I finally spoke, I could hardly hear the words. "And what if he still doesn't hear me? What if . . . what if we're just doomed to always live in the mold people place us in?"

She paused. "Do you really believe that?"

"I don't know. Maybe," I told her. "I think sometimes you hear people talk about you long enough, you start believing what they say. You start acting the way they expect, because why not, you know? Saying stupid shit because everyone thinks you've got a big mouth anyway. And then before I know it, I've become the exact kind of guy my brother thinks I am."

"You're not, though. You're not." She sniffed again, and the thought that Ruby Tate would lose any tears over me made me feel like tearing at my own skin. "You are wonderful, Griffin. I wish you could see it."

My eyes burned at the plea buried in her voice. "I think you've made me better, Ruby. So I guess I owe you a thank-you too."

"Me? I didn't do anything."

"You gonna argue with me about my emotional growth?"

"Well . . . no. But I don't think I can take credit for it either."

"You probably should. All this time, I needed my own little birdy to knock me back into line," I said lightly, but my heart was racing at the truth of it. I had to grit my teeth, claw my way back into some semblance of composure, because I was seconds away from asking if I could drive to her place, no matter how late it was. Seeing her would be enough to satisfy the craving that had throbbed constantly since I'd left. Touching her would send me to my knees.

"I don't think you needed me to put you anywhere," she insisted. "If anything changed for you, it's because you wanted it to."

I scrubbed my face as I sat up in the chair. Everything in my head was spinning out of control, and until I heard her voice, I didn't realize how bad it had gotten.

"Do you want to fix things?" she asked. "With your brother, I mean."

I want to fix things with you, I thought desperately. *Bring us back to where we were before.* I didn't spend my time wisely when she was right in front of me. Every night, I should've slept with her in my arms and memorized the perfect way she fit against me. Every day, I should've spoiled her rotten, kept her warm and safe, held her hand in the dark and felt the steady thrum of her heart under my cheek while I curled my body over hers.

I chose my words carefully. "It should be easy, shouldn't it? To put yourself out there with someone who . . . who means a lot to you."

Ruby was quiet for a moment. "It should."

My eyes pinched shut. "But what if they don't want what you want? What if you give them a glimpse of what you've been hiding underneath all the bullshit and they still walk away?"

Through the phone, I heard a trembling breath escape her mouth, and I had to tilt my head back to fight for control.

"I think you have to decide what you'll regret more," she said slowly. "If the risk is worth it."

It was a humbling thing, to admit how much of my life I'd been held back by a fear of truly disappointing people. Oh, I'd done that in spades, but it wasn't me trying to be the best version of myself. Wasn't me trying at all, really.

But when you finally find someone who makes you want to be better? The fear becomes a looming shadow you can't escape and you can't ignore. I didn't want to just be better for Ruby; I wanted her every fucking day I could have her, and there was no denying it anymore.

A flash of her face looped through my mind, when she'd asked me to teach her. When she'd set down her own fears and asked for help. When she'd risked something important because the regret would've weighed too heavy at the end of the day.

Sitting there in the dark, underneath the blue sky and the bright stars, I knew that when it came to Ruby Tate, I'd regret doing nothing. I'd regret it until the day I died.

"I'm going to change the subject for a second," I warned her.

"Okay."

"Will you come to the first day of training camp? Players invite friends and family, and . . . and I'd like to have you there." My chest expanded on a deep breath. "I don't usually have anyone out there for me."

Ruby let out a shocked noise. "Really? I . . . Are you sure? That seems like a big deal."

"It is," I admitted slowly, heart hammering. "For me, it is. I've never asked anyone, but . . . will you come? It's not for another couple weeks, and . . . I know you're busy, and so am I. But I'd love to see you. Maybe you could come over after and see my place. Climb up in my tree and test it out."

"If that's a euphemism, you need to work harder."

I laughed deeply, the smile in her voice sending a warm jolt through my veins. "It's not, but I'll take that into consideration."

"Okay," she said shyly. "Text me the date, and I'll . . . I'll see if it works in my schedule."

Hope bled through my chest, and even though half of me wondered what the fuck I was playing at, I knew I had to do something. Anything.

After so many weeks, she hadn't faded from my mind in the slightest, and I knew one thing for certain: I wasn't willing to be nothing to her anymore.

Chapter Twenty-Eight

RUBY

Me: I don't know about this, Lauren.

Lauren: The outfit is HOT. Men love it when you wear something with their name on it. Makes them feel all primitive and shit.

Me: I'm not trying to make him feel primitive. I'm going to support my friend.

Lauren: Mmmkay.

Me: Don't say it like that.

Lauren: Fine. If you want to kid yourself that he's making this effort because you're just friends, I'll play along. But I promise . . . this is a man showing you that you're important to him.

Lauren: I'll be there in twenty. Just finishing up my makeup now.

I tossed my phone onto my bed and sighed, standing again in front of the mirror in my bedroom. On Lauren's advice, I tied the jersey off by my hip, a slice of my stomach showing above the waistband of my denim cutoffs. When I turned to the side, the sight of his name on my back sent my pulse sky-high. She'd found me a brand-new Griffin King jersey somewhere in Denver when she was visiting Marcus. It was expected, she told me, that when you go to training camp to support someone in particular, you wear their jersey.

Apparently she knew everything now, even though she and Marcus refused to define their relationship. The man had literally tattooed her name on his ass a couple weeks ago, but they couldn't call each other boyfriend and girlfriend. Their visits were usually limited to once a week, due to his busy schedule heading into the season. But still . . . they'd each made the effort. And all that time, I'd been here, wondering why the less-than-two-hour drive to Griffin's new place made it seem like he lived on a different planet.

It wasn't like I didn't want to see him.

Sometimes fear made for a stronger leash than we were willing to break.

My hands shook while I finished pulling back my hair. I'd braided it off my face, anchoring it to the nape of my neck with a dark-blue ribbon. And no matter how badly I tried to ignore it, my heart had been thrashing erratically all morning.

Anxiety, as it turned out, can do that to ya.

Even knowing it was nothing more than that—anxiety about seeing a man who'd climbed deep under my skin—I sat heavily on the foot of the bed and laid both hands on my chest. The curse of being the type A responsible one was only feeling comfortable in situations where the outcome was known. Where it was expected.

It didn't really matter if the outcome occasionally changed; it was walking into something and owning a relative degree of confidence. Like Griffin. If I'd known how it would all turn out, would I have indulged even a hint of that relationship?

Staring at my own reflection in the mirror from my seat on the bed, I wanted to say no. I wanted to admit that I never would've walked the same path, but I'd be lying to myself.

The thought of never having Griffin in any of the ways I'd had him made my bones ache and my heart hurt in a different way than it had ever hurt before. Sometimes I closed my eyes and pictured his face—his wide smile and bright eyes—and it was all I could do not to burst into tears.

Was this falling in love, then?

Not being able to get them out of your head. Missing them like a limb. Replaying all the bursts of time where they made things better. Where their absence felt like a small sort of death to be mourned.

It was awful.

My phone buzzed on the bed where I'd thrown it, and assuming it was Lauren again, I grabbed it and tapped on the message bubble.

Mom: Look what popped up in my memories today. Glad you're healthy and strong. Love you, my girl.

After that, she included a broken-heart emoji and a string of pictures that sent my stomach sinking down to my feet. It was my last hospital stay before they found a donor for my transplant. I didn't even know my mom had taken these pictures, and looking at them had my chest going hard and cold, my throat tight.

She wasn't doing this to hurt me—my parents were unfailingly pragmatic, just like me—but I felt it like a knife to the gut all the same.

In the first few, I was sleeping in the hospital bed, hooked up to wires and machines, a sickly pallor to my skin, and my arms and legs were painfully thin. Off to the side of my bed, my dad was slumped in a chair, his head resting on his hand as he slept in a cramped position. There were bags under his eyes, and it looked like he hadn't shaved in days.

A tear spilled over onto my cheek before I knew I was crying, and the slow build of unease crawled up my skin as I looked at the other photos. I'd turned twenty-four not too long before I was in that hospital bed, and I remembered thinking that I likely wouldn't see twenty-five. Making peace with the fact that I wouldn't. Telling my mom that I'd prefer to be cremated because the thought of a coffin made me want to scream.

My eyes slammed shut when I imagined having a conversation like that with Griffin. Imagined him sitting where my dad sat. Imagined trying to make peace with any shortened life if he was the one I was saying goodbye to.

My fingers started tingling, and my breath came in choppy, short bursts. I dropped my phone and sank my head into my hands while I struggled to calm my breathing, waiting for the cold, prickly wave of anxiety to pass.

It didn't.

It built. And built. And soon my legs were trembling, my head staticky and loud and horrible.

Bruiser came into the room, nudging my arms with his nose and emitting a low, distressed whine. I sank onto the floor and wrapped my arms around him, pressing my nose into the sleek fur of his neck, tears coating my face while I told myself over and over that this would pass. It would pass. It would pass.

After a few minutes, the grip on my lungs eased, and I sucked in a deep breath. Bruiser whined again, licking my face.

"I'm okay, buddy." I scratched behind his ears and kept breathing until my head cleared and my hands stopped tingling. After a few more minutes, when I felt like my legs could hold me, I stood from the floor and went to splash cold water on my face. My makeup was ruined, and I couldn't find it in me to care. All I wanted to do was crawl under the covers and sleep until the next day. Or stare at those pictures and remind myself why being alone was so much easier.

Griffin's face tore through that thought, and I swallowed a sob.

It will pass.

It will pass.

Whatever I was feeling for him, it would pass.

With a hand still on my chest, I let the steady thump of my heart ground me as I sent Lauren a text. Then Griffin. Jaw tight with resolve, I silenced my phone, peeled back the blankets on my bed, toed my shoes off before climbing in, and tugged the covers up over my head.

GRIFFIN

"Quit looking at the sidelines, asshole. You gonna play or not?"

Liam smacked me on the back of my helmet when I wasn't listening inside the huddle, and I set my jaw, trying to focus on the play we were lining up.

"Sorry," I told him. "Just . . . looking for someone."

He eyed me, the rest of the defense watching our interaction carefully. "Need to sit this one out?"

I raised my chin. "No."

"Good." He leaned in. "All right, we're moving to the Miami 4-3, got it? I need you, you, and you," he said, pointing to me last. "Crash the left side of that line. Don't let the tight end get past you."

We stuck our hands in, and when Liam called, we clapped once before we jogged into position. The atmosphere of training camp always felt a bit like a party, especially on days like this, where the practice fields were filled with spectators with signs, family members dressed in the team colors. Balloons danced in the air, and music played over the speaker system. Media mingled along the sidelines, and even with the massive influx of faces, I couldn't find the one I was looking for.

I exhaled, anchoring my hand on the grass, grinning at the way Marcus growled at me from his tight-end position.

"Good luck trying to catch me, dick," he said.

I laughed.

The center snapped the ball into the QB's hands, and our left side pushed in hard against the O-line. Marcus tried to run a post route but bounced off my chest, and I shoved him back, where he tripped over his own run protection. I spun around an offensive lineman, hands reaching for our quarterback, who danced back and tucked the ball under his arm just before I wrapped my arms around him. In a real game, against a real opponent, his ass would be on the ground, but flooring my own quarterback was generally frowned upon.

"Damn it," he laughed. "You're too quick, King."

I tapped his helmet. "That's the point, isn't it?"

He tossed the ball back to one of the coaches and whistled for the offense to take a water break.

Liam approached, holding his fist out for a tap. "Nice work. You do that every game, and we'll be just fine."

"Thanks." Someone handed me a bottle of Gatorade, and I took a long drink, eyes skating over the different groups of people. But there was no sign of messy blond hair and big gray eyes anywhere to be seen.

"Looking for your girl that's not your girl?"

I sighed, tossing the Gatorade bottle back to the boy who'd handed it to me. "Yeah."

"She's friends with Marcus's . . ." He paused. "Whatever the fuck he's calling her. Heard him say something about consensual monogamous sex and cuddling partner, and I kinda wanted to gouge my eyes out."

"Yeah, Lauren is her friend." My brow furrowed. "Why?"

"Isn't that her?" He nodded over to the opposite sideline, and I caught a glimpse of Lauren laughing at something Marcus was saying to her.

My heart jumped into my throat as I jogged over there, but still . . . there was no sign of Ruby.

Lauren saw me and laid a hand on Marcus's arm. She whispered something by his ear, and he gave her a quick kiss and a smack on the ass and went to talk to the media.

"Hey," she said. "Good to see you, Griffin."

Under any other circumstance, I'd attempt polite conversation. "Where is she? Did she come?"

Lauren blew out a slow breath, narrowing her eyes a little as she looked over my shoulder. "I'm guessing you didn't check your phone?"

"No. I left it in my locker. Why? What'd she say?"

Lauren gave a small shake of her head. "I don't know what she sent you, exactly. But the gist of *my* text was that she freaked out. Couldn't do it."

"Do what?" I asked, feeling more than a touch exasperated. "It's training camp."

"Don't be obtuse; it doesn't suit you."

I slicked my tongue over my teeth. "I'm not trying to be. It was just . . . I wanted to see her."

Her eyebrows arched slowly. "Is that all? You didn't mean anything by this invitation?"

I pinched the bridge of my nose and then let my hand drop. Lauren's gaze was unflinching, like she was daring me to brush this aside, to make it less than it was. Make Ruby less than she was.

That, I wouldn't do.

"I meant something by it," I admitted in a gruff voice. "I don't know what she's even open to, or . . . if she's willing to try. But I fucking miss her. And I'm sick of feeling that way."

Lauren exhaled quietly. "It's gratifying to know that I didn't read you wrong." She leaned in, angling us away from the crowds of people with a gentle touch of her arm. "Ruby isn't just cautious, Griffin. She's terrified to get hurt. To hurt *you*."

"How would she hurt me?"

Her smile was sad. "I think this is a conversation you should have with her."

It was the sadness in that smile that had my chest caving in on itself.

"Her heart. She doesn't think it makes sense to fall in love with anyone." I ran a hand through my sweat-soaked hair, my muscles humming with the need to run and find her and kiss her and try to take this away for her. Humming with the need to tell her I was in love with her and I'd never leave her if she let me stay.

Lauren didn't give me any verbal affirmation. She didn't need to.

"Fuck," I muttered. "That's a hell of a reason not to want a relationship, Lauren—especially for a guy who doesn't know how the fuck to be in one."

She gripped my arm. "She's never had anyone try to push past that. She doesn't know how it would feel if someone cared enough to work through her fears." Her eyes were hard, and I had the distinct feeling that if I took one wrong step, Lauren would castrate me with a smile on her face. "You just have to ask yourself if you're strong enough to be the one to do that for her. Do that *with* her. And if you're not, then leave her be, because she doesn't need someone playing games because they're bored."

"That's not what I'm doing."

"I'm glad to hear that, but I'm not the one you need to prove that to," Lauren warned. "All she knows is what you've told her. That you didn't want serious either. That you wouldn't fall in love with her. You think you're scared to admit how you feel? Imagine how it feels for her."

All it took was conjuring the image of her face, and a pang of love tore through me so strong that it almost knocked the breath from my lungs. Was I still scared? Hell yeah, I was.

But it was nothing—*nothing*—compared to how I felt about her.

Ruby and I, we could be scared of this together.

"Thank you," I told her, then kissed her hard on the cheek.

Somehow, I kept my head through one more play, then bolted to the locker room when Coach said we were done with official team activities. Marcus yelled my name. So did Liam. I ignored them both.

The building was quiet when I shoved through the door, so quiet that all I could hear was the blood roaring through my ears. Inside the locker room, I ripped my bag open and found my phone in the side pocket as I tore off my sweaty practice gear with my other hand. As I shucked off my shorts, I tapped the home screen and saw her text come into view, throat clenching when I did.

Ruby: I'm sorry. I can't come today. It's . . . too much. It shouldn't be, but it is, and I don't know how to change that. Please don't hate me.

The text from Ruby didn't make my heart stop. Didn't make my stomach sink. A smile spread over my face before I could stop it.

She loved me.

She fucking loved me, and it scared the absolute hell out of her.

I took the fastest shower known to man, then yanked on my clothes while my skin was still damp. As I left the locker room, I hit the screen to call her. While the phone rang endlessly in my ear, I jogged toward the exit. Why were the parking lots so fucking far away? The ringing stopped, and I swore under my breath while I waited for her voicemail to pick up.

"Ruby? It's me. God, I don't hate you. I could never fucking hate you, birdy." I sucked in a breath, but it was almost impossible because my heart was racing so fast. "I'm coming to you. I just . . . I need to see you. Please, don't shut me out because you're scared, sweetheart. I'm scared too. Just talk to me. I'll be there as soon as I can, okay?"

I love you.

The words were on the tip of my tongue, but I swallowed them. She deserved so much more than a frantic voicemail to hear them from me for the first time. I hopped into my truck and cranked the engine on, fumbling with my seat belt as I threw the gear into reverse.

I eyed the clock, hoping I could get there in less than ninety minutes. I'd be there before dinner. We'd have all night.

I didn't care if we didn't kiss, if we didn't have sex. I'd sit on that couch and do nothing more than hold her hand and be the happiest man in the universe.

It was that thought that had me distracted as I pulled the truck out onto the road, going too fast.

The blare of a car horn was what I heard first, and then the sickening crash of glass before everything went black.

Chapter Twenty-Nine

Ruby

If there was any upside to an anxiety attack, it was that you got a hell of a nap afterward. The moment I yanked those covers over my head, I slept like the actual dead. If not for Bruiser nudging me in the shoulder blades hours later, then nosing around the covers to snuffle loudly against my ear, I might have slept the entire day.

"Bruiser," I groaned. "Stop it."

He shoved his nose into my ear, and I squealed, pulling away from him to tug the blanket tighter around my head. When he started nibbling on my arm through the blanket, I laughed helplessly, turning onto my back and flipping the comforter down so I could wrap my arms around his big, blocky head.

His body wiggled as he flopped onto his side and angled for belly rubs. I complied, burying my face into his neck while I scratched his stomach. For a few moments, I lay there and let the fog of sleep clear from my head.

I hadn't napped like that in years, and there was no doubt it was the emotional drain from earlier in the day. The last time I'd had a panic attack was about four months after my surgery, and in the moment, I genuinely thought I'd die right there on the kitchen floor. It ended in an ER visit and a promise to my doctor that I'd start seeing a therapist.

I did, for a couple of years. And during that time, it helped me understand a lot. But it had been at least a year since I'd spoken to her. *Might be time to schedule a session,* I thought, playing with the frayed edge of Bruiser's collar.

He wiggled on his back and I smiled, finally lifting my head to check the time. My eyes bugged out when I realized it was past dinnertime.

"No wonder you woke me up," I said to Bruiser, sitting up and yawning loudly. "You're hungry, aren't you?"

His ears perked up when he heard *hungry*, and he bounded off the bed, scrambling through the house toward his food bowl. I left my room, ignoring my sleep-rumpled reflection in the mirror, and I filled his bowl with two scoops of kibble. The container of his food went back under the counter in the laundry room, and I glanced down at the jersey. The knot had fallen apart in my sleep, and even with the smaller size Lauren had picked, it fell down over my hips, nearly covering my shorts.

The thought of Griffin waiting at training camp made my stomach squeeze uncomfortably, and now that the cloud of my earlier meltdown had ebbed, I knew I needed to do a better job of apologizing. Of explaining.

I rubbed my temple and made my way back to the bedroom to change and check my phone. It was still sitting face up on the nightstand, and it lit up when I came into the room. My eyes narrowed when I saw the sheer number of missed calls. Voicemails. Texts.

All from Lauren, except one. At the very bottom of the mass of notifications was a missed call and a voicemail from Griffin. My heart clenched, and I almost tapped on it, but then I noticed the first few texts from Lauren—and the ground disappeared from beneath my feet.

I sank weakly to the bed as I scrolled through them, the most recent one coming in less than twenty minutes earlier.

Lauren: Ruby, call me, NOW.

Lauren: RUBY! I've called you three times and I don't know what the hell you're doing but this is important.

Lauren: Okay, I left you a voicemail, but maybe you're not checking those right now. Please call me, it's an emergency.

Lauren: Griffin was in a car accident. I don't know how bad it is. He's at Centennial Hospital.

I was off the bed before I'd made a conscious decision to move, sprinting through the house, my purse and keys in my hand before I'd registered a single rational thought. Fear tangled cold around my limbs, and I had a moment where I pictured ice hanging heavy from my legs and arms and hands. I paused, wondering if it was safe to drive.

There was a sharp pounding on the door, and I yanked it open to find Kenny—red-faced and panting. His car was running in the driveway, the door left open, and behind him was a cop car with the lights on.

"Kenny, what on earth—"

"It's . . . it's Griffin," he panted. "Lauren called me while I was at my family reunion."

"I know! I just saw her text and I . . . I have to get down to Denver." I tilted my head. "Did you get pulled over in my driveway?"

He shook his head frantically. "It's my brother. He said he'd take you."

"Really?" I grabbed his face and laid a smacking kiss on his cheek, sprinting past him toward the cop car.

"Ruby!" Kenny yelled.

"I don't have time, Kenny!"

"You're not wearing shoes."

I froze, glancing down at my bare feet. "Oh."

He darted into my house—where I'd left the door open—and threw me some flip-flops. I stepped into them and blew him a kiss before disappearing into the passenger seat of his brother's patrol vehicle.

"Thank you," I told Kenny's brother once I was buckled in. He wasn't in uniform, but he was wearing a Denver jersey, too, and for a second, the sight of it almost had me losing the tenuous grip on my emotions.

"Where to?" he asked, flipping the display screen to enter in an address.

I brushed at the tears under my eyes, trying to scrub at the mess of mascara left on my skin. "Centennial Hospital." I shot off a text to Lauren, letting her know I was on my way. The car took off, and I stared down at my screen, at the sight of his name on my missed-call list. Slowly, like the words on the screen might bite me if I moved too quickly, I touched the voicemail notification and brought the phone up to my ear.

When his deep voice filled my ears, my eyes pinched shut, squeezing hot tears down my cheeks.

"Please, don't shut me out because you're scared, sweetheart. I'm scared too. Just talk to me."

I laid a trembling hand over my mouth, crying quietly after the voice message was done.

"Just talk to me."

This wouldn't pass.

It would never, ever pass. And more importantly, I didn't want it to.

The waiting room down the hallway from Griffin's room was full of very big, very somber-looking men. Lauren saw me get off the elevator and extricated herself from Marcus's lap, tugging me into a tight hug.

The door to his room was slightly ajar, and I stared at it over her shoulder.

"Can I go in?" I asked. "Is he awake?"

"He was for a little bit. He's sleeping now," Marcus said, sliding a hand up Lauren's back when we separated. He was as serious as I'd ever seen him. "You're the only one he asked for."

"Really?" I whispered.

Lauren nodded. "None of us have been in there yet. They had to take him down for X-rays on his arm and ribs, but when they wheeled him from the ER to his room, he asked if you were here."

My chin trembled, guilt gnawing mercilessly at my insides. "What happened?"

Marcus cleared his throat. "He got T-boned. Right outside the facility parking lot—that's how we all knew so fast. One of the security guards saw it happen and ran in to tell us after he called nine-one-one. We got here right behind the ambulance." I opened my mouth to ask another question, but the big man just lifted his chin toward the door. "Go. Maybe his stubborn ass will wake up, knowing you're here."

The walk from the waiting area to his room felt like it would never end, only the pounding of my heart to keep me moving forward.

I carefully pushed open the door as I sucked in a fortifying breath. Griffin was asleep in the bed, his chest rising and falling, and I swallowed a small sob at the sight of him so still and quiet. His head was wrapped with white gauze, and there were two butterfly bandages on his eyebrow and cheek. His arm was wrapped, too, held tight to his body in a sling. An oxygen cannula was hooked around his face, wires snaked underneath the hospital gown, and my eyes flew to the screen showing his vitals, the up-and-down lines showing a steady, strong heartbeat.

I wandered closer, my fingers shaking as I pressed them against the monitor and stared at that line until my eyes started blurring. Life was filled with heartbreak. There was no escaping it, no matter how firmly we built up the walls around our life. If something had happened to him before I told him what he meant to me, I never would've forgiven myself.

All the protections I'd built up over the years, torn down by this one man. Feeling them fall away was freedom, and I took a deep, cleansing breath while I studied every inch of his face. Tears slid hot down my cheeks as I took a seat in the chair next to the bed and carefully traced the skin over his knuckles.

The veins mapping the back of his hand made him look so strong, so capable. Eyes fixed on his face to make sure I didn't wake him, I carefully wound my hand around his and lifted his fingers to my mouth, kissing them as softly as he had when he'd done it to me.

Could he feel what I felt in that moment?

If he could, I hoped that it imbued his body with something powerful and sweet, a tenderness that I associated only with him.

"I'm sorry," I whispered against his skin, my eyes pinching shut while I tried to stem the tide of tears. "I'm so sorry I wasn't here. I should've come. I shouldn't have been so scared."

Resting my forehead against the front of his fingers where they curled around mine, I let myself release all the emotions pressing against my insides. I cried until I felt the pressure valve release, my whole body melting from the tension finally escaping.

"Don't cry, birdy," a quiet voice rasped from the bed.

My head snapped up. "Griffin? Are you okay?"

His eyes were still closed, and he licked at dry lips. "Water?"

I stood quickly, striding around the bed to get the Styrofoam cup with a lid and straw, easing the straw to his mouth. He let out a small grunt when he was done, resting his head back on the pillow. I kept the water with me and returned to my seat. Instantly, his hand sought out mine again, sighing when our fingers twined together.

"Do you need me to get a nurse?" I asked.

"No. Stay." He tightened his hand in mine, finally prying his eyes open enough that I could see they were glossed over with unshed tears. "I just need you."

I lost it, dropping my head to the bed, unleashing a torrent of shoulder-racking sobs. Griffin made small shushing noises, his hand pulling from mine so he could cup the back of my head while I cried.

"I'm okay, baby," he whispered. "Look at me."

Sluggishly, I lifted my head, and when he smiled his crooked smile, I felt my heart tear clean from my chest in the most perfect, miraculous way.

It was his.

Every inch of my body, every ounce of blood running through my veins, whatever I was made of, was his.

"I'm okay," he repeated, cupping my face tenderly. "My arm hurts like a bitch, and I broke a rib, and I might forget who the president is for a couple days, but I'm going to be fine." Then he deepened his smile, the dimple popping in his cheek. "Now, will you get into this bed with me so I can hug my girl?"

I let out a choked sob, climbing carefully against his good side. He winced when I shifted too close but wouldn't hear of anything other than a full-body hug. I placed my arm gingerly across his midsection and sighed when he curled his good arm around my back.

Griffin kissed the top of my head and exhaled heavily. "That's fucking better."

I smiled into his chest, then raised my head, setting my chin down so I could look up into his face. "I got your voicemail."

His eyes searched mine. "Yeah? I didn't really stop to think about what I was saying. I just . . . I wanted to see you. I've missed you."

Absently, I skimmed my thumb along his bottom lip. "I missed you too."

"Can I ask you something?"

I nodded.

Griffin pulled in a slow breath. "If it were me in this hospital bed for a long time, for something serious," he said, refusing to drop my gaze, "would it make a difference in how you felt? If that car accident took my legs or my arm, or I was in a wheelchair for the rest of my life. Would you choose to walk away because it made things easier?"

My throat was impossibly tight as I shook my head. "No," I said, voice trembling.

He slid his hand up my back, cupping my neck in a firm grip. "I don't care if I have one year or five years or ten, Ruby. I want all of your days. Every single one, because they're so fucking precious. I will love you through every sunrise and every sunset because we've already missed too many. Do you understand me? I'm not going anywhere."

I could hardly see him through the tears, but I surged up to kiss him, and he groaned into my mouth, his tongue teasing mine just before I pulled back to rest my forehead against his.

"I love you," I said against his mouth. "I love you, and I'm in love with you, and nothing can change that, Griffin King. No more missing anything," I promised.

He exhaled shakily, stealing another deep kiss while his arm curved around my waist, hitching me tighter against his body. I sighed into this perfect, sweet kiss, until the beep of the heart monitor had me pulling away.

I laughed. "I think someone's getting too excited."

He stared into my face, the adoration in his eyes making my world expand at every seam. "Your fault."

A nurse popped her head into the room, frowning when she saw us on the bed. "Oh, come on now, have some sympathy for those of us who have to walk in here."

"Sorry," he said with an unrepentant grin.

"Mm-hmm." She winked at me while she checked his vitals and the IV bag on the hook. My face flamed hot, and I pressed my cheek into his chest while she maneuvered around me. "Need anything for the pain, Griffin? Doctor should be in shortly to talk to you about surgery on your arm."

He frowned. "Will I be able to play at the beginning of the season?"

She gave him an incredulous look. "You fractured your humerus and you think you'll be playing next month?"

"Maybe? Can't I just . . . play in a cast?"

I rolled my eyes.

She shook her head. "Bless you, honey. I admire your optimism. He always like this?" she asked me.

"Yes."

"What about sex?" he asked. "Can I resume normal activities soon?"

I slammed my eyes shut while the nurse laughed. "We get you cleared of that concussion, and yes. No funny business with the arm, but as long as your rib can handle it, you two can do . . . whatever you want." She patted my arm. "Good luck with him, by the way. I think you'll have your hands full."

Griffin patted my backside. "Oh, she loves it. That's why she's my consensual monogamous-sex-and-cuddle partner."

The nurse's eyebrows popped up, and she lifted both hands in the air. "On that note, I'll come back when the doctor's done."

When I pinched him in the side with a hissed warning, he laughed.

"I can't believe you said that." I eased up onto my hip, shaking my head as I looked down at him. My fingers whispered over the butterfly bandages, and he sighed, catching my hand and pressing my fingertips to his mouth.

"I've had a head injury. Go easy on me."

I hummed, leaning down to kiss him again. Griffin tried to tilt his head and deepen the kiss, but the oxygen tube got in the way. He ripped it off his head and nudged me closer, teasing my tongue with his.

"You're going to be the worst patient in the world, aren't you?" I whispered against his lips.

"Oooh, can you wear one of those nurse outfits and spank me if I'm bad?"

I tipped my head back and laughed. "We'll see," I said. "We've got time to figure it out."

Griffin's eyes warmed. "Yeah, we fucking do."

Chapter Thirty

GRIFFIN

Seven weeks later

"Nope. No clothes allowed on Tuesdays."

It was like I hadn't even spoken. Ruby shot me a dry look, pulling one of my T-shirts over her head, the sleek line of her naked body disappearing underneath clothing that was far too big for her. I frowned as she walked away.

"That's a house rule, birdy," I called after her.

"Not one I agreed to." Her head popped back around the corner of the door. "Besides, this isn't my house. If you'd like to walk around naked, feel free, but you might traumatize Eileen when she gets here."

I let out a disgruntled sigh, settling my head back down onto the pillow and closing my eyes again. The sound of her footsteps coming back into the bedroom had me peeling them open. Her hair was wild around her face, like it always was after she woke up.

She split her time between my place outside of Denver and her home in Welling Springs, adjusting her work schedule so that her days off allowed us to have three straight days together. She arrived with Bruiser on Saturday evenings, after closing up the library at noon. Sundays, we went to Denver's home games together—the only ones I was attending, given my stupid broken arm meant I couldn't play until after Thanksgiving.

On Mondays, she worked remotely at my house, and I'd happily conceded one of the extra bedrooms to become her office. Not long after, during one of her return trips to Welling Springs, I had floor-to-ceiling bookshelves installed, then handed her my credit card and told her I didn't think she'd be able to fill them in two weeks.

It took four days, and her triumphant smirk when she slid the last book into place made me so fucking crazy that I slung her up over my shoulder with my good arm—ignoring the screaming pain in my rib in a way that would piss off my doctor—and marched her right back to our bedroom, her breathless laughter filling the room until I commanded her to sit over my face and let me kiss between her thighs until she screamed my name. It was a tactic that I'd found very successful.

And since Tuesday was my day off during the season, I was trying to institute a mandated no-clothes, sex-only day. I had a bit of convincing to do.

"See, I knew you'd change your mind about naked Tuesdays." I patted the empty side of the bed. I'd spent four eternal weeks sleeping in a recliner with that evil sling on my arm and now dedicated a substantial bit of energy to trying to be in bed with her as much as humanly possible. "Come back in, birdy. We don't have to be at the airport for another hour."

Instead of taking pity on my poor morning hard-on, Ruby tossed something at me—not the shirt, unfortunately—and I caught it before it hit me in the face.

My lip curled at the sight of the sling.

I hated that fucking thing and would burn it at the first-possible chance.

Holding her gaze, I dumped it right back onto the floor. "That is not sexy, and not what I was hoping to start my day with." I sat up and motioned for her to come closer. "You. Come here."

Ruby set a hand on her hip, and it bunched the T-shirt up just enough around her waist that I got a mouth-watering glimpse of her thigh. "The doctor said you have to wear it. I know it's feeling better, but—"

"My arm is fine." It hurt like a bitch the night before, but there was no *way* I was admitting that now.

She narrowed her eyes. "I know what your pain face looks like. Don't you lie to me, Griffin King."

I growled. "It makes me crazy when you say my full name. Get back in bed, baby."

Ruby stayed right where she was. "I will if you put the sling back on."

"You know what's not feeling better?" I pointed to the bulge underneath the sheet. "He's not. I can finally do normal sex positions and sleep in bed with you, and I'd like to set a record for most times getting you off in a week, okay? This is practically a charitable endeavor on my part."

Her eyes never strayed from mine, but she rolled her lips in, trying to hide the smile that threatened. "Do not try and distract me. You promised me you'd be a good patient."

I flexed my arm as I reached out to her—it was still slightly skinnier than the other, since the permanent cast had come off the week before. "I am a good patient. The best. I did all my PT this week, didn't I? You should come give me a kiss as a reward."

Ruby's grin broke free, and when she leaned down to plant a kiss over my waiting mouth, I knew I had her. "You really should have warned me about how much affirmation you need. I might not have agreed to this cohabitation deal," she said against my lips. What a crock of shit. She always wanted it, just as bad as me.

My hand curled around the back of her thigh, fingers tickling lightly up underneath the hem of the T-shirt.

Slowly, I pushed my hand up, and when I found her slick between her legs, I nipped at her bottom lip. "You should have warned me how insatiable you are. I would've made you move in sooner."

I surged forward and clutched her around the waist, swallowing her surprised squeak with an open-mouthed kiss as I deposited her on my lap. Ruby's sigh of concession had a smile breaking open over my face, and she slung her arms over my shoulders as we kissed lazily.

After a few minutes, my hands coasting up the length of her back underneath the damned T-shirt, Ruby pulled away with a dazed expression. "We don't have time," she moaned.

I kissed her again, deeper this time, my hand digging into the mass of her hair. "Yes, we do." She tugged at the sheet, the only thing separating us, and heat surged through my veins. *Got her.* "And once they get here, you're going to be impossible to please."

She pulled back, eyebrows arched. "Me?"

With a hum, I leaned in to nip along the line of her jaw, slowly working the T-shirt up with my hands. I would make Naked Tuesdays a thing, so help me. When I pulled it up over her head, she sighed, fixing me with a mock glare when I grinned in triumph.

"Yes, you," I told her. "It's not my fault we have sex all over the house. I won't be able to boost you up on the island. Or have you in the pool after dark. Or on the kitchen table. You love it when I do that," I whispered against her lips.

"I do." She pushed one of my hands up to cover her breast, arching her back when I dragged my thumb over her hard peak. Watching her face when I teased her there was one of my new favorite hobbies because her breath always hitched in the most delightful way. I ducked my head and kissed along the length of her scar.

Ruby dug her hands into my hair and tightened her fingers, tugging my head up so she could slide her mouth over mine in a searing, impatient kiss.

My girl.

We'd come a long way in seven weeks. There was no hiding what we wanted from each other, and through some difficult, emotional conversations, Ruby admitted that her greatest fear was leaving me behind—hurt and alone.

That fear might never go away, but every single day we spent together, it made us both realize that happiness wasn't some lofty goal we were forever chasing. It wasn't trying to heave the imaginary boulder up over the barrier and be done with it.

Happiness—true joy—was soaking up the tiny moments we had with each other, seeking contentment in living everyday life with a person we loved, no matter how long that might be.

Forever wouldn't be long enough, not if we had another fifty years, but even what I'd had with her was the best time in my entire life. The car accident, and broken arm, had turned out to be a strange gift of time for the two of us. I wasn't living most of my waking hours with the team; instead, I got to spend most of my days with her. Football would be there when my arm healed, but getting this much time early in our relationship was fucking gold.

In between physical therapy and time in the gym, helping the team review film, my life was coming home to Ruby, helping her make dinner (or as much as I could with only one good hand), taking baths and swimming and napping and watching movies and taking Bruiser for daily walks. It was checking the progress on the gardens and spending quiet days in Welling Springs, sharing muffins on the bench while we watched the space transform into something even more beautiful.

Everything about our life was beautiful.

Maybe it was more beautiful because we didn't know what the future held, but God, I wasn't taking anything for granted.

Not making a mess in the kitchen because I couldn't crack an egg with one hand or having her at my doctors' appointments, not falling asleep next to her, and definitely not moments like this—where we so easily got lost in each other.

Tightening my grip in her hair, I angled my head to deepen the kiss. The slick winding of my tongue around hers had her whimpering into my mouth.

"Come on, baby," I told her. "Let's start this morning right."

Eyes locked on mine, Ruby lifted up, sinking down over my length, and we groaned in unison. My arms wrapped around her waist while she worked herself slow and sweet against me. It wasn't fast and it wasn't hard. It was a torturous build, each rock of her hips and dent of my fingers in her flesh had my heart hammering behind my chest.

Mine, it said. She was mine. And I was hers.

She tipped her head back and let out a decadent sigh as she came, and I fixed my mouth on her neck, groaning my own release against her skin.

Ruby slumped against my chest, burying her face into the side of my throat. "Naked Tuesdays might not be a bad idea," she murmured.

I smacked the side of her ass. "I'm very smart. I keep telling you this."

She pulled back to grin at me. "Too bad we can't start today, huh?"

"Why not?" I couldn't think straight with her still warm and tight around me. She pulled up with a hiss, and wouldn't you know it . . . it was the perfect height. I tugged her closer so I could kiss the tip of her breast again, licking across her chest to give the same treatment to the other.

Ruby laughed, cupping my face so she could kiss my forehead, then the tip of my nose. "Forget scarring Eileen—your niece and nephew might not appreciate a nudist household when they get here."

Shit. Sex with this woman scrambled my brain something fierce. You'd think I'd be used to it, but I still wasn't. All she had to do was smile at me, and I swear, I forgot my own fucking name.

I blinked. "Right. They're landing in"—I glanced at the clock with a wince—"forty-five minutes."

Ruby picked up my sling off the floor and handed it to me. "On."

"Bossy," I grumbled.

"I'm taking a shower first." She paused before entering the bathroom. "Do not join me, because you know what'll happen."

I gave her a grave nod as I stood from the bed. "Insatiable, I'm telling ya."

Ruby sighed. "Put the sling on."

Before she walked away, I grabbed her hand and swung her back in my direction, cupping her face with both hands. "I love you."

Her eyes softened. "I love you too."

We kissed, Ruby's hands sliding along my stomach. I swept some stray hair off her face. "Thank you for pushing me to ask for the visit."

She touched my chin with her thumb. "I'm glad he said yes."

"Me too." I wrapped her in a hug, sighing happily as I rested my chin on the top of her head. Ruby pressed a kiss to my sternum. "It'll be a good week. Do you think they'll like the rooms I set up?"

Ruby smiled. "They'll love them." She glanced over at the clock and grimaced. "Come on. If you keep your hands to yourself, we can save time and shower together; otherwise you'll smell like me when you pick them up."

I bent at the knees and swung Ruby up into my arms as she squealed in shock. "If you keep your hands to yourself, birdy, I'll be very put out."

Ruby wrapped her arms around me as I strode to the bathroom, her mouth curled into a contented grin. "What am I going to do with you, Griffin King?"

I rested my forehead against hers. "Just love me, baby. That's all I need."

"That, I can do," she whispered.

Epilogue

RUBY

Eight months later

"You are the hottest bride ever," Lauren proclaimed.

My eyes met hers in the mirror, and I smiled. "You're just trying to keep me from crying before I see him."

It was a lost cause, but I gave her props for trying. I'd been weepy the entire day. My makeup was tear-proof, according to the makeup artist who'd done her magic on me a couple hours earlier. Lauren had been in charge of my hair, curling it loosely and then pulling it back off my face, weaving tiny white flowers among the curls that fell to my shoulders.

The moment my mom had finished buttoning the back of my dress—a high-neck A-line dress with a lace overlay that hugged my upper body and flowed gently away from my hips—I took one look at myself in the mirror and promptly burst into tears.

I didn't realize how much I'd grieved having a moment like this until it was finally in my grasp. It was crazy how you could trick yourself into thinking you'd made peace with something, and really . . . it was simply acceptance of a fact, not true, down-to-your-soul peace.

The makeup artist touched up my face one more time before she left, and Lauren and my mom, red-eyed and smiling, told me I had to try not to sob my way through the entire day.

"Or maybe I'm trying to keep myself from crying." Lauren adjusted her strapless bra underneath the blush-colored dress she was wearing, grimacing when she had to tug on her very plentiful cleavage. "Good Lord, my tits are obnoxious right now."

"Well, maybe you shouldn't have let Marcus plant his Viking seed inside you, then," I pointed out. "Pregnancy has a tendency to do that."

She blew out a harsh breath, cupping a hand over her six-month bump. "Once. The man mentions *once* that we should have a kid, and of course I get pregnant the first week we try it without protection."

"Yes, I've heard all about how virile he is."

Lauren grinned. "He's such a dope. It's stupid how much I love him."

"Aren't you glad I gave him your number?" I asked.

She rolled her eyes. "I suppose."

Lauren reached into the cooler on the floor and removed the bouquet of white peonies. It was tied with a pale-pink ribbon, and stuck just inside, where no one could see it but me, was a minuscule tuft of hair from the giant stuffed bird Griffin had won for me at the fair.

From the moment I woke up, the day had felt like it progressed in a dreamy sort of haze. My mom, Lauren, and I had breakfast with Griffin's mom and Maggie while Griffin and the dads played a round of golf with Marcus, Bryce, and a slightly hesitant Barrett.

Barrett's girlfriend hadn't been able to make it . . . and that pairing? None of us saw *that* one coming.

Things weren't fixed between the brothers, but they were slowly— *very* slowly—getting better. At least they could be in the same room without fighting now. It wasn't much, but it was progress.

Maggie burst into the room, eyes widening when she saw me in my dress. "You look like a princess, Aunt Ruby."

I tugged her close for a hug. "Thank you, sweetie." As she pulled away, I held her arms out and smiled. Her makeup was subtle, her father agreeing to some mascara and a little blush to go with her full-length dress with delicate lace cap sleeves, in the same blush color as Lauren's. "That dress is perfect on you."

Maggie was standing up for me with Lauren, and Bryce was standing up with Marcus. The time they'd spent with me and Griffin over the last eight months had cemented them as two of my favorite people in the world. Maggie still warranted being on an FBI watch list for all the things she knew how to do on her own, but I'd take a bullet for those two kids without blinking.

"Uncle Griffin is going crazy waiting for you. Marcus and I started a betting pool on how long he lasts before he starts crying." She glanced down at her phone. "So far we have ninety-nine percent of the guests taking part."

"Maggie . . ."

She shrugged. "What? It's not illegal. And if I win, I can get that Taser I've been eyeing. Dad refuses to buy it for me."

Lauren chuckled under her breath. "Come on, kid. Time to line up. We can talk weapons another time."

The two hustled out of the room, and I was left in the quiet. For a moment, I heard the string quartet playing out in the church, and I tried to imagine Griffin waiting for me at the end of the aisle. My smile was easy, my heart rate strong and steady as I left the bridal room with a bright flurry of anticipation taking wing in my stomach.

My parents waited for me by the doors, but instead of walking me down to Griffin, we'd agreed that because of my journey to get here, it made the most sense that I'd take the trip down the aisle on my own. They were both teary-eyed when they kissed my cheek, and my dad didn't even try to wipe the tears off his cheeks when they went into the church to take their seats in the front row.

I let out a slow breath, my thoughts as clear and sharp as I'd ever experienced as the doors opened into the church.

There was music playing, but I couldn't hear it.

Romantic lights and lush flowers decorated the front of the church, but I didn't notice any of the details.

There were people in the rows, smiling and oohing and aahing as I made my entrance.

I saw nothing but him.

Griffin stood tall and proud at the front of the church, his hands clasped in front of him as tears streamed unabashedly down his face while he watched me. His hair was freshly cut, but I'd begged him to leave a little stubble on his face. I didn't want him looking too proper, because that certainly wasn't the man I fell in love with. It was his wild heart, the one that made him love so deeply, that made him perfect for me.

The cut of his deep charcoal-gray suit accentuated his broad frame, and when his chest rose and fell on a deep breath, it was all I could do not to sprint to the front of the church and throw myself into his arms.

When I came to the end of the aisle, his eyes locked on mine and he mouthed, *I love you.*

I love you too, I mouthed back, swiping at the stray tears on my cheeks.

We'd opted for a short ceremony with a small group of our closest friends and family, but as I handed my bouquet to Lauren and felt Griffin's fingers slide between mine, we might as well have been alone in that room.

It was just me and him, our gazes never wavering, and my chest filled with the warm contentment of a life that was so much better than I could've imagined. It was just the vows we were making—my voice trembling and thick as I promised him my loyalty and my support and my love for the rest of my life. My eyes filled with tears again when he promised to be my protector and my confidant, my best friend, for the rest of his.

Griffin pushed a simple diamond wedding band onto my finger, sliding it into place next to the two-carat cushion-cut diamond he'd given me six months earlier, bringing my hand up to his mouth to press a kiss onto my knuckles with his eyes pinched shut. I cupped his face for a moment before easing the black metal band over his finger.

He sighed in relief when it was on, and I grinned up at him.

"You're stuck with me now, baby," he whispered, tilting his head down toward mine.

"Good."

His eyes locked on my mouth while the pastor pronounced us Griffin and Ruby King, and the moment he said, "You may now—" Griffin swept me up in his arms and stole a fierce, breathless kiss while attendees yelled and whistled and clapped. His tongue wound around mine, and I moaned helplessly at the sudden rush of heat, knowing that he was mine—*mine*—forever.

It wasn't about taking his name or signing a piece of paper. It was so much more. Making promises we would never break, and proclaiming to the world that he loved me and I loved him and nothing could separate us—that's what it was about. It wasn't just saying we loved each other—it was showing it. Choosing each other, through all the hard.

Griffin broke away from the kiss, tilting his head back to give a triumphant shout. I clutched him around the neck and laughed, my feet dangling off the floor as he held me tight against his chest, burying his face into my curls.

"My wife," he murmured. *"My wife."*

We stayed like that for a few more moments—my eyes closed and my heart soaring—while the love in the room spread like sweet wildfire through my bones.

This is life, I thought. And I was more than ready to live it.

Second Epilogue

GRIFFIN

Ten years later

"I told you, no peeking."

Ruby huffed, arms outstretched while I cupped her shoulders and led her into the room. "I feel like I'm going to trip on something."

With a smile, I wrapped an arm around her waist and steered her past a plush ottoman. "Would I let that happen?"

"No."

She sounded so pouty that I laughed. My hand snapped against her ass, and she squeaked. "Almost there, birdy."

In front of us was a big, overstuffed chair for two—large enough that even I could fully extend my legs. With my hand guiding her arm, I eased her outstretched palm onto the back of the chair. She felt around, and I could so clearly imagine the furrow in her brow while she tried to figure out where we were.

Maggie had taken her out of the house that morning for a shopping trip, then surprised her with a trip to the salon to get her hair and makeup done.

Our tenth anniversary.

God, and what a fucking decade it had been. Life with this woman was so much sweeter than I'd ever planned, and even now I couldn't get enough of her. When I retired from playing, we built a house in Welling Springs, preferring the quiet pace of life there over the busyness of Denver.

We'd built a damn-good life after we got married. I played for two more years after my arm healed, and even though my body could have gone another year or two, I told Ruby that I was ready to be home with her. Instead of practices and travel and hours of game film, I shifted my focus to helping Ruby start a foundation for early literacy in underserved communities in eastern Colorado.

I still commuted to help the team a couple times a week during the season, but for the most part, my life was centered around one thing—loving Ruby Tate. And I was damn good at that.

We'd seen so much of the world over the last ten years. Her favorite place was Great Britain, and Greece was a close second. My favorite was anywhere I got to go with her. Watching the wonder in her eyes when she explored a new country was fucking addicting.

Bruiser lived until our sixth anniversary, and on our seventh, I surprised her with a monster of a puppy I'd found at an adoption event held by the team—he grew to be a hundred pounds of dopey, drooling cuddle monster, and we'd named him Tank. He had a horrible tendency to hog the bed and dig into the garbage when we weren't looking, but he was still our baby.

Kids weren't in the picture for us, but as Uncle Griffin and Aunt Ruby, we stayed busy. Not just because Marcus and Lauren popped out three kids in five years and we constantly had those little red-haired psychos over, but because Maggie and Bryce turned out to be two of the greatest surrogate children we could've asked for. We spent as much time as we could with them, along with my parents, Barrett and his wife, and their younger kids.

"Are we at the house?" she asked. "Did you bake muffins? The last time you tried that, you almost burned the kitchen down."

"Lies." I eased both arms around her so I could nibble at the line of her jaw. Ruby melted into my embrace, sliding her arms over mine and sighing. "Ready to see your surprise?"

"Yes."

Careful not to tangle her hair, I untied the blindfold. In our family room, I'd set up a massive projection screen, flanked by paper lanterns flickering with warm yellow light. There was one chair in the middle of the room, where we'd be able to snuggle in tight next to each other.

She exhaled a quiet laugh when she saw the small end table holding a plate of blueberry muffins. Ruby leaned over and picked one up, turning to give me a devious grin. "What is this?"

"A re-creation," I explained, gesturing to the chair in front of us. "If you don't mind, I need to sit first."

Ruby plucked off a piece of the muffin, sighing happily as she swallowed. "So good."

I sat back in the chair and spread my legs, patting the space between. She climbed onto the chair and settled herself in between my legs, her back plastered to my chest. Wrapping my arms around her was a flimsy excuse to snag the muffin, and she scoffed when I ate half of it in one bite.

While she got another piece of the second muffin, I pressed play on the remote, and when the opening credits began—soft, romantic light filling the screen—Ruby laughed in delight.

"You didn't," she said, turning to smile up into my face.

I leaned down to give her a lingering kiss. "I needed to re-create this first date."

Her eyes were soft and happy and warm, the flush of pink in her cheeks making me want to ditch *Pride & Prejudice* for tenth-anniversary sex in a really comfortable chair while her mouth tasted like muffins.

Later, I reminded myself. There was a blue lace number waiting upstairs on our bed, and a sleek diamond chain I wanted to drape over her skin while I kissed every inch of her body.

Spoiling her was also really fucking addicting.

"Why?" she asked.

I held my hand out, and Ruby slid her fingers in between mine, dragging lightly over the skin on my palm before pressing our hands together. "Because I knew that night," I told her, nuzzling in closer to the side of her head. "That you were special. And I needed more."

"You did?"

I nodded, my heart overflowing with the need to give her pretty words that I never quite seemed capable of. These days, I didn't spend much time worrying about the future. She was healthy and strong, and her doctors were optimistic that Ruby would be one of those people you read stories about—who live a long, healthy life. On days like this, it wasn't fear that had me looking back.

It was gratitude.

She pushed me past my fears—allowing me to be more myself than I had my entire life—and I helped her do the same with hers. Wasn't that what the best relationships always did?

It wasn't as simple as people made it out, where you know the bullshit you carry around and make a decision to drop it. Sometimes it took the right person, seeing through your armor and knowing that what was on the other side was worth fighting for.

"Ten years, I've been able to wake up with you as my wife," I told her quietly, holding her as tightly as I could. "And I wish I was the kind of guy who could make flowery, grand speeches. I know I could take you on an expensive trip or buy you just about anything you asked for." I swallowed, closing my eyes against the wave of emotion filling my chest. "But that's not what you want from me in moments like this, is it? You just want to see my heart, because you gave me yours, and it's the best fucking gift I've ever been given."

She sniffled lightly, brushing at her cheek as she slowly turned on the seat, sitting on her haunches to face me. I cupped her face, using my thumb to wipe away a single tear.

"And your heart's here, at our home?" she asked, eyes wide in her face. She had more wrinkles now, around the eyes and on her forehead, a couple of gray hairs at her temples, and she was the most beautiful woman I'd ever seen.

"My heart's with you, baby. Always. Doesn't matter where we are. I keep thinking about the beginning, you know? Thinking about how we started, what got us right here, and I just wish I could do it all over again and tell you I love you from the very fucking start." I held her gaze. "From day one, it was you and me, wasn't it?"

She nodded, surging forward to kiss me. When she broke away, I was glossy-eyed too.

"Let's do that, then," she said. "Go back to the beginning. You can burn me dinner and pester me over books."

"I still do those things," I pointed out.

Ruby smiled, and I felt it like a sweet ache in my bones.

"What do you think?" she asked.

"I like it." I held her close and kissed her again, breathing in her familiar, calming scent as I said a silent prayer of thanks for this beautiful woman whom I got to call mine, and for this amazing life that was ours. "Because you know what, birdy? We've got all the time in the world."

ACKNOWLEDGMENTS

Thank you to my family, who were endlessly understanding when I had to disappear during the summer to meet this deadline. I quite literally could not do this without you.

To Maria Gomez, Kelli Collins, and the Montlake team, as well as ME Carter for helping shape the story. (You can thank ME Carter for chapter 30 because she would not let me end this book without it.)

To my readers, for everything.

And last but not least—to Mona Kasten, whom I do not know, but who wrote *Maxton Hall,* which I binged this summer and after which I felt a powerful need to write a prickly, smart girl and a too-charming-for-his-own-good boy falling in love against the odds. Your storytelling is addicting, and I thank you for the overwhelming inspiration.

My flesh and my heart may fail, but God is the strength of my heart and my portion forever.
—Psalm 73:26

ABOUT THE AUTHOR

Photo © 2018 Perrywinkle Photography

Karla Sorensen is the author of the Wilder Family series, the Best Man series, the Washington Wolves series, and many other novels. She refuses to write or read anything without a happily ever after. When Karla is not devouring historical romance, reading Dramione fanfic, or avoiding laundry, you can find her watching football (British and American) or HGTV or listening to Enneagram podcasts so she can psychoanalyze everyone in her life, in no particular order of importance. With a degree in advertising and public relations from Grand Valley State University, she made her living in senior health care prior to writing full time. Karla lives in Michigan with her husband, two boys, and a big, shaggy rescue dog named Bear. For more information, visit www.karlasorensen.com.

CONNECT WITH KARLA ONLINE

Instagram

www.instagram.com/karla_sorensen

Facebook Reader Group

www.facebook.com/groups/thesorensensorority

Website

www.karlasorensen.com

Newsletter

www.karlasorensen.com/subscribe